or

S.L. Bhyrappa (b. 1931) is an eminent Kannada novelist whose works span twenty-four novels, six critical discourses and an autobiography. With an honorary doctorate from six universities, he is a best-selling author for over five decades, beginning with *Vamsha Vruksha* published 52 years ago. He received the Sahitya Akademi Fellowship in 2015, and was awarded the Padma Shri in 2016. He was also the recipient of the Saraswati Samman in 2010, and most of his novels have been translated into almost all Indian languages, including Sanskrit and English. His most well-known works include *Vamshavriksha, Grihabhanga, Daatu, Parva, Saakshi, Saartha, Tantu, Aavarana* and *Uttarakanda*.

He lives in Mysore.

Sandeep Balakrishna served in the IT industry for over seventeen years. He is the author of the bestselling history book *Tipu Sultan: The Tyrant of Mysore*. His other books include *Madurai Sultanate: A Concise History* and *70 Years of Secularism: Unpopular Essays on the Unofficial Political Religion of India*. He has translated S.L. Bhyrappa's bestselling Kannada novel *Aavarana* into English as *Aavarana: The Veil*, currently in its tenth reprint. He is also a columnist at various English and Kannada newspapers and magazines, and a contributing editor at *Prekshaa Journal* and the founder and chief editor of *The Dharma Dispatch*.

Sandeep is Fellow at the Indian Council for Philosophical Research and lives in Bangalore.

orphaned

S.L. BHYRAPPA

TRANSLATED BY
SANDEEP BALAKRISHNA

RUPA

Published by
Rupa Publications India Pvt. Ltd 2019
7/16, Ansari Road, Daryaganj
New Delhi 110002

Sales centres:

Allahabad Bengaluru Chennai
Hyderabad Jaipur Kathmandu
Kolkata Mumbai

ISBN: 978-93-5333-786-5

First impression 2019

10 9 8 7 6 5 4 3 2 1

The moral right of the author has been asserted.

Printed at Parksons Graphics Pvt. Ltd, Mumbai

A WORD TO THE READER

The question of where the village described in this novel is located in the globe might naturally arise in the mind of the reader. I have purposely omitted mentioning the names of its Taluk and District, as well as other geographical details because I did not want it to become a specific place. The village Kalenahalli that appears in this novel may very well be the native village of any reader. The reader can visualize the Arunadri Hill that neighbours Kalenahalli as a hill next to his or her own village.

If the village's dialect is altered according to a specific geography, the action in this novel can take place in any village located to the south of Kolar and all the way up to any village in the north, for example, in the districts of Bidar and Kalburgi. Or we can consider the phrase, 'At the centre of this Earth where lies the celebrated country of Karnataka' that occurs at the beginning of the timeless folk song of the cow. In this, if we substitute 'Karnataka' with 'Bharat', and read the novel, the action in this work can equally be located in any village of Hindustan. In such a case, it won't be difficult for a reader endowed with imagination to alter the names of a few other villages and towns that are mentioned in the novel.

This novel was first published as a serial in the Kannada daily, *Kannada Prabha*. I would like to thank its editorial staff, especially K.S. Narayanaswami.

The character of Tayavva in this novel has been depicted as someone who is born mute. I have personally known one such lady in real life. This character is not a person created to be a specimen for medical science. Readers will, on their own, understand the literary purpose behind depicting her as a mute. That should suffice.

My gratitude also goes out to my friend M.S.K. Prabhu who read the manuscript and helped to make corrections in a few places, and to the publisher, M. Govinda Rao.[*]

---

[*]S.L. Bhyrappa, 1968.

THE SONG OF THE COW:
TRANSLATOR'S INTRODUCTION

Our present age can be accurately characterized as one of rapid technological change and an overwhelming—and almost indispensable—dependency on machines and massive information overload. This phenomenon is unprecedented in the annals of human history. But the more significant part is the fact that this phenomenon—which can be termed the Regime of Technology—has spared no nation and no corner of the earth including India.

In spite of this, the role, place and reverence for the cow continue to endure as one of the central and sacred pillars of India's ancient civilizational and cultural ethos. It is also the main reason for including the protection, nurturing and preservation of the cow—generally speaking, cattle—in the Constitution of India. This reverence for the cow in the Hindu ethos also comes in direct conflict with and has given rise to endless and fierce debates and battles over cow slaughter by those who regard it only as food.

Dr S.L. Bhyrappa's novel *Orphaned* deals with these issues, among numerous other fundamental questions and problems. The context for the novel is set by the celebrated Kannada folk song titled *Govina Haadu* or 'Song of the Cow'. Using this song as a backdrop of sorts, the novel obliquely explores the roots of India's culture. The song itself belongs to unknown antiquity and became popular sometime around the fifteenth century in the NaDugannada, or Middle Kannada, period of its history. It is composed in an easy, versified form employing simple language, and continues to remain an immortal cultural and literary heritage of the Kannada language. Until a few decades ago, it was compulsory for primary and middle school children in Karnataka to memorize this song. It has also found its way into films, and is the subject of numerous learned treatises and commentaries.

The gist of the Song of the Cow is rather straightforward. A cow named Punyakoti is part of a large herd of cattle owned by a cowherd called Kalinga Gowda or Kalinga *Golla* (cowherd). Punyakoti abides by the lasting values of truth, non-violence, compassion and dharma. One day as she goes grazing on Arunadri Hill, she's accosted by a hungry tiger who wants to eat her. She pleads with him saying her infant is hungry and that she will feed him one last time and return. After much persuasion, the tiger is convinced by her fidelity to truth and lets her go. After she returns to the cowshed and feeds her infant calf, she informs him that she has to go back to the tiger. When the infant tries to dissuade her, she tells him it's wrong to break the word that one has given and tells him the value of pursuing truth for its own sake. When she's bidding him her final goodbye, the memorable line, *Tabbaliyu neenaade magane* (literally: 'My child, you're orphaned') occurs in the song. This line is the title of Dr S.L. Bhyrappa's novel.

Punyakoti returns to the tiger's cave and addresses him: 'Here, take my muscles, flesh, and the warm blood of my heart. Consume them all and be happy and live well on this earth.' The tiger, not only astonished at her steadfastness to truth but overcome with remorse, tells Punyakoti that he'll incur a great sin if he eats someone as noble as her. He says in repentance that she is akin to his elder sister. He bids her a final goodbye and leaps to his death from the top of Arunadri Hill.

Although this backdrop is not mandatory to follow the novel, it, nevertheless, provides a cultural context to the heavily rustic, raw physical setting in which the plot unfolds. Additionally, the author has used several verses from the Song of the Cow verbatim in the novel. These have been translated for the benefit of the reader. The foregoing story of Punyakoti would also help the non-Kannada, and especially the English-speaking reader, connect these verses to her story.

Sandeep Balakrishna
2019

1

At the centre of this Earth
where lies the celebrated country of Karnataka
lives the cowherd Kalinga
how shall I narrate his ways?

There is a huge difference in the way this song is recited at the Ochayya's Matha, or ashram, by the boys studying in government schools, and by our Kalinga Gowda from the village Kalenahalli. For the boys in school, this song, starting with these lines, narrates the story of the cow, and is just one poem in their textbook. However, for Kalinga Gowda, it is a true incident that occurred during the lifetime of his ancestors.

The cow named Punyakoti, thinking about her child, was walking in happiness when—

Today I got my food
said the cruel tiger
came afore, surrounded and blocked
the cow.

And to the tiger,

A prayer O King among Tigers
My baby is at home
I will take but a moment to give him teat
and then return and stand here.

Said the cow.

Must you die Mother?
Must you make me orphan?
Stay back here
said the child to the mother.

Truth is our mother and father
truth is our relatives and friends
God will not be pleased
if we stray from the word of truth.

The cow thus preached Dharma to her child and from there she walked amidst the spread of the highlands up to the slope of the mountain where Arbuta the tiger lived, and said—

Take my flesh, take my meat
drink the hot blood of my heart
eat well and you be satisfied and
live happily on this earth.

The tiger is pleased with her steadfastness to truth.

You're my elder sister
what do I gain eating you?
I will fall at your feet
and take leave of my life.

And the tiger,

Folded its hands to the Three Gods
looked in the eight directions
jumped up skywards
and left its life.

When Punyakoti, the cow returned to its barn and said, 'Shiva granted *Moksha* to the tiger and spared my life,' the owner of the barn, Kalinga fell at her feet. Then the cow,

The cows of my lineage
the cowherds of your lineage
at the Sankranti festival must
worship the beautiful Krishna.

S.L. BHYRAPPA

He said—

I will and my lineage will, every year
make during Sankranti festival
one milk-pongal sweet
and he celebrated a festival there and then.

2

There is enough evidence that Kalinga Gowda from Kalenahalli descended from the same clan of Kalinga *Golla*—or cowherd, who owned the ancient cowshed—which had housed Punyakoti. Indeed, the village obtained its name 'Kalenahalli' after the same Kalinga *Golla*, the Gowda-headman of the village. This fact has been confirmed even by the British rulers who researched and wrote the geographical history of the district. Our Kalinga Gowda even today is the Village Gowda, or headman of Kalenahalli. It is the tradition of his lineage to give the name 'Kalinga Gowda' to the eldest son of the second generation. This is affirmed by the family tree that exists in his house. Our Kalinga Gowda's grandfather's name too, was Kalinga Gowda. Our Kalinga Gowda has named his grandson—he's one year old—Kalinga. This child will become the Gowda after he grows up and takes charge of the barn.

There is yet another incontrovertible evidence testifying to the fact that our Kalinga Gowda is indeed the descendant of the Kalinga *Golla* lineage, and that the story of Punyakoti indeed occurred in the village of Kalenahalli—

Arunadri Hill in common parlance
exists in the land,
clutching the sky, it
causes amazement to the sight.

Kalenahalli, the village where Punyakoti's story occurred, lies at the foothills of the Arunadri Hill. If we suspect that Arunadri was some ordinary hill named thus by somebody, we learn that it has an even greater, definitive distinction—

In this Creation, Arunadri Hill
circumscribed by seven other Hills
an extent of twelve Yojanas
lay a dense jungle.

The Arunadri Hill is surrounded by seven other hills in an area spanning twelve *Yojanas* or ninety-six kilometres. Climbing to the top of Arunadri on a cloudless afternoon, all the seven hills are clearly visible. Not much evidence is needed to confirm the fact that the mountain-chain was covered with thick forests in the past. When our Kalinga Gowda's contemporaries were still boys, a forbidding jungle existed there.

Rose-Chestnut, Mango, Black-Plum,
Teak, Chennangi, Shami, Paadri
Tamarind and Bael
bent and touched and celebrated in that forest.

The forest playfully embraced
the Banyan and the Pipal, the Fig and the Orange,
the Jaali, the Tidigilu, the Agiley, the Sandalwood,
the Wood-Apple, the Aloe, the Bamboo and the Silk-Cotton.

Kalinga Gowda himself had seen all these trees in the forest. However, when he was twenty, that is, thirty years earlier, they had begun to cut the forests and were done with it. Teak trees went into building homes in big cities. Mango, black-plum, shami and paadri went on to burn as firewood in the homes of city-dwellers. Sandalwood trees went to sandalwood oil factories to become oil and soap, and reached foreign shores. And so when the major male trees vanished, how would their female counterparts like the rose-chestnut, bael and silk-cotton survive? Neither the pipal nor its wife, the neem tree, survived. However, a few banyan trees have still lived on, scattered here and there.

Our Kalinga Gowda is now fifty. However, he still rises in the early hours, has his river-bath, puts the *tilak* on his forehead and knots his hair elegantly. He wears striped long knickers, and then wraps the *dhoti* around his waist. He wears the locket-chain around his neck and slips the signet-ring on his fingers. On festivals and special occasions, he wears a saffron shirt, wraps a sapphire turban over his head and gracefully dons the resplendent, moon-hued shoulder-cloth.

The house right at the gates of Kalenahalli village belongs to Kalinga Gowda. Behind his house is his cattle shed. Indeed, we can say that his entire house is itself a cattle shed. His family lives in the portion that faces the street. The entire backyard houses his cattle. It is only for the purpose of cooking that his family—with his wife, son, daughter-in-law, and his one-year-old grandson—live in the portion that faces the street. At all other times, they live in the barn. Indeed, is it a mean task to take care of the hundred cattle-strong cowshed?

Behind the barn stands the ancient mango tree even to this day. Sitting under this tree, this *Golla* Gowda plays his flute and calls out to his herd. His barn comprises three parts. One houses the plough and the oxen, which pull his cart. The second houses the calves. The third houses only cows. Kalinga Gowda knows the name of every single cow in his shed. And every cow knows its own name. The moment our Gowda calls out the name of a cow, she immediately lifts up her head and looks in his direction. If he waves his hand at her, beckoning her to come near him, the cow goes close to him, smells his body and affectionately licks the uncovered parts of his body. When he takes them to the grassland reserved only for cattle grazing, he calls out the names of all his cows countless times. He yells, 'Hoy Paaroti, don't go towards the field. Hoy Lakshmi, come here, come here.' 'Ganga! Come! Kabhuuyy!' 'Gowri! Why are you dancing? Something wrong with you?' His cows are all named after Goddesses—Ganga, Gowri, Tungabhadra, Parvati, Saraswati, Dharmadevi, Ranganayaki, Sita, Kamadhenu, and so on. His tongue, which calls out the names of all these cows at least ten times every day, thus invokes the names of these Goddesses innumerable times! He is of the firm belief that he continues to accumulate *punya* every day in this manner, and has no doubt that he will attain *Moksha*—the Virtuous End or Liberation—and never go to Hell.

Punyakoti, who returned to the tiger's cave from her cowshed in order not to betray her promise to him, was saved by the grace of Lord Shiva, and returned alive. Her descendants still adorn Kalinga Gowda's cowshed. They are tall but of even build, pure white in colour, and although long, their horns are slightly bent so that even when they headbutt, they pose no danger to anyone. When they walk, their hooves leave a clear imprint on the ground. Their tail resembles the long, thick tresses of an auspicious married woman. Even when one looks at them from behind, the full udders between their legs appear heavy for their build. They are endowed with an elongated chest, with delicate folds of skin dangling underneath their long neck. Punyakoti's stock was always born with these physical characteristics. They would neither gore when you approached from the front nor kick when approached from the rear. The female of her stock would never withhold her milk from any baby that put its mouth to her teat. The male exhibited similar nature—it was always at the forefront where work was concerned. It never gored anybody, it was unaggressive, and chewed cud with a cheerful expression on its face.

When Kalinga Gowda was angry, he'd scold other cows. He would threaten them profusely with, 'Have you lost your mind?' or 'Just wait, you'll get a beating!' However, he would never even dream of chiding any cow of Punyakoti's stock. After all, wasn't it their ancestor who went to the tiger's door, not deviating from the truth of the word it had given? Even now, when the milk-pongal festival was celebrated on the day of Sankranti, he first worships the cows of Punyakoti's stock.

3

By his *jati*, Kalinga Gowda is a *Golla*—a cowherd. In his own words, he alone doesn't belong to the *Golla jati*. Every man is indeed a *Golla*, and every woman is a *Gollati*—the female counterpart. A woman who offers puja to the cow is a *Gollati*; a man who nurtures the cow is a *Golla*. The great rishis and munis nurtured cows. Their wives used to perform puja for the cows. And so, weren't they *Gollas*? There might exist hundreds of sub-*jatis* like the *Gangadikara, Dasagowda, Nonaba, Banajiga* and *Haaruva*, but all of them were within the same *Golla* family. Whether they wore the *tilak* or applied *vibhuti*—the sacred ash—was there ever a *Golla* who did not offer puja to the cow?

Kalinga Gowda is not illiterate. He recites the versified story of Punyakoti and can explain its meaning. He is also capable of narrating a few important chapters from the *Jaimini* Mahabharata. Although he had not formally learnt the *Gadugina Bharata*, he can decipher its meaning if someone recites it. A Brahmin *Jois*—an astrologer— lives in an *Agrahara*, two miles away from Kalenahalli. He is the *purohit,* or the priest, for the surrounding villages. People from faraway towns and villages claim that Narasimha *Jois*, younger than Kalinga Gowda by five years, has not only learnt Sanskrit, but is well-versed in the Vedas and Puranas. When Narasimha *Jois* visits Kalenahalli or when Kalinga Gowda visits the *Agrahara*, he places this challenge to *Jois*: 'Narasappa, you've studied the Vedas, you tell me, aren't our rishis and sages *Gollas*?'

'Yes, yes,' *Jois* agrees with him. Not just that, he cites a mantra: '*Maataa rudranaam duhitaa vasoonaam, swa saadityaa naamam amrutasya naabhihi* [She is the Mother of Rudra, She is the Daughter of Vasu, She is the treasure of Amrita, and because all the thirty-three crore Gods reside in Her, whichever God one worships, it is equal to worshipping the Cow. All those who offer puja to God are *Gollas*.'

Kalinga Gowda never reared cows for their milk. Does anybody take care of their mother because she gives milk? He has his own chain of reasoning in this regard: We are born because of our mother and develop love for her milk. However, can we get a mother simply because we are greedy for milk? And, even if we do get a woman in that manner, will she become our mother? The cow is the same; it is greater than one's mother. Indeed, *Gomaata* (Mother Cow), *Bhoomata* (Mother Earth) and the biological Mother who gave birth to us—indeed, who can receive, who can give these three?

He does not accept it when somebody tells him that the cow exists only to provide milk for humans. Why don't our mothers who birthed us, give milk to calves? Similarly, the milk of a cow is generated for its calf. However, the *punya*, the merit accumulated by *Gomaata* is greater than that of a human mother. Her breasts are far bigger. That is the reason why even after she finishes feeding her calf, her breasts still have milk for humans. For Kalinga Gowda, this meant that only the milk left over after the cow has finished feeding her calf, belongs to us. Whenever Kalinga Gowda and his family wanted to milk the cow in his cowshed, they wouldn't take the calf away from the cow and tie it separately. The calf would drink milk from the two udders on one side, and Gowda's wife or daughter-in-law would draw milk from the two udders on the other side into a large container.

There was a separate, large and roofed structure inside the barn to tie the cows. Each cow had its own enclosure and trough. However, calves were bundled together inside the living room itself. In the night, Gowda, his wife, son and daughter-in-law would get the really tiny infant calves to sleep next to them on the bed of blankets. Sometimes when the calves urinated on the blanket, none of them would get annoyed. 'Don't our children urinate? It's the same with the calves. The urine of the calves is better than the urine of human children. After all, it is one of the sacred *panchagavya*'—the fivefold sacred mixture of cow milk, curd, ghee, cow urine and dung. This was their deeply held conviction.

Gowda would not get sleep at night unless he got his back licked at least once a day by either a cow or a calf. Sometimes when he awoke mid-sleep as he changed sides at night, he would caress the calf by his side, talk to it and then go back to sleep, snoring gently.

In the morning, he would wash his hands and legs with the large mug, pray to the Lord of the East and free the calves so they could drink milk. No sooner had he freed them, each calf would unfailingly go straight to its own mother and start suckling. Kalinga Gowda would remark, 'Unlike humans, they do not forget their own.'

4

One morning, Gowda's wife, Lakkamma, was milking the cows in the cowshed. Sitting nearby, her daughter-in-law, Tayavva, had parted her blouse to feed her crying one-year-old infant. The baby didn't stop crying in spite of suckling at its mother's breast. When Lakkamma said, 'Give your breast properly', Tayavva looked at her confused, not being able to comprehend what she was supposed to do. Tayavva could not speak. She was born mute.

∽

Tayavva was married into the family to fulfil a promise Kalinga Gowda had made many years ago. Tayavva, the daughter of Kalinga Gowda's

S.L. BHYRAPPA

younger sister, was only three when Gowda's son, Krishna, was eight years old. The relation, bonded by siblinghood, was considered a good match in every way. On some occasion, Gowda gave his word to his sister and brother-in-law that he would get their daughter married to his son. At that age, this young girl still hadn't started to speak. Of course, Gowda knew that it was common for three-year-olds not to have developed their faculty of speech. Besides, there was no special reason for him to think about it. However, even when she turned eight, she was unable to speak. Special vows to God, mantras from sadhus, tantric rituals from Malayali priests, nothing worked. Her tongue remained mute. It was clear to everyone that Tayavva was born dumb.

Gowda did not give much thought to the promise he had made to his sister, Dyavakka. But, when she initiated the conversation of her daughter's marriage, Gowda asked, 'Sister, the girl is dumb. You tell me, how can I get her married into my home?'

'My dear brother, when we spoke about her marriage, who knew she would be dumb? You agreed that she would marry your son. The match was fixed. Now, will you break your word, just because she is mute?'

How could Kalinga Gowda break his word?

Truth is our mother and father
truth is our relatives and friends
God will not be pleased
if we stray from the word of truth.

Didn't Punyakoti, the cow who returned to the tiger to honour her promise, belong to the barn owned by his ancestors? This was the same barn that was now his, and inhabited by cows of Punyakoti's lineage. Gowda thought to himself, 'If I break my word, how will I be able to face them? And, what about the cows? The Sun and Moon deities reside in their eyes. What is that which is not visible to them?'

His sister Dyavakka had put him in a spot. But what could he do? 'Ok, my dear sister. I'll bring your daughter to my home in marriage. Let's ask the *Jois* and fix the marriage', he told her.

But then, the task of convincing his wife Lakkamma to agree to the marriage also fell on his shoulders. It was not that she wasn't aware that one shouldn't break a promise. The custom of parents deciding siblinghood marriages for their respective children at an early age was also not rare. Although, in this case, nobody was at fault, Lakkamma asked Gowda, 'What happiness would a mute wife provide our son?'

Gowda answered, 'What's the problem if she's mute? She's beautiful. She does all the chores well. It's just that she can't speak. Tell me, is the Mother Cow mute?'

'How can she be mute? Isn't she the Mother of all the Gods?'

'Exactly. But can she speak?'

'No.'

'That means not all those who cannot speak are mute. This girl is the same. The cows in our cowshed speak. They come to me when I call them. They lick my body. When I make an eye-gesture, they instantly understand it. They certainly know how to speak even when they don't speak. And why should they? Are they human beings, who require speech? Why should the Gods speak?'

Lakkamma didn't quite know how to respond to this, as Gowda asked, 'Tell me, who is your mother-in-law?'

'It has been many years since your mother passed away.'

'Not that mother. My mother means the Mother Cow. Think of her as your mother-in-law. Does she torment you? Does she complain against you to me?'

'No.'

'Likewise, if you get a cow-like daughter-in-law, she'll be unable to make harsh, unfair complaints against you to our son. You'll be happy. Everybody will be happy. Just agree.'

Lakkamma consented to the marriage. And so, the thirteen-year-old Krishne Gowda was married to the mute, eight-year-old Tayavva, his paternal aunt's daughter. The wedding ceremony took place at night in accordance with ancient *Golla* tradition. Krishne Gowda didn't utter a word saying he didn't want this tongue-less girl. He wasn't old enough to say something like this. Besides, matters of marriage were completely in the hands of parents. Children had no say in it.

Tayavva was smart in work and life. Although she couldn't speak, she completely understood what others spoke. She came to stay in her marital home six years after marriage. Three years later, she was pregnant and gave birth to her first child, a boy. *So what if she's mute, is there a greater joy than this?* thought Lakkamma.

⚘

The baby didn't stop crying even after she fed it alternately, first from her left breast and then the right. With his tiny hand, the infant pushed away the breast it was suckling as if saying—'I don't want it.' Meanwhile, after milking one cow, Lakkamma applied castor oil to the udder of another and began tugging at it with a *sorr* sound. Her grandchild kept wailing. For a minute, she stopped milking, turned towards her daughter-in-law and asked: 'Why have you loosened? Can't you give your breast firmly?'

When the daughter-in-law made a hand-sign, she understood. Tayavva was telling her that her milk had depleted since the last one week and there was absolutely no milk in her breast this morning. 'The milk must be stuck for some reason. Press with your fingers and check', said the mother-in-law.

When Tayavva complied, no milk emerged. 'Did the milk stop in just one year? The same thing had happened with your mother too. What sort of womankind is yours if you can't feed milk to your child for at least three years?' At Lakkamma's rebuke, the daughter-in-law cast her eyes down in helplessness. The cow that her mother-in-law was milking made a *borr borr* sound as its milk filled the large pail, the top portion of which was swelling with white froth.

Although the infant was accustomed to drinking milk from a spoon, it was unwilling to let go of the joy of suckling its mother's breast; it began to bawl incessantly—nothing could pacify it. Not even when his grandmother held him in her arms and put a small bit of jaggery in his mouth. The task of milking the cow stopped right there. When Tayavva saw her child in her mother-in-law's arms, she took over the milking.

Kalinga Gowda had awoken at dawn and headed to the fields. The rainy *Aashaada* months of June and July had given way to the ongoing *Shravana* months, and farmworkers were planting ragi saplings to be harvested in spring. In the East, the Sun God, the Swami, had risen up to a height of four grown men when Gowda returned home. The infant was still bawling. When he asked, 'Why is the baby hollering like this?' his wife said, 'Tayavva's breast has stopped giving milk. What kind of a good woman is she whose milk dries up in just a year? The same thing happened to her mother too.'

Gowda was aware that Lakkavva had fed milk to her own child for three full years. But then he couldn't tolerate it when she referred to her daughter-in-law's mother—his own younger sister—as 'what kind of a woman is she?' True, Lakkavva was a superior woman in this respect. But not all women are alike. That's why she shouldn't have spoken in such a derogatory manner about his younger sister and her daughter. He scolded her, 'Will you just shut up now? Are all cows alike? Do all cows give milk equally?'

Lakkavva had no answer. She handed over the infant to Gowda and went towards the kitchen. Her daughter-in-law was already grinding the spices to mix in a broth of hyacinth bean. Pacifying the baby was a considerable problem for Gowda. When he went in and asked his wife what to do, she said the same thing she had said earlier—'It's become completely attached to breast milk. It won't stop until it gets breast milk.'

Gowda went to the calf-shed with the infant. He left it to play with the calves, but to no avail. Then, he went to the ox-shed and seated the infant atop the back of an ox. The child still didn't stop crying. Finally, an idea struck him. Isn't the *Gomaata* greater than the Mother who has given birth to us? Isn't her teat bigger than our Mothers' breasts? *That's right*, he thought, and headed to the cowshed. All the cows had been milked. Besides, if the child puts its mouth directly on the udder, not all cows will take kindly to it.

But Gowda had immense faith in the lineage of Punyakoti. No matter what time it was milked, it would, without trickery, give whatever milk it had. Although their udders had milk, other cows would play cunning games by withholding it, but not one cow of the Punyakoti stock would do this. That apart, it had never gored or kicked anybody ever. Now, Gowda's shed had three milch cows of the Punyakoti stock. One had just delivered its first calf. This *Shravana* month marked one year of its delivery. This bull-calf was the same age as his grandson. Having drunk its mother's milk, it was blithely prancing around near the outer wall of the cowshed. Gowda caught it and then brought it to its mother. The calf put its mouth again to its mother's teat. For a moment, the cow stiffened its hind legs and urinated: meaning, it loosened its teats. Gowda held the toddler in a leaning position and put its mouth to the teat on the other side. For a minute, the baby hesitated to drink the milk. With his other hand, Gowda gently squeezed the end of the teat that was in the baby's mouth. The moment the warm, tasty milk gushed into its mouth, the baby's suspicion vanished and it began to suckle happily. Punyakoti stood still without once lifting or moving its legs this side or that.

By then Gowda's wife had come to the cowshed and witnessed this. She wasn't surprised. As a *Gollati*, infants drinking milk directly from the cow's teat was common knowledge to her. But it troubled her as to why this idea, which had occured to her husband, hadn't come to her. After the baby had finished drinking milk, Gowda lifted it up, touched its head once to the cow's foreleg and addressed it: 'Mother, from today, you are its Mother. Each time it cries, you must give it your teat and nurture it.'

As he held up the baby and turned around, his eyes spotted his wife who had come near him. He blurted out instantly: 'You don't know how to pacify a baby which cries a bit. What kind of a woman are you? What's the big fuss if Tayavva's breast milk has dried up? Didn't you know how many cows we have at home?'

His wife felt humiliated. Her head lowered, she walked away.

From that day onwards, the toddler began to drink Punyakoti's milk.

After she gave birth to a calf, the Punyakoti stock would yield milk for two-and-a-half years. For the next one-and-a-half years, the infant joyously drank from her teat. On several occasions, it didn't need any adult to accompany it. The two-year-old would walk unaided and alone amidst all the cows, unerringly recognizing its own Mother cow and put its mouth to its teat. The cow would never gore or kick. The child would bend down below the cow's stomach and suckle till the time it was content, and then return to the house with traces of milk-froth on its cheek. By the time the cow had completely stopped producing milk, the child's desire to suckle had been satiated.

VOLUME 2

1

Lush green grass grew on the body of Arunadri Hill and in its foothills too. It was the time of the last rains of the season when the grass grew rampantly in the foothills and the cows feasted on this bounty to their heart's content. They gave milk, enough to fill a massive pitcher. Beginning with the rainy months of the *Aashaada* and after the passing of the *Karthika* months of October and November until the cold *Margashirsha* month of December, the entire region would be enveloped in green. Although the dense forest of the past no longer existed, yet, after the rainy season elapsed, the *Kakke* and *Bikke* trees would bend over with flowers and explode their seeds. The newly born and neatly growing *Palasha* plant sported its red flowers.

The tigers, which had inhabited the caves of the Arunadri Hill when the forest was dense, no longer existed; neither did the hyenas and the cheetahs. However, in the summer season of *Greeshma* and the autumn season of *Sharada,* some hyenas would wander into the hill. At times, it would pounce upon the cattle, goats and sheep, from the neighbouring villages that grazed in the foothills. However, it would never pounce upon humans. And if two or three cowherds were around, it wouldn't dare appear anywhere in the vicinity.

Kalinga Gowda had his own pasture of hundred and fifty acres, which he had inherited. He oversaw and preserved the grass in his pasture, but took his cows to graze at the foothills till the *Karthika* months. People from surrounding villages did the same. Of late, his son Krishne Gowda would go to the foothills. Now over fifty, Kalinga Gowda found it difficult to traverse up and down the uneven and rough terrain of the foothills. Besides, it was the season of supervising farm work. The father would oversee work in both farm and wetland while the son would undertake the responsibility of the cattle. Although they had employed labourers for cultivation, they would always look after the cattle personally.

Like his father, Krishne Gowda was tall and rugged. Barring the large moustache that sat on the father's face, his overall dressing and adornment resembled that of his father. There was always a *tilak* on his forehead, locket-chain around the neck, and signet-rings on his fingers. But, the son played the flute much better than his father. He could also whistle in a manner that mimicked the melody of the flute. He had his own betel-nut pouch, which contained nutmeg, clove, cardamom, tender betel leaves and limestone. He would wrap this pouch and tie it around his waist. He chewed a mouthful of betel that reddened his lips. As he joined together his lips to play the flute, the grazing cows would come and stand near him. When he took them grazing to the foothills, he carried a long bamboo staff in his hand. He had stuck a sharp spike on one end of the staff, making it a sort of spear.

One day, he had taken the cows grazing to the western slope of the hill. The tender grass here had grown waist-high because cowherds from other villages hadn't yet brought their cattle to this side. For Krishne Gowda's cows, this was an enormous feast. Krishna leaned against a boulder and napped for a while. Then he led the cows to the stream and let them drink water. After this, he left them at the bank of the stream and sauntered around. The cows resumed grazing and walked farther afield towards the cluster of *Palasha* trees. Cows belonging to the village folk from other villages as well were grazing here. Krishna too, arrived at the spot and saw about five or six folks. He chewed betel again and played the flute upon their request. By now daylight had receded, and in the west, the sun was setting. The other cowherds began driving their cattle back to their villages. Krishna too, turned his herd towards his own village. They began to make their way back, slowly grazing along the way.

Then at an incline, Krishna climbed down, crossed a stream and then let the cows climb up the slope first as he stood behind them, exhorting—'Huyyi! That's enough now, hurry up!' Suddenly, he heard a cow scream in fright from behind. Before he could scan his entire cattle for a count, the anguished scream *Ambaa!* emanated yet again. It didn't matter which cow it was or to whom it belonged; the hyena must have pounced upon one of them, thought Krishna. Gripping the staff in hand, he hastily climbed up the incline and saw one of his own Punyakoti cows standing beside a boulder nearby, shivering in fright. The hyena which emerged in a sprint from the opposite direction was about to pounce on it. Krishna looked at the hyena. It was of an extraordinary size. For a moment his heart trembled. But if he delayed, the Mother's life would be finished. By the time he twirled the spike of the staff and rushed forward, the hyena had already leapt on the cow and with a vicious swipe of its claw, smacked it across the face.

'You motherfucker!' yelled Krishna, and with lightning speed he jumped up and aimed his spear at its back. And missed. Unharmed, it let out a roar and jumped on Krishna. Now, Krishna aimed the spear at its chest and stabbed hard. The spear was stuck in its heart. But one of its front claws was embedded in his face and the other, in his chest. Blood gushed out from both places instantly, but he wasn't scared. He pulled out the spear and stabbed its chest again. Blood began streaming out from where the spear was lodged. When Krishna tried to pull out the spear to stab it once more, the hyena leapt on him and delivered the final, fatal blow.

2

When they saw the cow's face dripping blood, the other cows too, were frightened. They bolted hastily till they reached their home— the cowshed, which was located at the start of the village. Kalinga Gowda was astonished—every day, he was used to seeing them walk in with a leisurely gait, swaying their bodies sideways but today they had skedaddled here in panic. But when he closely examined the cow whose face was dripping blood, he clearly saw the deep gashes made by four claws that had dug in there. And even as he thought 'This is surely the work of the hyena', he immediately remembered that his son hadn't yet returned home. *How could Krishna abandon this wounded cow? Couldn't he just apply rose-leaf juice to its wounds right there on the spot? Of course, had he seen this, he certainly wouldn't have left it this way. Or, had he simply left the cows to graze on their own and sauntered off?* Gowda was angry at his son for a minute. But suddenly he felt scared and suspected, *what if the hyena attacked him?* He went to the back of the cowshed and checked there. Krishna wasn't there. He went inside the house and asked his daughter-in-law. No. He hadn't come home yet. Gowda's heart began to beat faster.

Immediately, he went inside the village. About fifteen or twenty men who had returned from the fields and wetlands had assembled there. Evening had already descended. Together, they lit torches made of dried coconut leaves dipped in oil. Armed with clubs, spears and scythes, they ran towards the the hill.

After crossing the bund at the periphery of the village, they split into smaller groups of three or four people and went off in different directions. Even as each person yelled 'Krishnaaa! *Lei*, Krishnaaaa!' at the top of their voice as they walked along, there was no response. Anxiety filled Kalinga Gowda's mind. His left eyebrow twitched and jumped up three times in tandem with his left shoulder. He urged the others, 'Look around! Walk faster!' He too joined one of the groups, walking with them. By the time they climbed up and descended down the boulders, crossed the small streams, searched in the clefts of trees and carried on forward, the darkness of night had already fallen. Gowda had specifically instructed them to search in places that showed traces of grazing, as these would be the places the cows would have gone to earlier in the day. Even as Gowda's group moved along the right flank of the hill, they heard a loud yell from the group behind, calling out to them: 'Kalinga Unclllle!!! Come here all of you, he's here!' They heard the yell rather unclearly in the dignified silence of the night. The 'he's here' words that Gowda heard evoked hope in his mind. 'He must be wounded. I reckon he's lying down, maybe unable to get up. Some medication and diet, and he'll be just fine', thought Gowda to himself and turned around with his men to walk towards the group that had given the call. From the movements of the torches, they could see that the other groups too, were heading in that direction.

When Kalinga went closer and saw the sight in the light of the torches, darkness enveloped his eyes. Krishna was lying down dead. Blood that had oozed from his face and heart had clotted and was turning black. The hyena had torn off his right cheek with its teeth and chewed on it. Flesh from both his thighs had been ripped apart by its mouth. All of his clothing was drenched in blood, and exposed to air, was now turning brown. The white hollow of his right eye was torn, blood trickling down. Gowda slumped as it were and collapsed on his son's corpse. The men who had accompanied him watched this sight, their grief overflowing. Kalinga Gowda was the Chief Gowda of the village. Krishna was his only son. Nobody could play the flute like he did in the entire village. Nobody could match the speed with which he raced the oxen during *Kaaruhabba*, the harvest festival. And now the only son of the Chief Gowda of the village had fallen, a dead victim of the hyena's onslaught. How could anyone mollify the Gowda? Two men ran to a stream, dipped a head-cloth in water and slowly patted Gowda's head with it.

Although Gowda regained consciousness after a while, he embraced his son's corpse even tighter, 'Where have you gone, my son?' he wept, his wails shattering the silence of the foothills. The eldest among the men, Kottigemane Chinnayya, took Gowda's head on his lap and consoled him: 'Kalinga *Anna*, there's no point in weeping now. That hyena must be around somewhere nearby. We need to kill it. Get up. Some of us will take the body and return home. The rest must search and kill that hyena.'

'My son is already gone. What's the point in killing the hyena?' said Gowda amid sobs.

'Yes, your son is gone. But if that hyena stays alive, who knows how many cows it'll kill! If it's killed, we'll at least earn some merit. It has killed Krishna, we mustn't let it get away with it.'

Now Kalinga Gowda was furious. The hyena. He sat up suddenly. 'You watch over the corpse. Wherever it is, I'll find it and make sure its blood flows', he said, standing up.

Meanwhile, one of them said: 'We didn't find Krishna's spear anywhere.'

Kottigemane Chinnayya thought quickly and said: 'Krishna didn't die just like that. He has pierced it with his spear. It must still be stuck in its body. It must be lying somewhere nearby. Come on, let's go search.'

Despite their protests, Kalinga Gowda joined the group that

embarked on the search for the hyena. Four men remained behind to watch over the corpse. Chinnayya's guess was correct. About a hundred metres from there, the hyena had fallen under a bunch of flowering thorns. There were two holes each on its chest and stomach from where blood was still flowing. The spear was still stuck in its chest. Because it would hurt if it moved this way or that, the hyena had placed all its four legs to one side and was lying curled up. When it saw so many people with torches, not only did it panic but the fury caused by facing this mortal threat escalated. It immediately stood up, and disregarding the pain caused by the spear, it bellowed once with such intensity that the sound enveloped the entire foothills.

'Fuck your mother!' said Kalinga Gowda, snatching the spear from the person next to him and charged at it. The hyena too, fell upon him in the same moment. The others shouted, 'Kalinga *Anna*! Kalinga *Anna*!' and before they could land their spears on the hyena, not only had Gowda's spear lodged inside its chest, but Krishna's spear had broken loose, and blood began to spurt from that location as well. The hyena was unable to touch Kalinga Gowda. It had fallen about five feet away from him, and before it could roar again, Gowda retrieved his spear and skewered it again, this time in its face. Although life hadn't yet gone out of it, the hyena's story had ended.

Gowda's grief had now subsided a bit when he saw the fate the hyena had suffered at his own hands. He told the others, 'Get this too, to the village.' A few knocks from the spears took out whatever life remained in the hyena. Then they tied its legs with vines plucked from the *Kattaale*—the agave plant—and gave it support on four staves. Two men carried it on their shoulders and then put it down near the place where Krishna's dead body was lying.

Now, when he saw his son's body, Gowda's mind, filled with rage, was overcome by grief. He beat his chest as he sobbed uncontrollably.

3

Nobody slept that night at Kalenahalli. Some villagers left to inform Gowda's relatives of the news, and to bring them to the village for the burial. Gowda, Lakkavva and Tayavva sat around the body, weeping continuously. The three-year-old toddler who understood this tragedy only partially, wept for some time and then lay down on his mother's lap and slept.

By the time the Swami, the Sun-God had climbed up five or six feet in the sky, relatives from far-off towns had arrived. The body couldn't be left for long in that state, with its flesh and muscles torn, as it would begin to rot and stink. They placed it on a bier made of bamboo. Before eight in the morning, they had buried it in the centre of Gowda's vast grassland and returned. Once home, Kalinga Gowda slept in one corner. Lakkavva and Tayavva lay down in another. Despite the insistence of several people present there, they did not touch even a drop of water to their mouths. Neighbours had taken the child to their home. Kalinga Gowda was the head of the village, the elder who had read *Jaimini* Mahabharata, the Gowda who was present in all their sorrows and joys, who had always offered them wise counsel—if he slept like this, who could speak the words to offer him solace and comfort his mind?

Earlier, Chinnayya had approached Gowda and said, 'This was God's will, Kalinga *Anna*, you please don't weep.' Gowda had lashed out furiously, 'Which bastard God is he? *Will!* That whoreson's piss! Was he filled with shit to *will* my son to die?' God-talk was of no use. Equally, talk of Karma, and previous birth didn't work. None among them had the wisdom enough to speak to Kalinga Gowda in this matter.

Two hours before sunset, Narasimha *Jois* from *Agrahara* arrived in Kalenahalli. It was past afternoon when he had returned home from a visit to another village, to accept *daana*, an offering traditionally made to Brahmins. The moment he stepped into his home, his wife told him the news of Kalinga Gowda's son's death from a hyena attack. Although *Jois* quickly finished his bath, he was unable to eat anything. There was a generational bond of mutual trust and affection between his and Kalinga Gowda's family. This bond remained alive in this generation as well. He drank a glass of *Gangodaka*—the Sacred Water—and completed the distance of two miles, sprinting along until he reached Gowda's house. Gowda was still lying down, but sat up when he saw *Jois*. Someone in the throng that had occupied Gowda's house, offered a wooden plank to *Jois*, who said, 'It's fine, brother', and sat down on the floor. Gowda didn't speak. Gowda's wife came near *Jois*, narrated her plight and began to weep loudly. The daughter-in-law, Tayavva, didn't have a tongue to cry loudly. But her face was a mass of flesh after all the relentless weeping she had done.

'What is the news?' *Jois* asked Kottigemane Chinnayya. Chinnayya recounted the happenings since yesterday in vivid, eye-arresting detail; not only that, he described all his efforts since morning to mollify and comfort them. His head bowed, *Jois* was thinking deeply about something for about half a minute. Then, he said, 'How is the condition of the wounded cow now?'

'Who would see that now, Swami?' said Chinnayya.

'Come, let's go see it', he said, and rose to head towards the cowshed. Chinnayya followed him. That day, nobody had taken the cows out to graze. The servants had put some straw in front of them in the grass-trench and filled their water-trough with water drawn from the well. The cow that had suffered the blow from the hyena's claw was standing there with an expression of shock and depression. The parts where the claw-nails had struck and drawn blood were swollen. It had neither touched a blade of straw nor a drop of water since yesterday. 'If its calf comes near it, it begins to kick... *budd, budd budd*. It had never kicked anybody till now', said Gowda's servant. When *Jois* went closer, it made a menacing sound as if to gore him. But the moment he stood a little afar, it cast its melancholic face downwards.

'It's stricken with fear, *ayya*', Chinnayya deciphered its behaviour.

Jois went in and told Gowda: 'Gowdayya, come to the backyard and look into the cow's eyes. Nail marks are deeply embedded on its face. Come and inspect whether that spot has turned poisonous. Only you must inspect it. Nobody else has the knowledge to do it.'

'How does it matter to me what happens to it?' said Kalinga Gowda, and wiped his eyes.

'Can *you* say this Gowdayya? Who else apart from you is well-versed in diseases related to cows? Your son is gone. And now, will you kill the *Gomaata* with your own hands by not giving her medicine, by not giving her treatment? Should this home be hit with this sin too?' he asked. Turning to Lakkavva, he said, 'Gowdamma, get up, go to the shed and see for yourself. You're the authority of this house. Couldn't you at least look at the cow since morning?'

By then, Kalinga Gowda had stood up. *Jois* followed him. Gowda's wife too, joined them. This cow that had never kicked anybody whether she was approached from behind nor gored those that approached it from the front, now shook its head to gore Gowda. But then he caught its leash and closely examined its face. He told *Jois*, 'It has turned poisonous. Need to go to the farm and get some herbs.'

'Send someone.'

'Nobody knows. I must go get it myself. I'll go immediately. You stay at home', said Kalinga Gowda and quickly exited from the backdoor of the barn. *Jois* went inside, uttering words of comfort to Gowda's wife.

When they saw their Kalinga *Anna* going out of the village alone, a couple of folks followed him into the farm. But he kept them at a distance when he started to pluck the herbs. There was an age-old dictum that forbade plucking medicinal herbs in full view of other people. He put the herbs in the folds inside his *dhoti*, came home, added a bit of garlic, clove and other medicines, and ground the mixture into a fine paste, and applied it to the wounds on the cow's face. When he learnt that it hadn't eaten grass or drunk water since yesterday, he took some grass to feed it with his own hands. It refused to open its mouth. He called to his wife who was inside, 'The cow's become like this because of fear. Light some broomsticks, we'll get rid of its fear.'

She went back in and returned with a broom made of yellow-grass sticks and waved it three times in a circular motion before the cow's face. Then she lit the front end of the broom and placed it before the cow. The broom burnt making a *cht-cht-cht-cht* sound, as the flame brilliantly lit up the entire barn, frightening not just the injured cow but the entire herd. 'Now the fear will go away', said Gowda.

The cows hadn't been milked that morning as well. The servants had left the calves to suckle. Lakkavva instructed the servants to allow them to continue suckling.

Gowda, who had returned to the house, told *Jois*: 'Narasappa, don't go to your village now. Boil some rice for yourself here, if you want.'

'Who needs rice Gowdayya? I'll stay here. Send someone to inform

my folks that I'll return tomorrow morning. That should be enough.'
A servant carried a lighted torch and set out for his house.

4

Kalinga Gowda wanted to drink water. He called for it, finished three-fourths of the pot in short quick gulps and dried his moustache with his forearms. He hadn't eaten betel nut since morning. He ordered for his betel nut pouch, then tossed two betel nut pieces into his mouth, spread a whit of limestone on the betel leaf with his thumb, and put it in his mouth. He then dropped some tobacco on to his palm, rubbed it to a powder, filled his mouth with it and asked *Jois*, 'What crime had my child committed to suffer such a horrible death so young?'

Jois answered: 'Gowdayya, you're so knowledgeable about so many things. How can you say this? Your son attained an honourable death. You mustn't say "horrible death".'

'Is it honourable to die from being bitten by a hyena?'

'He didn't simply die from the bite of the hyena. He fought to save and protect the *Gomaata*. The Shastras say:

gavaarthe brahmanarthe vaa varnanaam vaapi sankare |
grnhii yaataam vipravishau shastram dharma vyapekshayaa ||

'For the protection of the cow, even a Brahmin and a Vaishya must take up arms. Given this, your son is a cowherd by his *jati*; he went to save the *Gomaata*. And, he *did* save her. If he hadn't charged ahead, would the cow have survived? Like a man, he stabbed the hyena with the spear. Even if you hadn't gone there and killed it, it would've died anyway. Although he died unfortunately, he's sure to attain a virtuous end. Think of it as your fortune. The cow was saved.'

'What's the point if it's been saved! Will my son return?' replied Gowda as he stood up, went out to the veranda, spat the tobacco juice into the gutter and came inside. He called out to his wife and daughter-in-law, '*Lei!* Come here, Narasappa is telling us about the Shastras, come and listen.' Both Lakkavva and Tayavva sat down, leaning against a wall.

Narasimha *Jois* said: 'You mustn't think like this; you mustn't say—what's the point if it's been saved? It is written in the Shastras, *Yadgruhe dukhitaa gaavah sa yaati narake narah.* The person in whose house a cow is unhappy, that person goes to hell. If that cow had died, wouldn't its calf be sad? Then the previous seven generations and the next seven generations of your lineage would have gone to the *Raurava Naraka—* Hell. Indeed, your son would've definitely gone to Hell had he watched on silently like a coward fearing for his life even as he saw the hyena attacking the cow. But your son showed great courage, and he saved your ancestors; he saved you, too.'

As she heard these last words, Lakkavva wiped her eyes and sat erect. Tayavva too, began to listen to his words with greater attention. *Jois* said: 'Don't you know? In the past, there was a great Rishi named Chyavana. When he was seated in deep meditation on a riverbank, a great flood occurred and he was drowned in the river. But this did not disturb his meditation and he stayed inside the river in the same state. One day, when three fishermen cast their nets to catch fish, he was caught in their net. The fishermen reckoned that this was an enormous fish, but when they pulled it ashore, they found the Rishi. The fishermen were scared. But the Rishi himself told them: "You have caught me, thinking I was a fish. There's no mistake on your part. Sell me to someone."

'But who would buy such a great Rishi? News reached the king. He came over, prostrated before the Rishi and pleaded with him to come to the palace. "I will come. But first give these fishermen my price", said the Rishi. When the king asked: "But how do we fix a price for you?" the Rishi answered: "You're the ruler of this country, you think it over and make a decision." Poor thing, the king didn't know what to do. He said he would offer his entire treasury. To this, when the Rishi questioned, "That's all my price?" the king didn't know what to say. When the king said he would give his entire kingdom, the Rishi again replied, "That's all my price?" What else do you think should the king do now?' said *Jois*, looking at Lakkavva's face.

After she said, 'What would I know? You tell me', Narasimha *Jois* looked at Kalinga Gowda's face.

'I got it', he said.

'Then say it.'

'Didn't the Rishi say, "Give a *Gomaata*?" Right?'

'See that? You found out the answer. The Rishi did indeed say that. "A cow is equal to the entire Cosmos. And I am just one living being in that Cosmos. Even if you include crores of Rishis like me, it wouldn't be equal to the price of a cow," said the Rishi.'

Gowdayya told his wife and daughter-in-law: 'You heard that? Now drill this properly into your heads.'

Jois said: 'You've heard the name of Janaka Maharaja, right?'

'Sitamma's father, right?'

'Yes, the same. He was known as a Rajarshi. Although he was a great emperor ruling his kingdom seated on his mighty throne, he was akin to a Rishi. He had committed no sin. When he was really old, he discarded his body using his Yogic powers. That means, he left this body and went to a higher world. But his soul was taken to the gates of hell. When Janaka asked: "I have done no wicked deed. Why have you brought me here?"

To this, they said:

Ekadaatu charantiim gaam vaarayaamaasa vai bhavaan |
Tena papa vipaakena nirayadwaara darshanam ||

'What does that mean?' asked Gowda.

Narasimha *Jois* continued: '"Sometime in the past, you had stopped a cow that was grazing. It is owing to this sin that you were taken to see the door of hell", they said. Else, Janaka Maharaja would have gone straight to Heaven.'

'Heard that? You folks are lazy at times to take care of the cows properly', Gowda said to his wife and daughter-in-law.

Jois did not sleep that night. He began by telling them that thirty-three crore Gods inhabited the cow's body and explained the greatness of *Gopuja*, the puja offered to the cow, reciting *slokas* and explaining their meaning. By daybreak he said: 'Gowdamma, you must know this. You mustn't weep. Your son shed his life while protecting the cow. He died killing the hyena to save the cow. You have your next generation here, this boy-child—it will be protected by the virtue your son has earned. Now you must not cry. Nurse that injured cow. Comfort your daughter-in-law. Gowdamma, you must now get up and take charge of everything.'

Jois had not eaten anything since yesterday. 'Gowdayya all of you clean yourselves up and eat something. You must put in hard effort, heal the cow's wounds and save it. I don't know if it slept well last night. Go, check that. See if it needs any other medicine, diet, whatever', he said and left for his village.

Gowda got up and went to the cowshed. His wife followed him.

The swelling of the cow's wound had subsided. But it hadn't touched grass and water. It was standing as it were, in the same position, its body crumpled as if inside a pigeonhole, still badly frightened. After caressing its face with his fingers, rubbing its body gently and uttering comforting words, he turned to his wife, 'I'll go to the farm and get some herbs. She hasn't eaten anything. You soak two kilos of rice in water, put two coconuts, mix it well and keep it ready. She has fasted for two days. It doesn't bode well for the home if things are like this.'

Gowdamma left to get rice and coconuts. Gowda took the wounded cow's calf to suckle the teat of another cow and once it was done, left for the farm to get the herbs.

5

On the Eleventh Day, the entire house was wiped clean with water mixed with cow dung. Relatives were given the sacred *panchagavya* and cows were given as *daana*—this was how Krishna's last rites were completed. More than 10,000 people were fed a feast comprising ragi *mudde*—a large, solid ball made of ragi—a millet—and various other delicacies. After the feast, those who had arrived for the last rites from other places, returned.

Now everyone in Kalinga Gowda's house was struck with anxiety. The wound inflicted by the hyena on the cow had completely healed. But it still hadn't emerged from its depression. It still didn't touch grass and water. Its eyes did not shine with the same energetic light as before, but appeared like those of a lifeless animal. Anxious that it would die of starvation, folks in the house would soak two kilos of rice in water, add some coconut to it, stir it well and feed the mixture to it twice a day. It had no food apart from this force-fed rice mixture and water that it was forcibly made to drink. Gowda nursed it with every medicine he had knowledge of. There was nobody else in the surrounding villages in a vicinity of thirty miles who knew more than him about cattle medicine. The cow was also treated with various mantras and tantras and the entire cowshed was sanctified with pumpkin. But no cure was visible.

The cow became thinner day after day and finally, even stopped getting up. They fed it rice flour and gave it water even while it was lying down. And in the same position, it would drop dung and urinate. But prolonged periods of lying down tore the skin off its chest and the sides of its belly. Gowda knew the medicine to treat and heal such a wound. But because the cow continued to lie down on the same wounds, they wouldn't heal even after the medicine was applied.

The family was consumed with worry. 'Mother, my child gave his life for you. At least you live. If you don't, it'll appear as if my child has died in vain.' Gowdamma had uttered these words to the cow several times.

'Tell me what's happened to you, Mother. If you just sleep like this quietly, how'd we know? I've treated you with all the medicine that my brain knows. Now you tell me in your own words what's there in your mind', Gowda too had asked it tens of times.

Tayavva did not know how to speak. She had kept the sorrow of her husband's death within herself. Apart from weeping, she didn't know how to show her sorrow. Although her parents asked her to stay with them, she didn't agree to go. She would affectionately rub the cow's body, hug its neck and try to offer it comfort. She didn't know how to speak and the cow too, wasn't speaking anymore.

Twenty days passed like this. Towards the end, the cow didn't drink the rice flour mixture. If it was force-fed, it would simply vomit. Everyone in the house lost hope. At night they stayed awake and took turns to tend to it. Before dying, it didn't wriggle; it didn't even thrash its hands and legs. Like a body that was already dead ere, but which was merely completing an unfinished business, it put out its breath for the last time and didn't take it back in. Although all of them already knew that death was certain, they all wept loudly when it actually died. The sorrow of losing the son twenty-two days ago had become old in the face of this fresh sorrow. Gowdamma hugged its dead body sobbing, 'So you finally died, didn't you?'

It's not that no cow had ever died in the past in Kalinga Gowda's house. But typically, his cows hadn't died prematurely owing to disease and ill-health. Indeed, in the surrounding villages too, he would go out and provide medical treatment to any cow that was affected by disease, and he would cure them. It didn't matter if the cow was his or someone else's—even his enemy's. The moment Gowda heard that a cow was suffering from disease, and he didn't immediately go out to treat it, just the thought of the kind of hell he would fall into after his death, made him sweat. On several occasions, despite the best medicines and treatment, cows in his shed would die. But throughout his life, not one cow had died from an attack by a tiger or hyena. Now this cow—especially one from Punyakoti's stock—had died because of a hyena attack. The poison in the wound from the hyena's claws had healed. Despite this, the cow had shed its life due to depression. Mantra, tantra, rituals, medicine, nothing had yielded fruit. *Why did the cow die? Was it a lie that my son died protecting it? Did he sacrifice his life in a cowardly state of mind? He was a man, oh, he was a man! There was no cowardice in his mind*—thought Gowda to himself.

Now the dead cow had to be buried. The usual custom was to bury dead cows in the farm or the field and plant a sapling on top. But Gowda put this cow's corpse on his bullock cart and drove it to his pasture. He got the land next to his son's grave dug up and placed the cow's body to sleep there. He draped it with a new sari and blouse, placed a pound of rice, salt and a few coconuts next to it, poured a bowl of water on it, and covered the grave with earth.

Then he touched the grave with his hand, touched it to his forehead, joined his palms together in namaste and said: 'Mother, your son is sleeping next to you. He gave up his life to save you. And you died grieving his death. Having lost your son, you lost the desire to live. You are a blessed woman in all ways. Despite my son gone, I'm still alive, unlike you who gave up her life. I know you'll look after him in joy and sorrow, that's why I've put you to rest next to him. From now on, he is your responsibility.'

6

Another worry awaited Gowda.

The servant who was looking after his cowshed came to him and said: '*Ayya*, that male calf of Kapila has thinned down for some reason. It's not eating grass or drinking water properly.'

Gowda went in and checked it out. It was a male calf with four teeth. It had thinned down to the extent that it appeared shrivelled. Its eyes were dull. When Gowda asked, 'Why has it become like this?' The servant said, 'Although it has four teeth, it was still attached to its mother. I reckon it's become like this after its mother departed. I don't know clearly.'

The calf was three years old. Its mother had delivered another calf just two months earlier. On the day of his son's last rites, Gowda had given the cow and the new calf to Narasimha *Jois* as *daana*. The mother had given birth to another calf, but this one was still attached to her. Although it was tied at night in the bull section of the shed, come morning, it used to go near its mother. Mother and son would sniff each other for a while and lick each other's bodies. Now the mother was no longer there. Gowda instantly understood the reason why the calf had shrivelled. But what could be done now? Its mother had already been given away in *daana* and couldn't come back to this shed again. Gowda had planned to put this boy to the yoke by next monsoon, when planting would begin. But like a milk-drinking infant-calf, this one was shrivelling because it was missing its mother.

Kalinga Gowda spent the entire day in thought. The same thought persisted even at night. *What if he dies missing his mother? What then?* And so the moment he awoke at dawn, he got up, untied the rope of the male calf and took it along with him, walking in the direction of the *Agrahara*, the village of Narasimha *Jois*. En route near Ranganahalla, he tied it to one of the *Lakki* trees, went past the bunch of these *Lakki* trees, finished his morning ablutions, washed his hands and legs and cleaned his face in the stream there. Although the Swami, the Sun-God, wasn't yet visible in the East, he prayed to his charioteer, Aruna, and walked to the *Agrahara* with the calf.

By the time he reached there, *Jois*' wife Subbamma was milking the cow that had come to her house as an offering. Their five-year-old son was standing behind his mother waiting for the milk. *Jois* had gone to the tank bund to pluck flowers and *Tulsi*. They used to tie the cow in the front yard of the house. The moment it saw its calf, the cow loudly mooed once. At the same time, the calf recognizing its mother rushed forward and put its mouth to her face. Because the cow took a few steps forward, Subbamma stood up with the milk-bowl in her hand. 'How can the umbilical bond of the mother and child be forgotten!' said Gowdayya and narrated everything to the *Jois'* wife.

Presently, when the *Jois* came home and learned of what had happened, he said: 'Some mothers and children are deeply attached. We must not separate them. Do one thing.'

'Please tell.'

'You've given me this cow as *daana*. That which is given as *daana* must not be taken back just like that. Give me one silver rupee as its sale price and take it back.'

'*Ayya*, one rupee or one lakh rupees, that cow which has been given as *daana* mustn't be taken back. Instead, do what I say. I'll give this male calf as *daana*. You keep it. Mother and son must be together. Does it matter where they are?'

Jois thought about this for a minute. Then he said: 'That would've been a possibility. But one must consult the Shastras, which say:

Yuvaanaamindriyopetam shatena sahayoothapam |
Gavendram Brahmanendraaya bhoori shrungamalankrutam ||

This is a male calf—that means he's a *Yoothapati*, the leader of a group of hundreds upon hundreds of cows, by being capable of giving them his seed. That means this is not a cow, it is the Lord of Cows. And only a Brahmanendra—a person who's eligible to be called the Lord of Brahmins—can take him as *daana*. That means only a Brahmin who has the capability to become the progenitor of a new *gotra*—a lineage named after him—can accept this male calf. A *Vrishabha* or bull is equivalent to half a herd of cows. One *Vrishabha daana* is equal to a hundred *Godaanas*. Only a person who has the capacity to accept a hundred cows can accept a bull. An ordinary Brahmin like me, for whom it is hard to accept one *Godaana*, how can I accept that male calf?'

For a moment, Kalinga Gowda was answerless.

Then, suddenly, he said: 'Narasappa, remember when you accepted that *Godaana*? There was a male calf that came with it. How did you accept that?'

'Whenever we speak of *Godaana*, it's always implied that the cow is a lactating cow. How can a cow that doesn't have a calf give milk? And so, no matter whether that calf is male or female, it always comes along, together with the mother, and never as a separate *daana*. By the time the calf weans away from its mother's milk, the cow itself would've stopped giving milk. One should not give as *daana* a cow that doesn't give milk. That means it is forbidden to even give such a calf as *daana*. You're now telling me that you want to offer a calf that's weaned away from its mother's milk, that is, a bull, as *daana*.'

Gowda didn't know what to say. He removed his head-cloth, placed it on the ground and just sat there saying nothing. Was there no solution to this? Meanwhile, the male calf and its mother, each licked the other's body three times.

Gowda asked: 'Was she missing her son?'

'I couldn't clearly understand what it was doing. But one day while she was out grazing, she tore at the rope and ran in the direction of your village. I had to go and bring her back. I reckoned she'd run off because she was missing the house she was born in.'

'Maybe. That's possible. It could be that she might've also missed her calf. Now tell me, what should be done to unite mother and son?'

Jois thought for a minute. Then he got up, went in, returned with one silver rupee, placed it before Gowda, and said: 'Get up, hold the calf by its leash and sell it to me. Take this rupee.'

Gowda agreed to this. He took the rupee and put it in the folds of his *dhoti* at the waist. He stood up, held the calf's leash and went and stood under the edge of the roof of the house. The morning sun had now climbed up the height of three adult men. He lifted up the leash, held it up to the sun, put it in the hands of *Jois*, and said: 'I have given this in sale to you. The Swami rising up in the sky, and its mother, the *Gomaata* standing here and watching this are the witnesses.'

VOLUME 3

1

Three years rolled by. The centrepiece of Gowdayya's home now was the grandson. Now six years old, its name too, is Kalinga. The tradition of naming the first grandson after the grandfather's name existed in Gowda's lineage since generations. This is why the name Kalinga Gowda, who had lived during the time when Punyakoti returned alive from the tiger's cave, still survives in this lineage. If the grandfather is Kalinga Gowda, the grandson too, is Kalinga Gowda. But as long as the grandfather and father were alive, the 'Gowda' honorific was not applied to the grandson's name.

But the women of this house couldn't address this grandson as 'Kalinga'. In Gowdamma's case it was the name of her husband, for Tayavva it was her father-in-law's name. The village folk addressed him as 'Putta', or the 'Little' Kalinga. For the purposes of this house, his name was simply 'Putta'.

At age six, Putta goes to the pasture with his grandfather. He visits the fields and the farm with the servants. The cow of the Punyakoti stock whose milk he used to drink earlier has given birth again, and is now lactating. Even now, in the pasture, he puts his mouth to its teat and drinks its milk on occasions. No matter at what hour he puts his mouth to its teat, the cow doesn't move one bit. Apart from prattling non-stop with his grandmother, he would pick up and eat butter directly from the earthen pot in which it was being curdled. Sometimes, he would jump on his mother and ask, 'Why can't you speak?' Not understanding her reply in sign language, he'd ask his grandmother for the answer. If she replied, 'God has taken away your mother's tongue, Putta', he'd climb on his mother's lap, forcibly open her mouth, insert his finger, look inside and tell his grandmother, 'You're lying. Avva's tongue is right here!' Both women would look at each other and laugh.

Ever since the grandson was born, Kalinga Gowda was keen to

get him properly educated. Gowda was educated enough to read the *Jaimini* Mahabharata. To get his son Krishna educated, Gowda had brought in a full-time master exclusively for the purpose. But Krishna had learnt nothing although the knowledge of playing the flute had come to him untaught by anyone. The number of Yakshagana dances he had performed would amaze anybody. He'd chew his betel leaf and perform Yakshagana from time to time, and he topped the village in *Kolaata*, which was the group stick-dance performance set to folk poetry. The rest of the time, he'd play his flute as he grazed his cows. He had no interest in anything else. If he'd read the *Jaimini* at least once, Gowda's desire would've been fulfilled and he'd be a contented man. But he wasn't terribly disappointed when that didn't happen either. He'd himself say on occasion, 'Why does a *Golla* need more knowledge than what Krishna has learnt?'

He could've taught Putta how to write and copy the Kannada alphabet—*a, aa, e, ee*—but as a Vokkaliga, who didn't have the authority to impart knowledge, he refrained. Now, about four years ago, a new government primary school had opened in the *Agrahara*. Ochayya, who had been appointed by the government had not only taken charge but had also put wooden planks for the children to sit. Although they beat the children, they didn't thrash them so severely that warts would form. And so, convinced that his cherished grandson wouldn't suffer much from the beatings, Gowda decided to admit Putta there. When he asked Narasimha *Jois*, he gave the same opinion. *Jois'* son, the eight-year-old Venkataramana, went to the same school.

In the morning, a servant had to escort Putta to school and return— that was enough. He'd have his lunch at the *Jois'* home. In the evening, a servant would bring Putta back home. This was how Gowda fixed the arrangement. The *Jois* consulted the *Panchanga*, the Almanac, and fixed an auspicious date following which Gowdayya clothed Putta in a new shirt and shorts, took him to the school, made him prostrate before Ochayya, gave him ten coconuts and five kilos of butter as *guru dakshina*, folded his own hands in a respectful namaste and got Putta enrolled in the school. There was only one person for the entire school, the self-same Ochayya. Out of curiosity to know what lessons he would teach, Gowdayya sat for a while on the stone bench outside the school and opened his tobacco pouch. The *Jois* who had accompanied him left for a nearby village to obtain *daana*.

From where he was sitting outside, Gowdayya could hear Ochayya instruct Putta to copy the Kannada alphabets ಅ ಆ (a, ā). For a minute, he experienced a feeling of fulfilment. Then Ochayya was saying: 'Class Two students, open your books. Recite the poem you learnt yesterday; your recitation must be clear. You must recite with me.'

Even as Gowda speculated that it must be *Jaimini*, the teacher recited a different poem:

> *'pon ejecting I became dung, 'pon patting I became dung-cake*
> *'pon burning I became the sacred ash for the forehead*
> *applied without patting, I became manure*
> *what good have you done to anyone, O Human?*

Gowdayya's ears perked up instantly. This was indeed the cow's song. *Not bad for a government school. They teach well,* he thought, clicking two fingers to produce a *chit* sound even as Ochayya was reciting inside:

> *'pon extracting I became milk, and became curd 'pon hardening*
> *became butter when curdled.*
> *I became fine ghee when heated*
> *what good have you done to anyone, O Human?*

By then the recitation had stopped. The teacher was saying: 'All of you write down the meaning of this. Tomorrow, I'll teach you the next portion. There shouldn't be a single mistake.'

Gowdayya got up, went inside the school and asked the teacher: '*Ayya*, that song is very good. Please teach me some of it.'

Although he was taken aback for a bit, the teacher took out a book of Class Two, placed it in his hands and said, 'If you know how to read, you can read it yourself. Else, I'll teach.'

Gowdayya read the subsequent poems on his own. There was nothing in there that he didn't understand. Not so tough as *Jaimini*. Still, *how nicely it's written!* he thought to himself as he read. When he read the last poem, his eyes moistened:

I seek dirt and grass on the wayside and on the streets and
Munch on them, return home and give elixir.
And drinking it you betray me. Tell me
what good have you done to anyone, O Human?

After he had finished reading, Ochayya said: 'If you like it so much, I'll write this down on a piece of paper and send it through your boy.' Gratitude welled up within Gowdayya. He made enquiries about him. Not only did Ochayya know the complete *Jaimini* by heart, he also possessed the eloquence to narrate the *Gadugina* Mahabharata. He also knew Sanskrit and was well-versed in astrology and rituals. He folded his hands and told his grandson, '*Lei* Putta, go with Narasappa's son in the afternoon and eat lunch at his house. In the evening, Dyaava will come and get you', and left for his village.

Throughout the entire journey back, one question kept troubling his mind.

I seek dirt and grass on the wayside and on the streets and
Munch on them, return home and give elixir.
And drinking it you betray me. Tell me
what good have you done to anyone, O Human.

He drinks the Gomaata's milk and betrays her, his own mother... what good has he done to anyone? Field, farm, house, possessions... he wants everything. Goat, fowl, sheep, kid... he needs them all. He rears a dog only because it guards his house. He keeps the Gomaata only to consume her milk. What good has he done to anyone? Thoo! The human birth is the worst birth. Blessed is the cow's birth. Who knows how many virtues one needs to accumulate to get a cow's birth! God, will you give me the Gomaata's birth next time? Gowda prayed to God in his mind. *But have I committed no sin at all? So, if I merely ask for a cow's birth, will it be granted to me just like that? To get a cow's birth means to truly become God. But then, isn't the cow greater than God? I'm a bungling fool indeed. Where do I have the virtue of being born a cow in my next birth?*

∽

After the school finished at eleven in the afternoon, *Jois'* son Venkataramana took Putta with him to his home. Leisure period was between eleven and two. *Jois'* wife Subbamma served meals to Putta on a plate of stitched leaves. After eating, he threw the leaf and cleaned the floor. Starting that day, he ate lunch every afternoon in their home. Subbamma served him with great affection. Her son Venkataramana, three years older than Putta Kalinga, was in Class Three. Apart from school lessons, he has also learnt Sanskrit from his father. In the evenings, *Jois* teaches Vedic mantras to his son. Before his *Upanayanam*—the sacred thread ceremony—a year ago, he was already learning Sanskrit grammar, *Amarakosha* and *Nitishataka*. Now he's engaged in Vedic studies as well. 'If you don't go to the government's school, it'll be difficult to earn a livelihood in future,' was the perspective from which the *Jois* sent his son to the government school.

Putta was an intelligent boy. Apart from what Ochayya taught him at school, Venkataramana used to teach him other subjects in the afternoons. And, so, within fifteen days, Putta was able to write the fifty-two Kannada alphabets as well as read and write simple words like tree, home and son.

2

One afternoon after finishing his lunch, Kalinga Gowda washed hands and was drinking buttermilk, when a servant of the Hobli's *Sheikhdaar*—the Zonal Administrative Head—came to him and handed him a *hukum*, a government order, after taking Gowda's signature on it.

'What's this, son?' asked Gowda. The servant said, 'Nothing grandpa. You have that reserved grazing pasture of one hundred and fifty acres? A *hukum* from the top has come, which says that it needs to be cleared for cultivation. If you don't clear it on your own, the government will snatch it from you and give it to someone else.'

'Why's the government angry with me, boy?'

'It's not just you grandpa. Kottige Chinnayya has fifty acres of pasture, right? He's also got the same kind of *hukum*. And *hukums* are getting ready for pasture-owning farmers in other villages too. The number of people in the country has increased. People don't have enough to eat. And so, the government decided that instead of keeping pastures exclusively for cattle, if that land is cultivated, people will at least have something to eat, and that's why it has passed this *hukum*.'

'Which bloody son of which of my wives is the government?' roared Gowda in fury.

'You must not talk about the government like this. If you say such things before others, they'll put you in jail,' the servant counselled. He asked for water, drank it in his cupped palms and left for Kottigemane Chinnayya's house to serve him the *hukum*.

After he was gone, Gowda tried to read it once. But he found it difficult to read the carbon copy of the Sheikhdaar's cursive handwriting. And he was the only person in the village who was considerably literate. So if he couldn't understand this, who else could? Then, Chinnayya came running, holding in his hand the *hukum* that he was served with. He too, had received the same paper, in the self-same cursive handwriting. Both of them decided that only Narasappa *Jois* could read this and sprinted to the *Agrahara*.

Jois who read the whole thing including the notification, narrated the same summary: People don't have enough food now. Agricultural land must be increased. The Honourable Government has decided to provide government-owned pastures for cultivation at its own expense to farmers who were willing to till such land. Those zamindars who owned pastures were given the option to voluntarily use them for cultivation; else the government would forcibly take them over and then distribute them either on a sale or auction basis to applicants who had agreed to cultivate them. The pasture-owners concerned had to visit the Presence of Taluk *Amaldaar* Sahib and give an undertaking.

By then, the schoolmaster who had also arrived at *Jois*' home, read it and repeated the same summary.

'You see, noble souls earn merit by leaving behind pastures so that they provide grass for cattle. These bastards are stealing existing pastures. If the existing land is properly tilled with hard labour, will it say it won't yield a good harvest?' asked Gowdayya.

The master said: 'You go to the Taluk *Amaldaar* and make an appeal. He's a good man. He will bestow something favourable to you so that you're not in trouble.'

But Chinnayya and Gowdayya couldn't go to the Taluk on their own. So when they told him, 'Please come with us,' the teacher replied, 'I'm a humble government employee. I shouldn't come. If *Jois* comes along, it'll be all right.' Besides, as it was already getting late for school, the master left the place.

Chinnayya was thoroughly illiterate. He knew nothing about the government, laws and the rest. Gowdayya and *Jois* discussed these topics for a long time. 'Why did the government get this twisted mind? It was certain that no good would befall the guy who ordered this *hukum*', thus went the train of the discussion. One shouldn't be tardy in such matters. They both decided to visit the Taluk tomorrow. Chinnayya nodded. But his feet shivered slightly at the thought of going to the Taluk and standing in front of the Sahib.

3

The next day both of them arrived at the *Agrahara* by the hour the crow cawed. They had to go to the Taluk from there. The three of them traversed the twenty-kilometre distance into the town without stopping anywhere, and arriving before the sun had risen over their heads. *Jois* was not carrying anything. On his body was the *dhoti* that he wore, and the shawl around his shoulders. In another Sanctified Dhoti, he had a scraped coconut and a fistful of *Akshata* or Sanctified Rice. Gowdayya had carried six kilos of butter in an urn. Chinnayya had carried five kilos of butter in an earthen pot whose mouth was tied with a rope.

Jois had seen the town earlier. He also knew where the Taluk office was located. When the three of them went there, all doors and windows of the office were closed. Only two policemen tasked with guarding the treasury were standing there with guns. When *Jois* approached them courageously and asked, one of them told him that it was a Sunday, and government offices had a holiday on Sundays. *Jois* knew that government offices were closed on Sundays. But when they had decided on this journey, it hadn't occurred to them. But the time of their departure as per the Almanac that he had consulted yesterday, was certainly auspicious. But now this has happened. Gowdayya said out of disappointment: 'Why has the government kept holiday on Sunday? Isn't Monday the holiday for the entire country? In the villages nobody ploughs nor ties the yoke on Monday. The Shastras say that nobody should tire out *Basavanna* or, bull, on a Monday.'

Of the two, the policeman who wore the sacred ash and had applied *kumkum*, or vermillion, said: 'Gowdayya, you speak the truth. But the government is of the Europeans. He has made Sunday as holiday according to the convenience of his *jati*. The Monday of your village doesn't work in government.'

Jois asked the policemen: 'Can you please show me where the *Amaldaar's* house is?'

They pointed to the brick bungalow situated between seven or eight massive trees next to the huge compound of the Taluk Office. The *Jois* took along both of them, and after crossing the compound, reached the gate of the garden in front of the bungalow. A householder standing there asked them: 'What do you want? Why have you come here?'

Jois looked at the person who asked this. Not only did he sport the sacred ash on his forehead, he had also applied *kumkum* right in the centre of his brows. The sacred thread across his shoulder was also visible from under his thin undershirt and there were red pearl-studded earrings on his ears. He wore a four-span silk *dhoti* that shone like gold, and although he'd crossed fifty he had a well-built physique. *Jois* reckoned that he was the *Amaldaar* Sahib and spoke instantly: 'I am a Vedic *Purohit*, a priest, from an *Agrahara* under your rule. I have come here to bestow royal blessings upon you.'

'Who're these two?'

'Farmers from our village. They have come here to prostrate and pay their respects to you.'

Catching the hint in *Jois*' words, both Gowdayya and Chinnayya put their vessels down on the grass, touched the ground and prostrated. 'Come in,' said the *Amaldaar* to all the three as he went inside. Gowdayya and Chinnayya crossed the outer door. They didn't enter the inner door. In the large living room in the inner door, the *Amaldaar* sat on one of the four chairs and pointed the *Jois* to another. But the *Jois* didn't sit. From his Sanctified Dhoti, he extracted the coconut and *Akshata* and holding it in his right hand, melodiously chanted the mantra meant for royal blessings and sprinkled the *Akshata* on his head. After this, the *Amaldaar* himself got up and accepted the coconut with both hands and did namaste.

'Have you finished your *Sandhyavandanam*, your daily ritual oblations to the sun?' he asked. To which, *Jois* said, 'Briefly. I awoke early, finished my bath, and left my village.'

'Let's have lunch first,' said the *Amaldaar* and turned to the other two, 'Please sit. Have some lunch.' When he said this, Gowdayya and Chinnayya felt incomprehensibly happy. They hadn't in their wildest dreams thought that they would eat a meal in *Amaldaar* Sahib's house. The Sahib got up and went inside. His cook came out with a huge hindalium vessel and received the butter they had brought.

4

After they had all finished lunch, the *Amaldaar* occupied a wooden chair in the inner courtyard. *Jois* sat on a bamboo chair. Opposite the Sahib, Kalinga Gowda and Chinnayya sat on the floor near the wall, submissively, in a crumpled-up posture. The *Amaldaar* said: 'Gowdayya, over lunch I told *Jois* the same thing. This law has originated at the top. The government formed a committee of the European Red People to find out what can be done to increase the production of food. They said: "All pastures must be given for cultivation. Else, convert all private pastures to fields and wetlands. Pass a *hukum* to this effect and give it to the pasture-owners." This was the decision endorsed by the committee. Accordingly, the Diwan Sahib has passed this order through the Revenue Commissioner. Nothing is in my hands.'

Jois requested: 'We do understand Your Excellency's words. We are not big enough to see the Diwan Sahib. That's why as the *purohit*, I will inform you. You may write it as such to your higher authorities:

Tasmaadgavaam prachaaram tu muktvaa swargaanna heeyate |
yashcinatti drumam punyam go prachaaram chhinatyapi ||

Meaning, anyone who leaves pastures meant for cattle won't be denied from going to heaven. Those who obstruct the lands meant for cattle, or those who use such lands for selfish purposes, or those who cut down trees, twenty-one generations of such a person will fall into the

S.L. BHYRAPPA

Raurava hell. This is what the Shastras say.

Gokulasya trushaartasya jalaante vasudhaadhipa |
Utpaadayatiyo vighnam tamaahu brahmaghaatakam ||

'"Those who cause trouble to the cow's grass and water are termed as Colossal Sinners," says the Mahabharata.'

The *Amaldaar* was listening to *Jois'* words with great interest. He was a devout *Sanatani*, a pious Hindu who performed *Sandhyavandanam* and puja daily, and had immense bhakti towards the Shastras and Puranas. *Jois* further said:

Dhanuh Shatam parihaaro graamasya syaat samantatah |
Shamyaapaataastrayo vaapi triguno nagarasya tu ||
Tatraaparihrutam dhaanyam vihimsyuh pashavo yadi |
Na tatra pranayeddandam nripatih pashurakshinaam ||

'It is said that around the village, land amounting to about half a kilometre must be allocated for cattle. If it is a city, three times this land must be allocated. And in this area, if anybody makes a field, tills and grows crop, and if a cow eats his crop, the king must not penalize the owner of that cow—the Shastras say this as well. We must not deceive the *Gomaata* and use Mother Earth, the *Bhoomata,* for our purposes. Although the *Gomaata* eats the grass that grows on the *Bhoomata's* body, it transforms into milk and indirectly reaches us in the end. To whom else does a mother's milk reach but her child?'

The *Amaldaar* nodded his head as if agreeing with this, and said: 'What you say is true. As I'm listening to you, I feel a growing interest to formally learn in-depth all the Shastras related to this. You saw for yourself when we went to the backyard to wash our hands and legs—there are about four or five cows in my house at any time. At least two cows are always lactating. In fact, my wife doesn't give a drop of milk even to my grandson without first doing puja to the cow after her ritual bath early in the morning. But what to do? Those who rule the government are different people. The experts who give them advice and recommendations are also different people. They're all people from England. Or, they are those who have gone there and returned. Will the Diwan listen to me, a mere Taluk *Amaldaar?* What can I do in this situation?'

When he watched the *Amaldaar's* courtesy and adherence to dharma, the fear that had emanated in Kalinga Gowda from the notion that the *Amaldaar* was his boss, vanished. He butted in addressing him in the singular: 'My man, please listen a bit to what I say.'

Jois immediately retorted: 'Gowdayya! How can you address His Excellency in the singular? You've not learnt even a bit of refinement!'

But the *Amaldaar* himself said: 'It's ok, it's ok. He's speaking out of genuine goodwill. Tell me, what is it Gowdayya?'

Gowdayya said: 'It was my mistake, my man. I will not talk to you in the singular. If you so wish, please come to my village and enquire. In all, I have a hundred-and-fifty acres of pasture. This Chinnayya has fifty acres. For namesake, these lands are in my name and his. But till now, it has been that anybody in the village can bring their cows for grazing there. After the fodder has been exhausted near the hill, the other cows in our village come to our pasture and graze in it. We haven't shooed away a single cow so far. We haven't chided its owner. It's, after all, our *Gomaata*—does it matter who she belongs to?'

The *Amaldaar* nodded his head in admiration when he heard these words. Gowdayya continued: 'My name is Kalinga Gowda. You surely know the Punyakoti Cow Song. I belong to the lineage of that Kalinga. It was during the time of one of my ancestors that the Punyakoti cow went to the tiger and came back, alive. My village is at the foothills of the Arunadri Hill. My cowshed till today has cows from the Punyakoti stock. My son has given his life to save a cow's life.'

Jois interrupted: 'Right, right, what Gowdayya is saying is absolutely true! This is the same lineage as of *that* Kalinga Gowda. Kalenahalli is a sacred place. Your Excellency must please visit once and see this Gowdayya's cowshed, which houses the Punyakoti stock, and is no less sacred than Kashi or Rameshwaram.'

Now, the *Amaldaar's* interest was heightened. 'When I come to your Zonal Headquarters for the next round of assessing taxes for the Taluk, I'll surely visit. Since it's a sacred place, my wife will also accompany me. If one does puja to a cow of the Punyakoti stock, one's life is fulfilled. We'll inform in advance. You must perform the puja with due ritual ceremony. We'll get the necessary material for the puja.'

It was indeed true that the *Amaldaar's* devotion towards Gowdayya's cowshed was kindled. But he was powerless to protect the pasture. And neither was his devotion restricted only to Gowdayya's pasture; it extended to all pasture-owners. He genuinely wanted to save the pastures, but didn't have the necessary authority. He thought for a long time and said: 'See, my man, according to the law, I cannot do anything. But I'll tell you of a plan by which no harm will come to your pasture. I've converted my pasture into agricultural land. But there's lot of *poot-kharab* in there—that means it's untillable for the most part. But wherever possible, I've done some cultivation. Write me an application on these lines in six months. Get the signature of the *Shanubhoga*, the village accountant, on this application. In the *pahani* or accounting record of your pasture, tell your *Shanubhoga* to write a report saying that nothing much grows there except some beans and chillies. That should be enough. After that, I'll pass an order fixing a tax of twenty-five paisa per acre. That means Gowda must pay an extra tax of thirty-seven-and-a-half rupees to the government every year, and Chinnayya will need to pay an extra twelve-and-a-half rupees. Your pasture will remain intact. I can't do anything beyond this. I'll offer the same solution to the owner of any pasture under my jurisdiction, who brings a similar appeal to me.'

Jois said: 'Our Gowdayya, Chinnayya are well-versed in dharma and karma. I don't know if other pasture-owners will do what they're doing. In the present situation, what Your Excellency has recommended is correct. Gowdayya, please follow what he says.'

His Excellency's suggestion sounded good both to Gowdayya and Chinnayya. Paying an additional tax of thirty-seven-and-a-half rupees annually wasn't a huge burden to Gowdayya, and neither was the sum of twelve-and-a-half rupees a trouble for Chinnayya.

Gowdayya and Chinnayya did namaste to the *Amaldaar* and requested His Excellency to visit their village along with his wife. To *Jois*, the *Amaldaar* offered a *dakshina* of coconut, some fruits and a silver twenty-five paisa coin, all arranged neatly on a plate. *Jois* accepted it, and chanted the *ashirwada* mantra to bless him, and left for his village with his companions.

1

When the *Amaldaar* came for his next Taluk tax drive with his family, not only did he do a puja to all the cows in Kalinga Gowda's cowshed, he also visited the cave of the tiger Punyakoti had returned to in order to keep her word. It was right in front of that very cave that the tiger had told her: 'You're my *akka*, my elder sister; what will I gain by killing you', and had given up its life. The *Amaldaar* looked around and suggested that a *mantapa* or shrine be built there, and that once a year, a *Gopuja* be performed there only by the Kalenahalli village folk. And to indicate that he was the first, he also gave a donation of twenty-five rupees. For the *Gopuja*, his wife had brought about forty kilos of rice, twenty-five coconuts, jaggery blocks and bananas. She soaked this mixture in water and fed it to each cow in the cowshed. The *Amaldaar's* family was staying in the village Basavanna temple along with their family cook. Kalinga Gowda got a feast cooked for them and before they left, gave them a pot full of butter.

The pastures in Kalenahalli survived intact. But folks in the surrounding villages cultivated their pastures. Some of them sowed horse gram while others planted ragi. Some owners of private pastures had already cultivated portions of their pasture much before the government's order. But they would mention it as pastureland in government records. The only benefit from this was that they would save tax. After the order, government-owned pastures were changed to fields belonging to several people as per the records. Although only few folks cultivated and took out harvests diligently, everyone ploughed their field by sprinkling some horse gram only in order to safeguard their land rights.

The pastures of Kalinga Gowda and Chinnayya suffered the consequence of this. The pastures of the surrounding villages were now destroyed and had become fields. The cattle of those villages now had no place to graze. Their stomachs wouldn't fill by merely walking along the edges of the fields. And so everybody took their cattle to the Arunadri foothills. But for how long would the grassland at the foothills sustain this sudden onslaught of a massive number of cows grazing all at once? In exactly a month, it became barren, right from the roots. Now, the villagers shunted their cattle towards the pastures in Kalenahalli.

In the beginning, Kalinga Gowda didn't notice this. He never objected cows belonging to others grazing on his pasture. 'Who am I to object if the *Gomaata* grazes on the *Bhoomata*', used to be his attitude. Besides, why would folks who had their own pastures, send their cows to others' pastures for grazing? But when Chinnayya found out and told him what was really happening, Gowda was livid. 'Thieving bastards, their fields must grow crop, their cows should give milk, as well. May the progeny of these bastards be destroyed! *Lei*! Come, let's go stop the bastards tomorrow', he said. The next day, he took some of his servants and Chinnayya along with him to his pasture around grazing time.

When he reached there, he saw his pasture crowded with cattle. They didn't belong to just one village or locality. The folks who had accompanied the cattle were smoking *bidis* and whistling randomly. 'Who's the guy that sired you? *Lei*! Will you take these cows and back off or no?' he roared. The men froze for a moment. But those among them who could respond, did, 'If this is your land, put a fence, grandpa.'

'Who puts a fence around a pasture, you idiot? What, were you owning cattle since your father's time, asshole?' asked Gowda. One of them retored, 'Hey, Gowdayya, hold your tongue a bit before you speak. The government has itself passed a law asking all pastures to be cultivated. There's no longer anything like a pasture or whatever. If this is your field, put a fence.'

Gowdayya was incensed. He swung the staff in his hand and flung it towards the guy who said this. But that guy bent low and escaped the blow. Chinnayya's son Yangta began to chase away the cows. But Kalinga Gowda told him, '*Lei*, because these sinful bastards commit sins, will you also beat the *Gomaata*? Whether it belongs to him or you, they're all *Gomaata*. Take that stick and club that whoreson's skull properly.'

The force with which Yangta charged forward with the stick made the cowherds scamper away. Gowda and his party then chased the cattle away.

But the stealthy grazing activity didn't stop even the next day. Folks from the surrounding villages continued to send their cows clandestinely to his pasture.

2

This year, there was a genuine problem of availability of raw fodder for Kalinga Gowda's cattle. Gowda always stocked up two years' worth of grass, so that even if his cattle didn't find enough to eat outside to fill its stomach, there was always ample supply of straw at home. But the joy and pleasure of leisurely meandering around in the open field and grazing the raw, green grass couldn't be found in chewing straw in the barn. Not only would the body of the cow fill out, radiating health, it wouldn't produce milk to its fullest if it didn't graze in the open. This year Gowda would somehow manage with the straw stockpile, but what would be the fate of his cattle next year if the grass of his pasture went to other people's cows like it was happening now? Besides, those in Kalenahalli who didn't have pastures of their own but had three or four cows would also face difficulty.

One day, Kalinga Gowda and Chinnayya were discussing this issue. Chinnayya said: 'Next year, if they try to sneak their cattle into our village's pastures, we'll murder a few of them. After that, they'll get scared and no son of a bitch will come this side.'

'Hey, moron! Is your brain damaged? If you murder, the government will haul us up on the noose.'

'Then why doesn't that government teach a lesson to these thieving sons of bitches?'

The mention of government reminded Kalinga Gowda of the *Amaldaar*. At the same time, he also hoped that the *Amaldaar* could help him in some way if he met him. One-and-a-half years had elapsed since the *Amaldaar* had visited Kalenahalli. Kalinga Gowda was unaware whether he was still in the same Taluk or if he'd been transferred. The next day, he went to the *Agrahara* and enquired about the matter with the schoolmaster.

'He's still here. Indeed, the transfer order had come. But then, his retirement time has neared. "I'll retire. Why do you want to transfer me elsewhere, Swami? I'll stay right here for the next one-and-a-half years", he requested his superiors. That's why they've left him here. He'll stay for the next six months', said the schoolmaster.

In any case, I need to talk to the big man. I'm such a dunce! It'll be nice if our Jois is with me, thought Kalinga Gowda, and one fine day, he set out for the Taluk together with *Jois* and Chinnayya. As a mark of respect, both of them carried butter. Like before, *Jois* carried a coconut and *Akshata* wrapped to the end of the *angavastram* that he wore as his upper garment.

That day too was a Sunday. *Jois* had purposely chosen that day because he would be able to talk to the big man directly in his house. When they reached at eleven, the *Amaldaar* indeed, was in the house.

'Welcome, welcome. Even I couldn't make it to your village again after that day. Nor could I learn anything further about you since then. How far has the work of constructing that *mantapa* progressed?' he asked by way of welcoming them.

After the three of them had had their lunch, he brought up the topic of the *mantapa* again: 'To tell you the truth, a temple itself needs to be built. Else, a *mantapa* at the least. How's the progress?'

Gowda said: 'All folks in our village have pooled in money. Money can be arranged somehow. We had called Sivalingachaari from Chandrenahalli. He has come and seen the place and everything. "It's not enough to merely build a temple. A water tank must be dug opposite it for cattle to drink water from it", he said.'

'That's an excellent suggestion. Yes, yes, please go ahead. It doesn't matter if you incur more expenses. If required, I'll find a way to raise more money. If the work can be done before I retire, I'll raise donations from the businessmen and government employees of this town.'

'*Ayya*, folks of our village will put money for building the temple in their own village. I hail from Kalinga *Golla's* lineage, right? The Punyakoti cow is from my own barn, right? Be it even ten thousand rupees, I'll give the money from my own pocket. Money is no cause for worry. One man and one woman from each home in my village will go do the construction work themselves.'

'Then why hasn't the work started?'

'At the moment, Sivalingachari is busy building an Ishwara temple in Nagenahalli. After six months, he'll come to our village. The real problem is with the stone that we need for building the temple. Apparently, the stone found at our hill is not suitable for building the temple. Sivalingachari has strictly forbidden using it for the inner complex of the temple. We must get the stone from the Bettikere Hill. It's twelve miles from our village. *Ayya*, no matter in which town you are, will we perform the temple consecration without you?'

The *Amaldaar* was overjoyed, and said: 'Very good. Dig the water tank such that it is substantial. In future, you can host a cattle fair every year at that spot. Remember, the Punyakoti cow asked your ancestor to prepare the milk-pongal sweet every year on the Sankranti festival. On that day, let there be a grand festival along with the cattle fair. If there's enough convenience of water, shade and food, people even from faraway villages will get their cattle to the fair.'

Gowda's mind brimmed with great happiness at this new idea. His imagination already visualized the scene of the cattle fair.

'There's ample shade at the spot where the tiger's cave once stood. If we plant banyan trees around it, it'll spread out even more. We can conduct a grand cattle fair under it', added Chinnayya.

The *Amaldaar* asked them the reason for visiting him now. After Kalinga Gowda explained the issue, he said: 'I had a prior inkling that it would turn out this way. If all the villagers cultivate their land and grow crop, there would be no theft in anybody's farm. But, if everyone neglects their land, the rest will cast their eyes on the land of the one who ploughs and grows. The same thing has happened here. Folks in your surrounding villages have cultivated their pastures. Now there's no more grass for the cattle. These people don't want pastures, but they want cattle.'

'Don't these bastards have any brains, Swami?' asked Gowda.

'You must put this question to the government. People want more food, and for that more land needs to be cultivated. And for that, more cattle is required. Greater quantities of cattle manure are required. But the grasslands needed for cattle to graze must be eliminated. Indeed, the eminent people in the government themselves pass such orders. What can one do?'

'My dear sir, only you can show a way out.'

The *Amaldaar* thought to himself for five minutes, then asked: 'Don't you have a cowshed in your village?'

'Yes it's there. I have the largest cowshed. Chinnayya too has one. There are a couple of other small ones. The rest of them tie their cattle in stalls within their own homes.'

'That's not what I asked. I asked whether there's a shed to tie up rogue cattle, which grazes farmland.'

Jois said: 'What His Excellency is asking about is what we have in my village. It's what Rangay Gowda has done with the land he got in auction. That kind of cowshed is not there in Kalenahalli.'

Gowda and Chinnayya understood. The *Amaldaar* gave a suggestion: 'Give me an application stating that you require a cowshed for your village. You'll need the signature of the Village Police Patel on it. I'll sanction it. Call for an auction in your village. Let someone in your village buy it for ten rupees. In any case, your pasture is registered as a farmland in government records. And so, if cattle from any other village strays either in your pasture or any other land in your village limits, lock it up. The owner has to pay eight annas per cattle per day as fine to retrieve it. If nobody comes forward to retrieve it after eight days, call for a Panchayat and announce an auction of the cattle. Deduct the charges of keeping it in the cowshed and pay the balance proceeds to the government treasury. Do this for four or five cattle. After this, nobody will dare send a single cow even in the direction of your village.'

Jois said that this was the best solution. Gowda and Chinnayya agreed to provide an application requesting a government cowshed for their village, and to return after obtaining the signatures of his village folk on the application.

3

Kattemane Shingri Gowda got the cowshed contract for twelve rupees at the auction. As per the law, drummers went around the surrounding villages with this announcement: 'A new cowshed has arrived in

Kalenahalli. If anyone leaves their cattle on any land in Kalenahalli, it will be caught and locked up in the shed. There's a fine of eight annas per day. After eight days, the cattle will be auctioned.'

Yet, after the next monsoon, cattle from other villages didn't stop grazing in the pastures of Kalenahalli. And so, one day, the villagers of Kalenahalli got together and caught the cattle which had strayed into their grasslands. The village folk also travelled beyond their village limits up to the foothills and caught the cattle they found there. In all, they locked up 300 cattle. The owners arrived the same evening and threatened to start a fight. But Chinnayya's son Yangata quickly ran to the Hobli and brought two policemen with him. Those who had arrived spoiling for a fight were now scared. In the end, the owners paid a hundred-and-fifty rupees to the cowshed at the rate of eight annas per cattle and retrieved their bovines. The policemen who had come from far away simply pocketed hundred rupees and left. The contractor Shingri Gowda was left with fifty rupees, which was no mean profit. The amount he paid to the government was only twelve rupees.

From that day onwards, it appeared that Shingri Gowda had found a new vocation. Each morning, he would scout around all the fields in the village. He would also scan the foothills. Perchance he found even a single cow, it was an earning of eight annas. It was impossible for any cow to now escape Shingri Gowda's keen eye. For those who enquired, he claimed that the entire Arunadri Hill belonged to Kalenahalli, and that the *Amaldaar* had himself issued an order to the effect. And so, he earned little more than two or three rupees daily.

In about two months, cattle from the surrounding villages completely stopped going this side. Shingri Gowda's earnings too, halted at that point. But then how could he be known as a contractor without any earning? One day, he caught two oxen belonging to Kalenahalli and tied them up in his cowshed. The oxen were grazing in Kalinga Gowda's pasture. When the owner questioned him, he asked him to pay one rupee to get them freed. The owner approached Kalinga Gowda.

When Kalinga Gowda told the contractor, 'You must not tie up cattle belonging to our village', he replied, 'If you say this, how do I make an earning?'

Kalinga Gowda was furious. 'Have you grubbed out? Have you become a pauper?' Have you now begun to earn your living by tying up cattle? I'll get you your twelve rupees by pooling money from the village folk. You must lock up cattle only when one of us brings them to you. Else no! A son of the soil, this man, instead of toiling in the field, has resorted to earning money by locking up cattle!'

Shingri Gowda said nothing in response to this reprimand. But he thought to himself, *From now on, I won't catch any cattle that come this way from elsewhere. This old man is growling only because I made some security arrangements for myself.*

One day, Shingri Gowda caught a pregnant cow from a different village and locked it up in his shed. Even after a day had elapsed, nobody came forward to claim it. When he heard the news that it was a pregnant cow, Kalinga Gowda himself went there, and upon inspection found that the calf was due anytime. It would deliver today or tomorrow. The contractor had given it neither grass nor water since yesterday. When Kalinga Gowda saw the cow, not only did his eyes fill with tears, he was livid at Shingri Gowda. He stormed all the way up to his house, and exclaimed, 'Are you really a father of children? Will your children survive if you commit this kind of sin? You ungrateful son of a whore! You take eight annas every day, don't you? Don't you have the sense even to feed grass to the cow? There is a government law which says that you must give it grass.' In response to this lashing, Shingri Gowda brought the keys to the cowshed and flung it before Gowda, and said, 'Grandpa, I neither need this contract nor this trouble. I didn't take this contract to feed grass to the cattle of strangers. You take this cowshed.'

'Your horrid life will be your own witness, you bastard!' said Gowda. He took the keys, got the cowshed opened and ordered grass and slop from his own home to feed the cow who would deliver anytime. The cow first drank two pails-full of slop and then began chewing the grass. Gowda began to caress and rub its neck, stomach, abdomen and back, while muttering angrily, 'Can't those sons of whores who rear cattle have the sense to search for it if it's missing? Why should such bastards even rear cattle?'

By then the cow stepped sideways and began to lift and thrash its hind legs. It stepped forward angrily to gore Gowda who until then was rubbing it. 'Aha! Look at her! Did you overeat?' he said, holding its nose-knot and then tied it with a rope to one side in the shed. As he watched, he observed signs of the cow passing into labour. 'Wait, Mother, just wait. Give birth to your baby right here. Don't you worry, I'll give all the care you need', he addressed the cow. The cow shook its head twice as if in agreement.

Kalinga Gowda went home. Lakkamma was making ragi balls. He conveyed the news to her and then returned to the cowshed with two lemons, a raw thread, turmeric, a wet cloth and a pail of water. To the left of where it was tethered, the cow looked at Gowda with eyes resembling balls of burning coal, shaking its head violently as if to gore somebody. Gowda sat a distance waiting. Even after an hour, it didn't deliver.

By then Lakkamma arrived there. 'I've been waiting for a long time. She still hasn't delivered. She's glaring at me as if she'll gore me', said Gowda. At this, Lakkamma neared the cow and investigated. It was almost time for the calf to emerge. She turned to her husband and said: 'Does your brain understand anything at all? Will the cow deliver her baby in the presence of a man? Won't it feel embarrassed? You go out.'

That's true. It didn't strike me, he thought, cursing his own foolishness as he stepped out of the cowshed and sat under the shade of the banyan tree opposite it. After a while, Chinnayya arrived. When he asked, 'What's this now, Gowdayya? Why are you sitting here', Gowda narrated the behaviour of the cowshed contractor Shingri Gowda. Chinnayya agreed, 'Even I'm aware of it. That bastard thinks that this cowshed is only meant for earning money. Tell me, that bloody sinner takes eight annas! Can he starve cattle?'

Chinnayya and Kalinga Gowda thought for a bit and came up with a solution for this: Shingri Gowda must be removed from this contract. Instead, Chinnayya's son Yangata must take over the contract and provide grass and water to the cattle that was seized. They decided that a worker must be appointed at a salary of ten rupees per year to draw and supply water to these cattle. After deducting the cost of grass and the twelve rupees that had to be paid to the government, any balance that remained

S.L. BHYRAPPA

had to be given towards the construction of the temple near the hill.

Shortly after, Gowda's wife emerged from the shed and said: 'The cow has delivered. It's a very beautiful bull-calf. I need some more water to wash the cow.'

Chinnayya returned with two pails of water. The cow which had just given birth wasn't allowing anyone near it. Yet, Gowda held its nose-knot. Lakkamma and Chinnayya thoroughly washed its body clean. Lakkamma also washed the calf's body. After this, they applied turmeric and *kumkum* to the cow's forehead and horns and then, made a circular motion with a coconut in front of its face to ward off evil eyes. She then cracked the coconut open on the ground. She also took some soot from a cart outside the shed, rubbed it all over the cow's face to ensure no evil eye would harm it. But how could they leave the nursing mother and her baby alone in this shed? Lakkamma picked up the calf. Kalinga Gowda held the mother's nose-knot and led it to his home. The new mother was incessantly licking the body of her baby in step with Lakkamma who was holding it in her arms and walking ahead. Chinnayya who stayed back in the shed took a large dustpan and cleaned up the post-delivery mess.

After reaching their own cowshed, Lakkamma smeared turmeric all over the cow's body as a preventive measure against poisoning. Gowda went to the farm, plucked some leaves and herbs and applied the paste to the cow's vagina. The new mother must be kept cool. As instructed by her mother-in-law, the mute Tayavva soaked two kilos of rice mixed with two tender coconuts and fed it to the cow.

Then, the cow's owner arrived there. When he saw the twenty-five-year-old owner, Gowda burnt with rage: 'What kind of a *Vokkaliga* are you, you son of a bitch... to sit peacefully for two days forgetting a pregnant cow? You drink milk but you can't take care of the cow?'

'We honestly didn't know it had come here, grandpa. We kept searching for it all this while in the direction of Swaarenahalli and Suragihalli.'

'Which is your village?'

'Dyavalapura.'

Dyavalapura was about three miles. Gowda didn't want the new mother to walk such a long distance, and said: 'Let the cow and her calf stay here for two more days. Come back here day after and take them. Now, have some food.' Gowda fed him and sent him back.

When he returned to take his cow and calf on the third day, Lakkamma applied *kumkum* to it and prayed. When the owner took out two-and-a-half rupees, the fine for five days, and asked him the expenses incurred for the delivery, Gowda grew angry: 'What, you think only you've got money? She came here for delivery like the daughter of this home, and is now returning with a son. Should I take money for that?'

The owner of the cow fell silent. Kalinga Gowda said: 'Look here. You don't need to hold the cow's rope. Just don't make the calf walk. Lift it up, hug it, hold it in your arms and walk. She'll come behind it on her own.'

VOLUME 5

1

After Putta Kalinga had completed four years in the Primary School of the *Agrahara*, the *Jois* suggested that he be sent to the Taluk to study English. Gowda didn't like the idea of sending his only grandson there. What would he accomplish by learning English? *His grandson is capable of reading poems from the Nalacharitre just after finishing his education at the Agrahara school. The only thing now remaining is the Jaimini. If he was taught this under somebody's tutelage, his education was as good as complete*, thought the Elder Gowda. However, the *Jois* insisted, 'What's the harm in learning a bit of English to be in tune with the times?'

The *Jois'* son Venkataramana was now studying English in the third year in the Taluk school. He had already undergone the Sacred Thread ceremony and undertaken Vedic education to a good extent from his father. For food, he takes *bhiksha* and stays in the *mantapa* located in the compound of the Narasimha temple. The *mantapa*, which had doors and locks, also housed four to six other Brahmin students. Venkataramana also studied Sanskrit in the classes conducted within the temple in the mornings and evenings. The front portion of his scalp is cleanly shaven and the long hair at the back tied in a thick tuft; his forehead sports the *gopichandana*—a sacred, yellow ochre mark on his forehead; his left hand carries a white knapsack and his right a broth-bowl. When he goes around for *bhiksha* like this, he resembles a *Vatu*—a student studying in the ashrams of the rishis of yore.

The *Jois* told Gowda: 'Gowdayya, admit your child there. They have built a hostel for Vokkaligas. If you give fifty kilos of ragi, five kilos of beans, ten kilos of rice, and twenty-five rupees every year, it seems they serve some extraordinary food. My son Venkataramana will supervise and take full care of your grandson. And just like here, he will teach him and help him with his lessons. Don't you worry about anything.'

And, so, Gowda admitted his grandson to the middle school. The

Taluk was no insignificant place. It was the place of the *Amaldaar's* office. The previous *Amaldaar* had retired and returned to his native Srirangapattana. Gowda himself loaded ragi, beans and rice on a bullock cart, gave it to the hostel authorities, and made arrangements for his grandson.

Now, Gowda had only one worry. He had to construct a temple and dig a large *kalyani*—a water tank—in front of the cave where Punyakoti had gone to meet the tiger. But in the interim, Sivalingachari from Chandrenahalli had gone in the direction of Nanjanagud to build a temple. 'Why do you worry? Just arrange for the stones like I said. The rest of the work is mine', he had assured. Despite this, Gowda had no faith that the work would actually get done until Sivalingachari was physically present before him.

Putta Kalinga was learning English well. Because Venkataramana was teaching him advanced lessons, there was no need to appoint a teacher separately. Gowda was not only appreciative of his grandson, but actually proud of him. *Indeed, English wasn't trivial. It seems you had to know English to become an Amaldaar. In future our Putta himself might become an Amaldaar. Or, he might go even higher. Then, he'll issue a hukum prohibiting everybody from cultivating pastures which would decree that people should only cultivate land, which is left after the Gomaata has had her fill*, dreamt Gowda at times. Indeed, there was a reason for such a dream. After grasslands began to be cultivated, the price of grass shot up steeply. When he was a young lad, nobody used to sell grass in his surroundings. But even later, when grass started to be sold, one entire stack used to cost just two rupees. Now, the price for ragi grass has escalated to ten or twelve rupees. And because the price of grass has increased, it seems the cost of milk, curd and butter too, has increased in towns and cities. 'These bastards deserve this. Indeed, it's them who made that law ordering the cultivation of pastures. I hope they don't get any butter to eat', he'd curse.

In just two years after he had enrolled for English, Putta would speak a few bits in the language before his grandfather. *Isn't this the language of the Amaldaar?* the grandfather would think. By this time, Venkataramana had completed his middle school and was now in Mysore. His father had admitted him to the Mysore Sanskrit *Pathashala*—the school for advanced Vedic education, astrology and Vedic rituals in the traditional manner. Alongside, he also attended the high school. Because he learns Sanskrit, they provide him charity meals at the Maharaja's hostel.

Putta is now deeply familiar with the Taluk. He walks to and from there on his own. He knots the mouth of the vessel which contains the ghee that his grandmother has melted for him and carries it till there. Before sitting for his meals, he pours two spoonsful of ghee on his plate. When he comes to the village, he takes the cattle out to graze.

He talks to his grandparents. He mingles with the servants. But he neither talks to his mother nor goes near her. Tayavva was grieving in her mind for this precise reason. When he came home, she'd go stand near him with such love and expectation! But he would never speak with her. At times, she'd have tears in her eyes. One day when Lakkamma saw her daughter-in-law's tears, she directly asked her what the matter was. She described her sorrow with hand signs. Lakkamma understood and informed the matter to her husband. Although Gowda said, 'childish behaviour', he asked his grandson directly the next time the boy came home: 'My boy, why can't you speak to your mother when you come home?'

'How does one talk to her, grandpa?'

'How? In the same way... how do you talk to us?'

'You speak, and I speak too. She's mute, right? How does one speak to a mute?'

In that instant, the Elder Gowda could think of no answer to Putta's query. The question of how one spoke with a mute haunted him as well. He took the cattle out for grazing that day. The question still haunted him. He spent the entire afternoon thinking about it. In the interim, some cattle strayed from the pasture and rushed towards the fields. He yelled just once, 'Hey! Where are your senses?' They returned to their places. Presently, two cows came near him and shook their necks over his head. They wouldn't be content if they didn't have the soft, loose skin under their neck caressed by him every day. 'Oh! I'd completely forgotten. You've come yourself', he said addressing both of them. In response, they sniffed his face and licked his back. He rubbed their necks even as he spoke to them. Suddenly he recalled the Rama and Sita of the *Kole Basava.*[*] How well the two speak! If you asked, 'Lord Rama, will you marry Mother Sita?' the Basava, the ox would nod his head in a 'yes'. *Which son of a bitch said animals can't speak?* He thought to himself.

In that moment, Kalinga Gowda found the answer to the question tormenting him since morning. His daughter-in-law Tayavva might be a mute, but from the day they brought her home, everyone has been speaking to her. She too, speaks to all of them. 'Does one need only a tongue to speak? Can't our Putta understand this simple thing? Can't he learn this simple lesson even after going to the English school?' he grumbled to himself. As far as he was concerned, he spoke even to cows, and the cows spoke to him. His daughter-in-law Tayavva too spoke to him. It never occurred to him that she was a mute. He had to teach this to his grandson.

When he returned home that evening, he called his grandson, made him sit close to him and asked: 'Hey Putta, you say your mother is a mute, but don't I speak to her?'

'You talk to her, but does she reply?'

'She definitely replies to me. Her brain is sharper than your grandmother's. Do you know, I always listen to her advice in practical matters and dealings?'

Putta Kalinga said nothing in response. The grandfather continued: 'You must not call her a mute. When your father was alive, he never once called her that. He'd always chat with her. She too would chat with him. To her husband, she was not a mute. To both of us, she isn't a mute. But she became a mute to you, born from her own womb?'

The grandson didn't know what to say to this. For a while, he looked crestfallen. The grandfather said: 'Mad child! You're still a small lad. How

---

[*]A folk tradition hailing from antiquity in which an ox and cow are paraded before each house in a village or town by a team—typically a husband and wife—of people who carry out this profession for a living. The animals are dressed in vivid colours, their horns painted brilliantly. The animals are trained to obey specific commands and enact a scene from Hindu epics, typically the Ramayana as described in this novel. The ox is designated as Lord Rama and the cow as his wife, Sita.

can you understand these things? The mother who's given you birth is the same, the *Gomaata* is the same. The *Gomaata* too can't speak. Understand this well. Don't think your mother is a mute.'

In that instant, Gowda didn't understand the full import of what he had spoken. This happened to him on several occasions. He'd just speak on the spur of the moment and then dwell on its meaning later and unable to find it, would worry. His grandson too, didn't understand anything and just sat there blinking his eyes.

2

In two years, Putta finished the Five Rupees Examination of the middle school. Like Venkataramana, he too wanted to enrol at the high school in Mysore. But his grandfather said that this education was enough. Finding no other way out, Putta Kalinga went to the *Agrahara* and confided his desire with the *Jois*. When the *Jois* came to Kalenahalli and informed this to Gowda, he said: '*Ayya*, am I getting younger by the day? Am I not already running sixty-three, having completed sixty-two years? How much longer can I work with the aid of servants? Isn't it fine if he doesn't become an *Amaldaar*? Let him look after the cowshed.'

Putta had tears in his eyes. The *Jois* renewed his recommendation. 'If boys who're blessed with the gift of acquiring learning are deprived of schooling, Saraswati, the Goddess of Learning will be angry', he quoted from the scriptures. His own son Venkataramana is in Mysore. This is his final year of high school. He will personally look after Putta. Putta will have all the facilities in the Vokkaliga hostel. After continuing in this vein for half a day, Gowda finally relented.

Putta left for Mysore. Before leaving, he spoke to his mother as well, 'Mother, I'll take your leave.' Hearing his son address her, Tayavva felt very happy. After he was settled in Mysore, Putta didn't visit home even for the Navaratri holidays. Indeed, when the entire country would land up in Mysore to watch the Dasara procession, how could he miss that and come home? Gowda consoled himself. 'He's still a lad. He's studying.'

When he came to the village for the summer vacation, the demeanour on his face had altered. When he had gone to the Taluk, his face exhibited a sense of vivacity. Now there was a sense of superiority, a sense that exuded a know-it-all attitude. When his grandfather asked, 'Ai, what do they teach you at school? When will you read the *Jaimini?*' Putta replied, 'They don't teach the *Jaimini* there. How fire is caused, what all gases are there in the air, how did animals originate, how do people in different countries live and behave... they teach all this.'

'Ai, what's the use of knowing all that? What joy is there when you don't learn the *Jaimini?* It seems the *Jois*' son Venkataramana learns Sanskrit. It seems he studies Ramayana and Mahabharata in the original in Sanskrit. It seems he explains the meaning of any verse in the *Jaimini.* When will you learn all that?'

'He is the son of a *Jois*, he needs all that. Why do I need all that? Just leave it. I'm studying Science.'

'What's Science?'

'Didn't I tell you? How fire is caused...'

'If you rub with a flint, it's caused. Do you need to learn it in school?' Gowda closed the topic at that.

Putta was already fourteen. He had to be married off. When his father Krishna was just ten and armed with a spear in hand, he would take the cattle for grazing all the way up to the foothills all alone. In those days, hyenas would come to the caves in the hill occasionally. After Krishna died, hyenas have never set foot in the region. But after Putta returned from Mysore, he has never taken the cattle for grazing on his own volition. When the grandfather asked him one day, the grandson said, 'I feel bored there. You tell me, who can stay there all alone till the evening? There's no company either.'

'Aha! Why should anyone be with you? Won't the cows be with you?'

'If cows are around with me, does it mean I have company? Are cows humans?'

The grandfather couldn't think of an answer immediately. If somebody questioned a truth which was deeply rooted in experience for which no evidence was necessary, how could one answer such a question instantly? And in Gowda's case, it was much more difficult. He answered his grandson using a different approach: 'If you feel bored, play the flute.'

'I neither know how to play it nor do I have any interest in it.'

The grandfather felt hurt by this. He said: 'You're corrupted. Being born a *Golla*, a cowherd, you say you don't know how to play the flute? And you say you're not interested in it? What do you think this means? A cowherd must serve the cow as his mother. And then if he plays the flute so melodiously that she forgets herself in joy, he attains *mukti*. Lord Krishna has said that a cowherd who plays the flute forgetting everything, forgetting even himself even for a moment, attains *mukti*.'

These words elicited laughter from the grandson who was studying in high school. He said: 'At times, when I go visit Venkataramana in Mysore, he'll be chanting mantras. If I ask him what it is, he says it's the Veda. Apparently, if one learns its meaning, fully concentrates one's mind on it and chants it completely even once, one obtains *mukti* and attains the feet of God, too. This is what Venkataramana says. And you say that just by playing the flute, one reaches the feet of God. So, which one of these is true? Both are lies.'

'Don't say that, you stupid son of a whore. What Venkataramana says is the truth for his *jati*. For our *jati*, the flute is the truth. Do you know how well your father used to play the flute? With his lips red after chewing the tender betel leaf, when he stood there playing the flute, he was both Krishne Gowda and Lord Krishna at the same time! If he played the flute, even the most mischievous bull-calf would tuck its tail between its legs and drift off to sleep. Because he could play it so well, he charged in to save the life of the cow and gave up his life. One who doesn't know how to play the flute... does he have the guts to give up his life? That's why your father could summon such courage. God beckoned him to his feet because of his devotion.'

When he heard this about his father, Putta Kalinga experienced mixed feelings of sadness and affection. But his father had died after being attacked by a hyena. Is this what grandfather calls as going to the feet of God? It seems only one who can play the flute is endowed with the sort of courage his father had had. How were these things even related?

When he asked this question, the grandfather said, 'Didn't your father give up his own life to save the cow? If you don't play the flute how will you get the mind to save the cow's life? You'll think of saving only your life, right?'

'Grandpa, I can't understand a word you say.'

The grandpa himself mulled over everything he had just spoken. Even he couldn't fully understand the meaning of what he himself had said. Still, he felt that he had uttered something deeply profound. If he asked the *Jois*, he would explain the meaning in detail. This had happened numerous times. The old man Gowda would say something randomly. He himself wouldn't fathom its meaning. The *Jois* would assign a meaning and tell him that his words were indeed lofty, at which Gowda would laugh and say, 'I'm a cowherd and a simpleton. The words came to my mind and I uttered them. What's there in them but mud—enough mud spread over three passages!'

At any rate, Putta Kalinga took the cattle for grazing that day. But he felt really bored till the evening. No matter how much he tried to play the flute, his mind simply was not in it. Even when the cows came near him, he had nothing to say to those dumb animals.

The first year of high school was complete. After the vacations, he had to select optional subjects: Humanities or Science? His love veered towards Science. Venkataramana kept saying, 'Learn Sanskrit, I'll teach you.' But by then Biology and Chemistry had already become dear to him. He had no interest in learning Sanskrit.

3

Putta Kalinga passed the high school examination. Because he knew that his grandfather wouldn't accede to his desire for studying further in college, he approached the *Jois* in advance. Like earlier, there was some discussion, but in the end, Gowda agreed.

After the high school examinations, Venkataramana continued his studies in the Sanskrit *Pathashala* full time. He got up at the *Brahmi* hour—at about four-thirty in the morning—followed by ablutions and *Sandhyavandanam*. Then, there were Veda and Upanishad lessons, followed by classes according to the *pathashala's* syllabus. He had no free time except during the *Anadhyayana* period: specified days in a year during which no lessons were taught in accordance with the ancient system of Vedic education. But these days wouldn't coincide with Sundays which was when Kalinga had a holiday. Thus, the two scarcely met each other. And even when they met, they had no common topics to discuss except the rains and harvest back in their native villages. One wouldn't understand anything about Biology and Chemistry that the other was studying, who in turn had no taste for Puranic stories and Upanishadic secrets. Even now Venkataramana ties a thread made of the *munja* grass around his waist. He wears a *langot* inside and drapes a *lungi* on top of it. He has never worn knickers till date. If he combs his hair all the way behind his head and knots it, the bulk of the knot is as big as a peeled coconut. Except when he goes out, he wears only a towel-like cloth to cover his upper body whether he's in his room or in class. It is rare that he requires a shirt.

Kalinga was studying at the City Christian College. Apart from academics, he also took part in college sports. By the time he passed the Intermediate Examinations, he was renowned in the college as an excellent sportsman. He occupied the top spot not just in volleyball and kabaddi, but in running and jumping events as well.

When he was studying Junior B.Sc., he was sent to participate in inter-collegiate sports competitions attended by all colleges in Mysore. Even there, not only did he emerge first in kabaddi and in the running race, but was adjudged the best volleyball player as well. For that year's M.G.S. Tournament, they had even sent him to Bangalore to play. He took the first prize in the running race for the entire university, and was declared as the best player in kabaddi and volleyball.

Thus, not only did Kalinga's name become famous in the sports circles of colleges, he also became a favourite of the college principal. The principal was a Padre who hailed from America. If other students wished to see him, they had to first send a note requesting permission. But Kalinga would simply walk through the flap door of his office and talk to him.

When he was in the Senior B.Sc., he was the captain of his college's volleyball team. When a match against a Bangalore college had to be finalized, the principal had to sign a letter that had to reach Bangalore urgently. But the principal still hadn't come to the college, so Kalinga hopped onto a bicycle and went to his bungalow. He was about to have lunch. After signing the letter, he asked, 'Boy, did you have your lunch?'

'Not yet Father', he replied truthfully.

The Father asked him to have lunch with him. When Kalinga refused out of shyness, the principal insisted. Kalinga said yes.

The butler laid a table for him near the principal's and served food in porcelain plates. The principal began to eat using a spoon, knife and fork. Kalinga knew how to use a spoon, but did not have the practice to hold a knife and fork. The principal said, 'If you don't want the fork, eat with your fingers, like your country's custom.' He began to eat with his fingers. It was non-vegetarian food. Kalinga was not fully vegetarian. On occasions like the Maramma festival, they used to cook the meat of goat and sheep at home. But that cooking was done in the bathroom located outside the house. For that specific purpose, a large earthen pot was placed on a hanger in the bathroom. The meat was cooked in that pot in the bathroom oven and eaten there. It was not allowed in the kitchen inside the house.

After lunch, the principal left for college in his car. Kalinga left on his cycle, put the letter in the postbox and then attended his classes. He detected a certain kind of difference between the meat he was used to eating in his home and what he'd eaten that day. When they cooked meat at home, they would grind a mixture of cumin, pepper, coriander, cinnamon, chili and other local spices. This emitted an intense aroma, and except when one ate it, one couldn't distinguish just from its aroma whether the *sambar* or broth—to which this mixture was added—was a mutton *sambar* or a horse gram *sambar*. The latter was also prepared by his grandmother in the winter months after grinding the spices to a consistency his grandfather loved. But not much masala was added to the meat in the principal's house. Nor did it feel as if the meat was fully cooked. For some reason, he experienced a sort of disgust. Half an hour later, he had a sudden thought: the principal was a Christian, besides, they were Red people. They eat the meat of a cow. He perhaps fed me the same today! His stomach churned at the mere thought of this.

After the bell rang, marking the end of the period, he didn't sit for the next class. He came out of the class, climbed atop his bicycle and reached the principal's bungalow. The local butler who was fast asleep awoke at the sound of the electric doorbell that he rang, and opened the door. Kalinga stepped inside and asked him directly, 'The meat you served me today? What was it?' The butler who was unaware of anything replied, 'Beef.'

'Beef eh? Cow's meat? Why didn't you tell me?'

Still unable to comprehend, the butler said: 'What's in it to tell you? What's there to tell you?'

Kalinga had no response to this. The butler asked, 'Why? What happened?' But Kalinga made no reply. He came out and climbed his bicycle. And by the time he had covered two furlongs, he felt sick and nearly lost his balance on the moving cycle. He alighted immediately, propped the cycle against a tree by the wayside and sat down on the ground. He felt the churning spread across the insides of his stomach and felt like vomiting. He inserted his fingers twice so they touched his throat and vomited. Not only did the cow meat that he'd eaten earlier in the day gush out, but also bits of potato and onion from the curry added to the masala *dosa* he'd eaten earlier at the hotel. In ten minutes, the sickness in his stomach subsided. But the disgust wouldn't go without gargling. His whole body was sweating. He decided it was best to have a bath. He climbed back on his cycle and went to the hostel.

After a bath, he felt better. But anxiety still remained in his mind. He belonged to Kalinga *Golla*'s lineage. The cow is equivalent to God. *And look at me, I've eaten the cow's meat today. These Christians, especially Padres from the country of Europe, eat the cow's meat. Why didn't this occur to me before I sat down to eat? What sin have I committed!*

No matter how much he tossed about in the bed, this single thought tormented his mind—sin. When his mind was completely filled with the feeling that this was a sin, he remembered atonement. Even as he pondered over the atonement for what he'd done today, he remembered Venkataramana. *He'd studied the Vedas and the scriptures, he was the Jois' son; he's the right person.* He got up, wore his shirt, climbed his bicycle and reached the Sanskrit *Pathashala*.

Venkataramana had no classes that day. He was in his room sitting on a mat, copying out mantras from a printed book into his book of blank white paper, dipping his steel pen in the inkpot. When he saw Kalinga, he said, 'Come, Kalinga, it's been three months since you visited.

Why are you looking dull? Are you unwell?'

Kalinga narrated all the events since morning: 'You must help me with the atonement procedure. Tell me what I need to do.'

Venkataramana thought for a moment and said: 'Why did you have food in his house? Are our scriptures false when they have ordained that one must not eat in the homes of those who don't have the notion of *jati*?'

'I didn't know. Had I known, would I eat there? Now what's happened has happened. Tell me what the atonement is.'

'This is not a sin that you've committed with your full consciousness. It has occurred without your knowledge. And so, it's not a great sin. Take *panchagavya* tomorrow morning. Till then don't allow even a drop of water into your mouth.'

'In that case only you must give it. I don't know where to get it or how to do the procedure.'

After thinking for a minute, Venkataramana said: 'We need to get cow's milk, ghee, curd, urine and dung—the five ingredients that make up *panchagavya*—all of these are in the palace cowshed. I'll get it for you. Tomorrow morning, let's both go to Pashchimavahini by the first motor bus. Take *panchagavya* after bathing in the river.'

The next day both of them went to Pashchimavahini near Srirangapattana. After both of them had their bath, Venkataramana performed his *Sandhyavandanam*. After this, he gave *panchagavya* to Kalinga. Kalinga gave a silver rupee coin as *dakshina* to Venkataramana, immersed a silver quarter in the river, prostrated before both the river and Venkataramana, and felt comforted that his sin had been expiated.

4

The *Jois* says that Kalinga Gowda is now sixty-eight years old. The Elder Gowda claims that he is actually seventy. Now he has only one worry: that of completing the construction of the Punyakoti temple. Although the contract cowshed isn't earning as well now, Yangata still has two hundred rupees from that transaction. Everyone in the village has agreed to give donations. He still has the twenty-five rupees that the *Amaldaar* had given him in the past. However, this amount isn't sufficient to build the temple and dig the *kalyani*—the water tank. 'It's the cow belonging to my lineage. The temple is a mark of its sanctity. I must bear all the expenses.' This thought occupies his mind. 'Stones for the inner portion of the temple will come from stone mountain at Bettikere. Our village folk will get them on bullock carts. For construction work, two people from each family will pitch in. I must bear all the monetary expenses,' he decided.

Meanwhile, the *Jois* had gone to a village to obtain *daana* and returned home carrying the bundle of *daana,* after walking under the hot sun. He asked his wife for some water. Subbamma was surprised. He had never drunk water in this state, without first purifying himself from his sojourns outside. She asked, 'Will you drink in this state, without purifying yourself?'

'Don't I know that much? Give me water quickly. I feel like I'm dying,' he said. She gave him a large copper goblet filled to the brim with water from the Ganga. He lifted it, and put it to his mouth in great haste. As he attempted to gulp it down, three-quarters of the water went in, the rest spilled out. He felt a pain in his chest; he clutched his hand to his to his chest, and collapsed on the ground, uttering 'Rama Rama'. Subbamma rushed to him saying, 'What's this?' When she shook his head, there was neither reaction nor response.

The *Jois* was suffering from no ailment. He was strong and healthy.

The Elder Gowda was the first to receive the news.

Even at his age, Gowda used to take his cattle to the pasture near the foothills under the hot sun. The *Jois* used to travel to various villages to obtain *daana*. Not only was it the traditional duty of his ancestry, it was also the source of his livelihood. But walking along with the grazing cows in the blazing sun wasn't the source of Gowda's livelihood, it was the dharma of his life. He had plenty of servants at home. Although he could have asked one of them to accompany the cows as they went to graze, he did not do this. Gowda never abandoned his life's dharma even for a day.

Gomootraanaacharet snaanam vrittim kuryaasca gorasaih |
Gobhirvarceccha bhuktaasu bhunjeetaatha govratii ||

Bathing in the cow's urine, earning livelihood using only the nourishment the cow provides in the form of milk, curd and others, always walking behind the cow, and eating only after the cow has finished eating. This was the lifestyle prescribed for one who had taken a sacred vow to serve the cow all his life. This was what Gowda had learnt when he was still a very young boy. In fact, it was this *Jois* who had taught him this mantra and explained its meaning. Gowda was unfailingly practising this sacred vow in accordance with the tradition handed down to him by his lineage, to the best of his abilities.

Now the *Jois* was dead. Gowda visited the family and standing at the forefront, consoled his wife and son, who had returned from Mysore. 'What is the *Atman,* or the soul? Like one casts off an old garment and wears a new one, the *Atman* casts off a worn-out body and searches for a new body—this is death. People who are wise must not grieve over it.' He consoled the mother and son with such words expounding the philosophy of death. Venkataramana had studied the Veda, Vedanta and *Tarka*—the traditional school of Indian Logic. In this moment of grief at his father's death, he couldn't recall any of these. But when the Elder Gowda spoke about these matters, he felt the truth of these words.

'Son, you have studied and learnt so much. Don't you know all this? He was neither in pain nor did he suffer. He died comfortably. Your father has earned *punya*. Carry out the next rites so that he crosses the Vaitarani river. You mustn't sit like this.' Not only did he console Venkataramana in this manner but also soothed Subbamma and spurred them both on the path of duty. He supplied them with the material they were short of, and also gave them money, grain and groceries, and ensured that the last rites were performed in accordance with tradition. Venkataramana who had fully shaven his head, gave a cow as gift on the Thirteenth Day and sent his father to Heaven.

Venkataramana had now finished ten years of studies in the Sanskrit *Pathashala*. Two more years, and his formal education would've been fully complete. If he wanted, he had the option of either joining as a junior teacher at the same *pathashala* or as a Sanskrit Pandit at some high school and earn a salary. There was no hurdle preventing him from finishing his last two years of education. He had residence in the *pathashala*, charity meals in the Maharaja's hostel, besides a monthly scholarship of twelve rupees. If there was a special puja or occasion in the Palace, he would be invited because he was a traditional *brahmachari*. On such occasions, he would be given a *dhoti*, goblet and two rupees as *dakshina*. If he sent seven or eight rupees to his mother every month from that money, her life would be comfortable for the next two years. They owned no property in the *Agrahara* apart from their house and five or six cows. Their livelihood was derived from conducting rituals and puja in the surrounding villages as long as strength and ability permitted. Else, there was nothing.

Putta Kalinga remained in the village since the day the *Jois* died. One day, after the post-death rites were completed, he came to the *Agrahara*. When Venkataramana discussed his future plans, Kalinga said: 'Look, you know how the times are nowadays. Faith in stuff like scriptures, rituals and relationships are dwindling among people. Your father's time was different. If anyone gives you a *daana*, what do you actually get? Two kilos of grain, one kilo of rice, one rupee as *dakshina*. For this you need to walk three or four miles in the sun. What kind of fate is this? Study for the remaining two years. If you become a Pandit in a high school, you'll have a comfortable life.'

Venkataramana found this advice acceptable. He made arrangements for his mother—she'd have to stay alone in the village now—and decided to leave for Mysore.

But the next day, the Elder Gowda came to the *Agrahara* and asked Venkataramana: 'Son, I heard you're leaving for Mysore. Is that true?'

'What else do I do grandfather?'

'If you leave, who else is there in our village to perform puja, rituals and forge relationships? The *Jois* ancestry has come down since ancient times. Instead of doing your ancestral work at the place of your birth, why do you want to wander around from place to place?'

'That's correct. But how can I make a living with this? Times have changed.'

'I've thought about that as well. I've a plan which'll ensure that you'll always have enough with no trouble.'

'Tell me.'

'I'll not say it in words. Come with me,' he said and led him to the backyard of the house. The Elder Gowda held the tail of a cow tied there and said: 'I'll do something. Just trust me. Don't leave the village. Get married. I'll make sure that your family doesn't need to depend only on *daana* from villages.'

Venkataramana's mother, who was standing there listening to their exchange, said: 'Son, listen to him. He's not an Elder, who's ever broken his word.'

'Please do as your mother says, son,' said Gowda.

Venkataramana didn't study further. He went to Mysore one day and explained the situation to his gurus. He took their permission and blessings, packed his belongings and returned home. Nobody knew what Gowda would do next. They neither asked nor did he talk about it. But one day, Gowda brought one hundred kilos of paddy and fifty kilos of ragi in his cart and giving it to them, said: 'This will be enough till the next harvest. After that, I'll do something.'

Everybody in the surrounding areas knew that Venkataramana was a greater scholar than his father. More importantly, his learning was perfect in the matter of examining the horoscope and predicting the future. Thus, he would earn three or four rupees daily by practising astrology and conducting puja and rituals.

5

One day, Sivalingachari from Chandrenahalli landed in Kalenahalli and told Kalinga Gowda: 'All my work is completed. Only yours is remaining. Let's finish the temple quickly. Are your preparations all done?'

Indeed, everything that was needed for constructing the temple was ready. The people required for labour, carts for transporting stone, and money: all these were ready. But the task of hiring specialist stoneworkers was pending.

'Leave the stoneworkers to me. I'll get them. We need to scout for the spot that will house the *Garbhagriha*, the sanctum sanctorum. Ask a learned astrologer who can fix that exact spot and decide on the total area of the temple. The rest of the business is mine,' said Sivalingachari.

The Elder Kalinga called Venkataramana. Together with Chinnayya and four other prominent people from the village, they all crossed the foothills and reached the spot where Punyakoti had gone to offer herself to the tiger. There was none in the group who hadn't seen this spot before. Sivalingachari asked Venkataramana: 'Respected Shastri, first please fix the spot where the sanctum sanctorum should be. Then I'll tell you the general plan of the temple's structure and layout.'

Venaktaramana who had now become a Shastri, an officiating priest, said: 'If it was some other place, we would first have to test whether the spot is auspicious. However, since the tiger gave up its life on its own volition, out of its respect for Punyakoti's devotion to truth, this place has become sanctified. Hence there's no need to test the purity of this site. Let the cave behind this place remain as is. In the front, you plan your layout so that it faces the east.'

'Absolutely, absolutely', said Kalinga Gowda, joined by a chorus of the villagers present there. Sivalingachari concurred. Venkataramana said: 'Now we need to inspect the best spot for the *kalyani*. Look to the east of the temple. See that spot, below, that shoulder? I think that should be suitable. Right there in that cleft there's enough space to fit thousands of cattle. There, I'll calculate the exact place to be dug and tell you.'

'Right. Now tell me how should the main *murti* of the temple look', said Sivalingachari.

'When the tiger gave up its life, "Lord Vishnu was pleased, as was Lord Shiva. Brahma Deva too was pleased and all the Gods instantly bestowed a shower of flowers. They remain compassionate," says the poem itself. So, let the Trinity of Brahma, Vishnu and Shiva stand in a line. Let Punyakoti stand before them. And in front, let the tiger lie down dead. Right?'

'Very good, very good', the Elder Kalinga was impressed with Venkataramana's suggestion.

Based on the dimensions the Elder Kalinga had provided, Sivalingachari described the general plan and layout of the temple. Everyone agreed. Sivalingachari said he would begin work exactly in eight days, that is, the *Bhoomi* puja and *Ayudha* puja had to be performed on that day. The task of transporting the stones from Bettikere could start tomorrow. Venkataramana took him home for lunch. His *jati* didn't allow him to eat food in Kalinga Gowda's home. Typically, orthodox people belonging to the *Vishwakarma jati* don't eat even in the homes of Brahmins. But Sivalingachari was an exception and would eat in the homes of Brahmins. The distance between the site of the temple and the *Agrahara* was one and half miles.

Putta Kalinga was not in town during the past eight days. He'd gone to Mysore. He hadn't said anything to his grandfather about what he'd do in future after passing his B.Sc. His grandfather had anyway decided that he had to carry on his ancestral tradition. Besides, there was the pending task of getting him married.

The evening after Sivalingachari finalized the temple work and left, Putta Kalinga returned to the village from Mysore. The moment he stepped into his home, he told his grandfather: He had received a scholarship to study in America. They would bear all the expenses including his travel. He must go there and study agricultural science for two years. The grandfather didn't like the grandson's words: 'How much more do you need to study? Just let it go. I'm now seventy. How much longer can I work? Just stay back home and look after the cattle shed.'

'Just two more years. You don't need to give any money from your pocket. They provide everything. My college principal has given the recommendation and helped me get the scholarship. It's not easy even for the best of them to get this. I have got it! If I study there and return, we can extract gold from our land.'

But the grandfather didn't agree. Putta Kalinga knew he wouldn't agree so easily. He figured that if Venkataramana spoke instead, he'd concur, and ran to the *Agrahara*.

Venkataramana was happy when he heard that Kalinga was going to America. But he had a suspicion: 'See, it is a country of Red People. It seems they only eat the cow's meat. Besides, it seems our food is not available there. How will you survive there for two years? You already ate the cow's meat once without your knowledge. But that happened due to ignorance. That sin was expiated through atonement. But now you have to eat it with your full awareness because there's no other option. Why do you want to attach this sin to yourself? Can't you stay back at home? Has God given you any less?'

It appeared that Putta Kalinga had already anticipated Venkataramana's questions. He gave him the answer he had already prepared: 'That's all untrue. The people of that country may eat cow's meat. But it's not like everybody who goes there must eat it. All those Brahmins who go there, do they eat it? Bread and milk are available in plenty there. For non-vegetarians, sheep and goat meat are available separately. I will most definitely not eat the cow's meat. If you want, I'll swear on you. Didn't I take *panchagavya* from your own hands for eating it just once by mistake?'

Venkataramana had faith in his friend's words. Then, Putta Kalinga explained his problem: 'You need to convince my grandfather somehow. If I study there and return, we can grow gold on our land. Moreover, if we learn science and do cattle rearing, we can get ten times more milk from our cattle. You've seen the cattle at the palace, right? In America, they teach us the science of making our cows like those. I'll learn that and return. Tell my grandfather to stay quiet for two years.'

Venkataramana thought about this. What Kalinga said was also right. If one did farming scientifically, it was possible to obtain more yield from the land. Besides, if one studied Science and reared cattle accordingly, milk from the cows would increase, and cattle could be better nurtured. Besides, the Elder Gowda didn't have to spend anything from his pocket. Why should one say no to an offer that has come on its own? All these years, the Elder Gowda had singlehandedly tended to the fields and the cattle shed. He'd somehow do it for two more years.

Venkataramana offered Kalinga an assurance: 'I'll talk to your grandfather to the best of my abilities.' After hearing this, Kalinga said, 'You must certainly convince him', and left for his village.

Venkataramana had decided to go to Kalenahalli the next evening. But in the morning, the Elder Gowda himself visited the *Agrahara* and raised the topic of his grandson. Gowda listened to what Venkataramana told him about how it was good to send him abroad because not only would the land yield more harvest but it'd also be good for the cattle. He said: 'Son, what you say is fine. But will Mother Earth give a bigger harvest if one goes to the Red Country? The land at the *Palasha* Stream? We can build a bund atop it. In the rainy season, all the water from the foothills will collect there. If we don't waste water and cultivate diligently, we can even reap two harvests of paddy. We have beech trees in the grove. The cattle shed daily yields two cartsful of dung. Mother Earth is fertile. If we collect water, which is Mother Ganga, if we shed our sweat, tie our oxen and plough the land, will Mother Earth refuse to give us a good harvest? And just for this, does he need to go to the Red Country?'

Venkataramana did not know what to answer in response to Gowda's question. But when he asked, 'What you say is correct. But what's the loss if he goes there to study?'

Gowda said, 'Son, you don't know transactional matters. He's come to you and you are recommending his case to me. If he was really interested in cultivation, there's plenty he could do at home. Hasn't he studied enough already? That fool is not one who can go out in the sun. That's why he's all set to study further. It was a mistake to send him to study in the college in the first place. I hadn't got my son Krishna educated even a bit. Wasn't he tilling?'

Venkataramana was continuously nodding. Finally, the Elder Gowda himself said: 'That son of a miser has seen city life. Now even if I say no, he won't relent. What can be done? I'll tell him to go and bless him.'

He went quiet after saying this. After ten minutes, he said: 'If he wants to learn this work, shouldn't he first learn it here and then go there? If the cattle falls prey to a disease, does he know what kind of medication would cure it? Has he learned it from me? One can prepare medicine for a cow from its own urine. Has he learned the various kinds of medicine that can be made from it?'

Venkataramana was now engrossed in serious thought. The Elder Gowda's words struck him as true. A person who hasn't learnt the knowledge that is readily available at home, what'll he accomplish by bringing knowledge from alien lands? After subtracting the loss from the whole, what part will remain as profit?

The Elder Gowda didn't speak again. He exchanged some pleasantries with Subbamma and returned to his village. Venkataramana thought of meeting Kalinga and talking to him. But someone visited his home in the afternoon to get their horoscope checked. Thereafter, more villagers visited his home. The next morning, he was scheduled to perform a housewarming ceremony in a different village. Thus, when he went to Kalenahalli two days later, Kalinga had left for Mysore. His grandfather had already given him permission to study abroad. It was also decided that he would leave in two months. Now, there was no use in speaking with him. Kalinga wouldn't halt his journey, he thought, and left it at that.

Because he was travelling to an alien country, Lakkamma was anxious about his safety. Although unable to open her mouth and speak, the mute Tayavva stood before Venkataramana. 'Nothing will happen. There's no cause to fear on the ship. A ship is like a large town. Sea water won't enter inside it. Don't be scared', he consoled her and returned to his village.

1

Although he had said he'd return in eight days, there was no sign of Sivalingachari even after three months. The Elder Kalinga arranged for a cart, took it to Chandrenahalli and returned along with him. Ten stoneworkers accompanied Sivalingachari.

Now the whole of Kalenahalli was immersed in work. All the stones required for the temple must be collected from Bettikere hillock, which is twelve miles from Arunadri Hills. The stones of the Arunadri Hills are soft and can be used only for the steps of the *kalyani*. Of the sixty agricultural settlements in the village, forty houses had their own bullock carts. However, it was not possible to make more than one trip daily after filling the carts with stones. First, male workers were needed to labour alongside the stoneworkers at the Bettikere hillock. Only experienced folk could load stone blocks and pillars onto the cart and then unload them at the temple construction site. Food arrangements also needed to be made for them.

The Elder Gowda took out all the ragi from his granary. The villagers made up for the shortfall by contributing according to their ability. They distributed ragi to all houses. The womenfolk of each home ground the ragi, made balls from it, cooked a broth of beans, and together with butter and buttermilk, took this food in a hamper to the temple construction site. There was no cash payment for unskilled, raw labour and stones. A payment of three thousand rupees to Sivalingachari, all inclusive, was fixed. Apart from the design and construction of the temple, it was his responsibility to build the main *murti* inside the sanctum sanctorum, the *Nandi* or Basavanna in front of the temple, the large door at the main entrance besides the pillars and beams. A total payment of four thousand rupees was fixed for the ten stoneworkers. It was their task to not only break and mould the stones according to the desired shape at the Bettikere hillock, but also to work according to Sivalingachari's instructions at the temple construction site. In addition to this, it was also their duty to break the stones at the site of the *kalyani*, and build and arrange its steps. For mortar work, another person was engaged for one thousand rupees. His job was to prepare the mortar and to deliver the burnt limestone that was needed not just for the temple but the *kalyani* as well. The smooth sand required to prepare the mortar was available at the stream below the foothills.

Food arrangements had to be made for Sivalingachari. It was cooked in Venkataramana's home and sent to the site.

But the total cost wasn't limited to just these expenses. Both Sivalingachari and his stoneworkers needed *bidis* and matchboxes. Sivalingachari himself calculated that once the temple was completed, a sum of at least fifteen thousand rupees would be required to carve the temple door and mould the large bells that would adorn the temple, as well as for conducting the ritual for consecrating the *murti*. When it came to money, Gowda flatly refused to collect donations from his village folk. Apart from the two hundred remaining from the cattle shed contract and the twenty-five rupees that the *Amaldaar* had given him thirteen or fourteen years ago, he didn't take any money from anyone. He began using the coins buried inside the large boiler located in the middle of his living room.

Six months had elapsed since Putta Kalinga had left for America. He would write letters informing that he was safe and well, but he never enquired about the temple work. Neither would the grandfather ask anything to be written about it. Although he knew how to read and write, the Elder Kalinga would get his letters written by Venkataramana. Also, the address had to be written in English. Besides, the Elder Gowda didn't know how an address was supposed to be written even in Kannada. All of this doesn't appear in the *Jaimini* studies.

After the work began, Gowda's house was overflowing with unprecedented enthusiasm. Although it was fatiguing to walk all the way and then climb the shoulder of the Hill, Gowda nevertheless used a bamboo staff for support or sat in a cart that was engaged for temple work. He was present at all times at the temple construction site, watching. He asked questions about *Shilpa Shastra*, the science of building temples to Sivalingachari. He gave betel leaves and chewing tobacco to the stoneworkers. While they were resting, he would recite verses drawn from the *Jaimini* describing Krishna's devotee, Sudhanva's battle from the Mahabharata. When the women from the village got ragi balls for the workers, he would yell, 'It's hot, cover your head with the end of your sari.'

Gowda's wife was younger to him by five years. But she didn't have his health and sturdiness. She would visit the spot once every two or three days. One shouldn't go empty-handed to places where such sacred work was being done, so she'd bring for the workers betel leaves and betel nuts wrapped in the folds of her sari. If that wasn't available, she would fill the folds of her sari with some sand from the stream flowing en route. Her service for the day would be complete after pouring it into the cauldron where the mortar was prepared.

Tayavva's joy was indescribable. Although her mother-in-law says no, she goes every day to the site carrying a hamper containing ragi balls, broth and buttermilk, and returns home. Using sign language, she talks profusely with the other womenfolk of the village accompanying her. Perchance someone who hasn't visited the shoulder of the Hill asks, 'How far has the work reached?' she describes the stage it is at, using hand gestures. One day, as she was carrying the food hamper, Yangata's wife Kallavva, who was next to her, showed her a spot and said, 'Hey, Tayavva, see, isn't this where Krishna *anna* died? Can you see that place down there? Wasn't it in that stream that the hyena was sleeping?'

Tayavva had tears in her eyes. She stood there in the sun and wiped her eyes with the edge of her sari. Kallavva said, 'Why do you cry? It's now eighteen years. Krishna *anna* is blessed. He got a noble death. My husband was talking at home: to build a temple, it's not enough even though you have money. It's not enough even if you sing and dance hollering that you'll build it. If you don't have the *punya* needed to build it, no matter what you do, you can't build it. This is what he was saying. Krishna *anna's punya* is there, that's why grandfather is building it. Right?'

Tayavva consoled herself. She felt proud of her husband. She nodded her head.

One day, Chinnayya asked the Elder Gowda: 'You're spending so much to build this temple, shouldn't a puja be performed here daily? What're you doing about it?'

Gowda smiled inwardly and said: 'Hey, are you saying I haven't thought about it?'

'So tell me what's it?'

'I won't say it openly. Just wait, you'll see for yourself.'

2

Abundant water was found on digging at the spot which Venkataramana had shown. Stone steps originating from the bottom all the way up to the top were constructed in all four directions of the square tank, which was one hundred-and-twenty-feet wide and hundred-and-twenty-feet long. On the bank, fifty troughs were carved in all four directions, which were filled with water for the cattle. It was dangerous for the cattle to directly step into the *kalyani*. The water too, would be spoiled. In that spot textured with stone, water was filled to the brim, crystal clear and akin to the taste of tender coconut.

The temple structure was now complete. The *murti* for the sanctum sanctorum that Sivalingachari had carved pleased everyone. Sivalingachari had sculpted the *murti* after examining in minute detail the profiles and features of the Punyakoti cows in Gowda's home— the *murti* reflected the most distinctive features of the cows of this lineage. The countenance of even the Basava—the bull—opposite the temple appeared as if it was born of Punyakoti's womb. The dome of the temple made from the *Panchaloha* alloy—zinc, copper, brass, lead and iron—stood there shining brilliantly and ready to ascend the tower of the temple. Sivalingachari had got the massive bell specially moulded at Mysore. It was truly enormous, difficult even for two strong men to lift, and when it rang from that height atop the hill, its melody reached all the ten surrounding villages during periods of quietude. He had it raised to the ceiling of the temple's outer compound and hung on an iron crowbar.

The entire responsibility of the rituals related to the *murti's* consecration fell upon Venkataramana. Although he was acquainted with the *Agama Shastra*—the theory and practical procedure of temple worship—he hadn't studied it systematically. And so he went to Mysore and invited his own teacher. Also, according to the Elder Gowda's instructions, he went to Srirangapattana en route and inquired about the now retired *Amaldaar*. He learned that he had died three years ago.

The date for the consecration was fixed for the *Sankranti* festival. It was also decided to begin the annual cattle fair on the same day. Drummers went around with this announcement, not just to the surrounding villages but all the way up to the Taluk. Venkataramana had also visited the *Amaldaar* and obtained a license for the fair. Lunch had to be arranged for the visitors arriving on the consecration day. They estimated a crowd of not less than ten thousand, and made calculations accordingly.

One fine morning before sunrise, ten days before *Sankranti*, the Elder Gowda along with Chinnayya took a cart and reached the *Agrahara*. He halted the cart in front of Venkataramana's house, went in and said: 'Son, I need to go to the Registrar's office for a bit. You come, too.'

'What's the work now, grandpa?'

'I'll tell you there, come. I thought of going there later. But it came to me last night that I *must* go today. I've got Chinnayya with me as well. We've brought ragi balls and broth. You pack some *roti* or something. Meanwhile, I'll go get the *Shanubhoga*, the village accountant.'

Venkataramana finished his bath in half an hour. His mother cooked ragi *thalipeth* and coconut chutney and packed it for him. By then, the Elder Gowda returned with the *Shanubhoga*. After they had all climbed onto the cart, Venkataramana once again asked, 'Why are we all going now? What's the reason?' The *Shanubhoga* replied on his own volition: 'The respected Gowda will not say it himself. I'll reveal it. Listen. I mean, what's there in this to hide? Now, the Elder Gowda has built the temple. Going forward, puja must be performed there without fail at all times. His wish is for you to take that up. From his lands, he will write in your name five acres of farmland, two acres of wetland and a fifty-tree coconut grove. You and your future lineage will enjoy all this land. Nobody in your future generation should sell it. The rights to the puja as well as the land will belong to the first son in your bloodline.

If he doesn't do the puja, it passes on to the second son. Basically, the puja at the temple must go on uninterrupted.'

Not only was Venkataramana astonished, but felt embarrassed and asked: 'Grandpa, I will do the God's puja, but why the lands?'

'The lands are for food, for livelihood. Is it possible to fast permanently with no food for the stomach? Hadn't I asked you not to go to Mysore but to stay back here? I'd thought about this back then. I hadn't spoken aloud because first God's work had to be done,' he said. Then turning to the young cart driver, he called out, 'Hey Honna, are you listening?' When the cart driver turned back and said, 'What's it grandpa?' Gowda continued, 'All the lands in the direction of the *Agrahara* will now belong to the *Jois*. The sugarcane field, the *Saavantri* wetlands near the *Agrahara* lake, the mangrove—I'll write all these lands in his name. You cultivate them on a sharecropping basis. You've worked in my house all these years. I'll build a house for you. I'll buy you a cart. I'll get you a couple of oxen and two cows. In the coming auspicious period, I'll look for a daughter from a good family and get you married. Till your land happily. You eat half and give the other half to him following the path of dharma. Got it?'

Honna was dumbfounded when he heard these words. He was from Kenchenahalli, ten miles away from Kalenahalli. His father and mother died when he was six years old. He had meandered from this village to that and reached Kalenahalli when he was ten. He'd been serving in this Elder Gowda's house for the last twelve years. He's never once asked for a salary on his own. Nor had Gowda given him anything. He gave him a stomach full of food and clothes to wear and treated him with affection. Proving himself to be trustworthy in all his work, Honna had also been tasked with supervising the temple work.

Chinnayya said: 'Fine, fine! If husband and wife work hard, they can buy two acres of field in four years. Honna breaks his bones and works. He's a tough man, not a lazy whoreson!'

After they reached the Taluk and ate their packed lunch by the lakeside, the *Shanubhoga* left, then returned with stamp paper and wrote a detailed deed.

The deed was registered. As they prepared the cart to leave for the village, the *Sheikhdaar* of the Hobli presented himself before them. He addressed the *Shanubhoga*: 'I was thinking of coming to your village. There's a case related to Kalenahalli.'

'Which one, My Lord?' asked the *Shanubhoga*. The moment they heard the name of their village, both Gowda and Chinnayya's ears perked up.

The *Sheikhdaar* said: 'A person named Kalinga Gowda has built a temple and a *kalyani* on top of the Arunadri Hill on government land without permission by illegally encroaching it. This matter has come to the notice of the top officials. I've been ordered to do a spot inspection and submit a report.'

'He is that Kalinga Gowda,' the *Shanubhoga* pointed to Gowda and asked: 'Gowdayya, hadn't you taken a *hukum* from the government before building the temple?'

'Why should I ask any government for anything to build a temple in the sacred memory of the cow belonging to my lineage who won over the tiger by her truth? Have I cultivated that land, harvested ragi and filled my granary?'

'Gowdayya, but you still need permission to do whatever you want to do on government land. If you talk like this, it might become a police case tomorrow.'

'What will the policeman do, my man?'

'If the government issues an order, the temple can be demolished.'

'Aha! The bastards!' Gowda was furious: 'Will he survive if he demolishes God's temple? One needs to accumulate virtue in order to build a temple. The lineage of the guy who demolishes it will perish. *Sheikhdaar*, what is your *jati*?"

The *Sheikhdaar* said patiently: 'You mustn't be angry like this, Gowdayya. I just told you the government's law. We can set everything right even now if you give an application. You must give some fees to the government, that's all.'

The *Sheikhdaar* took the *Shanubhoga* aside for a minute. When he returned, the *Shanubhoga* said, 'Gowdayya, he says he'll fix everything without a hitch if you give him a hundred rupees. What do we do?'

'Why should we give these whoresons anything? We're doing God's work.' Gowda stuck to his stand. But if this problem wasn't resolved, there was every possibility that there would be trouble during the consecration ceremony and the fair that was scheduled just ten days away. After the *Shanubhoga* involved himself in the negotiations, the Elder Gowda gave twenty-five rupees to the *Sheikhdaar*. He got the application filled by Gowda, met the *Amaldaar* and secured the record.

3

The consecration ceremony and the fair was a far greater success than Gowda had anticipated. First, the water of the *kalyani* was sanctified with the Ganga puja. The temple shrine was installed and then the *murti* was consecrated with due ceremony. Not just the Gowda, but none in the surrounding region had ever heard so many Brahmins chanting mantras for such a long time. Although the crowd turnout far exceeded what they had expected, the food they had prepared not only sated everybody but remained in excess. 'When one does virtuous deeds, food will never be in short supply. It's not just here, I've seen it in several places. When we first sprinkle the Sanctified Water on the mound of rice, that mound will ensure that it'll be available for any number of people,' said an esteemed *purohit* from Mysore. About seven or eight thousand cattle had been brought to the fair. The cow dung alone, which was auctioned by the government, fetched three hundred rupees.

The Elder Gowda now had no worries. Gowda wrote to his grandson informing him that the temple work was complete and that he had made over some land for its puja. In response, the grandson didn't say much except that he was also happy to hear this. In the *Chaitra* month beginning with the new moon of April, Honna got married. Because the lands were close to the *Agrahara*, the Elder Gowda built a house for Honna nearby, in the rear area, complete with a large cowshed. The cart and oxen soon followed. After the rains fell, Honna began tilling his new sharecropped lands.

It was two years since the *Jois* had died. The Elder Gowda stood at the forefront and got Venkataramana married. Two families were settled.

The New Type Middle School had now arrived at the *Agrahara*. An experienced English teacher who had completed the SSLC examination also arrived in tow. He was a pious, traditional man who performed the daily prescribed rituals without fail and had a daughter of marriageable age. He thought Venkataramana was the most suitable groom. The horoscopes, too, matched. Negotiations were conducted in the presence of the Elder Gowda. The wedding was fixed which took place in the *Jyestha* month falling in May–June.

The school wanted to fill a vacancy for another teacher who had passed the SSLC examination. Venkataramana had passed this exam and was suited for the post. His father-in-law himself put in the necessary efforts, approached the higher-ups, and after doing what was necessary, Venkataramana got the job. A salary of forty-five rupees a month. He wakes up in the morning, has his bath, completes his *Sandhyavandana*, and goes to the hill with flowers and leaves. From the *Agrahara* to the Punyakoti temple, it's a straight distance of one-and-a-half miles. He sweeps the temple, pours water on the ground, cleans it, finishes the puja, returns within ten and goes to the school.

Around the temple, the Elder Gowda's servants are growing bilva, oleander and other flowers typically used in puja. In the lower part of the *kalyani*, they've planted and are watering the stems of banyan and gunny. When he goes for the morning puja, the melody of the temple bell that Venkataramana rings wafts throughout Kalenahalli. In that moment, no matter where they are, the Elder Gowda and his family members unfailingly lift their folded hands in prayer, close their eyes and bend their heads.

VOLUME 7

1

Since the past month, the Elder Gowda's wife Lakkamma is bedridden. She often gets a fever. At times, the portion below her knee is swollen and then the swelling reduces and it becomes all right. All the responsibilities of the house have now fallen on Tayavva's shoulders. According to Gowda's calculation, Lakkamma has completed sixty-seven years. She doesn't understand that calculation. 'During the wedding, moustache had sprouted on our Gowda. I used to wear a scrap of sari. You make the calculation.' This was how she computed her age. Earlier however, she'd never been bedridden like this during any illness. Her hands and legs had never swollen like this. Gowda thought that she now had the Final Illness. They'd led this life. They'd lived well. The temple was built. What else was left, both for him and her, apart from death? At times, he regarded her illness with this sense of detachment.

But their only grandson still hasn't returned from the Red Country. *Three years have already passed since he left. He's written a letter saying he'd return in six months. Shouldn't he have even a bit of concern towards the village? He said he'd go for two years. Even if he returns, he'll do nothing here. He won't take care of the cowshed. He won't speak with his mother. He'll say what's there to speak with a mute? He'll go to some city and do some Amaldaar kind of work. In our village, we have our own headaches...* Gowda would fret within himself at times. Honna's wife is now pregnant. As is Venkataramana's wife. 'If he was married, we'd also have had a couple of kids by now. Where does he listen to us?' the Elder Gowda would confide to his wife sometimes.

They called the government doctor from the Hobli who gave her medicine by piercing her with the needle. But Gowda's wife decided that she was now stricken with the Death Illness. She wasn't unhappy because she was dying. But she longed to see her grandson before she died. An unfulfilled wish to get him married, and the chance to play with a couple of great grandchildren remained. Equally, the worry of who would care for her mute daughter-in-law after she was gone was troubling her. In his old age—after he had lost all his strength and would have to lay down weak—the question of who would look after her master and husband, the Gowda, also troubled her.

Also, because she lay down on the bed throughout the day, the skin on her sides would peel off and wounds would erupt. These would heal after Gowda applied homemade sandalwood oil, but soon a new wound would show up on another side. Each day, Venkataramana came home in the evening, sat for an hour and chatted with them. One day, the Elder Gowda told him: 'Son, your grandma is ill. If you don't come soon, you won't even be able to see her face—write a letter to Putta saying this. Let the whoreson come if he wants to.'

The next day, Venkataramana went to the Hobli and posted the letter.

Meanwhile, another trouble befell the Elder Gowda. There was news circulating that the government had decided to build a tar road connecting their Taluk and the neighbouring one. A motor would run on this road once every day. This meant that if people of the region wanted to go to the Taluk, they could do so hereafter by sitting in the motor. This news would've been of no significance as far as Kalinga Gowda was concerned. He had no work that entailed him to visit the Taluk. But, if he really needed to go and had no strength to walk in his old age, the bullock cart was sufficient. But when the news was confirmed, Gowda was agitated: the new road which would skirt the foothills of the Arunadri would cut through half of his grassland. It was being said that government officials had already taken the measurements. Chinnayya's son Yangata had seen them holding a tape and doing this. Although the pastures of the surrounding villages had all become fields, the Elder Gowda had managed to preserve his. Even though it was shown in government records as agricultural land—and he was also paying even agricultural tax for the last twenty or twenty-two years—it had, in reality, remained an undivided, single unit of pasture. Now, if a road cut through it, how much land would be lost? Besides, people and cattle would be free to roam on the road that cut through *his* land. Who'd be responsible for any stray cattle that grazed on the pasture that remained on either side?

By evening, the day after he heard this news, the peon of the Hobli's *Sheikhdaar* handed over a notice to the aged Gowda. When Gowda asked what was written, he said the same thing. The government will build a new road. The road will pass through Kalinga Gowda's land. The government will acquire that extent of Gowda's land and give him adequate compensation. If the landowner had any dispute in the matter, he could file an appeal within a month.

The Elder Gowda didn't sleep that night. The question as to why his pasture was being subjected to repeated troubles haunted his mind. Since the past month, the cattle in his village were stricken with disease. Although he gave medicine to all the cattle in Kalenahalli, two cows had died in his own shed. That grief hadn't fully subsided yet. Now a situation has arisen where his pasture would be split. *What'd happen if these bastards don't put the motor? Can't they sit on bullock carts and travel?* he thought to himself through the night.

Gowda's wife was lying on one side, but she was fully conscious. Tayavva too was awake, writhing. The elder Gowda confided his worry to them. But Tayavva didn't have a tongue to speak words that would comfort him. Although she attempted to say something, Gowda's wife didn't have the strength to articulate it clearly.

Gowda went to the *Agrahara* as soon as he got up in the morning. He showed the notice to Venkataramana. Both decided to stop this somehow. The notice was dated twenty days earlier. It had reached here after considerable delay. They went to the Hobli in Honna's cart. When they met the *Sheikhdaar* and the Sub-Overseer, they said, 'The road has to be done urgently. The survey is complete. Work has started from our Taluk. An Order has also been issued to acquire the private lands through which the road will pass. The government will give you some compensation for the loss of your land. You must write down the details of the land price, fertility etc. and give an appeal', the *Sheikhdaar* said.

'My good man, can't you do something and ensure that no harm comes to my pasture?' asked the Elder Gowda.

'It's impossible to do anything. The executive engineer has himself approved the plans based on the survey. Work has already started from both Taluks. Is the government insane to needlessly extend the length of the route?'

As no work could happen here, both of them reached the Taluk in the same cart. If the *Amaldaar* who was there twenty-two years ago was still here, he'd have done something. But who knows how this guy will turn out! Still, Venkataramana wrote an application. The aged Gowda held it in his hand and went inside. Venkataramana wasn't allowed to accompany him. *He's a schoolmaster: a government employee. 'How did you involve yourself in this matter? I'll report you to your department.' What'd be his fate if the Amaldaar yelled at him with this?* The aged Gowda handed the application and prostrated before the *Amaldaar*.

'Should the government change its plan because you want to save the pasture where your cattle grazes, oldie?' asked the young sahib.

'My good man, the land belongs to the *Gomaata*. Please save it somehow. You'll obtain *punya*.'

Whether it was because the aged Gowda had addressed him in the singular or because he'd spoken about *punya* or for whatever other reason, the sahib was furious. 'Don't you have any brains, oldie? Which is your village?' he screamed.

The oldie's courage deserted him. His tongue was dry. No matter how hard he tried, no words came out of his mouth. The sahib said, 'No matter what the government wants to do, the villagers invariably bring in some headache. Done. You go to your village now. I'll do everything later.'

'My good man, are you sure...' the Elder Gowda was saying.

'Didn't I tell you once? Now get out', he ordered.

He came out and wiped the sweat off his face with his head cloth. It was unnecessary to narrate what had happened inside to Venkataramana, who was standing outside the door and listening to everything.

Venkataramana escorted the Elder Gowda to the assistant engineer's office. He wrote another application, gave it to the Elder Gowda and when he asked him to go in and hand it over, the fear-stricken Gowda refused to go in.

'How can you refuse? Shouldn't the pasture be saved? Just because this *Amaldaar* is hare-brained, will they all be the same? You go in,' he infused courage. The Elder Gowda went in, placed the application on the table and prostrated.

The engineer read the application. He listened to him. He didn't yell. 'Okay, I'll think about it', he said. Afraid to talk further, the old man came out silently. Venkataramana approached the clerk, told him that if he got the work done, he'd get him some gift from the Gowda. He told the clerk that he himself was a government employee, and that when he came to collect his salary on the first, he'd see him again.

Now, both of them were slightly confident. 'God will definitely do good. If we pour some money into their mouth, it'll all be fine. You might need to spend fifty or hundred rupees', said Venkataramana to which the Elder Gowda replied, 'Let it cost whatever. It's enough if the pasture is saved intact.'

2

The condition of Gowda's wife was worsening. Everybody felt she wouldn't survive. But none could say when she would die. Although in bed constantly, she was conscious. The expression on her face suggested that she understood what the other person was saying. At times, when she had strength enough, she'd emit an unintelligible word or two from her barren lips; else, she'd spread the fingers of her right hand as if wanting to say something. Tayavva would understand this sign quickly. Accordingly, she would pour milk or water into her mother-in-law's mouth; or she would shift her body on the other flank. At times lying with her eyes open, she could understand the signs her daughter-in-law was making.

More than fifteen days had elapsed since the Elder Gowda had been to the Taluk with Venkataramana. Because the final days of his wife were approaching, he never ventured anywhere outside now. The servants took the cattle out for grazing. Venkataramana came in the evenings and sat talking for some time.

One afternoon, the servant Ninga came home and said: 'My man, I'd been to cut some leaves by the stream. On my way back, I saw that they've begun to cut the road crossing our pasture. They're cutting it from this end to the other. The road will go atop where your son, the Younger Gowda, is buried.'

The moment he heard this, Gowda felt a premonition of sorts. 'What's that?' he asked his servant, and when the servant repeated the same thing, he calmed himself down, took his stick, 'Come, let's go,' he said heading for the pasture together with the servant. He walked in the blazing sun, crossed the stream and made his way upwards through the farm there. When Gowda climbed the jujube knoll, he could see more than a hundred labourers working on his pasture. When he walked closer, his heart pounding wildly, he discerned that none of these labourers were from the neighbouring villages. He asked, 'Hey, why are you chopping here?' One of them signalled with his hands indicating that he didn't know the language.

All the labourers were Tamil speakers. But the *mestri*, the supervisor-in-charge of these labourers, knew Kannada. He spoke to the Gowda: 'Three days have passed since work has started here. The government people have given a contract for half a mile for each person. Our contractor—can you see that boulder over there?—he's got it from there up to this tree here.'

'But I'd given an application to not build the road inside my pasture?'

'I know nothing about that, Respected Gowda.'

The Elder Gowda's servant Ninga pointed: 'Look there my man. They've demolished our Younger Gowda's grave.'

The Elder Gowda went closer and had a look. Two large slab-stones sat atop each other on an elevated mound raised on the spot where his son Krishna and later Punyakoti, were buried next to each other. Barring the slab-stones, the rest of the place was covered with grass. But now, the labourers had not only tossed aside the slab-stones but had dug up the mound and levelled it. Like they'd done everywhere else, even here, they had dug about two metres into the ground and had left the soil right there. The remaining task was to pour gravel on this soil and flatten it with the road engine.

When he took in this scene, the Elder Gowda simply sat down. He couldn't think of anything to say. For all these days, Krishna had noiselessly slept next to his mother Punyakoti. In the last twenty or twenty-two years, this was the feeling that Gowda had experienced whenever he passed by this side. Krishna was the Man who had sacrificed his life to save the cow. His body too, was buried in this pasture. How could any tiger or hyena come this way as long as he was here? And by the way, no hyena had dared to raise its head in these surroundings after he had died. Now, these people have dug up his grave and will run the motor on top of it. For a moment the Elder Gowda felt dizzy and put his hand on his head to steady himself. Then he calmed himself, got up, went near the supervisor and beseeched: 'My good man, we'd buried my son and cow there. These guys have dug up that very spot. Is it possible to turn the road slightly this side? My pasture is anyway already broken. Do something so that at least this spot can be saved!'

The supervisor said in a sympathetic tone: 'Respected Gowda, the details of how and where the road must be made have already been planned and measured. The top people have done all this. No matter what we do, that won't change. You must first go to the deputy commissioner and get a stay order from him. After that you must see the executive engineer and get the road plan changed. Whether they'll do it themselves or whether it should come from the top, I don't know. But when we've got the *hukum* that the road must be ready for motor transport in two months, they won't change this.'

The Elder Gowda didn't speak after this. Maybe he understood that all talk was futile now, maybe he lost his strength to speak, or maybe he was enveloped by a sense of despair, he simply took his staff in his hand and left. The servant Ninga followed his master.

As they descended the knoll and walked over the farm, another servant Gorava who was searching for them, presented himself. Wiping his eyes, he said: 'Mother's gone.'

The Elder Gowda merely lifted his head and looked at him. When Ninga asked what the matter was, Gorava replied: 'I was right there when you said that they were doing the road on top of the Younger Gowda's grave. After you and Master left, Mother asked softly, "What?" I went near her ears and said, "It seems they're doing the road after breaking Krishna's grave. It seems they're also breaking the grave of Punyakoti who's resting next to him." After this she didn't speak anything. A teardrop fell from her eyes. I said, "Don't cry Mother, the Elder Gowda has gone to check it." Then, I left to draw water from the well to fill the trough. After a while, Tayavva came and called me. I go and see: Mother's life had left her.'

Ninga the servant wiped his eyes. But the Elder Gowda didn't speak a word. He continued walking ahead. By the time he reached home, people of the village had gathered. Tayavva was mutely weeping, holding with both hands her mother-in-law's body, which, over days of lying incapacitated, had transformed into a skeletal cage, and now, separated from its life force. Gorava who saw this sight said with tears in his eyes, 'Perhaps Mother wouldn't have died had I not told her that! Now it looks like I killed her by saying it,' he rubbed his eyes.

The Elder Gowda uttered no word. He leaned against the pillar for ten minutes, consoling himself. Although people surrounded him and spoke to him, he just sat there as if dumbstruck. Then, suddenly he stood up, 'What the hell! Why're you all sitting here like this? Can't you get up and make the bier? How long can we keep the corpse at home? Will the life once gone, come back?' he said.

Chinnayya's son Yangata, who was nearby, asked, 'Shouldn't the relatives arrive? Tell me, which all villages should I send the message to?' To which the Elder Gowda replied, 'There's no need for any relatives to arrive. Get up now. Let's bury the corpse soon', he said.

The bamboo bier was ready. The Elder Gowda said, 'Hey, she died as a *muttaide*, a married woman. Her husband is still alive. Apply lots of *kumkum* and turmeric. Deck her up with flowers. See where the new sari is.'

The womenfolk washed the corpse, wrapped a new sari, rubbed turmeric on the cheeks so that it was prominently visible, applied *kumkum* on the forehead, and stuck some flowers on the short locks that remained on the head. When the daughter-in-law fainted as the bier was lifted, the Elder Gowda told the womenfolk to console her and followed the corpse. As he had ordered, the grave this time was dug in the farm instead of the pasture. After the village folk who had accompanied him sprinkled grains of rice on the corpse, the grave was closed with earth.

By evening, several relatives, both from near and far arrived. The moment the news reached him, Venkataramana left school midway and sprinted over. The Elder Gowda himself didn't narrate how the grandmother had died. After the others told him, Venkataramana said, 'Shall we go to the district even now? No, not you. I'll go alone. The pasture has anyway been shattered. But I think they'll do our work if we appeal asking them to make the road by slightly skirting the grave.'

'No, no! Don't go', said the Elder Gowda.

'Not that. We need to make our attempt. The clerk at the Taluk engineer's office didn't do anything. We can catch him again and get at least this much done.'

'My son, you're hallucinating. Keep quiet', was the Elder Gowda's only reply.

Venkataramana dropped the matter there. Now the death rites of the grandmother had to be performed. If they had a son, he would automatically be entitled to the right of performing the rites after shaving his head clean. Now the grandson had to do this. 'Shall I send a telegram to Kalinga?' Venkataramana asked.

'What does that mean?'

'Writing a letter through the wire. If we say that this has happened, within a minute, they'll inform the post office of the place he is. If I go to the Taluk, pay money and write the message, it's enough. It'll reach him within tomorrow morning. If he comes in the aeroplane, he can arrive here in two days. Even if he reaches here before the Eleventh Day, he can perform his grandmother's last rites.'

After thinking for a minute, the Elder Gowda said: 'It won't matter if that whoreson doesn't come. We perform the last rites to reduce our Karma. What's the point if he comes?'

'It's not that. It's our duty to inform him. Once he hears the news he'll certainly come.'

'Fine. Then send the wire-letter. How much money will it cost?'

'Even I don't know exactly.'

As a rough estimate Venkataramana took one hundred rupees and left for the Taluk's telegraph office on the Elder Gowda's cart that night.

But Kalinga didn't come from America even on the Eleventh Day. Neither did the Elder Gowda talk about that matter again. But the relatives and well-wishers who had arrived for the rites discussed it. One of the relatives had his head shaven and performed the rites. About four or five thousand people were present for the night's dinner. Gowda performed his wife's last rites sparing no effort.

4

A kind of melancholy gripped the Elder Gowda in its thrall since the day he saw the road being built atop the graves of Krishna and Punyakoti. He no longer wished to speak with anybody. It appeared that strength had ebbed from his limbs. Until the last rites of his wife were finished, he forced himself to stay active. That was that. After the relatives and well-wishers had departed at night on the last day of the rites, he spread the blanket and just lay down. He spoke a few words of comfort to his daughter-in-law who came to see him from time to time. The rest of the time, he would lay down in silence. He had no fever, no chills—no specific ailment that could be pinpointed. *What's happened to me?* he would think to himself at times.

Venkataramana accurately grasped the Elder Gowda's state of mind. He would come there every evening and speak a few words from the lore of Vedanta. He'd ask him not to grieve over his wife's death—just like how a worn-out garment is discarded, the *Atman* discards one body and takes another. Now, the times are changing. Isn't this the *Kali Yuga*? After it is over, the *Pralaya*, the Terminal Deluge will occur. Then the *Satya Yuga*, the Age of Truth will start over. Then the cow will be worshipped everywhere throughout the earth. And devotion towards the cow will be reborn and thrive. Gowda would calmly listen to everything that he said. But unlike in the past when he would ask questions and learn things he didn't know, he wouldn't ask any question now.

What's happened to me? Gowda would think at times. He had no interest in food; he didn't care about his home and lands. Neither had he any concern for the cattle in his cowshed. Until now, he'd never once skipped the ritual of examining the water troughs of his cattle at least four times a day. Now there was no enthusiasm to even visit the cowshed. There was a gloom on his face that he could feel himself. He would eat the ragi *mudde* and broth made of legumes which his daughter-in-law forcibly placed before him on a plate. He'd wash this down with half a pot of buttermilk and sleep. However, the food that he ate couldn't prevent his decline day after day.

One day, as he thought about the road that was made on top of the graves of Krishna and Punyakoti, he recalled the manner in which Punyakoti had died. It had been struck on its face by the blow of the hyena's claw. After it returned home from there, he himself had treated the cow with medicine, but even after the wound had healed, the gloom that had enveloped it didn't go away. *And now, just like how my daughter-in-law is forcibly making me eat, all that rice and coconut mixture that we fed it didn't give it strength. It's the same gloom that's now on my face. There was no life in its eyes. The same thing has happened to me now. In Punyakoti's case, it could be said that she became like that—mortally fearful—after the hyena's strike. But, what has happened to me? What did I see that I've become like this—startled, scared? What has struck me?*

The cow, the human—aren't their minds the same? He'd often ask this question to himself and then answer it himself: After all, the cow's mind is better than that of the human's. They belonged to divinity. The human was base.

Chinnayya had died a year ago. His son Yangata was now the master of that house. One day, the Elder Gowda sent for Yangata. After this, he got his cart ready and they went to his farm where Gowda showed him the various greens and roots that had grown near the fence and canal. He then explained the medicinal properties of each. He taught Yangata the specific herbs that needed to be used for preparing medicine for specific cattle diseases, how they needed to be applied, the other ingredients that had to be mixed, the symptoms of different diseases, and other relevant knowledge. In the end he said, 'Any cow that's stricken with disease; you must go and give it medicine. Even if the cattle belong to your enemy, you mustn't decline. You mustn't take money for giving medicine. If you take money, your lineage won't survive.' Then, taking Yangata's hand in his own, the Elder Gowda took an oath from him. Then he sat in the cart, reached home and lay down again on the blanket. After resting awhile, he told Yangata, 'Who knows when that whoreson will come or not, or even if he'll come at all, whether he'll stay in this house. You take care of my cowshed.' To this, Yangata Gowda said, 'Why do you speak harsh words grandpa, just leave it.' He then took the Elder Gowda's hands once again in his own and made the oath.

Three days after this, the Elder Gowda told Venkataramana: 'Son, see if there's an auspicious day, either tomorrow or the day after. I want to perform the *Godaana*.'

'What's the special occasion now? The *Godaana* was performed during the last rites of Grandma.'

'Do we need a special occasion for *Godaana*?' Then, sighing deeply, he spoke slowly: 'Listen, I'll tell you the truth. All these days have passed. After I became the master of this cowshed, I must've performed some twenty or twenty-five *Godaanas*. But I haven't given away even a single Punyakoti cow as *daana*. Remember, I gave away two cows during the puja when the temple was consecrated? It occurred to me then to give away the Punyakoti cow. But does human greed go away so soon? So I gave away a different cow back then. I won't live much longer. But before I die, I'll give away a Punyakoti cow.'

Venkataramana made some calculations with regard to days and stars, and said that the day after tomorrow was auspicious. And so, on that morning, the Elder Gowda lay down in the cart and together with Tayavva, went to the Punyakoti temple. Two lactating cows of the Punyakoti stock followed the cart along with their calves. After the puja in the temple was over, the Gowda took water from the *kalyani* and performed puja to the two cows in tandem with the mantras that Venkataramana was chanting, and gave them as *daana* to Venkataramana. Then, Tayavva touched the feet of the cows and the Brahmin and took blessings. The Elder Gowda said: 'A burglar was occupying my mind all these days. Now he's gone. We should give as *daana* that which is dearest to us, isn't it?'

Venkataramana took the cows and returned to his village. The Elder Gowda returned home in the cart with his daughter-in-law. There were six more cows of the Punyakoti stock at home. He told his daughter-in-law: 'Child, any cow of any stock is equal to the Punyakoti stock. But this particular stock has been handed to our lineage. You must care for it properly. Understand this.'

Tayavva nodded in devotion.

Next morning, the *Kole Basava* visited the village. They enacted *Sita Kalyana*—the marriage of the God Rama and his bride, Goddess Sita—in front of Gowda's house. In response to the question, 'Rama, will you marry Mother Sita?' the bull enthusiastically straightened its chest and continually nodded its head. Then, in response to 'We won't give you the girl', it stepped back, sulking. Then, it bent its legs in the manner of Shiva's bow, which Lord Rama had bent as a precondition to wed Sita. After this, it stood next to Sita, the cow, on its own accord. Now, in response to 'My Mother Sita, will you marry Rama?', Sita merely bent its neck in the bashful manner befitting a young bride. The *Kole Basava* troupe then played the *Shobhana* raga—the auspicious tune played during weddings—on their *Nadaswaram* and completed the wedding rituals of Sita and Rama. Then as their procession stopped outside each home, the villagers gave them trays full of ragi and pulses. The womenfolk applied turmeric and *kumkum* on Sita and Rama.

After completing the rounds of all the houses in the village, the troupe came to the Elder Gowda's house. A match had been fixed between two members of their troupe, and both the bride and the groom were right there. However, they had no money for the expenses. If the Elder Gowda gave a loan of fifty rupees, they would return the money in two years. 'Because you're the Elder Gowda and you're the Headman, we're asking you. It's auspicious work. You'll earn *punya*, Elder Gowda', said the leader of the troupe.

When Gowda asked, 'What the hell! Who knows which village you're from? What's the guarantee I'll get my money back?' the leader didn't say anything in response. He beckoned a young man and a girl in his group. He escorted the Sita cow inside the house and made the couple hold her tail. Then he said: 'Respected Gowda, we're getting them married. Look, they have taken the oath on Mother Sita. If we don't give your money back, these two won't survive.'

Gowda didn't speak after this. He called out to his daughter-in-law and asked her to fetch fifty rupees. He counted it once more from where he was lying down and handed it to them. 'May auspicious things happen to this home. May it be filled with gold. May a thousand cattle be born in your barn.' The troupe left after uttering these and similar words of blessing.

The same night, the Elder Gowda sent for Yangata. When he arrived, 'Son, I badly want to listen to the flute. Go, get it', he said. After Yangata brought the flute, the Elder Gowda put his arm around Yangata's shoulders and walking slowly, went to the barn at the outhouse. He had Yangata inspect each trough to check if there was grass and water. After this, he spread his blanket and lay down on the bamboo cot tied in the middle of the barn. All the cows in the shed had finished eating grass and were now lying down, masticating. The oxen tied to the right, outside the parapet were still eating. The backyard beyond the slope of the roof was soaked with moonlight. Obeying the Elder Gowda, Yangata sat on a corner of the cot and started to play the flute.

Until the time his lungs had vigour in them, the Elder Gowda used to play the flute like none other in these surroundings. Then his son Krishna used to play in a manner befitting his father's name. Indeed, it was simply joyful to watch Krishna lose himself in the flute, after chewing *paan* until the juice dripped from his lips. Let alone the world, Krishna wasn't even aware of himself as he played it. Among the folks now, Yangata plays it well.

But despite playing for half an hour, his flute music didn't take on any colour. The Elder Gowda asked, 'What, haven't you taken *paan*?' When Yangata said no, he asked him to go inside and chew some. But there wasn't any *paan* in Gowda's house. Yangata went to his home, returned with a pouch of *paan,* and filled his entire mouth with the concoction. The nerves in his neck swelled after a short while. His body temperature rose. Then he put the opening of the flute to his lips. Now the music was infused with strength.

Now, even the oxen had stopped eating grass in the tranquillity of the night. From time to time, Tayavva was refilling the *mahua* oil and adjusting the wick of the small, lit earthen lamp. The melody of the flute was escalating. The song had no connection to any theory of classical music. Just as when Lord Krishna was a lad, he created *Maya* or illusion with his flute, this flute too, was creating illusion. Where's the world that isn't created by illusion? But only the *Maya* that Lord Krishna had woven is the actual truth. Other truths become illusory.

In Lord Krishna's time, the cows are lying down by the riverside, masticating in the moonlight. Nearby, the infant calves are jumping about, playing. The atmosphere is serene. Suddenly some mischievous bulls charge in. They gore one another, locking and smashing horns. The red dust caught under their hooves that rises upward from the earth, rings around the white of the moonlight. Blood dribbles from the bodies of the fighting bulls. Some have their horns broken. Yet, they don't stop their combat. The frightened cows together with their calves sprint towards the cowherd Krishna and take refuge in him.

Smiling, Krishna takes out his flute. He fixes his lips to it and blows it loudly once. The bulls stop fighting as soon as they hear the music. Rooted to the spot, they turn towards the person blowing it. The fury each had towards the other extinguishes on its own. The red dust abates, and the earth becomes clean. There's only the music of the flute everywhere. All the cattle close their eyes, perk up their ears and lie down. Even the river has stopped flowing, silencing its gurgles so as to not impede the music. The water has stopped flowing, and now resembles a solid lump. The moonlight is a heavy clot. The flute has stilled its melody, unwavering like the strand of a flame in an airless region. Is Krishna filling his breath into it or is he pulling it out?

The Elder Gowda was lying there listening with his eyes closed.

Yangata played till after midnight passed, and the legs of the cot were now visible in the skylight. He experienced a sense of absorption that day as he'd never felt before. *Indeed, who doesn't experience this sort of absorption especially when they play the flute in Kalinga Gowda's barn at the express wish of Kalinga Gowda!* By the time he stopped playing, the Elder Gowda had drifted off into a calm sleep. But Tayavva had been sitting there all this time listening to the melody till both her ears overflowed with it. After some time, Yangata asked Tayavva, 'Shall we wake him up and take him inside?'

'No, let him sleep there', she signalled with her hands. He asked,

'I'll go home. Will you stay here?' She motioned him to leave. Ninga the servant was sleeping in the front courtyard of the house. Tayavva poked him awake, then gestured him to go sleep near the cot at the barn. Sleepy-eyed, he got up, dragged his blanket along, and slept on the stone slab placed on the ground next to the bamboo cot.

The earthen lamp filled with *mahua* oil was burning sedately. Tayavva refilled oil to the brim. But she didn't manipulate the wick to increase the brightness.

The Elder Gowda was sleeping peacefully. Tayavva went inside to sleep but it eluded her. Memories of her husband arose each time she heard the flute. There was none who could play the flute as beautifully as he could. And as he was playing it, even the wayward cattle would silently come over and lie down all around him. But her own son never learned to even put his lips to the flute.

After tossing around a few times, Tayavva got up and went to the barn again. The oil had almost fully depleted and the lamp was burning feebly, though unperturbed. The Elder Gowda's face was visible in its light. It appeared as if he was still lost, listening to the music of the flute. Ninga who was sleeping down on the stone slab was snoring. She poured oil into the lamp yet again, then came in and lay down. After tossing some more, she drifted off to sleep.

5

In the morning, though the day had broken, Tayavva had not yet woken up.

'Tayavva, Tayavva!' Ninga yelled, waking her up, and said, panicking: 'Come, see. The Elder Gowda has died. He has died sleeping like how he was sleeping in the night.'

For an instant she went immobile in the spot she lay on, as if her heart had shattered. Then after Ninga called her name again, she slowly got up and then went to the barn. And what does she see? Ninga had untied all the cows and oxen and had now tethered them outside. The Elder Gowda lay there on the cot in the same manner as last night. His face bore an expression as though he was still listening to the flute. *When did he die? Was he already lying dead when she saw him last night or did his life leave him in sleep?* Tayavva didn't know. *Maybe he's not dead after all, Ninga might be lying,* she suspected. She went closer, touched his body. His hands and legs were frigid and stiff.

1

All the relatives who had turned up for Gowda's wife's final rites were also present for his. But back then, the Elder Gowda was alive to take care of everything. Now, apart from the mute Tayavva, there was not a soul to lead from the front. Although Venkataramana stayed there throughout from morning till evening, he hesitated to take independent decisions because money was involved. Tayavva brought out a large barrel containing rupees from inside the house and placed it before him. He counted them. Eight hundred and twenty rupees in all. The last rites had to be completed within this amount. But if the whole thing was spent for the rites, how would the family make do until the next harvest? He thought about this as well. But then again, the last rites of the Elder Gowda, who had lived such a dignified life, shouldn't be performed in a miserly fashion. At least eight or ten thousand people had to be fed. But now there was neither ragi in the granary nor paddy in the storage. It'd all been spent during the temple consecration and his wife's rites.

Relatives and well-wishers who understood the situation brought ragi flour, rice, jaggery and pulses from their respective villages. The drummer went around the neighbouring villages announcing the grand feast on the Eleventh Day. Arrangements began to be made accordingly. 'Is he an ordinary Gowda? He built a temple,' was the pride which brimmed not only among his relatives and well-wishers, but pervaded among others in the village too.

On the afternoon of the Tenth Day, the house was filled with relatives and well-wishers. For tomorrow's grand feast, work was in full swing in the vast field in front of the house—from digging out the earthen stove to washing the enormous vessels and other utensils. Then, a car arrived there, its body fully covered in dust. Even as the people looked in its direction in surprise, a tall, reddish-brown coloured sahib got out.

Dressed in trousers, coat, hat and boots, he directly went inside the Elder Gowda's house. None of the relatives could recognize him. But Tayavva instantly recognized him and beamed a smile. But she couldn't speak out and say who he was. He said himself, 'Amma, where's grandpa?' Everybody now knew; he was Kalinga who had gone to the Red Country.

Kalinga had the bedroll and trunk removed from the car's boot and got it placed inside the house. After he paid money to the driver, the vehicle left. He removed his trousers, coat, hat, and shoes, and changed into striped pyjamas and white shirt, and sat on the bed. Relatives were either shy or scared to talk with him. Presently Yangata arrived, 'When did you come, my brother?' he asked.

When Kalinga asked him, 'Aren't the last rites of grandma over?' Yangata narrated everything in detail—grandmother's rites were completed twenty-five days ago. Tomorrow, it was grandfather's turn.

Tayavva was relieved that her son had returned home. She gestured him to come inside and then, placing the money in the barrel before him, told him with her fingers that these were six hundred rupees. Perhaps she reckoned that her responsibilities ended at that! Kalinga returned to the bed, leaned on it and took rest. Yangata was sitting down on the floor talking continuously. In half an hour, Tayavva had cooked steaming hot rice, and asked them to come for lunch. She served the meal in large plates. Perhaps the food was terribly spicy for him. He drank water again and again, and abandoned the half-eaten rice mixed in broth. He ate curd rice and stood up.

Meanwhile, Venkataramana arrived. No matter how enthusiastically the relatives and well-wishers and village folk worked, it was Venkataramana's job to issue them the requisite suggestions and advice. When he saw Kalinga, he was both surprised and relieved. 'When did you arrive? Did you get my telegram?'

'I did. That's why I left everything and got here.'

'Why did it take so long?'

'I wasn't in town when the telegram came. There was some delay by the time it reached the place we were at.'

'Anyhow, you've come at least now. It's a huge relief for us. Everything is set for tomorrow. Together, all these folks are doing every single necessary task. You don't worry. I was thinking of a suitable person who could sit and perform tomorrow's rites. Now you've come yourself— you're the one actually endowed with the authority to perform the rites.'

They spoke for a long time. Venkataramana narrated everything that had occurred here after Kalinga had left for America. Given the occasion, he revealed only so many details. He covered everything including the temple construction and then the death of his grandparents. When he asked him about his life in America, he didn't seem too enthused to speak about it. His mind was engrossed in learning about the happenings here.

'You said you'd return in two years. It's almost four years now. Why?'

'I first studied agriculture. Then, I got another fellowship: to study animal husbandry, meaning the preservation of cattle, their diseases, their utility, benefits. I studied this for a year and got a diploma in it. All these days, I was in a farm getting practical training,' he said.

Venkataramana left for the *Agrahara* that evening.

2

Before seven the next morning, Venkataramana arrived with a bundle of *darbha*, the sacred dried grass. By then, the house had been swept clean and swapped with water mixed with cow dung. In the inner courtyard, the *Navagraha Dhanya*, the Nine Sacred Pulses, plantain and mango leaves, a *dhoti*, a copper vessel, and other utensils meant for *daana* were all kept ready. Tayavva had bathed a lactating Punyakoti cow and tethered it along with its calf outside the front door. This was meant for the *Godaana*.

Venkataramana prepared the *panchagavya* in a large vessel by mixing milk, curd, ghee, cow urine and dung and washed it with the *darbha*. Then about seven or eight Brahmins from different villages assembled at the spot. The relatives and well-wishers finished their bath. It was customary to first take the *panchagavya*, then perform the *navagraha* and other *daanas*, and finally proceed to the spot where the body was buried, and offer it water and ghee. As Venkataramana spread out the plantain leaves and was giving instructions to place the *navagraha dhanyas* in their allotted directions, Kalinga arrived, having finished his bath. Venakataramana asked Yangata, who was seated there, placing

S.L. BHYRAPPA

the Sacred Pulses on the leaves: 'Did you forget to call the barber?'

'I've called. He's sitting on the portico near the pillar.'

'In that case, Kalinga Gowda, go there and get your head fully shaved,' said Venkataramana, now in the capacity of a *purohit*, the priest officiating the ceremonies. Kalinga didn't say anything in reply. Five minutes later, when Venkataramana repeated, he asked, 'Won't the work get done without removing it?' All the Brahmins who had assembled there said, 'No, no, it's only after shaving the head that he'll be entitled to perform the last rites.' Among the relatives, one of the Elder Gowdas joined the chorus, 'How's it possible, my brother? You must compulsorily shave off your head.'

Venkataramana also pointed out: 'When my father died, I shaved my head. You've seen it yourself. This is the same. You've returned from foreign lands. If not fully, at least shave off a bit in the front like an arc. Till it regrows, you can wear a hat or a topi.'

Kalinga thought for a minute, and then replied: 'I don't believe in all that. You get the rest of the work done. It's fine.'

'How can the rest of the work get done without shaving your head?' asked the other Brahmins. Among his relatives, an old lady said, 'Son, what's infected your brain that you speak like this?' Kalinga's face darkened. Still, he didn't agree.

Finally, Yangata asked Venkataramana, 'Will it do if I shave off my head?' Venkataramana, the *Jois purohit* said, 'So be it. You're akin to the Elder Gowda's son. You get it shaved. But then, you'll also have to sit in front of the *navagraha* and perform all the rites. Is it ok, Kalinga Gowda?' Kalinga Gowda said okay. The problem was resolved. But nobody was happy. Tayavva was extremely unhappy. But she didn't know how to express it. Besides, how could she instil sense into her son in the presence of so many people?

Yangata fully shaved his head, wrapped around the new white *dhoti* till it touched only his knees, inserted the *darbha*-ring made by the *Jois* into the ring finger of his right hand and sat down. Then, as the *Jois* chanted the mantras, he performed puja first to Lord Ganesha, who was made from cow dung and dried grass, then to the urn consecrated as a shrine, and then to the *navagrahas*. Simultaneously, puja was performed to the *panchagavya*. Kalinga and Tayavva had to drink it first. Although Yangata sat in Kalinga's seat, it was not his *sootaka*—the death-related impurity—that had to be washed away. And so, Venkataramana called Kalinga, and when he came there and extended his palm, he made a spoon from a mango leaf, filled it, then poured the *panchagavya*. Just as he prepared to fill it again, Kalinga said, 'Once is enough.' Then he went behind the pillar, and when he tried to drink it, felt disgusted by the odour of the urine and dung it contained, and wiped it on the pillar. Although the others didn't notice it, Venkataramana observed it from the corner of his eyes. Tayavva who was seated this side of the pillar also noticed it.

Then Venkataramana *Jois* called Tayavva. She went there, bowed, placed her right palm atop her left and stretched it out. The *panchagavya* poured three times into her palm filled it to the brim. Closing her eyes in bhakti, she drank it on the spot, then wiped her palm on her head, circumambulated, and prostrated before the *navagraha*. After this, not only did the relatives and well-wishers drink it, so did the other village folk who had assembled.

Other mantras were then recited and the last rites were completed. The Brahmins were given *daana* and *dakshina*. Tayavva gave away the cow only to Venkataramana. By then, Venkataramana's mother, his wife and one-year-old daughter had also arrived from the *Agrahara*. Their job was to cook for the Brahmins assembled there. Subbamma had fed Kalinga as a boy and had taken care of his studies. When she spoke to him, 'Are you fine, my child?' he respectfully folded his hands and spoke to her courteously. He did namaste to Venkataramana's wife, Meenakshi and enquired after her welfare.

After offering milk and ghee to the grave, the relatives left for the Punyakoti temple. Venkataramana had already gone there, bathed in the *kalyani*, and performed a special puja. Every visitor who entered the temple rang the temple bell, and its sweet music resonated throughout the surrounding villages.

An impossible crowd had gathered for the evening's feast. Since it was the ritual feast in honour of the departed Gowda who'd built the temple, there were throngs of people even from villages that were not informed of his demise. Yangata who had assumed all responsibilities was slightly frightened. But Venkataramana who had stayed back, infused confidence in him: 'In a feast for God, food will never be in short supply. The last rites of the Elder Kalinga are akin to God's work. Don't be scared.'

In reality, everyone's stomach was full. Broth, ragi *mudde*, *paayasa*, rice, were all left over. Towards the end, when it appeared that there was shortage of betel leaves, only six or seven leaves were given to each guest instead of an entire pouch.

3

The next morning, Kalinga woke up late because he had slept late last night. As was the custom, the relatives who had attended the last rites, had gone back immediately after the feast, without the post-feast farewell formalities. Only mother and son remained in the house. Kalinga had to urgently write some letters. When he learnt that a post office had newly arrived at the *Agrahara*, he donned his trousers and went there. But that small office had no postal stationery that one could send to a foreign country. By the time he reached Venkataramana's house from there, he had already finished the temple puja and was sitting at home reading an English newspaper. When he saw this, Kalinga asked: 'What's this, do you also read the English paper?'

'It comes to our school. I've already been reading it from the past two years. I can understand it very well. Come, sit.'

Kalinga sat on the mat. Subbamma made him *upma*. Venkataramana told him that he'd inform the post office to get the foreign postal stationery he wanted by tomorrow.

Then they exchanged some transactional conversation. Kalinga asked: 'Amma told me that there's only six hundred rupees at home. So many relatives had filled up the house. Do you think something might be amiss?'

'*Che, che*, no, nothing like that. When the Elder Gowda died, there was eight hundred and twenty rupees. For the rites yesterday, the relatives themselves got the provisions and grains from their own villages, and finished the work.'

'I've never known how much money grandfather had with him. But then, a family that has all these lands, the barn, has only eight hundred and twenty rupees left? How's that possible?'

'Kalinga, are you suspecting someone? Tell me directly. You weren't home. After grandfather died, I used to visit your home twice a day to console your mother, and gave some advice on transactional matters. If I've eaten even a single paisa of your house in stealth, let my lineage not survive.'

'Venkataramana, don't mistake me. I'm not suspecting you. I know your father's character and yours as well. I'm telling you the truth. I now want to learn everything about my house. My mother can't speak. Who else is there apart from you to educate me on all that has happened in this interim?'

Venkataramana told him every single detail related to monetary affairs. After he left for America, it cost fifteen thousand to build and consecrate the temple. 'The Elder Gowda never once uttered a word about those expenses. The Shastras say that one must not make calculations with regard to money spent towards works of dharma. But I have an estimate because I've seen it being built all the way from the start', he said, and then told him about Honna's marriage, and later, the expenses towards his grandmother's last rites. 'The gold in your house has remained intact. But then, your house didn't have a lot of gold from the beginning. Your grandfather always used to say, "Why does the wife of a cowherd need gold?" Still, your grandmother's brooch, the golden chrysanthemum flower, necklace, that other round necklace... all of them are there. Your mother's jewellery is there as well. The solid gold bracelet and earrings that your father wore? Those are also there. Towards the end, your grandfather stopped wearing that hundred-and-twenty-gram gold arm-bracelet. That's there at home, too.'

Venkataramana also told him about the endowment that the Elder Gowda had made in his name after building the temple and assigning him the responsibility for its daily puja. Then Kalinga asked: 'Doesn't the government give any compensation for the road cutting through our pasture?'

'They need to give it. I've heard myself that they indeed give it. You make an attempt. Let's go to the *Amaldaar* or the deputy commissioner's office one day.'

They spoke till eleven-thirty. Venkataramana had to leave for school. So, Kalinga left for his village. Yangata was engaged in getting the vessels and other utensils washed and returning them to their original owners. They had been borrowed from various places for use in yesterday's ceremonies. Tayavva had prepared rice and broth for her son. He told her not to put that amount of spice in the broth and then ate his food. Using her hand gestures, she asked him a few questions about four or six times. He didn't understand.

He took the keys from her, went inside the inner dark room, and from the wooden trunk, extracted the land documents, and read all of them very slowly. He found the paper which said that about twenty-five or twenty-six years ago, their pasture had been converted into farmland, that it was entered in government records, and that tax had been paid. He kept it separately in his leather bag.

Next morning, he went to the pasture and surveyed the road that was built in its middle. The road cut right through the pasture. White stone was set using the road engine, gravel was put upon it and it was flattened again. They were now digging pits on either side of the road to plant banyan stumps. On the right side, they had erected the mile and furlong stones. According to its calculation, the Taluk was at a distance of sixteen miles.

When the coolies digging a trench for planting trees saw him attired as he was in trousers, boots and hat, they stopped work and folded their hands. The supervisor present in the vicinity ran towards him and said, 'Namaste *Saar*.' He delivered the news that the motor service on this road would commence in fifteen days, that is, on the first of the next month.

'Do you have a tape?' asked Kalinga.

'I do *Saar*.'

With his assistance, Kalinga measured the breadth of the road. He also took into account the width that the banyan saplings planted on either side of the road would occupy after they grew massive trees. After measuring the exact length of the road that cut through his pasture, he borrowed a scrap of paper and the pencil that the supervisor had tucked behind his ear and then noted down the calculations. He walked from there, climbed the shoulder of the hill and went to the temple. As he was climbing, the large temple bell emitted a clanging loud enough to peal the entire hill.

The temple door was open when he arrived. Venkataramana was plucking flowers and leaves from the oleander, *tanagdi* and other plants. Venkataramana felt happy at seeing him. 'Come, you've come exactly at the puja time.' When he descended to fetch water from the *kalyani*, Kalinga too, went with him. The expansive *kalyani* was three-fourths full. The water was clear and pure. The steps of the *kalyani* were sturdy. Kalinga was lost in some thought. Venkataramana went to the temple and immersed himself in the puja with sandalwood paste, flowers, incense and lamp.

When Kalinga returned to the temple, the puja was nearly over. Venkataramana was lighting the wick of the *arati*. His left hand held a small bell. When he saw Kalinga, he said, 'You came at the right time. I'll perform the *arati*. You ring the bell out there in the compound.' The bell was truly enormous. It was a fun experience to ring it: holding the rope fastened to the end of its tongue and tugging it till the tongue slammed the inner edge. He rang it with great energy till Venkataramana asked him to stop. Finally, he touched the *arati* that Venkataramana offered gave and held the flowers in his hand. Venkataramana brought a vessel made of galvanized metal and said, 'You need to take the *prasada*. Go, cut a *Palasha* leaf out there and bring it.'

'What's for *prasada*?'

'Boiled green gram, grated coconut, jaggery.'

Kalinga stepped out, cut a fine *Palasha* leaf from the tree nearby, washed it with the *kalyani's* water, wiped it with his handkerchief and returned. Venkataramana filled it first with the green gram and then sprinkled grated coconut and jaggery on top. Kalinga, who put just the boiled gram in his mouth, asked: 'This has pepper in it, right?'

'Yes.'

'Look, this is really tasty. In the Western countries they don't eat chillies like we do. They eat pepper instead. Chillies aren't good for the body. I couldn't eat the broth that my mother served yesterday and the day before. I should tell her to make it with pepper from now on.'

'You're accustomed to eating that country's food. It'll take a couple of months for you to get used to the taste here.'

After he finished eating the boiled gram, Venkataramana served some more.

'Do you prepare it every day like this?' Kalinga asked.

'It's not boiled gram daily. It could be a grain-vegetable salad or soaked grain. Sometimes it's sambar-rice or curd rice. If there's some inconvenience at home, I get just coconuts.'

'What do you do with the *prasada* daily?'

'Normally, some folks come here during the puja hour to offer fruit and coconut. I'll give it to them. Else, I'll keep some near the *Basavanna* in the front: for the birds. I'll eat a morsel and take the rest home.'

After this, Venkataramana locked the temple door and went home. Kalinga continued to roam around and inspect the land at the foothills that lay to the left after descending the *kalyani*. It was afternoon when he went home.

4

In the evening, Kalinga went to the *Agrahara* and obtained maps for Kalenahalli and the foothills from the *Shanubhoga*. The next day, he went to the Taluk in the bullock cart and from there, he went to the district centre by the motor. The deputy commissioner was in his office at one in the afternoon. He granted him an interview the moment he saw the visiting card that was sent to him: K. Kalinga, B.Sc; M.S. (Agri) Ohio; D.A.H. (U.S.A). Kalinga had worn a full suit with a tie and a hat on his head.

After exchanging some polite pleasantries and smoking a cigarette with the sahib, Kalinga spread out the map he had brought with him on the table, showing him the details and said: 'In reality, this is a field that was being cultivated. When I was abroad—because there was nobody to look after its management, my grandfather had left it just like that without taking out any harvest. These tax receipts are evidence that it was a farmland since the last twenty-five years. I've suffered enormous loss on account of the fact that a road has cut through agricultural land.'

'What's the estimate of your loss?'

'When we calculate the space that will be occupied by the trees by the roadside in future, a total of twenty-six acres of land would have been lost. Neither is this calculation restricted only to land. The land that was in a single holding so far has now been split into two. Also, since a public road has come in between, there's now no security for the crop on either side.'

'Meaning, what's the compensation you plan to seek?'

'I'm a farmer—a son of the soil. If you only give me money as compensation, it will be of no use. Instead, if the government gives me land, I'll extract harvest. My loss will also be compensated. The country will also have food.'

The deputy commissioner was happy when he heard these words. Kalinga said: 'I went to America with the sole purpose of learning the scientific system of farming. In my four years overseas, I studied not just agriculture but even animal husbandry. But by the time I returned, my cultivable field has been broken and lost. What do I do?'

'It is an auspicious sign for the nation that educated people like you have opted to do farming. Let's see, is there any other suitable land that can be given to you?'

Pointing to the map, Kalinga said: 'See this land at the foothills? Not only does this fall to the west of my existing land, it's also suitable for cultivation. It's about seventy acres in area. It'll be very convenient for me if the plot is given. But even then, I will need to raise an investment of twenty thousand at the least to develop it.'

The deputy commissioner said it would be granted. He instructed Kalinga to write his appeal in the form of an application and get it typed. He then said: 'See, the government has envisaged different types of loan schemes for developing farmland. The interest rate is low as well. After you get this land, make an application for loan. You'll get it easily.'

Then he asked a few questions about life in America and other related topics. One of his younger brothers was set to leave for America in three months. He asked some questions about food and dress in that country. He was slated to go to the Ohio University as well.

'You don't worry. I have several friends there. I have relatives even. I'll write them a letter in advance. They'll make sure your brother is comfortably settled,' assured Kalinga.

'Give the application for the land today. If you so wish, I'll get it drafted myself. Then it will be sent to the *Amaldaar* and then to the *Sheikhdaar*, who will visit the spot for inspection. I'll issue an order after obtaining his report,' he promised.

5

Kalinga inspected all the cows in his shed. Sixty cows in total. But only twelve were lactating. Ten were pregnant. Another thirteen were in a state where they would get pregnant if joined by a bull. The remaining twenty-three that had given birth to calves and provided milk all their lives were now old.

Among the oxen, only eight pairs were actually in working condition. Thirteen individual oxen, still in their four-tooth stage, had not yet fully attained youth. The remaining thirty-two had fully attained old age and were absolutely in no condition to do farm work. *What was the quantity of grass that these aged twenty-three cows and thirty-two oxen—a total of fifty-five cattle—consumed? What was the quantum of labour of the servants who oversaw them?* thought Kalinga. The next time he went to the Taluk, Kalinga met a Muslim engaged in the cattle business, called him, and sold all fifty-five cattle at the rate of fifteen rupees per head.

Selling cattle wasn't a new practice in their lineage. Not only in the Elder Gowda's own lifetime, but even his ancestors used to sell cows, oxen and bulls. They planted the two-ear maize in their farm and fed the tender but sturdy maize to the young bulls so they grew in strength and size, and then sold them at the cattle fair: this was the typical practice in vogue in their lineage. They also sold milch cows for the best price. But none in their village sold aged cattle, be it ox or cow. Besides, why would anybody buy cattle which could neither work nor provide milk? The one who bought them in their youth and extracted work from them or drank their milk had to care for them in their old age just like one cared for one's parents when they grew old. But of late, some villages had begun to sell aged cattle to Muslims. Those who bought them made profits by killing them and selling their flesh and skin.

Tayavva didn't comprehend anything when Kalinga sold all the fifty-five cattle on the same day. But in the evening when she saw that the barn was half-empty, she grew suspicious. When she gestured to her son what the matter was, he similarly gestured back, 'Nothing, you go in.' Tayavva couldn't restrain herself. She kept saying something with gestures. But Kalinga said nothing. She didn't relent. She went directly to Yangata's house and gesticulated. Yangata understood everything. Besides, he had heard that very afternoon from the boys of his house that the Muslim had taken away a large herd from the Elder Gowda's barn.

Now Yangata came to Kalinga's house and asked: 'What's this brother, does anybody give cattle to a butcher?'

'How can you say that he's a butcher?'

'Who else apart from a butcher purchases old cattle?'

It's not as if Kalinga was unaware of the matter. But he hadn't anticipated that outsiders would question him in this manner. But, he was furious when he realized that his own mother had gone out and called in outsiders to mediate justice. But without showing it, he said: 'It's over now, let it be.'

'How can we let it be?' argued Yangata: 'Do you give away your own barn's cattle simply because he gives you a few rupees? Had Elder Gowda been there, would he allow it?'

'It's not merely a question of its price. What's the cost of the grass that it daily ate for free and wasted?'

Yangata could think of no answer for a minute. He had never learnt how to calculate the price of the grass that either a non-milch cow or an aged cow ate. Who indeed calculates the price of food that family members eat? He said: 'It's a fine question you ask. Your mother's growing old. In a few days, even she won't be able to do any work. Will you then calculate the price of the food she eats?'

Now Kalinga was unable to find an answer. It wasn't as if he hadn't heard this argument about cattle from every villager. From his childhood days, he had heard these words inside and outside his home, as well as in the home of the *Jois* where he had eaten food. But his views had changed after going to America. Although he knew that the villagers wouldn't understand his views even if he articulated them clearly, he still said: 'Are you saying that the same thing applies equally to both humans and cattle? What are cattle for, if not for human utility?'

Yangata felt stunned by these words. He had never thought about the question of whether cattle existed merely for human utility or whether humans were born for the utility of cattle or whether one is born merely for another's utility. Just as how the male child born in a home works in the field, so does the young bull work in the field. Just as how a mother gives milk to her infant, so does the cow give milk to humans. Just as how the male child and mother eat food, so do the ox and cow eat grass. In all this, who benefits from whom? He didn't know how to respond. He said: 'You're educated. You must speak about dharma and karma to simple villagers like us. Instead, if you do such things yourself, your clan won't survive. Behave yourself!'

Although Kalinga was outraged by these words, he didn't show it in speech. Village folk were this way. They have no ability to think. If something is said that goes against their beliefs, they speak rudely. So, he said just this much: 'Fine, my brother Yangata. You mind the business of your home, I'll look into the affairs of my home.'

'Have I come to steal something from your home? When I've come here to utter some good words of counsel, this fellow is creating differences between us saying "your home and mine". Your home? Which is your home? I'll tell the whole village that this fellow has sold cattle to the butcher and ensure that nobody ever comes to your home. I'm quiet only because this is the Elder Gowda's home—understand that! No bastard of mine will fear you because you're educated,' said a furious Yangata, and left. He was nearing fifty. After the Elder Gowda's death, although there were three others in the village who were elder than him, none of them were as knowledgeable or well-informed. Besides, his cowshed was the largest in the village after that of the Elder Gowda. Naturally, he should get the leadership of the village. What was Kalinga's age? Twenty-eight perhaps. Yangata has a son who's twenty-eight.

Kalinga was crestfallen. But he consoled his mind on the strength of some deep-seated faith. Tayavva went to the shed and closely inspected every single animal. Three from the Punyakoti stock were included in the cattle that were given away that morning. Kalinga had sold even these to that butcher. Not only did she have tears in her eyes from sorrow, she also felt a sense of trepidation that something bad would befall her son. She went, stood before the cot on which her son was seated and expressed her feelings in sign language. *But what was new that she would express that Yangata hadn't already told?* thought Kalinga, and didn't pay her any attention. Mixed with these feelings was also the angst that it was she who had brought that outsider Yangata and got him upbraided.

6

In a month, the seventy acres at the foothills was made out in Kalinga's name. Together with the sixty acres of land to the west of the road it became a fertile holding of one-hundred-and-thirty acres. In the course of his visits to the Taluk and District offices in connection with this work, it eventually came to his notice that the records related to the temple and the *kalyani* that his grandfather had built had remained pending any decision. Being ignorant of the law, grandpa had built the temple and the *kalyani,* and also had trees planted all around on government land. When it had come to the government's notice, there had been an inquiry in the matter. The *Sheikhdaar* had simply swallowed the bribe from the Elder Gowda. He had merely frozen the records but hadn't resolved the matter.

Kalinga thought that whatever had happened was for the good and filed an application with the government to grant him the land on which the temple and the *kalyani* was located. This could be done by way of a *darkhast*—a government deed transferring non-agricultural land for agricultural purposes. He told the deputy commissioner who was now familiar to him: 'My grandfather built the temple for the sake of dharma. We're taking care of all its expenses. We've also given a grant of land to its *pujari*. Please grant that land in our name by way of *darkhast.*'

Kalinga took ownership of that locality after paying two hundred rupees to the government as the *darkhast* fees. This also meant that the pending matter was resolved. Additionally, this area was almost conjoined with the newly acquired land at the foothills.

After this, he mortgaged all his ancestral lands to the government and obtained a loan of twenty-five thousand rupees for farm development. He built a modest house at the centre of the foothill-land, and roofed it with a zinc sheet. After fitting it with windows and doors and finishing all other incidental tasks, he informed folks that he was going to the city for about three or four days.

The usual chores at home went on as before. Servants cultivated the farm and wetland and as was the practice, planted corn, which was the crop of the first rains of the season. The farm had to be ploughed in the monsoon. The first rains have just begun. Kalinga isn't sitting idle for even a day. He roams around the farm. He traverses the pasture. He visits the Taluk. The motor service is running daily on the new road near the village from the past one month. He travels back and forth in it once every two or three days as if that road and the motor were made and were functioning just for him. Attired in a suit and hat, if he puts out his hand, the khaki-clothed master in the motor stops it and then escorts him to the front seat. The villagers have developed not just surprise but fear and respect towards Kalinga. And especially after they learnt that he acquired from the government the entire land lying to the east of the foothills, astonishment has taken root in them. It seems that the Master at the District makes him sit on the chair—the *Shanubhoga* at the *Agrahara* himself told this.

Four days later, Kalinga brought a tractor. He drove it himself for the first two or three days, tilling the land at the foothills and the pasture beyond the road. Then a driver appeared and joined work under him. Emitting a *budd-budd budd-budd* noise that could be heard not just in the entire foothills but in the neighbouring villages as well, the tractor would plough away without the aid of oxen. Its large iron teeth would rip out the ground, prying out clumps of soil the width of a man's embrace. It does not ever get tired, no matter how long it tills. Even the fellow who runs it turns the wheel sitting comfortably on its red seat. There's a roof of rough cloth over his head to block out the sun's harsh heat.

When Kalinga started to run it for the first time, his barn's cattle were grazing in the pasture to the east of the road. Terrified by the extraordinary noise made by the tractor, the unaccustomed animals began to bolt helter-skelter. Ninga who was overseeing their grazing, was unable to catch them no matter how hard he tried. But then where could those frightened cows run? They scattered in various directions across the pasture and finally reached the cowshed after running and stamping over the fields and wetlands en route. Tayavva too was surprised when she saw these cattle returning so soon in the afternoon. Although even she would hear this uncommon noise, she had assumed that it was from a new kind of motor that had come to the road. Even she'd been to the road one day to see the motor. She had heard its roar and sensed a similarity with the thunder of this one. At first, she thought that the cattle wouldn't understand this. But suddenly her mind began to think in a different direction: *How can we understand what the cattle cannot? They're like Gods. It seems they know everything that'll happen in the future. But what'd happen in the future?* This they were unable to tell her.

Standing afar and displaying only fright in their eyes, the bodies and legs of some among them were shivering. Tayavva couldn't understand whether they were indicating that something bad would befall them in the future or whether they were shivering merely out of fear.

The name of the fellow running the tractor was Jamal. Food had to be sent to him through a servant. After running the tractor during the day, he would park it in the shed located at one side of the newly built house, where he also slept at night. But he would rarely step into the village. His status appeared very high in the village. On the one hand were these villagers who hoisted the plough on their shoulders and walked behind a pair of oxen all day long just to till half an acre each day, and on the other was this charioteer, seated with boots on his legs, and running this machine with a demon-like jaw, which ripped out entire chunks of earth as it rushed forward making the *budd-budd* sound! He wouldn't even wash the plate in which he had eaten. The other servants, who tilled using the plough, had to do that work.

Another machine arrived after seven or eight days. A few khaki-clothed workers came with it. By then, Kalinga had built a small brick house next to the *kalyani* near the temple. This machine was installed inside it. The workers drowned a thick pipe that was attached to the machine into the water of the *kalyani*. When the machine was started, it too, made the *budd-budd-budd* noise just like the tractor. Water from the *kalyani* instantly rose up and started to spill out of a large tap. It seems the name of the machine was irrigation pump. Nobody could pronounce it in that village. They simply stopped at 'pump'.

Each day, Kalinga was getting work done by the servants on the large new field. Canals were dug for water to flow. In some places, they buried iron pipes inside the earth itself. They erected a wire fence with spikes to prevent cattle coming from the road. Motors loaded with only sacks used to travel on the new road. It seems the name of these motors was lorry. Instead of cattle dung, white-coloured sacks of foreign manure stuffed into gunny bags arrived on the lorries. *What will he grow? Ragi, paddy, or some foreign crop?* The villagers would think surprised. If anybody asked, Kalinga would say, 'You'll see for yourself'. The name of his large field was 'farm'. The villagers would pronounce it as 'paa-ra-m', reasonably correctly.

VOLUME 9

1

Three years had passed since Venkataramana had joined the *Agrahara's* middle school. In the interim, his father-in-law had been transferred to a different Taluk. And, now, even he had received a transfer order and had to move within a month. After all, how can a government employee remain in the same place—that too, in his birthplace? But if Venkataramana left the village, what would be the fate of the puja in the Punyakoti temple? It was true that he actually didn't need to make a living by working at the school job. What indeed was the purpose behind the Elder Kalinga Gowda giving him the grant of the land, which provided enough for a family to comfortably eat?

Even then, Venkataramana did what he had to do at the inspector's office, and got his transfer done to Basavanapura, which was adjacent to the *Agrahara*. The distance between Basavanapura and the *Agrahara* was just a mile. While the *Agrahara's* school was now a *pucca* middle school, the New Type School had just recently been set up in Basavanapura. Venkataramana bought a bicycle so he could easily commute back and forth. He wrapped his *dhoti* above his knees, and after falling in the field by the lake and bruising his knees—he finally learned to ride it.

He continued to do the puja each morning. As always, before opening the temple door, he would chant this mantra, and vigorously ring the large bell in the front compound ten or twenty times.

Namo Gobhyah srimatibhyah sourabheyibhyah eva ca |
Namo Brahmasutaabhyasca pavitrabhyo namo namah ||

Salutations to the cow, to Srimati, to the daughter of the divine cow, Kamadhenu, to the daughter of Brahma, and salutations to the Most Sacred.

As the sound of the bell wafted through the hillside to the surrounding villages, he opened the temple door and began to sweep the dirt both inside and out. But the two machines that Kalinga had brought made the *budd-budd* noise simultaneously as if in competition with each other. If the tractor was wrecking the quietude that had always been present in the foothills, the din from the diesel-oil pump installed right beside the *kalyani* was rushing directly inside the temple. The time had come for the temple bell to compete with the noise of the diesel machines. It was becoming impossible for him to conduct the puja by chanting the mantras with feeling and devotion amid this racket.

Venkataramana would receive information about every stage of progress that Kalinga made on his farm. He was happy when he heard the news that Kalinga had got ownership of the land at the foothills. It was indeed a matter of happiness for anybody that the grass of such a vast fertile land was now available to the cows belonging to such a large cowshed. But he was upset when Kalinga began getting it tilled using the tractor. He asked Kalinga directly: 'You already have land near the village, enough to maintain servants and to feed an additional four families. Why are you getting this pasture—meant for cows—cultivated?'

'Why, to grow crops.'

'What will you accomplish by growing crops after snatching the *Gomaata's* food? After all, we get our food only if the *Gomaata* eats a full stomach. Right?'

'Venkataramana, you're still living in the age of my great grandfather. Our stomach will be filled even if the cows don't eat. Look at this tractor. Isn't the land getting tilled even without oxen? Likewise, we can obtain a bigger yield even without cattle manure. You just wait and watch for yourself the kind of harvest that the foreign manure that I've got will generate.'

Venkataramana didn't have an answer to this. 'So, does the cow exist merely for use in tilling? If that's not there, do you say that the cow's no longer required?'

Kalinga laughed to himself and said: 'That's it! But you definitely need cows for milk. We need to take care of them even better. You just wait and see how well I'll care for them.'

Venkataramana was pacified by this answer. After all, Kalinga had just told him that he would take care of the cows even better—that was enough.

But then he remembered how Kalinga had sold the fifty-five aged cows and oxen to the Muslim butcher. This distressed him a great deal. *Why did he do this? Has God given him any less?* He thought to himself. When he went to Kalenahalli on two consecutive days to discuss this with him, Kalinga was unavailable.

2

One morning, Venkataramana arrived at about nine for the puja. He didn't have school because it was a Sunday. After sweeping the inside of the temple and washing the ground with water, he extracted the sandalwood paste. By the time he began his puja, a *Dhamm!* sound from a gun reverberated throughout the hillside. Instantly he remembered that Kalinga had recently brought a gun. For several days now, Venkataramana was mentally struggling to feel a sense of devotion associated with the mantras amid the *budd-budd* noise from the pump. And now, the gun had arrived. *Will he also start hunting? But who'd hunt near a temple? Birds? Animals?* With this thought in mind, he finished the puja by mechanically chanting the mantras.

Kalinga came to the temple when it was time for the *arati*. He didn't have the gun in his hand. He had worn khaki knickers with his shirt tucked in and a thick leather belt around his waist. A hat on his head protected him from heat. When Venkataramana held the *arati* plate before him, he ran his palm over its lit wick dipped in ghee. After taking the flower he'd been given, he asked, 'Venkataramana, won't you give me the *prasada?*'

'Why're you asking stuff like this? I will certainly give the *prasada* to all devotees who come during the puja hours.'

'Not just the *prasada*. I'm very hungry. What have you made today?'

'Curd rice. Go get a leaf.'

Venkataramana put two large servings of curd rice, filling the large *Palasha* leaf that he had fetched from outside the temple. Sprinkled with green chilli seasoning, curry leaves and grated coconut, the curd rice made with cow's curd, was giving out a delicious aroma. Even after Kalinga had eaten his fill, the rice that remained was enough to feed two more people. Venkataramana took just a handful by way of *prasada*. After he went out, washed his hands, and returned, Kalinga asked: 'Look, it's been so many days. You never came to visit my newly built farmhouse even once. Why?'

'Every day, I am in a hurry to go to school after the puja.'

'But you could come in the evening. It seems you come to the village, you visit home and speak with my mother on several occasions in the evening. Why haven't you come to the farmhouse?'

'What's there for me to see? Sacks of foreign manure, farming implements… that's it, right?'

Kalinga didn't say anything for a minute. He was thinking within himself, then said: 'Look, you and I are friends since childhood. Don't you at least have the curiosity to see what new work I'm doing? Why are you showing negligence in my case?'

'It's not negligence. I just said it like it is.'

'In that case, it's anyway a Sunday today. It's okay to go home late. Climb down and come with me.'

Venkataramana wrapped the vessel of the *prasada* in his towel, locked the temple door, stuck the key inside his girdle, wrapped his shoulder-cloth so that it covered his head as well and left. He wasn't wearing any footwear. Kalinga wore his shoes that he had removed outside the temple. They crossed the *kalyani* and descended from the side from where the water pipes went down. The potato crop that was planted throughout the field was now sprouting. A few servants here and there were watering the crop in that vast farm. Upon reaching the farmhouse after crossing over the ridges, all of its interiors were visible to Venkataramana.

It wasn't merely a shed for storing farming implements. Neither was it as small as it appeared from the height of the hill on which the temple stood. On one side was a separate shed for parking the tractor. On another portion lay a large warehouse for storing farming implements. The portion right next to it contained well-furnished living quarters. The inside of the roof was fitted with thin wooden planks. The living quarters contained a veranda and three rooms; the kitchen and bathroom were at the rear. The house had taps and a water tank. Apart from the sofa in the veranda, the rooms had spring beds. After Kalinga had shown him everything one after the other, Venkataramana asked: 'Going forward, will you shift your family here from the village? This will suit you. But won't Tayavva feel bored here alone?'

'Sit down, let's talk', said Kalinga pointing him to the sofa. But because Venkataramana was still wearing the Sacred Garments and holding the *prasada* in his hand, he sat on a wooden chair. A gun was hung on the wall opposite. Recalling its sound while he was conducting the puja, Venkataramana asked: 'What did you get the gun for—hunting? In the olden days, it seems there were tigers and hyenas in this hill. It seems not a single wild animal has come this side after your father died. I go there daily for the puja. I haven't seen a single animal. Why did you get this?'

'Not for hunting. I'll stay here. A solitary family will be here all alone, day and night. There's the fear of robbers. I got it for my defence.'

Even as Venkataramana said, 'Tayavva...' Kalinga interrupted him mid-sentence and said, 'You still don't know. I haven't told anyone. I got married in America. I also have an eight-month-old baby boy. In five days from now, both my wife and baby will come to Mumbai by plane. I'll go get them.'

'None of us knew anything', Venkataramana who had started to say something stopped at that. Although Kalinga kept looking at him for ten minutes, he didn't say anything further.

Then Kalinga himself asked: 'Why did you go quiet? Aren't you happy to hear that I'd got married?'

'Wouldn't I be? Wouldn't I feel happy if you got married and the Elder Kalinga Gowda's lineage grows?'

'Then, why did you go quiet?'

'Nothing', he went quiet again. Whether he didn't know what he had to say or whether he felt that he had no right to say anything in this matter, or whether he had to say some random thing—but no matter how hard he tried, nothing came to his mind.

Kalinga said: 'I knew that the villagers wouldn't accept this. You're orthodox. Besides, you're the village *purohit*. Still, you're my friend. I'd thought that you would say congratulations the moment you heard this news.'

'My good wishes are always there with you. Whenever I perform the puja in the temple, I always pray that the Elder Kalinga Gowda's home should flourish prosperously. But then you could've chosen and married a suitable girl from your own *jati*. You're educated. Getting a girl who's even slightly educated in these rural surroundings is difficult. But in Mysore, you get educated girls even from your *jati*. If required, I'd have travelled myself and made a proposal with such a family and fixed a girl for you.'

'Venkataramana, if someone gets married, nobody in America asks the girl's lineage or clan. With an open mind, they immediately congratulate you. It's only in this country that we think of all these complicated *Puranas*. You even read the English paper every day. Can't you progress at least a little?'

'It's not just about me. What I say is this: if we get a girl who's been raised to follow the same traditions as us, she'll carry forward our family's traditions, customs, dharma, karma. For example, in the upcoming *Sankranti* festival next year, a fair needs to be organized at the Punyakoti temple. Had you gotten a girl from your own *jati*, that girl would have fasted, taken the *panchagavya*, and performed the puja and other rituals. Indeed, the wife, more than the husband, has to do puja to the *Gomaata*. I don't know if your wife from the Red Country will do all this. What's her *jati*? Aren't all people of that country Christians?'

Kalinga said, smirking: 'Even they are from the farming *jati*. The girl was studying agricultural science with me at the university. Her father owns a large farm. She has experience and practice working there. No less than any man, she sits on the tractor and works from morning till evening. The women of our country should feel ashamed, looking at the way she works.'

'Maybe. But don't lots of women in our own village take the plough and till? Aren't there women who drive the cart? Is it women or is it men who do the work of removing weeds and planting saplings? What I mean to say is this: your wife has learnt the farming system of her country. Our women follow our system. If they're taught how to do it, our own women who drive the cart and use the plough, can also drive the tractor. In addition to that, our women know all our traditions, practices, dharma and karma.'

Kalinga didn't know how to answer. But, neither was it possible for him to just accept Venkataramana's words without response. He said: 'You know, our points of view differ. Meaning, there's a difference in our respective perspectives. All right.'

Venkataramana didn't understand Kalinga's words. This Sanskrit traditionalist who was merely a middle school teacher didn't understand that the contextual meaning of 'all right' implied, 'we've spoken enough no further conversation'. Continuing the conversation, he said: 'Look, I'd been meaning to tell you this. But you were never available. You shouldn't have put the pump to the *kalyani* and used its water for farming. That water is meant for the deity.'

'Why? It appears that you're unaware. An inquiry had been conducted, a record had been created against my grandfather for building a temple on government land without authorization. That's why I took suitable steps and made that land in my name. The temple, the *kalyani*, the surrounding space including all the plants and trees, they're all now my private property and part of this farm. There's no legal hurdle for using the water of the *kalyani*.'

Venkataramana suddenly felt he had learned some new knowledge. He said: 'I'm not talking about matters related to law. In a way, I'm happy that this land is yours. But nobody should say "this is mine" with regard to any temple. No matter who builds it, a temple belongs to devotees.'

'Fine. You said I shouldn't have put the pump. Why?'

'It's the deity's *tirtha*—it was built for the deity's bath. It must be used by the devotees and cattle for only drinking its water. No matter who drinks it, they must drink it with the feeling that they're drinking *Tirtha*, the Sacred Water, as the deity's offering. You shouldn't have put the pump and used it for your own farming purposes. I'll say it even now. I'll myself investigate this land and find a spot that has a good water source. Dig a well there. You'll get ample water. Remove that pump and fix it here.'

'What's the loss if the *kalyani's* water is used for farming?'

'It's not a question of loss. That which has been built for the deity must only be used for the deity's work and for nothing else. Your grandfather built it as a work of dharma, as a pious deed. If you derive utility from it, it'll mean that you've repudiated his piety. Besides if temples are built on hillocks, hills, riverbanks and such other places, no work that will be of utilitarian value to humans should ever occur there. Those places should be dedicated to only bhakti, puja and such other activities.'

'Even I've heard this kind of stuff. But tell me', asked Kalinga sitting upright on the sofa: 'How much did it cost to build that *kalyani*?'

'I don't know exactly how much it cost. The Elder Gowda would never make calculations in the matter of carrying out works of dharma. Although he knew it, he never told another person. I know how much was paid to Sivalingachari and the stone workers for building both the temple and the *kalyani*. Oxen, carts, male and female workers, all of them worked for free. If we calculate all of this, in my estimate, the *kalyani* alone must've cost at least eight thousand.'

'How much would be the interest per year for eight thousand? Even by bank rates, it'll be at least eight hundred rupees.'

'When no calculation of money is made for God's work, where's the question of calculating its interest?'

'He didn't calculate. You don't know the transaction I've done. I've obtained a loan of twenty-five thousand rupees by mortgaging all our old properties with the government. An interest of twelve rupees for every hundred must be given towards it. All this is for developing the land. And where was the money for this tractor, pump, farmhouse, foreign manure, seeds? There's also a loan of ten thousand on the tractor and pump. Grandpa used all the money to do works of dharma. He emptied the house and died. Only six hundred rupees were left the day I came home. And now, if I need to dig a new well like that, I'll need another eight or ten thousand. Besides, what's the guarantee that we'll definitely get water at the spot we dig? Where's the money for that?'

Venkataramana didn't speak: not because he had no response, but because he was trying to find a manner in which to immediately articulate what was in his mind. By then, Kalinga himself continued:

'You say that the temple water must only be used for the deity's work and nothing else. This is an old-fashioned belief. Even if I draw water from it every day, the *kalyani* is filled by morning. Leaving it untouched means that it's a sort of luxury. In a poor country like ours, such luxuries are impossible. Besides, what's your point? That spirituality and worldly utilities must be kept separate. It's wrong to stay that way. Whatever is supposed to be meant for spiritual purpose, must also be utilized for daily life.'

Venkataramana stopped him at that and said: 'Let that be. You just said that there was only six hundred rupees when you returned home, and that you took a loan of twenty-five thousand rupees and then ten thousand more to do all this. What would you have lost, if you hadn't taken these loans? Is your ancestral property scarce? After keeping aside what you need for your home and selling the rest of the harvest, you would've gotten more than two or three thousand. Why did you need all this business? The cattle would've comfortably been grazing in this new land.'

Kalinga laughed at these words: 'Our country has remained backward precisely because of this mentality. Don't you know that the food grown in this country isn't sufficient for its people? Our country will never progress until the mindset of being-content-with-what-we-have vanishes.'

Meanwhile, the tractor driver Jamal stepped inside. He was wearing a khaki pant and shirt and his face was covered with sweat. After doing a *salaam* to Kalinga, he said: 'It's already twelve. Breakfast didn't come today. My stomach is screaming.'

This used to happen on some days. It wasn't always possible for Tayavva to prepare and send everything on time. Besides, Jamal didn't eat ragi *roti* like the others. It was the job of the other servants of the house to supply him breakfast and lunch here. On some days, they'd purposely refrain from bringing him food. Kalinga asked Venkataramana: 'It's already twelve. Will you eat the *prasada* that you have with you?'

'No. I'll go home and have lunch.'

'Then give it to Jamal. There's enough curd rice for two people. It's tasty with some nice seasoning. Eat it Jamal.'

As if alarmed, Venkataramana asked: 'Isn't he from among the Muslims?'

'Why?'

'This is the deity's *prasada*.'

'Is it written in the Shastras that the deity's *prasada* mustn't be given to Muslims?'

'It's not that. The *prasada* mustn't be given to those who don't come to the temple, show their devotion to God and take the *tirtha*. He doesn't even fold his hands before our Deities.'

'Venkataramana, why do you discriminate like this? Why all this Shastra to give a morsel of food to a hungry person?'

'If it's merely food, it can be given to anybody. Indeed, the Shastra itself says that one must immediately give food to a hungry person. But this isn't merely food. Do you remember? You used to have lunch in the afternoon at our home when you were studying in the primary school. Back then, we wouldn't serve you lunch on the death anniversary rituals of my grandfather and grandmother. The reason for that is this: According to us, our ancestors are our Gods. They don't become Gods for outsiders. Meaning, outsiders don't regard them as their Gods. The one who doesn't have a feeling that they are Gods also doesn't have the right to eat the *prasada* that is first made as an offering to them. On the day of the anniversary, people not belonging to our family don't eat food at our home, even if they belong to our *jati*. This too, is something like that. If Jamal regards the cow in the Punyakoti temple as God, he obtains a right over this *prasada*. Else, how can it be given?'

'Venkataramana, I merely asked you to give the food that's left over, but you are talking about some death anniversary-related Shastras of your father, grandfather, great grandfather,' said Kalinga. Turning to Jamal, he said: 'It's all right, there should be some bread in the kitchen. Eat that. Anyway there's no tractor work this afternoon. Go to the village, eat your lunch and get some for me as well.'

Jamal was about thirty-five or forty. He sported a moustache on his well-shaven face. He had been a lorry driver earlier. He was not in Kalinga's house as a servant staff: he was employed on a monthly salary. Now it appeared that his self-respect was wounded by the words of

Venkataramana *Jois*. Watching this *Jois* with contempt from the corner of his eyes, he walked in to the kitchen wearing his boots.

After a minute, Kalinga asked Venkataramana: 'This sort of discrimination exists only in our religion, right?'

'How do I know whether it exists in only our religion or in others as well? You've seen the Red Country. You tell me.'

Kalinga recalled as he thought to himself: they allow everybody inside the temple of the Christians. But they don't allow non-Christians to take part in the Holy Communion. They don't give the bread and wine, which is part of it. This was his own experience in America. He'd heard somewhere that even the Muslims had some similar practice. But he couldn't recall its details. By then Jamal had emerged from the kitchen, 'Sahib, the bread has dried up. I'll go to the village and eat. Then I'll also go to the *Agrahara* and return by evening. Give me a rupee for some expenses.'

He took money from Kalinga and departed. Venkataramana said: 'That means even you don't have any food now. I'll go to my village. You take this *prasada*. Get me a vessel.'

'There's anyway enough food for two. Let's eat together. There's a tap inside. Its water comes from the *kalyani*.'

'Okay. But I don't want the tap's water. Come, let's both go to the *kalyani*. We'll sit on the bank and eat.'

Kalinga locked the house. Both of them walked on the ridges, climbed the knoll near the pipes and by the time they approached the *kalyani*, the pump's machine was still running. 'Stop it for some time. We must have peace at least when we eat the *prasada* near the deity's *kalyani*.' Accordingly, Kalinga stopped it. Venkataramana served curd rice on the two large *Palasha* leaves that he brought with him. Both of them ate it once, then took the remainder and finished it.

As they were eating the last morsel, Kalinga asked: 'Venkataramana, if I touch the food on your leaf, will you still eat it?'

'It's true that you've returned from America. But tell me why would you touch it? Will your hands itch if you don't touch it? This is sheer mischief.'

Kalinga stopped at that. They were full. Both got down into the

S.L. BHYRAPPA

kalyani and drank handfuls of water. Because they'd come here again, Venkataramana went back to the temple, vigorously rang the large bell in the outer compound, opened the temple door, filled the still-burning lamp with the *mahua* oil, folded his hands before the deity, locked the door and came out. Meanwhile, Kalinga had descended down to the farm and was inspecting the potato crop. Venkataramana dipped the cloth tied to the vessel of the *prasada* in water, soaked it, placed it atop his head and began walking down in the direction of his village.

3

Venkataramana felt upset because Kalinga hadn't revealed for so many days the fact that he was married. *After returning from America, he doesn't share even one of his numerous plans with anyone. Others learn of them as he goes on implementing them. His mindset isn't like what it was earlier. Back then, he was like everybody. Why has he become like this now?* Along with this thought, another element of curiosity sprouted in Venkataramana's mind: *has he told his mother that he is married?* It was already ten or fifteen days since Venkataramana had been to Kalenahalli. Maybe he'd told his mother. He began to wonder what Tayavva would've felt about this.

The next evening he went to Kalenahalli. Tayavva offered him a wooden plank to sit upon. After enquiring after her welfare, he asked: 'Won't you get your son married, Tayavva?'

In reply, she touched her forehead and shook both her hands. Without fully understanding what she meant, he asked, 'Why, because he won't listen to you?' She nodded yes to this. He understood that she wasn't aware of the matter. He remained quiet despite the temptation to reveal it to her.

She confided her sorrow, recalling the loss of her in-laws. She also confided her grief at Kalinga selling off the aged cattle of their cowshed. Venkataramana had meant to ask Kalinga about this, but hadn't remembered it while talking to him yesterday. He decided to ask him the next time they met.

He met Yangata Gowda on the street after he left Tayavva. 'It's been so many days since you came. Please come, Holy Sir', he said and took him home. After enquiring about the prospects for rain that year and narrating the state of the crops, he asked: 'Did you see how he's lording over it all?'

'Hmm. I'm watching.'

'Seems he's drawing water by putting the machine in the deity's *kalyani*. Seems he's made out the temple, the *kalyani*... everything to his own name.'

'Yes. I learnt yesterday. I told him not to do that—that it's a wrong thing to do.'

'His grandfather built it for the sake of dharma. Have we laboured any less for it? Can't you go slap that bastard and uproot that machine?'

It hadn't occurred to Venkataramana to fight like this, using force. But it was his firm opinion as well, to get that water pump removed. Even as he was thinking of all the village folk going as a group to dissuade Kalinga, Yangata Gowda asked: 'Seems the whoreson has got a gun. Is that true?'

'Hmm. I've seen it myself.'

'Seems he sits on the chair with the Deputy Commissioner Master. True?'

'Hmm. I've heard the *Shanubhoga* telling me.'

'What can be done to such whoresons, Holy Sir?' Yangata comforted himself by merely abusing Kalinga. But he had no words for what needed to be done about this in the future.

Venkataramana himself said, 'All of you in the village get together, confront him, and tell him forcefully. He might get frightened to oppose scores of people together.'

'The villagers are scared of him, Holy Sir. You don't know.'

'Why should they fear him?'

'His attire, that tilling machine that he has, the gun, his sitting with the Deputy Commissioner Master. They merely listen to all this and get scared.'

Venkataramana was astonished. But then it was the truth.

But it was also true that the folks of Kalenahalli were endowed with manly courage. All houses had people who, at least in one generation or the other, had killed a tiger or a hyena with the spear. There were also people in the village that had fought a hyena armed with just a stick. Yangata Gowda wasn't any less daring. Even at fifty, he could traverse any number of miles on foot in the darkest of nights all alone. With just a single strike, he could put the longest of cobras to sleep. On several occasions, he had held live snakes by the tail and bashed them down like a washerman thrashes clothes. 'You're endowed with such indomitable manly courage. Why do you need to fear Kalinga's gun? If he shoots random folks simply because he's got a gun, the government people will put him to the noose. What? Is a gun crueller than a tiger or cobra? You hail from a lineage that has fought the most formidable tigers and hyenas!' said Venkataramana.

'But he's got that kind of machine, Holy Sir. It rips out the ground making that *budd-budd-budd* sound, tilling it.'

'Why should you feel afraid of a land-tilling machine?'

'Even we don't understand, Holy Sir. You see, the motor started to ply from near our village? Sometimes, the men of our village sat on it, went to the town and returned. From then on, they are scared of the motor, they're scared of Kalinga.'

Venkataramana didn't understand this. But, it was true. It wasn't his intention that the village men should get together and launch an attack on Kalinga. It was enough to summon him before the village folk, get him to remove the pump that he'd installed in the temple's *kalyani*, admit to his mistake of selling cattle to the butcher and make a promise that he'd never repeat it in future. He still had faith in the fact that no matter who he was, everybody had to fear the collective might of the villagers: even Kalinga would be frightened. But Kalinga had built his farmhouse one-and-a half miles outside the village. Looking at the sofa and the beds there, it appeared that he'd settle there with his Red wife. What could villagers do to a person who stays outside the village? There's no fear of the village for one who doesn't need it.

At the moment, he didn't know what to do. He spoke a few courage-infusing words to Yangata Gowda and returned to his village.

VOLUME 10

1

After stepping down from the motor on the roadside, Kalinga picked up the baby. His wife Hilda was holding a handbag. Jamal who had come to the road, made the servant Ninga carry the leather trunk on his head. Ninga was full of surprise. In his entire life, he'd never seen a woman who was so red. Neither had he encountered any situation where he could even imagine that humans this red could exist! Fear and respect welled up in him the moment he saw her. But he was also surprised as to why, instead of a sari, she was wearing a single shirt—he didn't know what it was called—that ran from her shoulder to her knees? Her legs are so red! The infant in Kalinga's arms is so red! 'The God Indra in the dramas doesn't look this red. Neither does his danseuse, Rambha!' he wondered in astonishment as he walked behind them carrying the trunk.

Hilda stood before the farmhouse, slowly turned around and deeply inhaling once, she said to Kalinga: 'My dear, how exciting.'

'Really?' he asked.

'You're so wicked. You didn't tell me it was so exciting', she clapped both her hands making a noise and held them pressed together.

She went inside, had a quick tour of the house, turned around, and said, 'Fine.' Kalinga was experiencing a sense of sanctity. By the time she finished her bath and wore a fresh skirt, Kalinga had spread jelly over the bread that they'd brought with them, and which he'd cut with a knife. Then he lit the stove and kept the milk on it for heating. They gave the bottle to the baby, and after both of them ate breakfast and drank milk, Hilda came outside. By then, seven or eight servants had assembled there just to look at her. Hilda didn't look in their direction. She walked towards the shed at the left where the tractor was parked. The baby was lying on the bed, drinking from the bottle. Kalinga was following her. 'What make is this?' she asked, climbing on the tractor and starting it. It began to move, making the *budd-budd-budd* noise. She ran it for some distance. Not only were the servants astounded, they experienced a feeling of surrender in her presence. She drove it around in the vicinity, brought it back to the shed, parked it, and hopped down from its height.

As Kalinga neared her, she held his hands and said, 'That thing visible there—is that the temple? Come let's have a look.'

'Take some rest now. We'll go tomorrow', said Kalinga, but that didn't deter her. 'It's so exciting. I feel romantic. Let's go right away!' she dragged him holding his hand. 'The baby is on the bed. Take care of it if it cries', Kalinga instructed the servants and followed behind her. The servants knew that the two spoke English to each other. But they felt an incomprehensible fascination for the language as well.

Together, they walked in the direction of the knoll that led to the *kalyani*. The Red woman was as tall as Kalinga. One of the servants asked: 'See how that woman is?'

'Looks like an ivory fruit. Saw how she ran that machine?'

Jamal who was right behind them said in a rebuking tone: 'Hey, what? You think she's your house-servant to speak about her in the singular? Their name is European ladies. You must call her madam. She knows how to aim and shoot with the gun. You know that?'

This generated greater fear and fascination in them. Jamal said: 'Madam sahib speaks English. Even I can speak it. I used to be the driver in the house of a European sahib earlier.'

Everyone realized that Jamal's authority would grow further because of this madam. But they didn't tolerate his authority. Ninga, the most intelligent among them, said: 'Madam herself drove that machine, so now what's your business here, after she's come? They'll throw you out. Will you then work the soil and plough it like we do?'

Jamal's face instantly went pale at hearing these words. This had never occurred to him. It was not even five months since he'd lost his job as a lorry driver. When he had no means for livelihood, he got this job as a tractor driver. Seventy-five rupees per month. Kalinga sahib had told him that he'd provide a place for his family to live as well. He was getting free food so far. Now, his job may be gone. Did the sahib lie to him? He began to worry immediately.

2

When she saw the *kalyani*, Hilda said: 'You wrote to me about this, right? The water's really pure. How's the water source?'

'No matter how much we pump, it'll refill within a night.'

'Very fine.'

She asked, standing in front of the temple: 'Is this the temple about which you wrote in your letter? How's the *murti*, the deity inside? What kind of *murti* is it?'

'The main deity is that of a cow. Then there are the *Trimurtis*, that is, the Trinity as well.'

'Dear, Trinity is all right. Does that mean the people of this country also believe in the Father, Son and Holy Ghost?'

'Yes, but in a different sense.'

'In that case, why do they worship this animal?'

'There's a story behind this: It seems it occurred in our own home during the time of our ancestors', said Kalinga, and narrated the story of Punyakoti and explained the background of his grandfather building the temple.

'So exciting. Very romantic. But we can accept it merely as a story. Accepting it as real and performing worship is superstition. Do you too, believe all this dear?'

'Of course not.'

'Good, open the door. I need to see how it is inside.'

'The key is with the *pujari*. My grandfather has given him a land grant as an arrangement for performing the daily puja here.'

'Funny. But it's very intriguing. We can see it tomorrow, right?'

'Hmm. We can see it by about eight-thirty in the morning. The *pujari* is my friend. He also knows English. He has studied all the stuff of the ancient times because it relates to this country's Shastras.'

She said 'interesting' about the Nandi or the Basava *murti* in front of the temple. From that vantage, their new farm, the government road beyond it, and their pasture spreading out beyond the road were clearly visible. But Kalenahalli, tucked behind the grove beyond that pasture wasn't visible. It would take two more months for the potato which had been planted in the ploughed farm to yield harvest.

Hilda asked: 'That open space is filled only with grass out there, beyond the road… why haven't you cultivated it and planted some crop?'

'I told you back then, we need capital to do all of it at the same time. We need to quickly repay the existing loan of thirty-five thousand rupees. We can't run the tractor there unless the next monsoon arrives. It needs a separate irrigation system. This water isn't enough. Besides, we also need place for the cows to graze.'

'By the way, where are the cows? I can't see them.'

'They're still there in the village. We need to build a shed for them eventually. There's still plenty of work to be done. We need to investigate the field in all places for chemical content and then decide the kind of crop that'll grow well. How can I do everything alone? Now that you've come, let's triumph over this land together. Let's exploit its potential. You're the brains behind it.'

'I'm so thankful to you dear', she said with gratitude and then standing in line with his shoulder, kissed him.

Later, Kalinga said: 'Darling, you forgot. In this country, you shouldn't do this at any random place. This is an extremely traditional country. People will ridicule you.'

'This must be a very uninteresting country then. How will this country progress? How will this poverty go away? And when will this poverty go away? Haven't you seen for yourself how open people in the Western countries are?'

Just then, Ninga was climbing up from the direction of the *kalyani* in a sprint. It was already evening, nearing sunset. Ninga came up and said: 'Baby is screaming continuously.'

'Didn't you guys pick it up and pacify it?'

'It doesn't allow us anywhere near it. If we try to lift it up, it shrieks like crazy.'

Kalinga translated this in English to his wife. Both descended quickly and sprinted over the ridges. The servants standing in front of the house were watching with curiosity the sight of her running ahead of her husband. The infant went quiet after she took it in her arms, played with it and seated it on the tractor. Then Hilda told her husband: 'This kind of body shape, people wearing this sort of dress might have appeared strange to Jack. That's why he cried when they tried to pick him up. Right?'

'Yes', said Kalinga, picking the baby up.

The servants were still standing there. He approached them and said, 'What've you all been doing for so long? The sun's set already. You've just been lazy for the last four hours. Hey, Ninga, see if the milk's arrived.'

The servants went away. Only Jamal remained behind.

'Jamal, not enough water has been put on the part of the field that's towards the road. Turn it only in that direction throughout the day tomorrow', when he said this, Jamal asked: 'Sahib, is it true that you'll remove me from my job?'

'Who said this?'

'"Madam sahib drives the tractor. What's your business now? Go home", Ninga said. Did you tell me that my job here would last only till Madam sahib arrived?'

'That Ninga is an insane bastard. And you listen to his words? Not only does Madam sahib know how to drive the tractor, she also knows how to repair it wherever it breaks down. But she won't sit on it ploughing the farm every day. She only does the management work. Look, I won't eat at the village henceforth. You must bring all the stuff that Madam sahib requires for her cooking.'

'Tell me what you need. I'll go to the town in the motor and get it.'

'You didn't understand? She needs *lal tarkari*, red meat every day.'

Jamal understood now. Delight showed on his face. Sporting a smile on his face, he said: 'There's a guy called Karim in the Hobli. I can't get fresh stuff every day. I can get stuff that'll last two days. It won't spoil.'

'Look, on that side of this farmhouse, we need to breed chicken sufficient for the home. I'll go place an order for some nice country chicken. We need eggs daily.'

'Okay sahib, I'll take care of everything', said Jamal and took this responsibility.

Meanwhile, Hilda came close to him and asked, 'What's the dinner arrangement for tonight?'

'You take rest today. Jamal will fix up something', Kalinga said.

3

The next morning the temple's large bell rang at about eight. Hilda who'd just woken up and was brushing her teeth asked: 'What's this, sounds like a church bell?'

'No. The temple's *pujari* has come. The puja will commence now. Will you come? Let's go see.'

After drinking the morning coffee and with the baby in tow, they climbed the knoll near the *kalyani* and then ascended the precipice towards the temple. By the time they reached it, the puja was in progress inside. Hilda saw the *murti* of the deity. It was a four-armed *murti*. In one hand there was a shape resembling the wheel of a machine. A conch in another. An arm below held a wrestling mace. Another held a lotus. The second *murti* had a beard. The third one was weird. The half-nude male *murti* was clad in coarse cloth sufficient only to cover its modesty. But the weapon in its hand made it appear like it was the statue of a jungle-dwelling uncivilized male. A cow stood in front of these three *murtis*. It was of a really small size. Its limbs, unlike the cows in America, were small-sized, like the cows in India. A tiger was fallen dead in front of it.

Even the *pujari's* attire appeared a bit bizarre to Hilda. He'd shaved off the front portion of his head and had tied the tip of his long hair into a knot at the back of his head The rest of his hair spread out. There were three horizontal white stripes on his forehead. Similar stripes covered his shoulders, arms, and hairy chest. Only the wide white cloth that he had draped around his waist appeared attractive.

Although he sensed that there was somebody outside, Venkataramana continued to perform the puja, chanting mantras. After offering sandalwood paste, flowers, incense, wick-lamp, and *naivedya*—an offering of food, fruits, and coconut—he came out and applied the *vibhuti*—the sacred ash—to the Basava, performed puja to it, and went back in. Then he lit the ghee-dipped wick placed in the plate and ringing the bell with his left hand, began to perform the *arati*. At that moment, Kalinga began to ring the large bell outside. Tempted to ring it herself,

Hilda took the rope in her hand and began to ring it slowly like a church bell. After the *arati* was finished, Venkataramana held out the *arati* plate in front of them. Then Kalinga ran both his palms over the flame of the *arati* and joined them together. When he told his wife to do the same, she asked, 'What's the meaning of this?' Even Kalinga didn't know what it meant. 'Whatever, but you need to do it like this, so do it', he said. She said, 'interesting', and did likewise.

After this, Venkataramana brought the *tirtha*. After he received it on his palm, Kalinga drank it, stood before her and filled the spoon with it. When she asked, 'What's this?' Venkataramana himself said in English, 'It is God's Sacred Water'. Kalinga appended a commentary, 'That *murti* was washed with water before the puja. It's that water.'

Withdrawing her hand, Hilda said: 'Please forgive me. I can't take such unhygienic substances.'

Venkataramana went inside without a word. By the time Kalinga went out and returned with the *Palasha* leaves, Venkataramana was preparing to leave for home. Unaware of it, Kalinga asked: 'What *prasada* have you prepared today?'

'*Rasaayana*', came the reply.

'Meaning, a mixture of bananas, jaggery, and grated coconut. Powdered cardamom is also added to it for fragrance. It's delicious', Kalinga explained to his wife, placed a *Palasha* leaf in her hand, and stood there waiting. But Venkataramana who came outside put the *prasada* only on Kalinga's leaf and turned back. Hilda felt slighted. Kalinga was embarrassed. He said in Kannada, 'Venkataramana, won't you give her the *prasada*?' Venkataramana stopped and turned to them. He was lost in thought for a minute. He looked very uncomfortable. Then, suddenly he said in English: 'There's no *prasada* for those who decline the *tirtha*. Those who don't believe our Gods, our *puja*, don't have the right to eat their *prasada* as well. I won't give it to her.'

He said just this much and went inside the sanctum sanctorum. He tied the remaining *prasada* in a cloth, placed the other cloth on his shoulder and came out. Then he noticed it: Kalinga's wife hadn't taken off the rubber slippers that she wore on her feet. When he said, 'Please make way, I need to lock the door', Kalinga was standing there silently, holding the leaf of the *prasada* in his hand. Hilda was watching Venkataramana's behaviour with contempt. After they stepped out the door, Venkataramana latched on the large lock, stuck the long key to the tip of his waist-string and left the place walking barefoot.

Kalinga stood there for five minutes, dejected. Then he told his wife: 'Darling, you go home with the baby. I'll talk to him and join you.'

'What's there to talk to that *pujari*?' she asked scornfully.

'You don't know. He must have mistaken something. I'll tell you later', he said, and without giving her an opportunity to reply, he came out, wore his rubber slippers and descended in rapid strides. The *prasada* in his left hand remained as it was.

After returning from America, Kalinga never divulged any of his plans to anyone, kept them to himself and carried on his work accordingly. But even if he did divulge them, there was none in this village who could understand. Even if there was opposition to his plans, there was nobody who could mount such an opposition after understanding them. Besides, he was also endowed with a sense that he'd studied in America and so what really was there that he could tell these folks who only led a life of tradition and superstition? Yangata Gowda who'd come to argue with him because he'd sold fifty-five bovines to the butcher had returned without establishing victory over him.

But on one occasion in the past seven or eight days, Venkataramana had said, 'I won't give the God's *prasada* to someone who doesn't bow before our Gods.' He had rejected Kalinga's request right in the presence of his own servant. From that day, Kalinga had felt a sense of admiration towards Venkataramana without his own knowledge. His mind was occupied by some feeling which he himself couldn't decipher. Till his wife arrived, he'd felt that he didn't need to fear anyone, that he could live here without needing anybody's friendship. But from the moment he had gone to Mumbai, brought her here, and stepped on this soil together with her yesterday, his mind was suddenly gripped by a feeling that he was all alone. Although he'd been intimate with his wife at night and discussed numerous topics with her, this feeling did not go away. Instead, it solidified with each passing hour. Although this wasn't the first time he was sleeping in this farmhouse, this feeling, akin to isolation, which he'd never experienced before, had gnawed at him throughout the night.

By about midnight, he had remembered Venkataramana. His orthodoxy, his tradition, his views weren't unknown to Kalinga. But his mind told him that only he could be a companion both to him and Hilda. No matter how many differences of opinion, there was nobody else there who could talk with them. Kalinga had thought of introducing Venkataramana to Hilda and to invite him to visit his house often. But that morning, his plan had turned to hostility at the very outset.

By the time he reached the steps leaving behind the *kalyani* to his left and past the *Pipal* tree, he spotted Venkataramana who had already crossed all of these and was walking near the *Pipal* grove below. Although he loudly yelled 'Venkataramana', he couldn't hear it. By the time Kalinga sped, running towards the *Pipal* grove, Venkataramana was crossing the stream. He heard Kalinga's voice. He turned around, and Kalinga came closer and said, panting: 'Venkataramana, why did you do that?'

'What did I do?'

'You spoke really harshly to Hilda and came away without talking even to me?'

'What's harsh in that? I just said it like it is.'

'She's from a different country. She doesn't know the traditions and practices. What'd you lose if you showed a little patience?'

Venkataramana went quiet for a minute and then said: 'You say she's from a different country. What work does someone from a different country have in this country? But once she comes here, she must respect the traditions and customs of this country. When I said that *tirtha* means God's Sacred Water, you immediately interpreted it to imply that it's the water used to wash the *murti*. But she behaved as if it is just water used to wash a piece of stone and isn't good for health. It's your fault.'

Kalinga felt slightly relieved now. 'Yes. It's my fault. I admit it. She doesn't know the manners here. You explain all that to her patiently.'

'Why should I? She's your wife, you teach her.'

Amid this serious talk, Kalinga suddenly felt like laughing. But he controlled it and said: 'You must tell her. Isn't your family the *purohits* for our family since the beginning? It's your job to give us guidance in any matter related to the Shastras.'

Venkataramana felt a dash of pride at these words. He puffed up a little at the awareness that Kalinga would accept him at least to that extent. After he said, 'Sit down for a while, I'll tell you', and both of them sat in the shade of the silk-cotton tree nearby. After placing the *prasada* in his left hand on the grass, Kalinga sat cross-legged before it. Seated three feet opposite him, Venkataramana said: 'Look, I made a mistake. I gave you the *prasada* today. I gave it to you the other day as well. It occurred to me on that occasion—you're not eligible to take God's *prasada*.'

The conversation had turned grave again and Kalinga turned pale: 'Why do you say that?'

'Back then, I'd myself come to the village on two consecutive days to talk out this matter with you. You weren't around. It seems you sold the aged cattle in your barn.'

'Look, I know the argument you'll put forward in this matter. You don't know how tough it is to maintain the rest of them if the aged cattle eat up all the grass at home.'

'This is your indication to not talk about this issue, right? I'll say nothing. But know this. This won't do you any good; it won't do good to your lineage. So far, each time I performed puja, I also used to pray that the Elder Gowda's lineage should grow and prosper. But if this is your mentality, it doesn't matter even if the Elder Gowda goes to Hell, but this lineage shouldn't grow.'

Kalinga felt a mixture of emotions including amusement, rage, disappointment, sadness when he heard these words. Venkataramana said, 'The *prasada* on this *Palasha* leaf? Don't eat it. No water has been sprinkled on it yet, I'll take it back with me. You don't have the right to touch it.' With this, he lifted it up in one hand and in the other, took the *prasada* vessel tied in the cloth, stood up and left the place.

Although it occurred in Kalinga's mind to shout out 'stop a bit', he found it impossible to speak. He'd never experienced this sort of humiliation and defeat.

Till his wife came to the village with the eight-month-old male infant, nobody in the village was aware that Kalinga had already been married in the Red Country. But the very evening of her arrival, the servants relayed the news all over the village.

'Red, meaning she doesn't wear *kumkum* at all—that's how she looks. Her colour is the same as the camphor dolls that come during the fairs. Her hair is the same colour. She's also wearing a skirt like that doll', described one of them to which another said, 'Saw how she jumped up on the tractor machine and ran it?'

'She's as strong as her husband, my man. There's no knowledge that she doesn't know', added a third.

There weren't too many people in that village who had seen the Red People. Although Yangata Gowda had seen a Red sahib once when he'd been to the district, he hadn't seen his wife. The earlier cowshed contractor, Kattemane Shingri Gowda's son Tammayya had been to Mysore once to watch the *Jamboo Sawari*. There he'd seen English ladies. Based on the memory of that evidence, he assumed Kalinga's wife looked similar and described her.

Ninga the servant said, 'Do you know, she takes up the rifle, aims and shoots even the bird flying in the sky?' When he said this, the curiosity that the village folk had about her intermixed with fear.

One day, Yangata Gowda came home and asked Tayavva: 'Seems, your Red daughter-in-law has come. Have you visited her?'

Tayavva shook her head saying no. Six days had already passed since Kalinga's wife had arrived. Let alone her, even he hadn't stepped into the village since that day. But the servants continued to milk the cows as much as they wanted. Some among the servants who worked in that machine field were on daily wages. Then a couple of them were house servants. Only they used to come home here for food. After Kalinga's wife arrived, the inconvenience of sending food not only to him but even to Jamal, halted.

Yangata Gowda asked: 'Seems even the grandson has come?'

Tayavva nodded yes. Gowda said: 'He had already married secretly.

A baby was born as well. So, how'll he feel the responsibility to return to the village soon? That's why he stayed there for so long. Look at him! It's already six–seven months since he's come to the village. Did he even open his mouth saying he's married? That sneaky bastard!'

Tayavva shook her head no. Yangata Gowda said: 'Couldn't we get a good girl in our *jati*? It seems the Red *jati* people eat cow meat. From now on, all the cattle in your barn will be useful to your son and daughter-in-law. Anyway, leave it.'

When she heard these words, Tayavva closed both ears with her hands. As far as she was concerned, even listening to such a thing was sinful. But she was helpless. Her son had sold the old cattle to the butcher. A person like that might as well slaughter the cattle himself and eat them. Yangata Gowda said that Kalinga had eaten it all these days in the Red Country.

Tayavva couldn't sleep throughout that night. She got up in the middle of the night, lit a small earthen lamp, went to the barn and returned after counting all the cattle there. There were a total of fifty-four cattle and nineteen calves. She went inside and returned with a small mud pot. Just so that her memory would remain intact, she put inside it twenty-two hyacinth beans denoting cows, sixteen horse gram seeds denoting oxen, sixteen castor seeds denoting adolescent bull calves not yet ready for tying the plough, and nineteen red grams denoting small and slightly grown-up calves, and closed the lid. From that day onwards, after the cattle returned to the barn, she would tally the count of the cattle with the seeds in that mud pot. After she made the tally in this manner for seven or eight days and found it to be accurate, her mind found some solace.

Even fifteen days after Kalinga's Red wife had arrived, neither she nor Kalinga came to the village. The servants would come here and take any provisions and other items they needed. Tayavva was keen to go see her at least once. Besides, all the servants said that the male baby was red and plump. The desire to at least see the baby haunted her continuously. But then, who invited her? Besides, the son had to bring his wife and child—doesn't matter what kind of wife she is—and show them to the mother. When the son himself doesn't care, why should she go there?

At times when she was alone, she would weep for a while over the fate that had befallen her, and wipe her eyes with the edge of her sari and console herself. *Perhaps he wouldn't have done this had his grandfather and grandmother been alive! But then, he got married there when they were alive! He hadn't disclosed that matter to the village. Couldn't she who called herself a daughter-in-law come here at least once and see her? Did I tell her not to stay here together?* These thoughts would torment her mind continuously.

5

But one afternoon at about two o'clock, Kalinga came home. However, Tayavva remained quiet without acknowledging him. He went to the barn and came back. He inspected the granary and storehouse. Then, 'In all these days, couldn't you visit us there and see your daughter-in-law and grandchild?' he said, as if he was addressing the pillar or the wall. Tayavva made some sign. He didn't turn in her direction. He said, 'Come, come there now.' She got ready to leave as is. He lifted his head up and saw her. Her hair hadn't been oiled in days. The sari that she was wearing was dirty. Because she'd just cleaned up the ashes of the stove in the kitchen, her right elbow was sooty. On her face, sweat which had flowed since morning, had dried up. 'Have a bath and wear a new sari at least', said the son. The mother went to the bathroom.

She scrubbed her body with a mixture of *shikhakai* and soapnut powder, washed her hair with it as well, finished her bath and wore a new sari. She scratched her hair with the coarse wooden comb to untangle rough strands and stood up, ready to leave. Although he thought of giving some more suggestions regarding his mother's attire, Kalinga couldn't recollect any instance where she'd dressed up beyond this. After locking the house, Tayavva followed her son.

There was no one in the village. Both women and men had gone to labour in the fields and wetlands. The sun was beating down. Kalinga had worn rubber boots on his feet and a khaki hat on his head. To Tayavva this wasn't heat in the least. She'd left her wet hair open for drying and walked behind him barefoot. She'd never once seen her

S.L. BHYRAPPA

son's new farm or the farmhouse. The tilling machine had come inside the village once. She'd seen it then and the enormous teeth behind it, and been astonished.

After they crossed the gate in the centre of the metal wire-fence at the perimeter of the road, the tilling machine was running making the *budd-budd* noise. As she neared it, she noticed that the person who was running it was that Red Lady. 'Was she her daughter-in-law!' Tayavva's heart began to beat faster with curiosity. Her arms and legs began trembling subtly with fear. Yet, she followed behind her son. When they went near it, it appeared as if the tilling machine was coming directly upon them, raising dust. Tayavva went askew. Then, Kalinga said something to his wife. The machine stopped. His wife leapt down from it. Tayavva couldn't make out if it was a woman or a man. The body structure was that of a woman, but clad in a *chaddi*—shorts up to the knees—and a shirt on the chest. Though there was no braid, the hair was considerably long and had been chopped off like the drama people. Kalinga said something in English. She came near Tayavva, held her hands and kissed the top of her right palm. Tayavva felt weird. She instantly withdrew her hands. Without noticing it, the daughter-in-law put her arms around her shoulder and hugged her. The mother-in-law transmogrified into a ball of shyness.

When the three arrived at the tin house, Jamal was playing with the baby. The infant was red like its mother. Its eyes were shining like blue glass. Its skin colour was redder than that of a cut papaya. The hair was curled like finger rings. Kalinga had looked like this as a baby. But his colour wasn't this red. It was white. He picked up the child and handed it to his mother. She held out her hands, took it in her arms and embraced it with great love. But it let out a piercing scream on seeing this new, unfamiliar human form. Not just that, it began to cry and its breath stuck. Although Kalinga lifted it up, its breath didn't return. Immediately, Hilda took her baby in her arms and uttered some comforting words in her language. The breath that had been stuck inside now came out in the form of a wail. 'It didn't recognize', Jamal said.

The infant went quiet in five minutes. But when Tayavva reached her hands out towards it once more, it began to bawl in a high-pitched voice yet again. This time, Jamal took it outside. The daughter-in-law went to the kitchen inside. The son pointed his mother to the sofa motioning her to sit. She sat on the floor. Even when he insisted that she sit on the sofa, she shook her hands as if to say, why do I need it?

Presently, the daughter-in-law brought cut slices of bread covered with jam, as well as biscuits in glass plates. There were also bananas and oranges. When a plate was placed before her, she shook her hands signalling, 'I don't want it.' But when the son forced her, she ate the bread and bananas, taking them in her hand. The son was seated on the sofa. The daughter-in-law sat next to him and ate from a plate kept on the teapoy in front. The mother-in-law was mute anyway. The daughter-in-law doesn't know the language. The son couldn't think of anything to say. After the snack was completed in silence, the daughter-in-law got coffee from inside. But the mother-in-law didn't drink it.

After sitting there for a while, Tayavva got up and went towards the temple. This was the first time she saw the pump installed in the *kalyani*. From there, she climbed the slope towards the temple and rang the large bell in the compound four times. She perambulated clockwise, then prostrated, touching her forehead to the threshold of the temple. Of the three bilva leaves that Venkataramana had placed on the threshold, she tied one to the border of her sari. Next, she touched the feet of the Nandi facing the temple, and then touched her hand to her head. She held his face and horns in both her hands, hugged it lovingly, touched her eyes with her hands and then sat on the temple's veranda, alone for about an hour. She began to reminisce of the time when the temple was being built: how her father-in-law was always present here, how her mother-in-law was in a festive mood at home, how she would carry food for the stone workers, and then the consecration of the *murti*. The cattle fair was held here only after the temple was built. The cattle had assembled down there, all over that place which these people have now tilled with the devil-machine and planted crops. Both her in-laws died within a year. Now the son has made a farm there and put a fence. From now on, no cattle fair could take place here on any Sankranti. The last Sankranti, Venkataramana had performed a special puja to the deity. Tayavva had fasted, then come here and taken the *tirtha* and *prasada*.

In the barn at their home, she had made sweet *pongal* and fed it to the cows after applying turmeric and *kumkum* to all of them.

When will the fair happen here again? Her mind began to worry. Meanwhile, she heard the tilling machine begin to run, making the *budd-budd* noise in the field below. Tayavva got up from where she was sitting, came forward and looked. Her daughter-in-law herself was sitting on it and driving. Tayavva bowed to the deity again, touched the Nandi, and began to descend. Instead of turning in the direction of her son's farm, she took the *Agrahara* route although it was longer, and from there, turned towards the village.

6

Tayavva didn't visit her son's farmhouse again. She stayed at home doing her usual chores. Each day, milk used to go to that house. But they didn't take even a single bovine. That was the only solace for the old woman.

One Friday afternoon at about three, she had wiped clean the floor of the entire house and was drawing *rangoli*. It was an age-old custom in every family in the village to wash and wipe the floor of the house and do puja to the cattle in the evening on every Friday. Tayavva was making a two-patterned *rangoli*-bed under the opposite wall of the inner courtyard. In the evening, she had to light an incense after making a cow stand on the *rangoli*. Just then, Kalinga and his wife came in.

Their visit was unexpected. Tayavva straightened her waist, aching from all that bending, and stood still. Her daughter-in-law was not wearing the *chaddi* today. She had worn a skirt that left her knees bare and a shirt over the upper body like the men. There was a wide hat on her head. As her husband had instructed, she left her footwear at the door outside, crossed the threshold and stepped inside. But suddenly, she withdrew her feet, stood on the threshold and asked her husband: 'What's this filth?'

'The house has been cleaned.'

'Meaning what? It smells of cow dung. Smearing cow dung all over the floor is called cleaning?'

'I've already explained you the customs of this country—the floor will become clean only when it's washed with cow dung. From that cleanliness, dharmic purity will also ensue. That's what is said in the Shastras.'

'This is a truly incomprehensible practice.'

'Cow dung possesses germ-killing and disease-killing qualities. That's why they do this', said Kalinga, trying to fit his analysis so that it would agree with her logic.

'Let them apply lotion for killing germs, let them put Dettol. Why should they put cow dung? What kind of dharma is this?'

By then, Tayavva signalled to her to come inside. She placed her feet so that the soles were flat and her toes were pointed upward and once inside, asked her husband: 'What are these designs on the floor?'

'It's Friday today. In the evening, a cow will stand at the centre of the design and my mother will perform puja to it.'

'Quite interesting.'

Hilda had wished to see the cattle barn. Of late, they were planning a project to start animal husbandry in the scientific method, together with their existing farming activity. She was curious to understand how people in this country bred cattle, and how they reared them traditionally. Kalinga had brought her here to show his family's cowshed, which continued to exist since the olden days. He took her along and went to the barn from the backdoor. She inspected the entire barn once and said: 'It's sufficiently large. But it's completely unhealthy. They tie the cattle in one portion of the house they live in, don't they get disease?'

'People here don't think that way. They believe that the cow's dung and urine are disease-destroyers. Besides, according to their belief, cows are akin to God. Look at this cot in the middle. My grandfather used to sleep on it at night.'

'The poor old man. I guess that's why he died early.'

'Not early at all. He was seventy-five when he died. Perhaps he would've lived longer...' said Kalinga and went quiet. The memory of his grandfather's death aroused discomfiture in his mind. Hilda too, didn't push that topic further. She stepped closer and examined the water trough and the grass-trench of the cattle. Some water troughs contained not only water with which rice was washed but also slop—water used to wash the earthen pot in which ragi flour was boiled. She couldn't tolerate its odour. From there she went to the door at the back of the barn, and after seeing its outer portion once, she held her husband's hand and said: 'Come, let's go.'

When they came to the hall, Tayavva was in the kitchen. Kalinga shouted, 'We're going.' She came out and signalled them to sit. Both of them sat on the cot for some time. Tayavva felt like offering them something to eat. There was nothing else in the house. There was food cooked in the morning: beans broth, ragi *mudde* and rice. She gestured with her hands, asking, 'Will you have a meal?' Not correctly understanding her gesture, Kalinga said, 'Sure, if there's something.' When Kalinga saw the two bronze plates that she got from inside, he said he didn't want food. Tayavva gave two cups of milk to each. They drank it and prepared to leave.

Dung had stuck to Hilda's soles. She asked for water to wash it. Tayavva brought water in a vessel like Kalinga had asked her to. Then Kalinga himself poured water on her feet. She rubbed her soles on the stone at the door and after she finished washing, Kalinga gave her a handkerchief from his pocket. She dried her feet with it, then wore her footwear and left. The husband followed the wife.

As she watched this spectacle, Tayavva was truly furious. Anyone who steps into the house from outside always washes the feet with water *before* entering. But this wife of her son has washed her feet before going out of the house. In any region, the wife pours water on the husband's feet. But this fellow himself poured water on her feet from the vessel. Her rage mounted as she thought about this. She wept once, lamenting at this misfortune of getting such a daughter-in-law.

1

When the season's potatoes were harvested and sold, nine-and-a-half thousand rupees remained after deducting the expenses towards seeds, manure, fuel for the tractor and pump, and wages for the servants. It was the first crop on the farm. Both Kalinga and Hilda were convinced that as the land became better, the crop yield would increase and greater profits would ensue. Because he got bulk business, a speculative businessman from the district who shipped to Mumbai gave thirteen-thousand-two-hundred rupees and put the entire potato harvest in sacks and took them away in a lorry.

The day after she came here, Hilda had minutely tested the quality of soil in every part of the farmland. Although she largely agreed with the test results Kalinga had made earlier, she also demonstrated to him that some of his decisions were incorrect. After considering the general climate of the region and the climatic conditions in different months, they decided to plant cotton in one half of the field and in the other half, Virginia tobacco that was used in cigarettes. Kalinga went to the District Agricultural Cooperative Society, took their advice and brought back the seeds and manure that he needed.

From the day the potato was harvested, Jamal was cultivating the land by driving the tractor for eight hours daily. When he needed rest, Hilda would drive it. And so, the soil was much purer this time.

After the cotton and tobacco were planted and the saplings began to sprout, Kalinga and Hilda had some free time to begin to think about other things. One day, Hilda returned from a stroll in the pasture beyond the road and said: 'The grass in that pasture is of ordinary variety. If optimum manure is given and arrangements are made for water, we can grow better quality grass in that place. In the same land, we can rear some seventy–eighty cattle.'

'We need capital to do all that. We can start that once we get the money we've invested in this cotton and tobacco. First we need to erect a fence for the pasture. Then we need to run the tractor, cultivate the land and then plant new grass. But before that, we need to make arrangements for water.'

Hilda estimated the cost for all of this and said: 'We've paid up the instalment for the government loan. That apart, we'll be left with three thousand after deducting the expenses till the cotton and tobacco are ready for harvest. Check the grains and pulses in the house in the village and sell it off. Even if that won't be enough, you said there's some gold at home—sell that. What's the use of that meaningless capital called gold—it doesn't contribute to any profit?'

'I can sell the grains. But my mother won't stay quiet if I try to go near the gold. She might rake up a huge ruckus throughout the village.'

'My dear, this country won't progress', Hilda conveyed her verdict. Kalinga too, agreed.

The sale of the grain that remained after setting aside the quantity required till the next harvest, yielded two thousand rupees. To this, he added the three thousand that he had at home and erected a metal barbed wire fence around the pasture beyond the road. Apart from this, he also constructed a large zinc-sheet barn, and in the nearby slope, dug a rough well. Because there was ample ground water, it filled up quickly. He transported one of the haystacks lying at the rear of the barn in his house on carts. After this, he shifted the milch cows here, leaving behind oxen and calves that had weaned off milk.

2

Twenty-two cows—sixteen among them were milch—and sixteen calves. In any case, from the cattle that went for grazing, thirty-eight were missing. When Tayavva noticed this, she questioned the servants about it. The servant said that they were all tied up in the new barn built in the pasture. Although the night lamps had already been lit, she took along a servant to the new barn. She'd neither seen nor heard about it. Although the servants were aware that the tin house was built in the middle of the pasture after it was fenced, they had assumed that it was meant for keeping the tilling machine and for human habitation. When they went there and looked, the cows were all tied separately. Servants were milking them. Perhaps because it was the first day, Kalinga was supervising the milking of the cows.

Tayavva who arrived at the barn, angrily asked Kalinga what this was all about. He hadn't anticipated that she'd come here in the darkness, at this hour. 'I built this because you'd be unable to look after all of them on your own. Each day, these guys will bring you the milk required for the house.'

Tayavva gestured with her hands saying, 'You'll kill these very cows and eat them.' He asked, 'Which slut-son told you this? That's all lies. Have you lost your mind?' She proceeded to untie the cows. 'Mother, will you just leave and go home? Or no?' he admonished her. Jamal who just arrived there comforted Tayavva, 'Don't be scared Mother. Nothing's going to happen to the cows. Think that it's my responsibility to take care of them.'

Tayavva was in a position where she could do nothing. Tears welled up from within her. Holding the face of a cow nearby, she sobbed, whimpering repeatedly. Although Kalinga felt sad watching this, he was also vexed at his mother's behaviour. He said: 'If you want, take two milch cows home.' Tayavva went out, not wanting even that. But Kalinga told the servant who'd accompanied her to untie two cows and take them with him. With or without his conscious knowledge, the servant untied two Punyakoti cows together with their respective calves and joined Tayavva.

Tayavva came to the village but didn't go home. She landed at Yangata Gowda's house. The servant who followed her tied the cows to the pillar at the door and went in with her. Yangata Gowda who'd just finished his dinner and was rubbing tobacco in his palm, greeted her and seated her on a mat made from date palm leaves. She narrated the matter using hand gestures. The servant who accompanied her explained everything in words. She gestured that they'd slaughter those cows and eat them.

By then four elders in the neighbourhood arrived. After they sent word, about seven–eight other prominent village folk joined in. All of them were already furious with Kalinga. It was true that the pasture belonged to the Elder Kalinga Gowda's ancestry since ages. But even those who didn't have their private pasture used to graze their cattle in it. None in the village had ever discriminated or claimed ownership of land where the cattle grazed. Now, within a year, Kalinga had fenced not just his pasture lying outside the road but had also fenced and cultivated the land at the foothills that lay beyond the pasture. The space in which the cattle could graze in the village surroundings had diminished. Now he's put the fence even on that portion of land at the perimeter of the road. What'd be the fate of those who didn't have their own pasture? Now, Yangata Gowda's small pasture was all that remained in the village. But if all the cattle in the village including that of Yangata Gowda rushed in, it wouldn't last for even a month.

Several village folk had seen the fence being erected around the pasture at the perimeter of the road. Kalinga's Red Wife held the big ruler—the one which the engineer sahib's servants held—took measurements, and was giving instructions for digging pits in specific spots. She got stone pillars installed in the pits and then like a supervisor, she gave instructions on how to insert and pull the metallic barbed wire out of the holes in the pillars. They all experienced an unknown sense of fear about her. Although several among them had a desire to see her from close quarters, they would stand at a distance, watch her fearfully and then return.

Now, Yangata Gowda asked everyone what could be done. Tayavva gestured, 'Go, cut that fence.' Yangata Gowda endorsed it saying, 'That's the best.' But the men of the village were frightened to commit an act of such aggression.

'She's got a gun, my man. What'll you do if she kills you with it?' asked one.

Another, 'She sits on that machine and runs it making that *barrrrooooo* noise. She'll bring that out and roll it right over you.'

'Murderous bitch, a filthy murderous bitch, my man. She looks like a man wearing that *chaddi*. Each pillar of her thigh is as tall as us. If she was a lady of our country, we wouldn't need to fear.' When another man said this, the fourth courageous guy added his own drop of wisdom: 'That Muslim whoreson out there? He's got a dagger with him. He'll come along with her.'

Yangata Gowda's son, Maata was now twenty-seven or twenty-eight. His wife had just delivered a second male baby. He stood up and thundered: 'All you sons of *Shikhandi*, you eunuchs, are you all wearing bangles? Come with me, I'll show you. She's got the gun eh? A gun? If all the village folk storm in with bludgeons, she'll scoot, her thighs shivering inside her knickers!'

Courage surged throughout the assembly at these words. Tayavva asked making a gesture, 'Have you all shaved off your moustaches?' But Kattemane Tammayya spoke pragmatism, 'Look, it seems he sits with the deputy commissioner and smokes cigarettes. If a brawl breaks out, he'll go tell the police people, who will come and cart off the entire village. Will your manliness work if they put shackles on your hand and throw you in jail?' Courage instantly deserted the assembly.

They spoke well up to midnight about removing the fence around the pasture. But no concrete plan occurred to them. Yangata Gowda's son Maata alone abused everyone as eunuchs and indicated the importance of employing muscle strength. But the manliness of the village had dissipated. Nobody present there could comprehend the reason as to why the inner strength of these men—the same strength, which had enabled them to fall upon tigers and hyenas and kill them—had dissipated in this manner. Nobody had the capacity to even think on these lines.

3

Of the fourteen milch cows, the milk from two cows was sufficient for Kalinga, Hilda, their baby, and Jamal with some milk remaining. As for the twelve other cows, even after their calves drank to their heart's content, milk measuring about thirty-five to forty litres in the morning and about thirty litres in the evening would be left over. What had to be done with all that? No matter how much was generated, nobody in the village sold milk; it would be given free of charge to the children in homes which didn't have milch cows. The remainder would be curdled and then butter would be extracted and stored. Even buttermilk would be given free of charge, like a *daana*, to whoever asked for it. Only that butter which remained at home after everybody had eaten it was sold in the weekly market. Thus, the milch cow wasn't a profitable business at all. Only when adult cattle was sold in the cattle fair or market that money would be visibly seen.

One day, Kalinga went to the Taluk in the motor and met the hotel owner at the bus stand. He told Kalinga to send any quantity of milk, and that if it wasn't diluted with water, he'd give ten annas for every two litres. The same day, Kalinga bought four large milk cans and returned. The next day onwards, he made arrangements for milking forty litres and filling it in two cans before the motor arrived in the morning. For the past three months, three motors were plying on that road. The evening motor came at six. He instructed the servants to finish the milking and dispatch it before it arrived. On the outside of the can, he stuck a paper note on which he'd written the measure of the milk that it contained.

Seventy litres of milk, that is, twenty-one rupees and fourteen annas every day at the minimum. Twenty-five rupees per month had to be paid for each motor. After deducting that amount, twenty rupees remained each day. Kalinga made a mental note. Animal husbandry was indeed a profitable business! But it had to be carried on in a manner that was financially secure. Had all the milk that his grandfather had simply given away as *daana* been sold, it would've amounted to four or five lakh rupees. He didn't do even that. *In the end, all he did was to spend all the money he had to build the temple and then die, making me beg for a loan from the government*, thought Kalinga to himself.

One day as the servants were milking the cows, Hilda arrived on the spot. The calves were drinking milk on one side of each cow's udder. The servant was milking the teats on the other side. When Hilda saw this, she asked her husband: 'Why do those calves keep drinking milk?'

'If the calf doesn't suck it, the cow won't release milk. Besides, the calf needs enough food as well.'

'Dear, do you too still believe this? If the udder fills up with milk, the cow won't feel comfortable till it comes out. Doesn't it feel uneasy until the urine that's filled up in the bladder comes out? It's the same with the udder. It's unscientific to say that a cow doesn't release milk until its own calf puts its mouth there. You've seen it yourself in America. Don't they put the rubber tube and completely suck out all the milk? Besides, no calf's stomach will be full with just its mother's milk. If the calf needs to grow healthy, other kinds of nutritious food needs to be given. From now on, tell the servants to tie up the calf before milking.'

Kalinga gave the order accordingly. But after the calf was separated from the teat, and when the servants tried to touch it, the cows began kicking. The calves began to scream, *Ambaaa* and struggle. Those cows were never used to being milked without their calves. But Hilda didn't relent. She was someone who'd scientifically studied the physiological mechanisms of how milk secreted from specific muscles, where and how they'd get stored, and the kind of discomfort that would ensue if it didn't come out.

Wooden platforms were built and the cows were put on them for milking. From the third day, the cows began to comply. They'd allow the calves to put their mouths to the teat for just a minute: this was before the milking began, and once it released the milk and till it finished urinating, they'd drag the calf and tie it in front of the cow. It would content itself, silently licking its baby's body. Then, once all the milk was sucked out, the calf was allowed to experience the joy of sucking at its mother's teat.

When they saw this new system, the servants who were engaged in milking the cows felt distressed. They'd never seen this method of milking cows in the Elder Gowda's family. Nor had they even heard of something like this. The elderly one among them asked Kalinga one day: 'My man, they say that if you snatch away the baby's mouth and milk the cow, the milk becomes poisonous. You shouldn't do this.'

However, there was no evidence to show that the milk would become poisonous. All that milk went to the hotel. The thousands who drank cups of coffee and tea prepared with this milk didn't die from poisoning. 'I don't need your Puranas. Just do your job', said Kalinga.

When the cows were milked after separating them from their calves, the quantity rose to seventy litres in the morning and to sixty in the evening. Kalinga enquired with other hotels in the Taluk. They said they'd give twelve *annas* for every two litres if he promised to supply undiluted milk without fail. The hotel at the bus stand agreed on their own accord to pay twelve annas for fear of losing the pure milk that they were getting all these days. They had a bigger hotel at the district bus stand as well. If they got better milk in greater quantity, they could send it there in the motor. 'Doesn't matter how much milk you have. Give it to only us, not elsewhere', they said. It wasn't important who took it as long as the money came on time and the transaction was honest. The bus stand hotel gave him an advance as well. Kalinga purchased four more cans.

Milk worth forty to forty-three or forty-four rupees was being generated everyday now. The amount that had to be given to the motor had increased to fifty or sixty rupees per month. Additional expenses were incurred on other nutritious food for the calves. But when the accounting was done, it turned out more profitable to tie up the calves during the milking.

One day, even as the cows were being milked, Hilda came there and said: 'Dear, if the cows are given better and more nutritious food, we can increase the milk yield. In any case, the capacity of these cows to generate milk is low. The cows of my country are much better from this perspective. Moreover, we also need to change the technique of milking. Instead of human fingers, if we fix rubber tubes and suck the milk out using the pressure of a machine, it'll be hygienic as well. You've seen this in our home in America, right?'

'Yes, I've seen it. But we need six more months to do that', said Kalinga.

The government had decided to provide an electrical connection from the preceding Taluk to this one. Two months earlier, the electricity department people had taken measurements for laying the poles. The row of poles passed right next to their farm. If they pulled a wire from it, not only would their farmhouse light up, they could also draw out all the water from the *kalyani* using electrical power instead of diesel, whose power was limited. And as Hilda suggested, they could even suck out milk from the cow's udder till the last drop.

VOLUME 12

1

The cotton and the tobacco crops were growing better than anticipated. Going by current market rates, it was certain that at least thirty-five thousand rupees would remain after deducting the expenses towards the seeds, manure, machine fuel, labour and other incidentals. After they began to send milk in the motor, there was absolutely no need to think about money. Hilda suggested that they buy their own van after harvest. First, they had to deepen the well at the cowshed, build a cement structure for it and install an electric pump. Kalinga's plan was to grow better quality grass in the pasture and fit an electric motor to the pump at the temple's *kalyani*.

Kalinga's prestige had grown considerably in government circles. He had become a role model for the Agriculture Department's wing that publicized scientific farming. He'd returned after studying in America; he had an American wife. It seems the wife was better learned both in agricultural science and animal husbandry. Once when the district's deputy commissioner had passed by this route while on tour, he had visited the farm, observed everything, and had chatted with his wife in English.

Yet, Kalinga didn't have peace of mind. Although Hilda was always there next to him, she was the brain behind the progress of his farm, the farm's supervisor, and the wife who provided intimacy, the sense that he was all alone continued to plague him. The government officials had seen and appreciated his achievements, but the villagers with whom he had grown up, hadn't. Apart from Jamal and the servants who worked for him only for reasons of subsistence, none from the village ever came to his farm. His own mother had come to the farm just once. That was it. Either she didn't like the environment or wasn't happy with Hilda's dressing and behaviour, in any case she never came in this direction again. After she came to the new cowshed, fought, wept and took two

160

cows away, she had also stopped cooking food for the servants. Kalinga supplied them with their share of ragi, pulses and chillies and made arrangements for them to have food in their own homes.

Even his childhood friend Venkataramana has not come in the direction of the farm in ten months—that is, since the day after Hilda arrived and he had returned to his village after castigating him. Every day at about eight in the morning, he comes to the temple for puja. The sound from the bell in the front compound is audible to everybody like a clang on the head. The moment they hear it, the servants working in the farm stop their work, turn in the direction of the temple, fold their palms and close their eyes. On several days, they go to the temple during the puja hour, take the *prasada* from Venkataramana and return. There were also days when *bhaktas* or devotees from other villages come with their wives and children to conduct a special puja. They take water from the *kalyani* to cook food that they eat inside the small stone *mantapa* situated at the rear quarter of the temple. The temple had become a place of pilgrimage. With each passing day, the glory of the temple's deity spread to faraway villages. This is what the servants discussed amongst themselves.

At the hour when Venkataramana came for the puja, Kalinga was unable to even walk in that direction. Perhaps it was fear, embarrassment or shame; he felt it difficult to show him his face or walk around in his presence. But the desire to talk with him was constant. He would often tell Hilda who was suffering from loneliness sans any social life: 'No matter how traditional he is, it's only Venkataramana who can give us real company here. At least he has the guts to criticize me directly to my face and cut all contact with me. Who else has that kind of character?'

Hilda would say: 'Isn't his traditional mentality a little extreme? Nobody can reform that, right?'

'According to him, it seems we need to reform. As far as he's concerned, there's no question of any reform on his part.'

'It's a sort of hubris that he has.'

Kalinga would nod to this.

Electricity still hadn't come to their house. Hilda would switch on the battery-operated radio to pass time. At night, Western music would play. She didn't like the music here. Kalinga had brought a gramophone and some music records. One day, she played a record and began to dance, holding her husband close. She had no other contact or activity apart from reading English newspapers, and working in the farm.

Of late, she had begun to practice Kannada by talking with Jamal. In the beginning, Kalinga had taught her a few words and sentences.

2

One day, Venkataramana and Kalinga unexpectedly came face to face at the Taluk bus stand. Without thinking, Kalinga spontaneously initiated conversation: 'What's this, have you come for the salary?' Just as spontaneously, Venkataramana said, 'No, I had some work at the inspector's office.'

A minute later, Kalinga said: 'I'd thought you won't talk to me.'

'Why, are you an enemy who's stolen my kingdom?'

'Not that. The other day, you took back the *prasada* that you'd given me.'

'Yes. You're not entitled to the *prasada*. But what's the objection in talking to you?'

Both had to return to the village in the same motor. And so both of them sat next to each other in the bus stand on the stone bench built for passengers. When Kalinga again asked the reason for coming to the Taluk, Venkataramana said: 'Initially, I was appointed to the school in my village. Then I got a transfer order. But I somehow managed to get it changed to the New Type Middle School in Basavanapura, next to my village. Now they've transferred me again to another village. I'd come here to get it cancelled and have it moved back to my own village.'

'What's your problem going to another village?'

'Puja.'

Kalinga smiled. Venkataramana who noticed this immediately said: 'Yes, the word puja sounds funny to you. That's why I shouldn't even speak to you.'

'I didn't laugh because of that My Lord. I remembered something else. Come. I know the *Amaldaar*. I'll tell him to talk to your inspector. If required, we can bring some influence on the District Education Officer', he said, getting up. Venkataramana followed him silently. Kalinga went inside the *Amaldaar*'s office alone, spoke to him, came out, and said: 'He's given his word. Don't get relieved from Basavanapura. In about five or six days, you'll get an order stating that you're transferred to your own village.'

Venkataramana felt grateful to Kalinga.

Later, both travelled in the bus together. Venkataramana got down at the *Agrahara*. Kalinga went a little further to his farm. The order transferring Venkataramana to the *Agrahara* reached him in a week.

~

One morning, Venkataramana was performing the puja in the temple. It appeared that someone had come from outside. Because it was common for devotees or people from neighbouring villages to arrive during the puja hour, he continued his puja without turning that way. He finished the *naivedya*, then lit the wick for performing the last *arati*. When he started to ring the bell in his left hand, the person outside began to ring the large bell. After he completed the *arati* to the deity inside and turned around to perform the same to the *Nandi* opposite the temple, he was surprised. The one ringing the bell was Kalinga's wife. Nobody else was around. He could see that she'd left her shoes outside the temple and washed her feet in the *kalyani* before coming in. He went close to the Nandi and finished performing the *arati* as if he hadn't noticed her. As he was returning, she said, 'Please hold it before me.'

'It shouldn't be held before those who don't believe in it', he said, walking away.

'If I tell you that I've come here in faith, you must believe me.'

Still Venkataramana went inside. But, he thought something for a minute and brought the *arati* plate outside. Hilda ran her palms over the burning flame of the *arati* and pressed them to her eyes. Venkataramana went in and brought the *tirtha*. Placing her right palm over her left, she drank the three spoonsful of the *tirtha* that he poured in it and then ran her right palm over the red hair on her head. Venkataramana who'd gone inside, was thinking again for two minutes. Later, as if he'd made a decision, he said, turning to her, 'I'll give you the *prasada*. Please get a leaf from outside.'

Hilda went out and returned with two leaves. On one, she accepted the lemon rice mixture that he served. She held the other forward and said, 'This is for the child.' After serving, Venkataramana asked: 'Where's Kalinga?'

'He's not in town. He's gone to place an order for the electric pumps.'

Not knowing what to say further, he went inside, wrapped the remaining *prasada* in his cloth and came out, getting ready to go home. 'I came here to speak with you. You're already leaving for the village?' she asked.

He was astonished not merely because she came here today in this manner and took the *tirtha* and the *prasada* with devotion, but because of what she said now.

'What's the matter?'

'What can I say if you ask me standing like this? Please sit. Else, please come to our farmhouse, I'll tell you.'

'I don't have time now to come there. I need to go to the school at eleven', he said and sat down on the platform of the temple. As she sat near him on the same platform, Hilda asked: 'It seems you and Kalinga are childhood friends and you have tutored him too. Is that true?'

Because she was sitting close to him, he moved away a little and answered: 'Yes.'

She smiled when she noticed this, then moved aside a bit herself, and asked: 'You say you're childhood friends. So, why have you kept him at such a huge distance? Some intellectual differences may arise. Should friendship end because of that? You must have a democratic approach to differences.'

Venkataramana remained quiet, not knowing an answer. After waiting for five minutes, Hilda asked: 'Isn't it?'

Now the answer flashed to Venkataramana. 'This is not merely a matter of differences. There might be differences in the matter of tobacco prices next year, but it won't come in the way of faith. This is a question of our faith. It's a question related to dharma, tradition and custom. It's not possible to treat it that lightly.'

By then, Hilda who'd begun to eat the lemon rice holding the leaf in one hand, asked: 'Won't you eat?'

'No. I'll go home and eat it with lunch.'

'It's very delicious. How do they prepare this? What all do you add?'

'Lemon juice, chilli powder, seasoning, curry leaves, all of that. In what manner, how much, the women know that. I don't.'

'Look, it's been almost a year since I've come here', said Hilda in a depressed tone: 'You've never come to our home even once. You haven't brought the woman of your home. Neither have you taken us to your home. How can we live alone?'

Venkataramana felt sad when he heard this. Yet, he said: 'When you don't want our lives, lifestyles and ideals, why should anybody come to your home? If you want to mingle with people, be like us. Else, be the way you are.'

'Friends shouldn't be this harsh. You agree that you're his friend. But you don't mellow down your mind. The ways of your country are strange. If somebody behaves or lives differently from you, you keep them out instantly. We don't do that. We include them with us. We discuss. We win them over to our opinion. Else, we accept their opinion.'

Venkataramana was silent. She asked: 'Did you get the substance of my words?'

'What?'

'You mustn't maintain distance like this from now on. Please visit our home. Whatever mistake you discern in us, show it to us through logical reasoning and correct us. It seems you're the *purohit* for Kalinga's lineage. Isn't it your duty to correct us?"

He felt a surge of pride when he heard these words. Earlier, Kalinga too had uttered these words. But when he heard these words emanating from the mouth of a foreign woman, a woman from a different race, a woman who had read so much, and a woman of stark Red colour and endowed with a confident gait, he experienced an incomprehensible exultation for a minute. She saw her watch and said to herself, 'The time is already ten. I guess you need to walk to your village, have your lunch and go to school!'

Venkataramana got up, locked the temple door, stuck the key in his girdle, rang the temple bell again, and walked down the hill barefoot.

On a Sunday, Venkataramana finished his puja, left the *prasada* and other items behind in the temple, locked it, climbed down and went to the farmhouse. The pungent smell from the ripe tobacco leaves pervaded throughout the farm. The fully grown cotton trees were standing to the left. The radio was playing inside. In the outer door, Kalinga's child was seated on a colourful wooden horse and playing. A new tin house had been constructed next to the tractor shed. At the centre of its door stood a middle-aged Muslim woman. It flashed immediately to Venkataramana that she must be Jamal's wife. Next to that house, tall meshes made of wire were erected and a few country chickens were being bred there.

With great affection, Kalinga welcomed Venkataramana who was visiting his home nearly a year after he had set up his family here. Because he was still wearing the Sacred Garments, Venkataramana sat on a wooden chair. 'You've anyway come from the temple. Couldn't you bring the *prasada*?' When Kalinga asked this, he didn't say anything in response immediately. Hilda who emerged from inside said: 'Remember you gave me that lemon rice the other day? It was very delicious. I asked our Jamal's wife, Bilkis how to prepare it. She taught me. But she told me herself that there's a difference in taste between the way you prepare it and the way she taught me to make it. Besides, we also add another ingredient which you don't.'

Kalinga said instantly: 'Darling, he's just finished his puja and come here wearing the Sacred Garments. You're uttering all this stuff indiscriminately. He might as well get up and leave this place.'

All this while, an odour that Venkataramana was unaccustomed to, was assaulting his nose. Now when he understood what it exactly was, he really couldn't sit there. He stood up and said: 'I didn't come here to sit. I came here to tell you both to come to the temple.'

Kalinga understood everything. He didn't force Venkataramana. He said: 'You leave now. We'll join you in ten minutes.' Venkataramana stepped outside. As he walked towards the hill, he keenly observed the tobacco plants that stood on either side of him. Each leaf was as wide as that of a plantain leaf. At least twenty leaves in each plant. Although he had seen tobacco plants in the past, he'd never seen a variety that grew in such luxurious abundance. *How many thousands would ensue in profits?* He made an estimation as he climbed up the slope of the *kalyani* and reached the temple. He felt hungry and although he wanted to eat the *prasada*, the spicy mixture made with soaked green gram that was inside, he recalled the invasive odour in Kalinga's home, and refrained in disgust.

In about half an hour, Kalinga and Hilda arrived. Immediately, Kalinga asked him again: 'Forgive me, Venkataramana. She doesn't know the background. She just speaks thoughtlessly. You had to unnecessarily come here instead of staying back at my home.'

'The porch of a temple is always better than the house, right?'

'Not that, but why're you this snooty about non-vegetarian food?' Hilda asked.

Kalinga interrupted: 'Why do you ask such serious questions at the outset? Couldn't you think of any other light-hearted topic?'

'Let her ask. What's wrong with that?'

'Look, Hilda. He's not scared of logical debates. He's studied Vedas and Vedanta for ten years in Sanskrit. Your knowledge in that area is really feeble. You haven't studied Vedanta. At the most, his English might falter a bit during serious debate.'

'I'm not saying all this with an intention of defeating him. He's knowledgeable. Let him teach me. If his English is a problem, you help out.'

Venkataramana felt his body swell up at these words. He recalled the years of his study at the Sanskrit *Pathashala* in Mysore and asked: 'Doesn't non-vegetarian food imply cruelty to animals?'

'It's not a question of cruelty. Don't animals exist for the purpose of providing food to humans? It's equally not against the view of religion to regard them as such.'

'Which religion says this?'

'I don't know your religion. In my Christian religion, we believe this. Animals don't have a soul as humans do.'

'In that case, the beliefs of your religion are fundamentally incorrect. Every animal that's ever been created in the world has a soul. In God's creation, nobody is born for the sake of another person's utility. It's an incorrect belief to regard only the human as the highest among all animals.'

Kalinga now intervened: 'I don't understand. I've heard you say yourself that the human birth is the best among all births. Now you say this?'

'What do you mean when you say the best? The human has the capacity of discrimination, which is something that no other animal has. The human is the best only in the sense that he can distinguish between what is right and wrong and conduct himself accordingly. That doesn't mean he can eat other animals. Is swallowing up someone inferior to you a trait of superiority?'

Neither Hilda nor Kalinga could think of a response to this. Venkataramana continued: 'It's nowhere said that only the human birth is the most superior at all times. The human birth is inferior to that of the divine birth. Lesser than the human birth is the demonic birth. But then, animals aren't demons. In several instances, noble people take birth in the form of animals.'

This was new to Hilda. She asked him the basis for these words. Venkataramana responded that she'd understand all that if she read the Puranas.

'How do we believe everything that's said in the old Puranas?' asked Kalinga.

'Each country has its own unique and bizarre Puranas or mythologies. If one proceeds on their premises, it'll become impossible to arrive at a consensus acceptable to all. Besides, a myth is an unscientific creation of artistic imagination. Therefore, we need to talk scientifically,' Hilda argued.

'You've studied physics, chemistry, and biology in high school, right?' Kalinga asked.

'Yes, I've studied them', said Venkataramana.

Then Hilda spoke: 'Then consider this according to zoology: the history of animal life shows that the weaker animal becomes the food of the stronger one. The natural lifecycle is itself structured in this manner. The small fish is eaten by the big fish, which in turn is eaten by a bigger fish. There's yet another animal that eats even this bigger fish. That animal doesn't necessarily need to be a human. Merely because the human gives up eating meat, the rest of the animals won't change their food pattern.'

Meanwhile, Kalinga said, 'Look here', pointing his fingers to the wall. Both turned in that direction: an insect was crawling on the wall. Right behind it, a lizard sped noiselessly, and with a calculated and stealthy gait, swallowed it in a flash.

'This is the example. It's the truth of the functioning of life forms everywhere. The state of life of every animal is its fundamental state of being, its fundamental truth, an inevitable truth. This truth applies even to humans. Why does the human even rear goats, buffaloes, sheep, cattle and other animals? But in this, the human isn't as selfish as other animals. Although he utilizes them for their meat, he's preserved their species from extinction by preventing them from falling prey to other cruel animals. He's bred their stock, nurtured them, and eaten only what he requires. In any case, he's preserved their species. Isn't this a service that the human has provided to animals?'

Hilda wanted to talk at length in greater detail. But she couldn't recall everything at that moment. Now she remembered something and started to speak. But Venkataramana signalled her with his hand to refrain. He was readying his response. After a minute, he said: 'You spoke of science saying that it's the natural order for all animals to survive by eating creatures weaker than them. That's a lie. Just as there are tigers, hyenas, dogs and vultures, there are also herbivores like oxen, horses, cows, parrots and doves in the animal world. The people of your country say that man is basically an animal. Even if we admit that as true, is man an animal who belongs to the category of dogs and vultures, or to that of cows and doves? You might say that he's endowed with teeth that can tear flesh and chew it. But he can equally eat fruit and greens with the same teeth. And so, in your opinion, tell me what sort of animal should the human be?'

Hilda was listening to him with intense concentration. Her blue eyes were fixated on him. Venkataramana continued: 'You said the human is preserving various animal species by preventing their extinction, and that thereby, bestowing a great favour upon them. It's indeed praiseworthy if it was done without expecting any return. But why does the human even do this? Because of the selfish reason that if all these animals entirely become prey to those cruel animals, the human wouldn't have any food to eat. Just like how he protects goat and sheep from the carnivores, why doesn't he also protect small carnivores like the leopard and chameleon? The science that you quote isn't capable of deciding the morality or otherwise of non-vegetarianism. Don't build your ethics on the edifice of human selfishness.'

The atmosphere had become tranquil by the time he finished saying this. Hilda was contemplating on his statement even as she was watching him. Because he had come for puja, he had worn the Sacred Dhoti made of fibre, the cotton Sacred Thread across his shoulder and he had covered his upper body with a flimsy cloth. His stomach and chest were visible. The long shiny tresses that hung down behind his head were dry. The bands of *vibhuti*—the Sacred Ash—applied on his shoulders, arms, chest and forehead had caked up and were falling. Kalinga asked: 'Did you take some *prasada* after you came here from our home?'

'No.'

'Why?'

'To tell you the truth, I felt a sort of disgust out there. Didn't feel like eating anything.'

'It's already twelve. Aren't you hungry?' Hilda asked.

'I can stay like this even till twelve tomorrow afternoon. Fasting isn't really a big thing.'

'He's a Brahmin after all, and he's studied Sanskrit.' Kalinga said: 'Fasting isn't a big deal for him. Neither does his strength diminish if he fasts nor does he lose patience. But it's impossible for us.'

'You don't need to only be a Brahmin to fast. Your grandfather fasted for the entire day before this very temple was consecrated. That day, after the consecration ceremonies were over and after all the devotees had finished eating and their plates had been cleaned—that is, till the sun set in the evening, neither he nor your grandmother touched even a single drop of water.'

'They're people from the olden days.'

'So which age is your mother from? If necessary, she can fast for three days and still remain serene. Even today, she doesn't touch a drop of water until the *Gopuja* is finished every Friday evening. Aren't you aware of it?'

Hilda recalled their earlier visit to the village on a Friday afternoon to see Kalinga's mother. Lost in some random thought, she said: 'Why do these people indulge in the self-torment of fasting in the name of religion?'

'And why do you people loudly justify the pain you cause to other animals when you can't bear even a bit of self-torment? Only a person who can withstand hunger can remain tranquil without killing other animals for satisfying his hunger.'

Kalinga was about to say something. But Hilda stopped him and said: 'Enough of this debate now. We'll talk another day. If we continue this, he'll fast all day. It could well be a state of inner happiness for him. But I can't watch that. There's some tiffin anyway. Why don't you eat that at least?'

'No. I'll have lunch at home.'

Although Hilda wanted to know the reason behind that, she refrained. After a while, Venkataramana got up, opened the temple door, tied the vessel of the *prasada* in a cloth and locked the door. He touched the door once and ran his fingers over his eyes reverentially, vigorously rang the massive bell in the compound about four to six times, and walked barefoot on the scorching earth in the blazing heat towards his village.

En route to his village, his mind experienced a sense of exultation. He'd never had this sort of a serious and logical debate with anybody in this village. Every day at home, he read some Shastra or Purana texts, but there was no one who could actually engage him in debate. But today, that Red Woman who was Kalinga's wife had made him talk a lot. He couldn't figure out whether she agreed with his opinion. He thought of asking her some other day.

4

One day when he was conducting the puja, Hilda arrived. Like she'd done on an earlier occasion, she took the *arati*, brought the leaf for the *prasada* and held it out. After Venkataramana served a sweet dish on the leaf, she asked: 'Why don't you eat something here?'

'I eat a handful everyday as *prasada*.'

'Not that. Eat the same amount as what you've given me. Wait, I'll get you a leaf as well', she said and returned with another leaf. He filled it up and sat on the porch. She ate a mouthful and asked: 'What's this called? How do they prepare it?'

'It's called *gulapoute*. They make it with semolina and mix jaggery, ghee, raisins and cardamom. I don't know the procedure.'

'It's very delicious. I'd told you the other day to bring your wife along to our home. You didn't. Neither did you invite me to yours. How do I learn to prepare these items?'

'Doesn't Jamal's wife teach you?'

'This question emanates from anger. You know that she doesn't know how to cook these sorts of dishes. You're saying this to tease me. Fine. But look, I'll tell you something: I'm an American. Our social life includes teasing and making fun of each other and generally having a good time. In all these days since I've come here, I had no one to talk to. And you, a friend, have remained far away from us in anger. Remember, this is the first time you've teased me.'

'But I didn't say that to tease you.'

'Really? Then did you say that in anger? Am I not qualified even to expect friendship from you? Is it only anger?' she said looking at him with questioning eyes. By then, her leaf was empty. Venkataramana saw that and asked: 'Shall I serve more?'

'I'll eat if you serve. But nothing will remain for you to take back home.'

'I don't bring this here so I can save something back for home. It's meant for the devotees who come here during the puja hour. It's enough to take back home just a handful as the *prasada*', he said, as he washed his hand and filled her leaf again. Then, he remembered and asked: 'Where's Kalinga? You've come alone.'

'He's gone to the district. The milking machines have arrived at the railway station by parcel. He's gone to collect it.'

'Milking machines?'

'Why, what's so surprising? In America, we don't milk with our hands. If the machine is used, it's comfortable for the cows and it's easier for us. Besides, it's a very hygienic method. You can see it for yourself once it comes here.'

A significant amount of the *gulapoute* remained even after he served her the second time. 'Take this for your child', he said, and then cut another leaf and served some more.

'Thanks a lot. You give us something to eat each time we come here. You haven't taken even a drop of water from us so far. Isn't this *jati* system really awful?'

'I haven't given you merely food. And it's not just you. I give it to any devotee who comes here during the puja hour. There's nobody today, so I've given you a lot more. As for the *jati* system, that's a different topic.'

'You're educated. You've studied philosophy. Do you believe in the *jati* system?'

'Hmm, I do. *Jati* exists in the human nature itself.'

'Apart from human nature, isn't it wrong to fix it based on birth?'

'Nobody can do anything about a tradition that has been passed down since centuries.'

'See, this is the difference between me and you', she laughed loudly once and said: 'We chop off anything that doesn't agree with reason and move on. But you remain stuck to something merely because it's been passed down through generations. Anyway. It's Sunday today. Your school has a holiday. Come home. It seems you take milk and fruit, if not anything else.'

'But I've to go home.'

'Your house will still remain there. You *must* come,' she said. As she got up, she held his hand and pulled him up. Not only was he startled because a lady had touched his hand in this manner, but he was in the Sanctified State. His mother ate lunch only after eating the *prasada* that he took back home in this Sanctified State. Now he was polluted. Right then, Hilda herself said: 'Forgive me please. People of this country feel offended if a man touches a woman as well as the other way round. It's not like that with us. Besides, it looks like you're in the Sanctified

State. Anyway, please come home now.'

Venkataramana made a plan. He left the *prasada* that was remaining inside the temple as is, locked the door and left with her. Both descended from the direction of the *kalyani*. The diesel machine attached to the pump had now been removed and an electric motor had been installed in its place. It didn't make a din but emitted just a *Bhmmmmmm* sound as it pumped up the water. The tobacco was all set for harvest in about a week. Although its overpowering pungent odour felt spicy to his nose, there was a sort of attraction in it. Hilda who was walking ahead of Venkataramana said: 'This must be harvested within a week. Else, we'll suffer losses.'

Hilda's house was locked. Jamal's wife who came there said that he'd gone to the cowshed carrying the baby with him, 'I was waiting for you. I'll go to the hills and get some twigs,' she said and went away. After Hilda opened the door, Venkataramana went in and sat on the wooden chair. She laughed and said, 'Your Sanctified State is gone now. Please sit on the sofa.' Still, Venkataramana didn't budge from the wooden chair. She went inside and returned with four bananas, a handful of raisins and cashews in a glass plate, placed it on the teapoy in front of him and reclined comfortably on the sofa opposite him. Although he claimed that he wasn't hungry, she keenly insisted that he must eat. He peeled a banana and with his right hand, broke off tiny pieces, and put them in his mouth so that his fingers wouldn't touch his mouth via contact with the fruit. When she saw this, Hilda said: 'How will people like you manage if you come to America? All these strict adherences to sanctity, pollution, tradition, vegetarian food. Won't it be tough?'

'First of all, there won't arise a situation where I'd need to go there. And even if I do go, I've heard that there've been people who remained completely vegetarian. It seems there is plenty of fruits and milk. Rice, flour and ghee is available everywhere. We can cook something.'

'In that case, you won't be able to learn anything by mingling with the social life.'

'Doesn't matter if I don't mingle. What's the loss?'

'Isn't it a loss? Isn't it a loss if you lose the potential opportunity to gain profit and return to your homeland empty-handed?'

'But what's the profit that you're talking about?' he asked, not understanding what she implied.

'Didn't you get it?' she asked, her eyes brimming with laughter: 'I thought your brain is sharp. The *pujari jati* doesn't have a nuanced mind in all areas. This applies to the *pujaris* of our church as well! Your friend came to our country and didn't return empty-handed. He mingled in the social life and returned after snatching something big.'

Now Venkataramana understood what she meant. He also felt embarrassed to speak on the topic. But Hilda herself said: 'The Sanctified Ones are often cheated out of such profit.'

Venkataramana asked: 'Even I'm aware that in the Western countries men and women freely choose and marry on their own. But our Kalinga is from a different country. He belongs to the race with black skin colour. How did you marry someone like that?'

'Why're you asking this question?'

'Because I felt like asking it. Please forgive me if it's a mistake.'

'You're very touchy. What's the mistake in this? It's always a pleasure for anyone to share with their friends the story of their marriage', Hilda said: 'I was studying at the Agricultural Science College. He was a good sportsman. I have great interest in sports. Even now both of us swim in your temple's *kalyani*. Didn't you know that?'

'No,' said Venkataramana. His mind was suddenly disturbed. Humans! Especially, a woman, swimming in the *kalyani* whose water was used for performing *Abhishekha*—offering the Sacred Bath—to the deity. He felt that it was an affront to the entire puja itself. He said immediately: 'Look, I'll say just this much. I'm not coming in the way of everything that you do. That water is meant for performing *abhishekha* to the deity. There's a rule which says that nobody should step into it or even wash clothes with that water. Going forward, you shouldn't swim in it. I was unaware of this till now.'

'Fine. I'll inform Kalinga. Now listen to the American story. This was how your friend and I were acquainted and then became friends. My father too is an agriculturist who has his own farm. Your friend used to come to our farm as part of his visits to experimental farms. On several occasions, he used to eat with us. He used to participate in dance balls and drinking parties. We eventually decided to get married.'

'Look, this question's been on my mind for several days now: no matter how openly and liberally men and women may fall in love and marry in your social setup, that might hold true only for the men and women belonging to the confines of your society. But you knew that you'd have to leave the country of your birth, your race, your parents, everything, and settle in an unknown country ten or twelve thousand miles away. Knowing all this, how did you still agree to this marriage?'

Hilda's red face grew redder, but it appeared that she was pleased by these words. 'If I've to answer this question, I need to tell you how we fell in love.'

Before she could speak further, Venkataramana said, 'Forgive me if there's a mistake in what I said. I didn't mean to ask this personal question.' His face was contorted with embarrassment.

'Why do you ask forgiveness? We openly discuss our love lives. And as we recount it with friends, there's a kind of romantic joy as though we're reliving that experience. You suppress everything in this country. I knew that just like many other countries across the world, even India is awfully backward in agriculture. The standard of food production in various countries of the world is broadly taught to us in college. Kalinga would often tell me about the condition of agriculture in this country. When he proposed marriage, he said: "I won't ask you to agree to this marriage only because you love me. I've decided to do farming in a scientific manner in my Hindustan, which is extremely backward. For any accomplishment that a man sets out to do, he'll require a companion who'll be the wellspring of his inspiration and the driver of his brain. And I haven't found any other companion like you anywhere. If not for my sake, think that it's for uplifting my country and marry me." When I heard these words, not only did my body shiver with excitement, I also felt that I was moving forward towards a lofty goal. I consented.'

Hilda narrated this with considerable emotion. Venkataramana asked: 'So that means you came here solely to uplift Hindustan?'

'I won't say that. But then, in a country filled with tradition, superstition and non-science, where can an enterprising experimenter like Kalinga find a suitable companion? Not only did Kalinga tell me as much while he was in America, he keeps saying it even after I've come here. The officials of the government's agriculture department themselves tell us that our farm has now become a model everywhere. With time, other farmers will also follow us and reform their farming methods. I told you because you asked. I have a certain sense of satisfaction that despite leaving behind my country, my race and my parents and coming to an unknown land, the people of a backward country are being uplifted to whatever little extent and even indirectly because of me. There's also this facet of a lofty goal behind your friend desiring me and I consenting.'

Venkataramana tilted his neck up and watched her face. Her blue eyes were brimming with pride and self-contentment. Hilda too watched his face with a fixed gaze. Turning his sight elsewhere, he asked: 'You just said that you came here with the goal of reforming this country's food production. You've now grown tobacco and cotton in your entire farm. Cotton is at least required for cloth. But then in the hot climate of Hindustan, there's no shortage of cloth. In the remaining half of your farm, you've only grown tobacco. It's true that it's a special variety of tobacco. But then does tobacco fill the stomach of this country's people? We'll only get some more beedis and cigarettes, right?'

Hilda hadn't anticipated this sort of question. She did not have an answer to it. But after a minute, she said: 'What's the explanation of the word agriculture? It means it's an endeavour of growing something on the earth and harvesting it. It doesn't necessarily need to be one word. A specific industry flourishes because of tobacco. This is the raw material for that industry. This too has a place in the country's economic progress. You must understand this in a wider context from the perspective of economics. If we give the tobacco of this country, some other country will give food in exchange.'

'I don't know the economics you're talking about. Neither have I studied it. But then, why have you grown this? Because there's more profit in this than in potato, paddy, ragi and maize. Right? And because it's a profitable crop, some folks in our villages also plant tobacco in half an acre or an acre. But nobody plants this in their entire arable land at the expense of growing food. Our backward village farmers believe that if one doesn't plant the seeds of food in the womb of Mother Earth and obtain a shower of food, Mother Earth will curse them. Your belief is different. Keep that aside. It doesn't appear that there's any lofty goal of coming to a backward country and freeing it from its woes of food production that motivated your love and marriage. Even you got married according to the customs of your society just like the other young men and women there, and you came with Kalinga just as a wife goes with her husband. You're helping your husband by driving that tractor just like how our village women help their husbands by carrying pails of cow dung on their head.'

Hilda experienced a complete loss of face upon hearing this. Today, she wasn't engaged in a logical debate with him on dharma, morality, ethics and other profound topics. She was experiencing the joy of friendship with someone by sharing matters which were personal and buried in the depths of feeling. It was for this reason that she'd gone to the temple in the morning and brought Venkataramana along. The discussion had turned serious without her knowledge. But this pujari is now sitting quietly, after bluntly telling her what was on his mind, without a care as to what the effect his words would have on her feelings. Suddenly she felt that she was a complete outsider here. She didn't have a single friend in this country apart from her husband. Neither was there a possibility of having any friend in these villages. From time to time, her husband would say that only this man could become a companion to them. But she hadn't thought that he could speak so rudely, with no value for her feelings. Over the past few days, she had met and spoken with him. Although he had held opinions completely different and even opposed to hers regarding religion and ethics, she had sensed a sort of attraction in his personality. She had genuinely felt that he was their friend. But perhaps he never felt even a shred of friendship or compassion towards her!

Feeling humiliated, Hilda's eyes filled up with tears. Because her self-respect would be shattered if she wept in his presence, she got up immediately and went inside. He noticed this as well. Although at that moment the realization dawned on him that his words might've hurt her, he hadn't spoken with that intent. Hilda didn't come out even after fifteen minutes. In the end, Venkataramana himself said, 'If you're hurt, please forgive me. It's getting late for me, I'll leave.' She didn't come out even after he waited for a minute. He got up and stepped out.

The afternoon sun was already sloping downwards. The shadow of the head was now at a distance of one cubit from the leg. The deity's *prasada* was still in the temple. But he felt anxious when he remembered that until he took it in his Sanctified State, his mother would remain fasting. But Hilda had polluted him by touching his hand. He went to the temple, got the metal pot, filled it with water from the *kalyani*, came to the shore and poured the water upon himself so that he was completely drenched from head to toe. Then in the soaked clothes—signifying 'sanctity'—he held the vessel of the *prasada*, locked the door, rang the large bell in the compound some seven to eight times, and with rapid strides on the burning ground, descended in the direction of his village.

5

All the cotton and tobacco crop had been harvested and sold. Thirty-six thousand rupees remained after deducting all expenses. Summer was approaching. Even if the sowing process was started immediately, no matter which crop, it would reel under the rains that would begin at the end of May and decay. So they decided to plant potato once more, and after it was harvested, to leave the farm empty for a month. Then they would plant high-quality tobacco yet again in the entire farm.

Of late, Hilda had become very inward-looking and was continuously thinking something within herself. In addition, her health wasn't all that good. She would suddenly feel dizzy and nauseous and was generally indisposed. If she felt extremely depressed, she would hold her two-and-a-half-year-old son, Jack, close to her and close her eyes tightly for a minute. Little Jack could speak English. He even spoke the Kannada that Jamal and his wife taught him. He could also speak in Urdu. Jack had no friends as well. Jamal was his only companion.

One day, Hilda hugged her husband tightly and said: 'Dear, don't worry about my health. It's really nothing. Jack will soon have a sister or a brother. You won't get angry, will you?'

'No, no. I'm not angry. You don't be depressed. But why are you always so dull like this? How many times I've told you! I know you don't have company here. But what can we do?'

'Dear, I'll never get any company in this country.'

Even Kalinga had become inward-looking. Loneliness was haunting him as well. Whenever he went to the village home he sensed that he was not merely lonely in this village but amid this entire race of people. It was only when he went to the Taluk or the District that he had the experience of a social life. At all times other than when he was involved in farm work, he would feel that this loneliness had encircled him and was strangling him. He said: 'Darling, Venkataramana used to visit us. Now, even he's stopped coming here. At least if he visits us, our boredom would perhaps reduce.'

'We can never find any compatibility with that man. In all these days, he's never taken me to his home even once. I respect him. But our lifestyles and outlook don't match at all. How can one find happiness in the company of a person who constantly opposes everything you say? This Jamal and his wife, only they can become close to us.'

Kalinga thought for a while and said: 'Look, our monotony will only increase if we constantly stay within the fenced confines of this farm. We need to take the initiative and visit a place where people gather, and try to have some social life.'

'But where do we go?'

'There's a village called Maarikere four miles from here. There's a huge temple for the village deity named Maaramma out there. There's a *jaatra*, a fair, scheduled eight days from now. You'll get to see a lot of interesting sights like mask-dancing and people walking on fire. Even Jack will have a pleasant change. Let's go.'

'That's a fine idea.'

S.L. BHYRAPPA

VOLUME 13

1

The glory of the Maaramma deity of Maarikere was renowned in the surrounding thirty miles. She was an angry deity whose eyes were burning coals; she had fangs that could tear into anything. Only Maaramma was endowed with the strength and power to hew and drive away any Epidemic Deity, which tried to set foot in the region including the plague, smallpox and dysentery. But, Maaramma wouldn't drive away an Epidemic Deity just like that. Her terrible hand would offer its succour to only those villagers and those homes that came to her on foot and offered her the requisite sacrifice. It was not her duty to protect the others. Therefore, more than the other serene deities, people would come to her *jaatra* in large numbers and offer their bhakti to her with great devotion.

This year, there was an even greater crowd than at any time before. The large field opposite her temple was filled to the brim as if it would burst open. This apart, shopping stalls and booths were scattered across the fields, now empty after the harvest. Everything was available: from new clothes, pots and pans to studios which would shoot photos for just one rupee. The entire fair was drowned in a complex array of noises emanating from the drums, horns and bugles in front of the temple, besides the whistles, flutes and trumpets from the kids.

Hilda, Kalinga and Jack came to the fair at about eleven in the morning on a bullock cart after their breakfast and lunch. To the people who had assembled at the fair, Hilda's Red colour, her height, her physique and her attire seemed a wonderment—just like the magic show, the mantras and tricks of jugglery that were performed there. There were several men at the *jaatra* who'd seen the Red people before but to most women, Hilda and Jack were marvels. It was twelve by the time they completed one round of the entire fair. Two police constables were clearing the crowd around the tall sacrificial pole that stood right in front of the temple. This created a vast and empty circular space. More than two hundred bulls were tied beyond the enclosure at the left flank of the temple.

Kalinga was coming out after showing Hilda the insides of the temple: the *murti* of the Maaramma Deity and the various ghosts carved on both the walls of the temple's inner courtyard. As he came out, Kalinga encountered a police officer who greeted him and shook his hand. After he introduced his wife, the officer extended his hand, held her right hand and shook it for longer than was necessary. Ever since Hilda had arrived in the village, this was the first time another person had shaken her hand. Although government officials like the deputy commissioner and others used to infrequently visit their farm, they would do namaste to her from a distance. This man was the inspector of the Taluk. He was a tall and well-built man who appeared to be a year or two older than Kalinga. His personality seemed accentuated in a khaki police uniform.

'What's this, you've come to the fair? Wasn't it enough if just the sub-inspector of the Hobli came?' Kalinga asked.

'I don't know if Madam Kalinga understands Kannada', he said in English.

'Thank you for the consideration,' Hilda expressed her gratitude.

Then he said: 'You're anyway aware of the bull sacrifice offered to this deity. This is the final year for that ritual. There's a government order, which henceforth prohibits sacrificing any animal as an offering to any deity. After the *jaatra* chariots are kept back this year—that is, from July onwards, we'll enforce this order even more strictly. Because this is their last opportunity, the devotees have combined all their past and future pledges to the deity and brought the buffaloes here. Two-hundred-and-thirty bulls have arrived so far. I anticipated that this would happen and came here personally. In such situations, people will attend the fair in greater numbers than they do each year. There's also the possibility of trouble erupting. Of course, my subordinate sub-inspector has also come. Twenty constables are also around.'

'How do they offer the bull as sacrifice?' Hilda asked.

'It'll happen right here. You can see for yourself. Come, how long should we stand in the sun?' said the Inspector and took them along to the *mantapa* of the *Utsava Murti*, or the Festival Deity that would eventually be taken around the fair. The *mantapa* was a tall structure and not only did it provide shade, but the sacrificial pole was clearly visible from there. The inspector sent for the Gowda of the temple and asked him to fetch them three chairs. Hilda sat on the one in the centre. The inspector sat to her left. Kalinga sat on the other, holding Jack. The sub-inspector come over for a suggestion. In his seated position, the inspector sahib accepted his salute and gave him the *hukum*. He sent for a constable and ordered him to get four tender coconuts.

The sacrifice began after a while. The inspector was narrating in minute detail every single development as it occurred, giving the necessary background information. He also added the specialities of other sacrifices that he had witnessed in similar fairs. Hilda was listening to him, looking in the direction of the sacrificial pole with wonder-filled eyes.

People had crowded around the pole at a distance of twenty feet in between. The summer afternoon heat was burning down atop everyone's heads. The men were wiping sweat off their bodies and faces and wore either a *dhoti* or a head-cloth on their scalps for shade while the women covered their heads with the loose end of their saris. They all stood looking towards the sacrificial pole. The *pujari* of the Mother Deity arrived. He had smeared turmeric and vermillion all over his forehead, arms, chest, neck and shoulders and like a woman, had worn a sari with its top end wrapped around his waist instead of bringing it around his shoulders. With a bunch of neem leaves, he sprinkled water on the pole. Two massively built men carried seven or eight broadaxes, with blades about two feet long, and placed them nearby. The sharp blades, freshly washed by the blacksmith the previous day glimmered in the sun. Their three-feet long handles were made of sturdy wood from the *Babool* tree.

After sprinkling water on the broadaxes and on the men who would slaughter, the *pujari* walked towards the spot where the bulls were tied up. The bulls, unknown to one another and impatient to be in a shady spot, were snorting. The *pujari* dipped the neem leaves in the water-vessel in his hand and swung his hands vigorously so that water drops fell on each of them. When the large water drops fell on the faces of some of the bulls, they emitted a sigh of pleasure. By then, the drummers who had gone elsewhere with the *Utsava Murti*, the Procession Deity, returned and began to beat the drums with intense ferocity.

A middle-aged giant of a man came running out of the temple, his face and body covered with vermillion, and stood near the sacrificial pole. The Gowda of the temple handed over a sheep to him. The lonely sheep was continually bleating even as that giant hugged it and planted his teeth to its neck. By the time he removed his mouth and fixed his teeth on another spot, blood was trickling out from its neck. Like a demon, he again opened his jaws wide, bit into the vein on its neck with his canine-like incisors, closed his eyes, chewed tightly, separated a ball of its flesh with his mouth and spit it out, as blood began to gush out from its neck. After a single *vaayin* shriek, the sheep's voice stopped. When he put his incisors to its neck yet again, the blood on his face flowed all over his body. The sheep had already reached the feet of the Mother Deity.

The drummers were now beating the drum at a faster pace. The giant opened his mouth, baring his teeth so that they resembled the fangs of the deity inside, hopped four times, leapt and then stood at one side. The people standing there moved ten feet back out of religious fear and devotion. By then stocky men were leading the bulls in a line. They tied the horns of the first bull together with a hefty rope and pulled it so that it directly faced the temple. Then they pressed its face to the sacrificial pole and fastened the rope around the pole. The *rav-rav-rav-rav* sound from the drum rose faster, surpassing the earlier pace of its beat. One of the strongmen held a broadaxe in his hand, touched its handle, then touched his fingers to his eyes, raised it high up and struck its neck. The axe plunged four or five inches deep inside, and the white protrusion above the muscle shattered. The animal screamed in agony, the sound drowning even the din from the drums. The second blow, delivered after extricating the axe which was embedded in the flesh of the animal, reached a further depth of four–five inches. The buffalo summoned all of its strength to its four legs and leapt up once. But by then, the third blow had landed and twisted its neck. The body fell down, and the head together with the horns, remained inside the rope with which it was tied to the sacrificial pole. Blood gushed out torrentially and began to make a culvert in the soil. The moment they saw this, the *madigas* who had assembled there for the task, threw ropes around its body and dragged it far away. Meanwhile, the face which had been stuck to the sacrificial pole had been lowered.

They immediately brought the next bull near the pole. Mortally scared from witnessing the previous scene, it refused to move forward and tightening its knees, began to holler. But four men experienced in taming and ruling over such animals through a variety of punishments, shoved it forward and leaned its face together with the horns against the pole and tied it up. Like the previous buffalo, its head was severed from its body after three blows. The culvert that was created by the blood of the previous buffalo was drying up but the blood that flowed from this one carried it forward. The *madigas* dragged away the head and the body of this buffalo as well. It was the turn of the third.

About twenty buffaloes were sacrificed in an hour. The bloody culvert flowed towards the stream at the left side of the temple and had solidified in a wide mass in the soil. Although the *madigas* were dragging away the bodies of the dead buffaloes and piling them up in a cart and transporting them, they were unable to keep pace with the rate at which they were being slaughtered. And so, a heap of corpses had mounted. So far, kites, vultures, and crows were circling above in the sky in a hunt for the sweets, *vada* and *pakoda* in the hands of the children at the fair, waiting for an unguarded moment. Now, guided by the odour of blood and flesh, they came near the sacrificial pole, making noises but remained flying overhead. They lacked the courage to savour the meat and blood by diving into the mass of people down there.

Hilda who was watching this scene, turned to her husband and said: 'Dear, enough of watching this barbaric scene. Come on, let's go home.'

Kalinga wasn't even looking in that direction. His mind was preoccupied with something else. He didn't hear her. But the inspector who was sitting on her other side said: 'Yes, lady. This is a truly uncivilized custom. That's why the government has issued an order to stop it. It's because this is the last time that so many sacrifices have been done. But you must watch the coal-hopping ritual in the evening. Look to your left, it'll take until five or six in the evening to clear all these buffaloes. Come with me till then. You can rest comfortably in the school and then return in the evening to watch the coal-hopping and the chariot rituals.'

Kalinga agreed. The inspector walked first. Hilda walked behind him and then Kalinga along with Jack. The crowd parted to give them way.

2

They remained in the school building, which was two furlongs outside the village, until five thirty in the evening. The inspector sent for the servant and got two benches joined together and told Hilda that she could rest if she wanted. Embarrassed by his extreme hospitality, Hilda reclined on a chair and relaxed. The inspector spoke to Jack as well in English. He praised him. Although he figured that she was pregnant looking at the lazy manner in which she stretched out her limbs, and the fact that she went out once and vomited, he still asked Jack, 'Are you the only child of your parents?'

At five-thirty, the three of them along with Jack left the place and reached another temple near the village. Both temples were built for the same deity. If the sacrificial pole stood outside the main deity's temple, the *Utsava Murti* was housed in this one. It was built near the spot where the village began. In front of the *Utsava Murti* temple was a heap of live charcoal resembling rubies, the result of burning thirty carts full of raw firewood. People had congregated around it. The same folks who had witnessed the buffalo sacrifice in the afternoon had gathered here.

The drummers arrived first. Behind them, four men carrying the *Utsava Murti* of the deity arrived and halted before the charcoal. Holding a copper vessel in the left hand and dipping the tips of mango leaves in the water inside the vessel and sprinkling it in all directions with his right, Venkataramana emerged from inside the temple. He was in the same attire that he wore every day to perform the puja at the Punyakoti temple on the hill. When she saw him, an astonished Hilda asked Kalinga: 'What's this, he's come even here?'

'He's the *purohit* for all the villages in the vicinity. Maybe he's come here because it's a special day,' said Kalinga. The inspector interpreted this instantly for the benefit of Hilda: 'Pollution from such massive sacrifices right in front of us has to be first purified by a Brahmin *purohit,* after which the deity will walk over the fire. Following that is the *Ratha Utsava,* the Chariot Procession.'

Venkataramana performed the *Punyahavaachana,* or the Purification Ritual for the deity. Then he sprinkled water with the mango leaves on everybody gathered there—from the men who carried the deity to the hundreds of men and women standing at the rear who had taken a vow to walk on the fire. He also sprinkled the Sacred Water on the fire which had now been lit evenly.

The drum-beating amplified. 'Now the deity will rush to the fire. Just see,' the inspector told Hilda and stood there watching the reaction on her face. Hilda was watching the carriers of the deity with trepidation. The deity rocked back once. The Gowda of the temple together with four or five other prominent men trooped in shouting 'make way, make way', and pushed back some folks who were standing nearby, clearing the spot. The sound from the drum had crossed the pace of a mere rhythmic beating and had touched a frenzied tempo emitting the *rav-rav-rav-rav* sound nonstop. The carriers of the deity came sprinting from behind and as if they were unaware that there was a spread of fire in front of them, simply charged ahead and walked over it. Hilda shrunk her face and watched the scene open-mouthed as if the fire had seared her own feet. The deity returned again and walked on the fire cinders for a third time. After this, all those who had taken the pledge rushed in and walked on the fire placing one step after the other. Hilda was looking at their feet. Then she noticed that Kalinga's mother was also one among those who were walking on the burning charcoals. Kalinga too noticed her.

After the whole thing was over, she asked: 'Why do they torture themselves in the name of God?'

'This is no torture. It doesn't burn a bit even when you walk on the burning coals,' the inspector said.

'I don't believe that.'

'In which case go step on it yourself. But then you need to have been fasting since morning.'

'Neither have I fasted nor am I a fool to burn myself over an uncalled-for challenge.'

'What you say is correct,' the inspector agreed and flashed a soft smile of obligatory friendship.

Now the deity will ascend the chariot. The inspector escorted them close to the chariot. With its enormous wooden wheels, the chariot was eighteen-feet tall. Colourful posters were wrapped all around it from top to bottom and there were four pillows hanging like swings from its four sides and it was decorated with tiny openings all over. To Hilda's eyes, the entire spectacle of the chariot, complete with the deity atop it being pulled by thousands of people appeared romantic. So when she said, 'It's a very romantic scene,' the inspector interpreted it differently and displayed an unusual expression on his face. Before the deity ascended the chariot, Venkataramana performed the *Punyahavacha* for the chariot as well. But he did not notice them in the crowd.

After the procession was over, the Mother Deity was still seated on it. The Yakshagana dance performance titled 'Devi Mahatme' or the 'Glory of the Mother Goddess' was scheduled to begin two hours later on the stage constructed with palm leaves directly facing the deity. 'You must watch it. I'll arrange chairs for you. Now both of you eat dinner with me,' said the inspector. But Hilda refused despite his repeated insistence. She was exhausted. The inspector had a jeep. He was ready to drive it himself and drop them home. But when Kalinga rejected his offer saying they had a cart of their own, he appeared a little disappointed. But he said, 'Fine. We'll meet again. Good night madam.' He then shook her hand for a long time, kissed Jack, waited till they climbed on their cart and bade them goodbye.

Several carts were moving in the moonlight. Lots of folks were returning to their respective villages on foot. Kalinga said to Hilda who was lost in thought: 'Wonder where that Venkataramana disappeared. We had this cart anyway. We could've travelled together. He could've gotten down at the junction of the *Agrahara* and walked just half a mile.'

Hilda spoke as though she hadn't heard his words: 'After all these days, it looks like we found someone who can mingle with us in friendship. That inspector is a good man, right? Why did you refuse his jeep?'

'You still don't know the mentality of people. It's only Venkataramana who can become a true companion to us.'

'Dear, haven't you still understood that pujari's mentality even after all these days? Have you seen him speak with us jovially at least once or even have a conversation without resorting to arguments and counter-arguments condemning us, humiliating us? Look at the inspector. He was with us since afternoon. Not a rude word. Not a single bitter episode. Even when a difference in opinion arose, he adjusted himself so well and remained pleasant! He has a quality contrary to police officers typically. Your friend Venkataramana's nature is completely adverse to what a priest should have.'

'Darling, you cannot understand the world that quickly. You were watching the pageant of the fair. Do you know what that inspector was watching?'

'No.'

'That's why I said you don't understand the world.'

'Really?' Now she understood. She felt embarrassed and felt as if she herself had committed some mistake. Holding her husband's hand, she said: 'Dear, I honestly didn't understand a thing. Forgive me.'

'It's not your fault', he said, pacifying her.

They lapsed into silence till the cart covered two or three miles. Then Hilda said: 'Everything that I witnessed since afternoon continues to haunt me. I don't understand the customs and beliefs of this country. These people engage in extraordinary animal slaughter in the name of God. The same people then go ahead and indulge in extraordinary self-mortification. Why kill a buffalo? Why step on burning coal? What's the meaning of all this?'

'You must ask Venkataramana. I don't know', admitted Kalinga.

They went to bed as soon as they reached home. But Hilda couldn't sleep. Her mind was disturbed by vivid reflections of those incomprehensible scenes. She decided to visit Venkataramana the next day. But he hadn't set foot in the farmhouse since the day when he had made her cry. Now her self-respect stood in the way of going to him on her own accord. She waited for several days in the hope that he'd come by himself. She had plenty to discuss. But even after three months, he didn't visit them. Now she was truly angry with him.

3

Venkataramana came to the farmhouse one evening at about four. Instead of the Sanctified Garments, he was wearing a *dhoti* and shirt. He was also wearing footwear. He had knotted his hair like an orb. Although she was furious that he hadn't visited all these days, Hilda welcomed him joyfully. 'Where's Kalinga?' he asked. She said: 'He's gone to the city. We wanted a van of our own. He's gone to order it. He'll come tomorrow evening or maybe the day after. You're still standing. Please sit.'

This time, even Venkataramana had planned to use foreign manure on his field and obtain a good harvest. He and his sharecropper Honna had decided to share the expenses of the manure equally. But it was only Kalinga who could assess the land and tell them which manure had to be used and in what proportion. He had come here to seek his advice in the matter. But he didn't disclose this to Hilda.

Hilda said: 'Please come, let's take a walk and visit our barn. Jamal told me there was some defect in the milking machine. I need to set it right.'

Venkataramana knew that they had bought the milking machine. Neither had he seen it nor was it something that would figure in his imagination. 'Sure, let's go. I haven't seen it,' he said getting up.

Hilda instructed Jamal's wife to take care of the house and left with Venkataramana. She was now in her fifth month of pregnancy. He was unaware of this. But anyone who saw her walking could figure it out.

She asked: 'It's six months since you came home. Why?'

'You know how it is—schoolwork. There's no free time for anything else.'

It didn't seem right on her part to press this issue further. 'Schoolwork aside, come home on Sundays at least. I don't do any work on Sundays.'

Venkataramana said okay. The young tobacco plants had grown throughout the farm. At a height of one cubit, they were all green and smiling. The odour wasn't pungent yet. They walked on the ridge and exited from the gate of the fence near the motor road. When they entered the gate of the fenced pasture, they saw that the grass had grown up to chest height. Venkataramana hadn't seen grass of that variety so far in his entire life. Hilda was explaining its special qualities and the method of growing it as she walked along.

When they both reached the cowshed, Jamal was supervising the milking from the machines. A servant was standing before a cow holding its calf in front of it. Four rubber tubes were fixed to each of the four teats of the cow with a clamp each to hold them in place. All the four tubes culminated in a large tube from which they jutted out. The large tube in turn, was attached to a small electric motor placed nearby. Its other outlet was placed inside a vessel a short distance away. The milk flowing through the transparent rubber tubes was visible to the eye. It was being drawn from all the four teats at once, then it stopped for seven or eight seconds, and resumed. Venkataramana stood there watching this with astonishment.

Jamal addressed Hilda: 'Madam sahib, this motor is making a *kra-kra* noise since yesterday. We need to dismantle it and see what the problem is.'

Hilda intently listened to the noise for a minute and said: 'We need to dismantle it and assemble its insides properly. You finish milking all the cows now or it'll get late for the milk to reach the bus. After that you go home and bring me the toolkit. I'll fix it in a quarter of an hour.'

Meanwhile, the machine had completely sucked the milk dry from the cow's teats. Jamal turned off the motor's switch and removed the tubes from the udder. The servant took the cow away and brought another one. Jamal fixed the tubes to its udder and turned on the switch. Like before, they placed this cow's calf in front of it. The cow was licking it. But the calf hadn't even once touched its mother's teat. Yet, milk began to gush into the tube like a fountain from all the four teats. Venkataramana asked Hilda: 'How does this machine work?'

'It's really very simple. This motor creates a vacuum inside the tubes. The pressure makes the milk from the udder flow out on its own. The vacuum that remains suspended during this time is created once again after the milk empties out in the vessel. The underlying principle of this machine is to create vacuum.'

'Will the cow release milk even if its calf doesn't drink from its teat?'

'Didn't you just see? It's true that the cow experiences a certain excitement from its calf suckling it. Milk flows generously owing to that excitement. But even without the calf, it can release milk. One only needs to get it used to this method.'

'So what's the difference between milking it by hand and using this machine?'

'It's quicker with the machine, and it's hygienic. Not just that, it'll milk it completely, not leaving behind even a single drop in the udder.'

'In which case, what's the fate of the calf?'

'It's not that the calf only needs its mother's milk. We give it other nutritious food. You've seen it yourself, haven't the calves grown healthy?'

Meanwhile, the milking of the cow was done. After Jamal removed the tubes, the servant took it away and brought yet another one. But this cow didn't have a calf. By the time Jamal had fixed the tubes to its teats, the servant returned with an artificial calf and held it in front of the cow. The toy calf which was made from cattle hide was as tall and as wide as a real calf. Its insides were stuffed with straw and it was stitched with gunny bags. Only its outer portion was covered in hide. The cow began to lick it. After the machine's switch was turned on, the vacuum in the tube began to suck the milk.

Venkataramana asked: 'Can we milk a cow without its calf?'

'Why, what's the relationship between milk and calf?' questioned Hilda.

'Is there no relationship between milk and calf? It's a grave sin to draw milk from a cow which doesn't have a calf. And even if it does have a calf, you're not giving it its milk. Why?'

'Aren't you aware? It isn't economically profitable to let the calf draw milk. Don't we breed and rear a cow only for its milk?'

'If anybody else had said this, one could've forgiven these words. But as a woman, *you*... you're already the mother of a child and you've given it breast milk. Now you're pregnant, you'll give birth to another child and feed it your breast milk. If you utter these words, I don't know whether to call it a sign of being uncivilized or a sign of ignorance.' As soon as he said this, Venkataramana suddenly closed his lips tightly.

After a minute, he said, 'I don't like to fight each time I meet you. It was my mistake to visit your home.' He turned to leave.

But Hilda who was standing close to him held his hand and stopped him and said, smiling: 'The Most Holy pujari. You mustn't run away in anger like this. You must debate when differences of opinion arise. Getting upset isn't a trait of friends. Please sit down. Even I have plenty of things that I need to talk with you.'

Although he felt for an instant that he shouldn't display his fury, Venkataramana didn't regret feeling it. But he controlled his anger and said: 'I can't sit here and watch this spectacle. Let's go somewhere else.'

'Jamal, finish the milking quickly. It might get late for the bus,' Hilda said as they came out. Both went near the newly built pond. Steps had been constructed and an electric pump had been installed. An overhead tank had also been built. Venkataramana hadn't seen it before. Neither did he ask her when all this had been done. He sat on a stone bench at the bank of the pond. There was another bench opposite him. But instead of sitting on it, Hilda sat next to him. Embarrassed, Venkataramana moved to the edge. She didn't notice it. She was lost in thought for a minute and then said: 'Look, each country has its own, different customs. In my country we do everything scientifically, calculatedly. In any industry, we calculate the cost for each item and we examine whether that cost is inevitable from the overall perspective of that industry. And if we find that it's not inevitable, we remove that item itself. For example, see: milk production is an industry. Is the calf inevitable for it? In the past, they had believed it was. But we learnt that it wasn't so, based on conclusions from modern scientific research. But then if we destroy all the calves, how will the stock of cows grow? Therefore, we preserve only that number of healthy calves required for breeding the stock and kill the rest of them. Else, what's the cost of all that grass that these remaining calves eat and needlessly waste?'

Venkataramana was watching her with raised eyebrows, in horror-filled astonishment. She continued after anticipating his response and getting none: 'But we don't slaughter calves without reason. They have another utility. Masticating animals have something called a fourth stomach. It's called a ruminant. We can obtain something called an enzyme from it. We need to add that in order to make cheese from milk.'

'How do you kill calves?' Venkataramana asked.

'The dairies which manufacture enzymes buy them from us and slaughter them. They might kill the calf by directly chopping its neck. Or they might kill it by caning it to death and then use its hide to manufacture soft footwear.'

'Meaning what?'

'Don't you know even that? They do it even in this country. I've heard that such factories exist in your Kanpur and other cities. The skin of tender calves is soft. It's securely tied to a peg and its body is beaten nonstop all over. Its skin swells up and blood oozes from its pores. By that time the calf might either die or it might still survive. But that's not important. After this, if the skin is peeled off raw and tempered, it'll be useful in making extremely soft footwear, bags, purses and other such items. But those are expensive products.'

Venkataramana couldn't fathom even in his imagination what she had just said, and he sat there as if bereft of speech. Then Jamal appeared there and said: 'Madam sahib, two cows have come to heat. Medicine must be given.'

'You might as well come with me,' said Hilda getting up. Venkataramana followed her. Hilda went to a room in the cowshed, opened the medicine chest, took out a thermometer, inserted it into the vagina of the cows that Jamal showed her, kept it there for a while, took it out, examined it and said: 'Yes, it's in heat. We need to give it the medicine so it gets pregnant. Go home and get me a tube from the refrigerator.'

'I've already brought it. I got it when I went to bring the toolkit.'

Hilda took the tube that he gave her and like an experienced doctor, filled half of its contents in a syringe. She inserted the syringe in the cow's vagina and filled it with the medicine. After repeating this procedure with the other cow, she told Jamal, 'Tie them up in their proper place.' She washed the syringe.

Venkataramana asked: 'What's this?'

'Didn't you understand something even this simple? These cows were in heat following their natural cycle. I administered them semen.'

Although she uttered these words with absolutely no embarrassment, Venkataramana found it tough to speak. Still, he asked: 'Why do you need to do this? Channe Gowda from the *Agrahara* maintains really virile bulls. He gives a bull for three rupees. Everyone in Kalenahalli has been sending their cows to Channe Gowda's bulls from time immemorial.'

Meanwhile, Hilda had opened the toolkit and was dismantling the motor of the milking machine. She said as she was working on it: 'That's a highly unscientific method. There's no guarantee that the cow will get pregnant through that method. Besides, we don't even know the breed of that bull! If the breed of cattle in this country needs to improve, you'll need to have superior-quality bulls. But then it's not profitable to use up all the semen of a bull on just one cow at a time. The government's department of animal husbandry imports the best breeds of bulls from New Zealand, extracts their semen, cultures and stores it in tubes like this. We got them four days ago and kept them in the refrigerator. We figured out from some symptoms that these two cows would be in heat very soon. Now I've administered it. Thanks to this procedure, you'll see for yourself the kind of stock that'll be born to these cows. If it's a female calf, you'll get to know in future the abundant milk that it'll yield after it grows up.'

Having said this, she removed the motor and examined its components. Her attention was now focussed on the internal architecture of the machine. Jamal also stood there watching it and trying to learn. Hilda said: 'Get the grease bottle. This needs to be wiped and refitted after applying grease.'

4

Venkataramana remained preoccupied thinking about these cows. Western countries take care of their cows in a scientific manner. Unlike the cows of Hindustan, they don't have the problem of malnutrition, they don't have troubles from epidemics, they aren't neglected. He had read this in an article in an English newspaper. But the picture that Hilda gave highlighted the appalling selfishness of those people. *No grass for cows that didn't give milk; they had no right to even live. Even the calf was unessential for milking the cow. They slaughter the calf to extract* some ingredient in its stomach and use it to make cheese. They spill its blood by beating it repeatedly with a cane, then skin it alive and make soft boots from it. They suck all the milk using that machine. If it's in heat they administer semen using a tube. It's unprofitable to get the bull to climb on it._ His eyes suddenly veered in the direction of her pregnant stomach. But in an instant, he shifted his gaze elsewhere.

Kalinga has implemented all these techniques in his own cowshed through this wife. These cows have been deprived of their natural joy of motherhood that comes from feeding milk to their own babies; neither do they have the pleasure of being joined by a bull when they're in their season. Venkataramana walked some distance and looked at the faces of the tethered cows. To his eyes, they appeared merely as brutes, nothing else. He was instantly reminded of the Elder Gowda's barn. To the Elder Gowda, cows were akin to his own mother, and calves were like his little brothers and sisters. Just like the milk in the breast of a human mother flowed only for her infants, the milk in the breast of a cow flowed only for her calves. The Elder Gowda's profound conviction was that a cow had to be given nutritious food so that it gave abundant milk and only after its calf had its fill, could humans milk the remainder. And just as the breast of a human mother would go dry after her infant died and until a new one was born, no one could milk a cow whose calf had died.

Venkataramana stepped closer and observed the food trough in front of each cow—these were marked with numbers—1, 2, 3, and so on. An aluminium badge with a number was tied around the neck of each cow and these numbers—on the badge and the food trough— matched. There was a bunch of paper charts on the wall above every trough, resembling case histories kept beside a patient in a hospital. Venkataramana examined one. The date on which the cow delivered, the quantity of milk that it gave daily and other related details were recorded there. In the Elder Gowda's time, each cow had a real name like Ganga, Gowri, Tunga, Bhadra, Kamadhenu, Sita and Savitri. Each cow was a Goddess on its own. But now in his grandson Kalinga's barn, each cow had become a mere number, and their supervision was in the hands of this foreign woman.

From where he was standing, Venkataramana stared at the Elder Gowda's grandson's wife. Although she uttered words such as semen, pregnancy and vagina purely in the context of cows, she had felt absolutely no sense of embarrassment while uttering them. Before his job at the school was made permanent, he had to go to the Taluk hospital for a medical check-up as was required by the government's law. The doctor had asked him similar questions and had also examined his private parts. He had endured sheer embarrassment. But then, at any rate, he was a doctor. He was also reminded of his biology lessons in high school. The teacher too, had uttered such words nonchalantly in the name of science. But shouldn't this wife of Kalinga have any sense of shame? Perhaps this was all science for her as well? He looked at her yet again. She had closed the top of the motor and was tightening the screw. Perhaps everything was indeed science in her eyes! Had Kalinga not gone abroad, and even if, perchance he hadn't married this lady, perhaps then the *punya* of the Elder Gowda's barn would've remained intact. It wouldn't have been eroded like this. 'When a person marries a lady, he also marries her beliefs.' He recalled reading this maxim printed on the top of the editorial page in an English newspaper.

They slaughter infant calves in the Western countries. That practice hasn't started yet in this barn. Had it been left solely to this woman's regime, maybe she'd have done it already! In the Western countries, nobody wants cattle for agriculture. But in this country, they do. We get money here by selling a calf that's just a year old. Else, this husband–wife duo would've killed all the calves! Venkataramana blazed with contempt. His stomach churned with nausea.

Presently, Hilda came there: 'What're you thinking? Come, let's go sit by the pond and talk.'

What was left to talk with her? He thought. He stood there saying nothing. 'Come, it looks like you're thinking something profound. Please share that with me. One shouldn't monopolize one's thoughts,' she said and tugged at his hands. Although he withdrew his hands, he followed her. After he sat down on the same bench as before, Hilda sat even closer than before and asked: 'Tell me, what were you thinking?'

He said nothing.

'Won't you tell me?'

'There's nothing to say.'

'See, now you're angry,' she placed her right hand on his shoulder and said in an affectionate tone: 'Friends should never get angry. Look at your face. Are you a small child that you're behaving like this? You come here very rarely. Why do you do this each time you visit us? Don't we deserve even a single person we can call a friend?'

When he heard these words of friendly warmth, Venkataramana's fury lit up like fire. He said: 'What kind of affection should I have for a person like you who belongs to the class of savages? You say that we need to debate and resolve any differences of opinion that may arise. We've been debating since the time we first met each other. There's been absolutely no change in your lifestyle and beliefs since then. In your eyes, a debate is simply another way of killing your boredom. Cruelty to animals doesn't prick your conscience even one bit. You, your race, your life-purpose, all these are thoroughly barbaric. You're crueller than tigers and hyenas! You're completely undeserving of human friendship.'

Meanwhile Jamal came there and asked, 'Shall I take the toolkit and go home?'

'Hmmm, yes, go,' Hilda sent him away. The evening had drowned, and darkness was falling. But Hilda listened with an amused smile as Venkataramana spoke in a derisive tone: 'Kalinga is a wretched sinner who hasn't upheld the honour of his ancestors' Dharma and Karma. And, *you* are a haughty woman who doesn't follow the customs and traditions of the home you've made as your own. Both of you belong to the home of that revered and noble soul, the Elder Gowda, but you are wrecking all his *punya*!'

'How do we belong to his home, Your Holiness?' she asked laughing mischievously. 'We've built a house outside the village amidst this forest and we're labouring hard to feed ourselves.'

'Look, I'm not talking to you to either poke fun at you or to become a laughing stock myself. I've now completely understood the exact perspective with which you view the cow and the appalling condition you've reduced it to. You proudly say that no cow in your country goes hungry. Even our papers here write the same thing. But here's the thing:

S.L. BHYRAPPA

half of the people in Hindustan live on half-full stomachs. It isn't a big problem even if God bestows this same fate both on humans and cattle in the future as well. Let our cattle perish of starvation. But it'll be enough if this depraved mentality doesn't arise in the minds of the people of this country... that cows are born only to satisfy the human's selfish need for food and the milk in its breast is meant only to fill its miserable stomach.'

'And what's going to happen if it does arise in their minds?'

'What's going to happen? The soul of this country will be decimated. Dharma and Karma will be pulverized.'

'Can you tell me in detail how that'll happen, Your Most Exalted Holiness?' she asked in a teasing tone.

Venkataramana didn't notice that. He said: 'What do you think that a cow exactly represents? It's the symbol of the entire cosmos. All the Gods and Goddesses who carry out and monitor the various activities of the cosmos reside in the cow. Brahma and Vishnu reside in the base of its horns. All the holy rivers lie on the tips of its horns. The Sun and the Moon in its two eyes, the Wind in its teeth, the Rain in its tongue; Saraswati, the Goddess of Learning in the *hoom* sound it makes, the Sunrise and Sunset in its two lips, the Four Dharmas in its four legs, the Sacred Ganga in its urine, the Four Seas in its teats, and a God each in the hair on its body making a total of thirty-three crore Gods. That's the reason the Rishis have said:

Vikrayaartham hi yo himsyaad bhakshayed vaa nirankushah
Ghaatayaanam hi purusham y Enumanyeyurarthinah
Ghaatakam Khaadak O vaapi tathaa yashcaanumanyate
yaavanti tasyaar Omaa Ni taavad varshaa Ni majjati

Meaning: whoever sells a cow for either eating or slaughtering it, or the one who gives permission for such a sale, such persons will drown in a special type of hell for as many years as there are hairs on the cow's body!'

'Really?' Hilda asked, showing her surprise.

'What else did you assume?' he asked in a firm tone.

Hilda guffawed loudly once in that serene night and asked: 'The imagination behind what you just told me is just fantastic. If we regard the cow as the symbol of the cosmos, then its organs will represent the Gods and Goddesses mentioned in your Puranas. But, why should that symbol be only the cow? Why can't it for example, be a dog or a buffalo?'

Venkataramana was infuriated by this question. He said standing up: 'What I'm telling you isn't as trivial as some joke that you seem to make it out. It's improper to even talk to you.' He turned to leave. But Hilda stood up, held both his shoulders and said, 'You cannot run away from a debate without giving an answer.' Apart from being embarrassed because she touched his shoulders this way, he was enraged as well. Still he controlled himself, sat again and asked: 'What's your debate?'

'You revere the cow as highly sacred, yet why do you treat the buffalo so pitilessly? Even I had been to this year's Maaramma fair. How many buffaloes were slaughtered there? What of the blood that flowed there, the fat that dripped from their bodies? The staggering number of animals slaughtered in the name of God or for pleasing that God—isn't this the other face of your religion? You claim that all animals are equal in *Ishwara's* creation. Yet, you gird yourself up to protect just one animal while being equally ready to slaughter another one. Why?'

Venkataramana couldn't think of an answer to this question. Still, he said: 'Look, that's the form of worship of the base people. The government itself has passed a law prohibiting animal slaughter, while offering puja to the deities. Animal slaughter hasn't been prescribed in the nobler Shastras. Still...' he remembered something and said: 'they slaughter the animal in the belief that it'll attain a Higher State.'

'My dear esteemed friend, do you realize the kind of bind you've now fallen into?' she questioned, looking at him decisively with twinkling eyes: 'You say yourself that that's the method of worship of the base people. But then why did you yourself sprinkle the Sacred Water on that deity and that fire and that chariot? It's true you weren't present when the slaughter occurred. But then even *you* took part in one of the facets of those festivities. So, no matter which facet you took part in and to whatever extent, you still must essentially bear the responsibility for all the lapses and errors of the entire process. Besides, you also just endorsed the government's law prohibiting animal slaughter in the name of God. Does this mean the government needs to interfere to reform your religious conceptions? You said that those people slaughter the animals out of a belief that they'll attain the Higher State. There's no answer stupider than that.'

As she was saying this, Hilda's voice had turned serious and towards the end, it was trembling with anger: 'You called me and my race barbaric. You first reform the barbarism within yourself and in your religion. Perhaps, only then will you earn the right to criticize another person's lifestyle.'

Venkataramana said instantly: 'Our fundamental view is always nobler. Every animal has the freedom to live. According to our belief, no animal has any sort of right over any other animal. Snakes and frogs, deer and tigers living together in mutual affection—this was the ideal of our forests where the rishis or the hermits performed penance. It's true that some base modes of worship involved the killing of goat and buffalo. That has ended starting this year. But you change your barbaric worldview that says that animals exist solely to fill the human's brutal belly. Till then it's meaningless to even talk with you.'

This time he simply stood up and walked away. Hilda immediately said: 'If non-vegetarian food is a sin, then all kinds of non-vegetarian is equally sinful. The people of your country eat goat, sheep, chicken and fish. But only the cow's flesh is prohibited. This is an illogical belief.' By this time Venkataramana was far away. The electric light was burning in the barn. Although there was a light pole near the pond, it hadn't been fitted with a switch. While it wasn't pitch dark outside, it was still sufficiently dark. Hilda yelled after him: 'Look, the servants in the barn have left for dinner. They'll return by nine. A lady, I'm all alone. How do I get home? I sent Jamal away because you'd be there with me. Won't you drop me home?'

'Where's the question of fear for blood-thirsty people like you? There's no need for me to accompany you,' he yelled back and trod forward. Hilda stood there for a minute looking in his direction with blazing eyes. Then she walked slowly to the barn, took the torch from the inner room and holding it in her hand, locked the main door and left all alone.

Then she saw someone walking towards her. She shone the torch ahead. It was Venkataramana. 'Come, I'll drop you home and then go home,' he said.

'Thanks. I don't need you. Please leave,' she said brusquely. He stood there quietly for half a minute and then walked away briskly.

5

Hilda's mind was consumed by anger like a serpent's hiss. Each time she and Venkataramana had spoken, it had always culminated in some argument, but in the end, they had always been able to recognize the differences in their opinions. And, no matter how many differences had arisen, Hilda had developed a sense of warmth towards him without her knowledge. She had felt a certain attraction towards the sheer force of his personality. But today all that had dried up and was replaced with contempt. Instead of debating with her patiently and then returning home, he had repeatedly berated her and her race as barbaric.

She couldn't sleep that night. So far, she had found the beliefs, customs and manners of the people of this country bizarre. Now they all appeared hypocritical. She got up at six in the morning and called out to Jamal and said: 'Look, I need some really good meat today.'

'Karim sent some last evening. Did it spoil?'

'No, that's not what I'm saying. I need the meat of a young cow.'

'Where do I get that sahiba?'

'In our barn. Get me a young cow. You kill it here and bring me its meat. Look, the servants talk about some Punyakoti cow. Bring me a young one from among that lot.'

Meanwhile, Jamal's wife arrived. She could understand Hilda's broken Kannada. She said: 'Amma ji, please don't do such things. Even if one person gets to know this, they'll dig up ditches and bury all of us.'

Jamal endorsed this and said: 'You don't know these Hindu people. They might remain quiet even if you kill one of them. But, if you kill a cow, all of them together will descend on you. Karim—the guy who supplies us meat, he killed a cow once during the Ramzan festival.

The news spread in town after eight days. All the men charged in and burnt down his house. If he hadn't run away in secret, they would've finished him off as well.'

But Hilda said in a tone of finality: 'I don't care how. I need it today at any cost. Go now and get me a cow. Nobody'll know here. Declare a holiday for the servants today if you must.'

As if she understood everything now, Jamal's wife said, her face beaming with a smile: 'Look, *Amma ji* has completed five months now. She's got the *khwaish*, the craving to eat it now. In her country, she was used to happily eat it every day.'

Jamal said yes and left for the barn. He strode quickly on the ridge that cut through the tobacco plants and reached the barn. He was supposed to have already been there, supervising the milking of the cows. The servants had already got everything ready when he reached. The moment he reached, he had the milk sucked out from each cow using the machine. He measured the milk, poured it in the cans and had them sent through the servants to the bus stop. The bus arrived and departed in fifteen minutes. To the rest of the servants, he announced, 'Go wherever you want. A holiday has been declared today. Tell the others that today there's no farm work as well,' and sent them all away. He told them that one of them had to come in the afternoon to take care of the grass and water for the cattle.

After everyone had left, Jamal untied a cow of the Punyakoti stock from its trough and led it out. It was the mother of a first calf, a new mother—only four months had elapsed since it had delivered. Its female calf had been tied separately to a peg near which it was lying down and watching its mother go. Looking in the direction of its baby, the mother followed Jamal, mooing.

By the time he got the cow, Hilda was already restless and fidgeting, waiting for him. It was past eight in the morning. There was a stone slab in Jamal's shed. On numerous occasions in the past, he had slaughtered tender sheep, goat and chicken there and after sorting their flesh, he had taken it in a plate and placed it on Hilda's kitchen table. Even now, he dragged the cow directly inside his shed. Not only was this place new to the cow, it was an atmosphere with no one around. It had never been alone till now. Jamal forcibly yanked it inside. Unaccustomed to opposing anything, it meekly submitted itself to his wrenching. Hilda was standing right there. Her two-and-a-half year-old son Jack was standing right behind her. Jamal's wife was standing at the door of her kitchen.

Jamal removed the rope tied to the cow and with it, made a catch around its four legs, then tossed it to Hilda and asked her to tug. When she yanked at it, he held both its horns and turned them. The cow which didn't even know how to resist, simply rolled over and fell down. He joined its four legs together and bound the hoofs tightly like a farrier does. The cow which fell down with the wail of *Ambaaa*, was now rolling its eyeballs all around, casting a look of utter helplessness. Jamal's wife went inside and returned with water in an aluminium vessel and a sharp knife. Jamal poured the water on the cow's neck, 'Get me a basin', he told his wife. When he pushed the basin under its neck, it screamed loudly. Jamal instructed his wife to hold its horns. She held them and stepped on it. Chanting 'Bismillah', he placed the knife in his right hand under its neck and sliced the vein across in one smooth motion. At that very moment, they heard the sound of the massive bell ringing from the temple on top of the hill. Jamal's hands trembled and his face broke out into a sweat.

The vein in the cow's neck had been cut and blood was gushing forth and spilling into the basin. In tandem with the loud sound of the temple bell, the cow emitted a high-pitched shriek just once. But its tongue which had come out remained hanging outside. After trying twice in vain to move its bound legs, it went quiet. By this time the basin was filled with blood and was spilling over; the cow's eyes had gone still and its sagging tongue had gone motionless.

Jamal said, thoroughly frightened: 'Madam, I'm scared listening to the bell's sound. If that pujari comes this way, what's going to be our fate?'

'He won't come to this house ever again. Don't worry.' As Hilda said this, her gaze naturally turned towards Jack, standing next to her. Jack wasn't crying. But he was shivering in fear. She immediately lifted him up and told him in her mother tongue, 'Why're you shivering like this, my baby? There's nothing to fear. Shhh... my child, quiet now,' she hugged him tight. But he still didn't stop shivering. She came outside carrying him. Nobody was around. She looked in the direction of the temple. She didn't see anyone. *That pujari must be standing inside, pasting flowers on that stone idol,* she thought. Then Jamal's wife came outside and said: 'The blood has drained out completely. He's asking whether he should cut the flesh.'

'You carry him,' she said, and handed Jack over to her. Entering Jamal's shed, Hilda closed the door so that nobody could come in. The blood completely drained, only the dead body of the cow lay there sleeping. Jamal had untied the rope on its legs. He watched her face.

She asked: 'Jamal, the pujari told me yesterday, have you heard? It seems the Sun and the Moon are in the cow's eyes. It seems the Four Seas are present in its teats. It seems there are thirty-three crore Deities in different parts of its body.'

'Yes madam, Hindus say that.'

'There, take that knife and gouge out its eyes, chop off its teats. Cut each organ one at a time. Let's see which Deities reside where!'

Jamal lifted his neck up and looked at her face to check whether she was joking or serious. Her face appeared severe. 'Why're you silent? What're you looking at my face for? Just do what I said. Or give me the knife. I'll cut it and check,' she said, and in the next moment, snatched the knife from the stone slab near him and pierced the cow's eyes. Then she poked its teats and slashed at it so that its udder tore away. She stabbed its stomach and checked. Lines of sarcasm appeared on her face for a minute and then she said to herself in her mother tongue: 'Duffers. Uncivilized, unscientific duffers! There's no scientific evidence for their beliefs.'

Jamal didn't understand what she spoke. She tossed the knife in her hand on the cow's body, opened the door and went out.

Jamal's wife was carrying Jack and ambling around. Jack had gone quiet now. Taking him with her, Hilda went inside her house and lay down on the sofa. She was completely exhausted. She hadn't had her breakfast or coffee; neither was she in a mood to take it now. When Jamal's wife came there a half hour later, she said: 'Look, I can't cook today. You get all that here and cook. But I'll teach you the method. Don't add the masala like your cooking.'

'Ok *Amma ji*. But so much of *gosht*, beef, is there. We can't eat all of that. What do we do with the rest?'

'Tell him to retain what's enough for all of us and give the rest away to someone', she said, then thought for a minute and said: 'Look, Jamal anyway goes to Karim's shop on his cycle to buy eggs. All these days Karim was giving us meat. Tell Jamal to give *him* meat today. Let everybody in his family eat—his wife, kids, grandkids. If he wants to make money by selling it, let him do that.'

By afternoon, Jamal's wife had finished cooking a meal made with the cow's meat. By then Jamal had also returned home. His wife took enough for both of them, closed the utensils, and went home. Later, Hilda went inside with Jack and sat for lunch. But she couldn't eat. There was no error in the cooking procedure. Jamal's wife had followed Hilda's instructions accurately. But by the time she ate two or three spoons, Hilda felt she had had enough. She hadn't had the opportunity to eat a meal with beef even once since she had flown in from America and landed in Mumbai and arrived here by train. Today, she had desired to eat beef till her stomach burst, owing to some fury unknown to herself. She had also consumed an ounce of liquor half an hour ago so that she could eat more. But how did this happen?

Jack ate his meal and got up. She got up as well, closed the lid over the utensils and wiped the table. Suddenly, she felt an unbearable sense of loneliness. Kalinga would return this evening, or maybe tomorrow. Even after so many days here, not a single friend in this country. She went in and lay down on the bed. Jack slumbered next to her.

But Kalinga came home at two that very afternoon. He had placed the order for the van that he had selected. The dealer had told him that he would deliver it within a year. It was troublesome to get even a motor vehicle in this country.

At lunch, Kalinga asked: 'What's this, the food tastes different today?'

'You tell me what it might be.'

He rolled the morsel several times in his mouth and asked: 'Beef. Where'd this come from?'

'Karim sent it.'

'A hugely courageous adventure. He won't survive if somebody gets to know. Send him a message asking him to never send it again.'

'Why, did you also develop these restrictions of dharma after you returned to this country, my dear?'

'It's not a question of d'harma. Yes, it's very tasty. But if they come to know that we're eating this, people in the neighbouring villages will be outraged and might do something. It's not a shrewd thing to do business wise.'

Hilda fell silent. Again, she was enveloped by a feeling of loneliness. Kalinga observed her sombre face and asked: 'Darling, why're you dull? It looks like you've not even eaten. Right?'

'Hmm. I couldn't.'

'Come, eat with me', he held her shoulders and seated her on the chair next to him. He handed her a set of spoon and fork and slid his plate between them. Both began to eat from the same plate. She was able to eat now. She said: 'If you hadn't come now, I'd have continued to starve my dear. I am able to eat only after you have returned.'

'That's natural. The women of this country don't eat until their husband has had his meal. The same thing happened to you.'

'Do you really think I belong to this country, my dear?'

'Why do you doubt it?'

'Nothing. Thank you. Thank you... very much', she said and filled the plate with another round of serving.

VOLUME 14

1

Notwithstanding how furtively Jamal did his work, news reached Kalenahalli within evening. From the moment Kalinga built a new barn and carted off the cattle, several folks in the village had begun to suspect that he'd commit cow slaughter. They had conveyed this suspicion to every single servant who worked under him and had instructed them to spy on him. The instruction had chiefly originated from Tayavva herself. The servants kept a mental record of the total number of cows in the barn, the number of calves they had delivered and other such details.

When the servant came in the afternoon to give grass and the new nutritious food to the cows, he noticed that one cow was missing. He informed another servant. When he ran and told this to Hilda, she said, 'It must've wandered off, go search.' When the same servant went to Jamal's shed and questioned him, he said, 'We've sold it.' But when he asked, 'But its calf is right there,' Jamal displayed his anger saying, 'Why do you want to know all that? Shut the crap up and leave.' The servant was suspicious now. Also his nose detected the stink of fresh blood and raw flesh. Jamal's wife had stored a sizeable amount of meat for tomorrow in her kitchen. The servant came out without a word. Jamal went inside his shed for lunch.

Meanwhile, another servant observed that a large ditch had been dug up at a spot in the farm with something buried in it. The patch of earth over the covered ditch was strewn with grass that was cut from the ridge. The servant ensured that he had not been spotted going in the direction and with careful steps, climbed the slope of the kalyani and reached the road. Then he turned left, went to the barn and informed another servant there what he'd seen. After serving grass, and the flour in the sack to the rest of the cows, both of them sprinted to the village. They'd never fathomed something like cow slaughter till now. Now it had occurred right in the Elder Kalinga Gowda's own barn. They've slaughtered and eaten the Punyakoti cow, which was the special preserve of the Elder Gowda's lineage.

Tayavva still hadn't eaten the afternoon's ragi *mudde*. When both of them informed her what had happened, her heart began to thump wildly. She signalled to them to get Yangata Gowda. He had gone to the fields. The servants went there, conveyed the matter and brought him along. The Gowda summoned ten prominent members of the village. When they were joined by the women and children of the village, it transformed itself into a large assembly. Honna who had come to Kalenahalli on some errand learned of the matter. He went to his Master Venkataramana's school in the *Agrahara* and informed him. Venkataramana let off the last period midway and came running to Kalenahalli.

When he reached, the assembly was in progress, animated with great commotion. Several folks discussed the important question that is the exact punishment to be meted out to someone who slaughtered a cow. One of them said that a fine of a thousand rupees had to be paid in the presence of the entire village. 'What's thousand rupees for those bastards, my man? He'll shut his arsehole up and pay any amount we demand. We need to do something more severe,' said another guy. When they saw that Venkataramana had arrived, the members appointed him as their head, offered him a seat, and asked him the question as to the nature of punishment that should be given to a cow slaughterer. Yangata Gowda's son Maata said: 'What's there to ask the Revered *Jois*? Isn't it said in the "Devi Mahatme" play that one who kills the cow must be killed? That's the punishment.'

But this punishment couldn't be implemented. The country's government, police and court have different rules now. Meanwhile, another guy said: 'You can do nothing to them. They have a gun. That Red Lady herself shoots the gun. And careful, that Muslim has a knife and dagger and all.'

At this point, the feverish heat in the hearts of the assemblage decreased a notch. 'I'll see what she can pluck from me using that gun,' said Maata pounding his chest. Tayavva who was quiet till then, shook her hands in Maata's direction applauding him.

Now Venkataramana spoke. Everybody listened to him in silence:

'We need to correctly understand what might've occurred. It's true, a cow is missing from there. They might've sold it. Let's go and ask, "Who have you sold it to?" It's their responsibility to show us the cow. If they don't show it, then we can conclude that they've slaughtered it. Let's also dig up that spot on the earth where they've buried it. One more thing: Kalinga isn't in town. That means it's his wife who's got this done.' When he said these words, he recalled the long and bitter conversation he had had with her yesterday. But he didn't reveal the incident and continued: 'Without Kalinga's presence, what can we do going there?'

'No. He arrived by the afternoon's motor. I saw it,' said one of them.

'Then let's all go. We'll ask him justice and get his wife to admit her sin and make her atone by consuming the *panchagavya*. They must pay a fine of one thousand rupees to the village. Another thing. They use the water of the *kalyani* of the Punyakoti temple for their tobacco field. Both husband and wife swim in the *kalyani*. I'd told them earlier not to do that sort of thing. They won't listen. They think the *kalyani* is their personal property. We'll discuss that matter as well and get their water pump removed. Nobody should dip even their feet in the water meant for the deity's worship. Given this, can they swim in it?'

'That's correct,' said everybody in unison and stood up.

'And if they don't listen, we need to pound those whoresons born to philanderers with a bludgeon,' Maata thundered with valour.

'Don't start a fight unnecessarily,' Venkataramana said loudly and joined them. Although nobody vocalized it, they allowed Venkataramana and Yangata Gowda to take the lead. The women and children of the village followed the men. Tayavva who was part of the group of women, was speaking with them using hand gestures. She wept in between and wiped her tears with the edge of her sari.

2

By the time they all descended from the hillside and neared the farmhouse, there was still evening light. When Jamal's wife saw so many people at once, she informed Hilda. Hilda came outside and watched: more than two hundred men, women and children descending in groups. Her subconscious instantly detected the fact that the villagers knew that she had ordered the cow slaughter. But betraying nothing, she asked Venkataramana, who was in front, in English: 'Are these guys in their senses? They're walking right over the tobacco plants.'

But, Yangata Gowda answered instead: 'You've killed the cow. We've come here to bring you to justice. Where's your husband? Call him.'

Hilda understood this. She replied in Kannada: 'Who gave you the right to enter our farm?'

The valorous Maata who was right behind his father yelled: 'You bloody whore, you dare give an asshole's reply when we demand justice? Call your goddamn husband!'

Venkataramana turned to Maata and said: 'Maata, you shouldn't use vulgar language. Be quiet now.' But Maata didn't listen. 'You think it'll work if we use polite language with such slutty bitches?' he asked.

Although she couldn't fully comprehend it, Hilda could deduce that he had uttered filthy obscenities. She stood ramrod straight and said decisively: 'You must all get out right now. Else I'll need to take out my gun and fire.'

'Look, he's still a young boy, and hasty. That's not important. Now sit for negotiations. Where's Kalinga? Call him,' Venkataramana said.

'There's no need to call him. I got the cow slaughtered. You don't have the right to question it.'

These words instantly incited the entire crowd. Some of them standing at the rear lobbed clumps of earth in the direction of the house. One of the clumps hit Hilda's shoulder with severe force. Venkataramana and Yangata Gowda turned around to pacify the crowd. Meanwhile, Hilda had gone inside. Kalinga wasn't home. For a second, she felt like crying. But she regained her composure in an instant, went into the bedroom and took the gun that hung there. She checked if it was loaded, came out and taking aim at the crowd, said: 'All of you disperse *now*. Else, I'll press the trigger.'

The moment they saw the gun, several folks began to run in panic. But those who were standing right in front remained standing. Tayavva who had been standing at the rear with the group of women, now came forward and stood beside Venkataramana, who yelled, saying: 'Don't threaten us with the gun. Are you aware of the consequences?'

Hilda pointed the gun towards the sky and shot a bullet. Those who had already scattered were mortally scared now. Those standing in front trembled as well. In a flash, Venkataramana moved, gripped her hands and called out to Maata. Maata, his father, Tayavva and others ran forward and held her. By then Kalinga, who came running from the side of the house, parted his way through them, rushed in and snatched the gun. Jamal came behind him. Kalinga had been to the barn. When he spotted from afar this mass of people descending the hill towards the farm, he had arrived here in great hurry. By the time Hilda's first bullet had been discharged, he'd already reached the flank of the house.

Unaware of anything, he said: 'What's all this Venkataramana?'

Yangata Gowda said: 'This is the bastard who asks this question now! He knows how to clean the whole world but pretends he doesn't know what's happening in his own backyard! You're asking what *this* is, you whoreson born to a debauch?'

Although this kind of language wasn't uncommon in rustic conversation, nobody had ever used it to his face directly like this. He felt humiliated. But, summoning patience, he asked: 'I honestly don't know anything. First tell me what it is.'

Venkataramana said: 'This morning, you've slaughtered a cow in your barn and you've eaten it. All the village folk have arrived now to demand justice for it.'

Kalinga instantly recalled the beef meal that he was served in the afternoon. With it he deduced everything that could've occurred as a consequence. He held his wife's hands and shoulders and asked: 'Hilda, tell the truth. Everything that happened. Don't lie.'

Already boiling with humiliation, the tears now freely streamed down from her eyes. But she straightened up and said defiantly: 'That's right, I got it slaughtered. None of them have the right to question *my* slaughtering of the cows of *my* barn or *my* eating it. I ordered Jamal to slaughter it and got it cooked.'

She said this much and went inside the house. The crowd's attention now turned to Jamal. But then he was already racing across the top of the field. Kalinga thought to himself for a minute and then addressed the village elders standing in front: 'I honestly was unaware of this. Now what's happened has happened. You tell me what needs to be done.'

Meanwhile, the people who had scattered hearing the gunshot now returned and formed a group. Maata and two other strongmen were in pursuit of Jamal. The headman Yangata Gowda asked everyone to sit down. After Kalinga had also sat down before them, Yangata Gowda said: 'You and your wife, both of you must take the *panchagavya*. You must pay a fine of one thousand rupees in the presence of the entire village. You must remove that pump machine that you've put to the temple's *kalyani*.'

'I'll give you the one thousand. The *panchagavya* pertains to each person's belief system. I might take it. But how can you force it on her? She's from a different *jati*.'

'How can her *jati* become different when she is married to you?' Yangata Gowda asked.

'Let's not discuss the issue of *jati* now. She just won't agree to it.'

'If she won't agree, sock it to her properly and get her to agree. Aren't you born to a man or what?'

Kalinga didn't respond to this. He asked: 'Why should I remove the pump at the *kalyani*? How's that related to this?'

'That *kalyani* was built for the deity's worship. How can you draw its water for your personal use?'

'I definitely have the right to use the water of the *kalyani* built by my grandfather. It's a well on my own land.'

Now Venkataramana spoke: 'You have a right over the self-earned property of your grandfather. But you have no right over something that he's given away as Dharma, as charity. Had your grandfather been alive, even he would have no right over it. The Shastras have declared as such.'

In a gesture endorsing this statement, Tayavva made a fist with her right hand and pounded it on her left palm. Yangata Gowda added: 'Your grandfather gave money only to the stoneworkers. Have you even bothered to find out who all got their bullock and oxen carts, who all laboured hard for building this? This work was done by the entire village.'

'What's the loss to the temple if I draw water from the *kalyani*?'

Venkataramana said: 'Look, you've argued this matter with me several times in the past. And I've given a just response based on the evidence of the Shastras. Don't ask the same thing repeatedly.'

Then the three guys who'd gone to apprehend Jamal returned. Blood was flowing from the shoulder of one. Maata who was holding a dagger in his hand stepped close and said: 'We chased that whoreson. We'd almost caught him just outside the road. Bastard took out this dagger from his underwear pocket and slashed it at us. It landed on Putta's shoulder. He started whining *Ayyyayyoo*. So we turned this way, and he scampered away. We couldn't see him in the dark.'

Kalinga went inside and returned with water, boric powder, tincture and cotton bandages and washed the wound, applied medicine and dressed it. The gash wasn't very deep. The three of them now sat near the Panchayat. Venkataramana said to Kalinga: 'Look, don't argue in this matter. Just remove the pump from the *kalyani*.'

After thinking for ten minutes, Kalinga said: 'Ok, I'll remove it. It might cost me about ten thousand rupees to dig a new well. That's not a big amount for me. But till the new well gets ready, what'll be the fate of this tobacco crop? So, I'll take this out after the new well is set.'

Venkataramana thought that was an acceptable solution. He was about to say yes when Yangata Gowda said: 'Doesn't work that way. You've to remove it *right away*. If you want water, get it from the well in your barn.'

But the well in the barn was at a slightly lower elevation compared to the farm. While calculating the height of the overhead tank, they hadn't factored in the possibility of pumping that water to the farm. Still, Kalinga reached a decision. The tank at the barn was an iron tank. If they raised the elevation of the structure beneath, its height would automatically increase and water could then be pumped to the farm. But a pipe had to be laid from underneath the road. This could be completed in the next eight or ten days.

When he said, 'Fine. I'll get it removed tomorrow', none in the group agreed. 'Pull it out now, come on.'

A deep sense of humiliation and helplessness filled Kalinga. But with foresight and patience, he got up, went inside his house and returned with a toolkit and crowbar and said: 'Come, you must also help me.'

A few strongmen including Yangata Gowda followed him. The electric light fitted to the pole was burning. He began unscrewing each nut and bolt of the machine. After removing them all, the strongmen carried down each part of the machine according to Kalinga's instructions. After this was done, they shifted everything to the tractor shed. The strongmen then broke the cement platform built for the pump using the crowbars.

Midnight had passed by the time all this was complete. Darkness had enveloped everywhere like a cave. By then the groups of women and children had returned to the village.

Kalinga went inside and returned with currency notes totalling one thousand rupees and placed it in Yangata Gowda's hand. The group dispersed after informing him that the husband and wife must come to the temple tomorrow morning and take the *panchagavya*.

3

Scared of staying alone in the shed, Jamal's wife lay wide awake in the veranda of Hilda's house. Hilda, too was lying on the bed awake, roasting in humiliation.

After everyone had left, and her husband came in and closed the door, Hilda said: 'You behaved like an absolute coward today.'

'What else should I have done?'

'Half the crowd had scattered after I fired one air shot. The other half would've scampered at the sound of the second one.'

'They wouldn't have gone. Didn't they fall on you and grab the gun from your hand?'

'What'd happen if I'd shot the group in self-defence?'

'All of us would've gone to the noose. Tell me, is it wise to act rashly in such matters?'

'Still, my dear, you behaved like a coward. Is there no police or government in this country? Why did you dismantle the pump and motor just because they asked you to?'

'Will the police guard us round the clock, at all times? You don't understand how villages here work. If they get all pumped up in outrage, they'll come here and annihilate the entire crop we've grown over a year in just one night. Which police will come here and guard us all year long? What did we lose by letting that *kalyani* go? It might cost us another ten or twelve thousand rupees. I'll cancel the van order tomorrow. We'll dig another pond or well. In any case, this nuisance ended just at this!'

'But you let me down, my dear, you didn't safeguard my respect.'

Kalinga felt slighted by this accusation. He had patiently borne all the defeats that he had experienced since evening and had behaved with transactional pragmatism. Now, enraged at his wife's denouncement, he said: 'What should I have done to safeguard your respect? Weren't you aware of the conditions in this place? And knowing it fully, why did you get that cow slaughtered?'

'Oh, that *pujari* provoked me. You simply can't imagine the kind of torture I've undergone since last evening!' she began to sob nonstop.

He lifted her head up, placed it on his chest and pacifying her, asked: 'Why, what happened?'

'He had come here yesterday for something. He came to the barn with me. He saw the cows being milked with the machine. "Where's the milk for the calves? As a woman, don't you understand its significance?" he asked me. I told him about how calves are killed in our country to extract enzymes. He admonished me saying I'm uncivilized, that my entire race is barbaric and said other nasty things. Then he said that there were Gods and Goddesses in every organ of the cow's body, and warned me and left. Tell me who can bear this kind of insult? I got a cow slaughtered this morning and examined its organs.'

'Did your insult vanish with that?'

'I can't say that. But I did experience a sort of relief.'

Kalinga didn't speak. His face creased as if this was his fate and he closed his eyes. Hilda too, closed her eyes and reclined, her head now on his lap. Her attention now drifted to her stomach which felt heavy. Then she suddenly said: 'Dear, please don't feel bad about what I'm saying. I've endured loneliness since the day I came to this country. And since yesterday, this loneliness has been throttling me and eating my individuality from within. And this evening, after you sacrificed my honour because you were sacred of the hooliganism of that group of savage, vicious brutes, I really feel I have no one to turn to, that I'm just a helpless, forlorn woman in this vast and unknown country.'

Kalinga's heart rued at her plight when he heard these words. He hugged her once, kissed her and said: 'Why do you say this, darling? You shouldn't ever get this feeling as long as I'm here. We just need to be a little shrewd in this atmosphere.'

She felt comforted to some extent. Embracing him, she said: 'I left my country just for you. I married you from a romantic zeal that I'll go to another country and grow gold in the barren land of that country using all my knowledge and my science. But when I come here, I see that apart from the earth and the water, no one here likes me.'

'Am I not there?'

'Yes, you are. I'm living only for you. I'm working only for your sake. In this farm surrounded by unknown, friendless villages, it's just the two of us grieving souls who truly love each other,' she said, getting up and then stepping outside the mosquito net that was hung over the bed. She returned with a drink for him as well. They straightened the net and then slept in each other's arms. Jack was asleep in the other room. In a few minutes, sleep enveloped Hilda. But Kalinga simply couldn't get his eyes to close. All sorts of fantastic thoughts and memories were gnawing at his mind in small bites. Memories of village life during his grandfather's time came flooding. The *Gopuja* during Sankranti, the bull race during the *Kaaru* festival, the Friday pujas... all of these and other festivals floated up to the surface. The reverence his grandfather, grandmother and mother had towards the cow stood right before his eyes like a solid, physical image. Even his mother had come as part of the group earlier that evening. And when Yangata Gowda was speaking, she was vigorously nodding her head and pounding her right fist on her left palm as if those were her words. She stayed back, standing with the menfolk until the pump at the deity's *kalyani* was uprooted and hauled back here.

Suddenly the feeling that he was all alone in this world welled up within Kalinga. As the grandson of his grandfather who was the Village Gowda—the Headman—he could've worn the crown of the Village Gowda. But today, all the village folk had come here and extracted the punishment-fine from him. Tomorrow morning, they'll call him at the puja hour and make him drink the *panchagavya*. *I'm the medicine for*

Hilda's loneliness. But who's the solace for mine? Neither Hilda nor Jack. His gaze shifted to Hilda's belly, which was still growing. His mind didn't find an answer even there.

As he changed sides several times, immersed in thought, he heard the sound of crows cawing outside. He switched on the torch near him and looked at his watch—already five-thirty in the morning. Without waking up Hilda, he gently got up, slithered out from the mosquito net, got down from the bed and stepped out of the house. Outside, dawn had more or less broken. His sight turned in the direction of the temple's *kalyani*. The electric lamp on the wooden pole in its vicinity was still glowing. Now that pole had to be removed as well. He had to scout for a spot where the new well had to be dug, he thought as he walked in the direction of the barn. By then the morning light was clear. And the sight that greeted him left him stunned: All the tobacco plants in the entire farm had been plucked out, trampled upon, and strewn around wildly.

Completely enervated, he dragged his feet slowly as he walked along on the ridges. Apart from a few plants which weren't visible in the early morning light, the entire tobacco crop had been destroyed. A loss close to fifty thousand rupees.

When did they do this? After we slept? Or even as the pump was being removed, other folks were busy with this work? Why did they still do this even after he paid the punishment-fine, agreed to the panchagavya, and removed the pump? Had they pre-decided this? Or, was it an act born out of an on-the-spur inspiration? He examined the footprints. It was clear that even women and children had participated in this.

Like Hilda had said, it occurred to him to complain to the police. But what would that achieve? He could catch a few folks and get their hands shackled with cuffs as a warning so that other village folk wouldn't summon the guts to do something like this in future. But then to do that, who all did he need to catch? He went to the barn with this thought.

A different scene awaited him in the barn. The main door was broken wide open. The cows remained where they had been tethered last evening. Five cows and six calves were missing. There was no servant. At this hour, the cows had to be untied from their troughs and the milking should've started. But Jamal who was in charge of the milking machine was missing. Not a single servant was around either. Kalinga noted the numbers of the missing cows. They hadn't gone in any particular sequence. Then it occurred to him in a flash. All the missing cows belonged to the Punyakoti breed. There were a total of six cows of that breed in the barn. And including the one that Hilda and Jamal had slaughtered, all the six Punyakoti cows were now gone. *That means, they had killed the Punyakoti cow yesterday. Apart from the five cows and their calves, they've also taken the calf of the cow that died yesterday.* But, this wasn't an act of theft. After the pump was removed last night, his own mother has come here and untied the cows. His mind guessed that the Punyakoti stock was akin to her Family Deity.

There were no servants to assist in the milking. And he felt it was too tedious a task to wash and clean each teat and then milk them using the machine all by himself. So he decided that there would be no milk that day. The loss incurred from not milking this one time was nothing compared to last night's loss of fifty thousand from the destruction of his crop. With this thought, he untied four or five calves and was in the process of untying the rest. But when the calves ran to suckle at their mothers' udders, the cows, unable to withstand this, began to kick wildly. All the calves that he had untied were the first calving of their respective mothers. After giving birth, these young mother-cows had never been suckled by their calves. They had only been accustomed to licking the calf in front of them and releasing milk, which the rubber tubes sucked from them, like urine. But the calves hadn't lost their instinct to suckle.

Kalinga tethered the calves again. He brought the cows one by one and quickly fitted the machine's tubes and extracted milk from all the cows. He filled the cans which had been washed and kept ready, carried them to the road in three trips and delivered it to the motor at the appointed time. He left the cows in their places, locked the front door of the barn, and crossed the road. It was eight-thirty in the morning when he reached home, looking at the ruined tobacco plants along the way.

Jamal's wife had returned to her shed after waking up. Jack was playing in front of her shed. Hilda hadn't woken up yet. Kalinga's eyes were burning like coal from not sleeping the entire night. His limbs were losing their ability to balance. When he went to the bathroom to wash his face, he remembered: the tank which was built to supply water for home use was full. But after it would have been emptied by evening, they would need to carry water from either the *kalyani* or the barn. He abandoned the idea of a police complaint regarding last night's crop destruction. And apart from the barn, there were no servants who would work in the farm as well. Unless he cringed in supplication before the villagers, he wouldn't get a single servant. *What do I do with this farm now?*

When he came out after washing his face, he heard the sound of the bell ringing in the temple. A boy standing in front of the house and said: 'They say everybody has come to the temple, and you both husband and wife must come together.'

He sent the boy away telling him that they would come. Hilda wasn't awake yet. His mind told him that she wouldn't come even if he requested her. She would say that she wouldn't agree to this humiliating atonement even if it cost her her life. He pulled the front door shut, took Jack with him, and reached the temple from the side of the *kalyani*. When he saw the place where the water pump had been, his mind was overcome with sadness.

Venkataramana was cleaning the inner courtyard of the temple. Outside, there were ten people including Yangata Gowda, Maata and others. The moment he saw him, Yangata Gowda asked, 'You came alone, where's your wife?'

'She's sleeping, she had the chills and fever all night. Give it to me. I'll take it and make her drink.'

Venkataramana instantly understood the background to Kalinga's answer. But he remained quiet. Gowda too, didn't object to it. Venkataramana began the puja. Yangata Gowda asked Kalinga, 'Have you washed your body?' After he replied 'no', Yangata Gowda asked for a pot belonging to the temple and led Kalinga and his son to the bank of the *kalyani*. After Kalinga removed his khaki shorts and his son's night suit, Yangata Gowda poured three potsful of water in rapid succession on their heads. Wearing just a soaked underwear, Kalinga went up with his son, his bare body shivering and his arms crossed in front. He stood at the temple door. Yangata Gowda retrieved a block of *vibhuti* kept on top of the inner door and smeared his three fingers with it. Then he applied it on the foreheads of both father and son. On Jack's red forehead, the white *vibhuti* resembled the colour of dull ash.

The puja was over in thirty minutes. Then Venkataramana emerged chanting mantras. He first gave three spoonsful of *panchagavya* to Kalinga. After Kalinga touched it to his eyes and drank it, he had three more spoonsful poured into his palm and made Jack drink it. Jack gulped it down with an expression as if he was drinking medicine. After this, Venkataramana poured three additional spoonsful into a cup that he made from the *Palasha* leaf and gave Hilda's portion to Kalinga. Then everybody who had assembled there drank the *panchagavya*.

A grand *arati* was performed for the deity, which was then passed around to everybody along with the *tirtha*. After this, he distributed the *prasada*, a sweet delicacy of banana salad, in the *Palasha* leaf. Venkataramana too, took the *prasada*, came out and sat. Then, Kalinga asked Yangata Gowda: 'Didn't I follow everything that you told me yesterday? And as if that wasn't enough, why did you uproot my entire tobacco crop?'

'What tobacco crop, my man?' the Gowda asked, completely ignorant of what had happened.

'Not a single plant has been spared in the farm. They've chopped everything and chucked them around. Fifty thousand rupees gone. How much I'd spent for the seeds, manure, water, current! What did you gain from that?' Kalinga's voice had grown heavy when he said this.

'Who's that thieving bastard who pulled out those tender green plants? *Lei*, you're sitting in the deity's temple, you better speak the truth,' said Yangata Gowda looking at everybody.

The twelve-year-old boy who had gone to fetch Kalinga said: 'When you were all removing that machine at night, then all of us boys and the womenfolk plucked it out together.'

'*Thoo*! May your houses rot, whoresons!' cursed Yangata Gowda in a continuous stream: 'Who asked you to do that?'

'Nobody. The boys started to pluck, then the elders also joined.'

Kalinga asked: 'Who took the cows from my barn?'

'How many are gone?'

'Five cows. Six calves.'

'Your own mother. Yesterday your wife killed a Punyakoti cow and ate it. That's why your mother decided that it's not safe to trust the cows of that breed with you, and yesterday while going back from here, she went to the barn and untied them. We were with her.'

Kalinga didn't speak again. After all of them had eaten the *prasada*, he asked Yangata Gowda: 'All the servants are absconding. And now, how can I even do farming? I gave the thousand you asked. I pulled out the *kalyani* pump machine. I took the *panchagavya* now. As if that wasn't enough, a harvest of fifty thousand is gone. Should the servants also abandon me?'

'Don't worry now. You've taken the *panchagavya*. We'll send for them and make sure they come to work,' said Yangata Gowda, reassuring him. After Venkataramana closed the temple door and rang the bell in the courtyard, everyone left for their homes.

When Hilda saw the foreheads of her husband and son who returned home at about eleven, she said derisively: 'What, you went there to shamelessly admit that you were wrong? What's that in your hand? Did you get it for me?'

'Hmmm.'

'Do you know what's happened here? Jamal sent someone to fetch his wife because it was dangerous for her to stay here. She went away. She didn't say a word where she's going. Not a single tobacco plant in the entire farm has survived.'

'I know all that. There's not a single servant as well.'

'Listen to me, my dear,' she said, looping her arms around his neck and locking them there: 'Nobody's here for us in this country. Let's sell all this. Come, let's go to my country. We'll buy land there and do farming. Else, let's take up jobs.'

'No. The anger of the villagers has subsided now. They'll send the workers. We shouldn't lose hope. This crop's gone. Let's dig a new well and plant a new crop. We need to behave with these people with some tact. If you go to the temple once, everything will become normal.'

'Your tact will only make me lonelier, my dear. You can play with these people either out of tact or for whatever other reason. But I really can't tolerate this isolation.'

'Hilda, you must bear it. You need to adjust a bit to this atmosphere.'

'No, no, no. I can adjust only with death. Thanks to what you've done, the village folk now have a feeling that they've won. Sometime in the future, they won't hesitate to do this kind of stuff even for a trivial reason. You need to complain to the police now. We'll be unable to live unless we infuse some fear in them.'

Kalinga thought to himself for a while. It occurred to him that there was truth in her words.

1

It was five in the evening by the time Venkataramana got his salary from the treasury at the Taluk. The last motor had departed by then. Because it was also market day, three or four carts from the *Agrahara* had come there. When he enquired, he learnt that all of them would depart after nine in the night. The cart drivers had cooked and eaten food and were in the process of getting the cart ready. With nothing to do till then, Venkataramana went for a stroll.

A speech was in progress at the Taluk public grounds. About five thousand people had assembled to listen to the speech which was being broadcast from the loudspeaker. He went there and sat down at a random spot. The speaker was from north Hindustan. His words in Hindi were being translated by someone standing next to him into chaste Kannada. The topic was, 'The tradition of the cow in Bharata and the present state'. He described in scholarly detail quoting from the Vedas, Upanishads, the Puranas and other tracts as to how our people regarded the cow. Venkataramana more or less knew everything about the topics he was expounding and the *slokas* that he was quoting. But when he started to describe the condition of cows in India in the modern time, a whole new world that Venkataramana hadn't known hitherto appeared before him.

He was saying: 'Because the population increased, the government converted all pastures into arable land. The consequence: no grass was available for the cow. Thus, faced with the situation of paying money for grass and water, people developed a mentality of regarding milk and butter from an economic perspective.

Even some Muslim rulers had a tradition of not eating the flesh of the cow. But it was only after the onset of British rule that beef consumption has increased. Because they have a shortage of food in their country, they began to send dried cow meat from this country. In some regions whenever there was a drought of grass, the farmers inevitably sold their cattle. Then the agents, who would collect and export cow meat to foreign countries, began to pay a higher price for cattle. The ignorant farmers had actually sold the *Gomaata* in their house to butchers. Although some cities have forbidden the killing of cows in their slaughterhouses, some Hindu members of the city municipalities themselves slacken the law after taking bribes from beef traders. This is occurring even today.

'My dear sons and daughters of the *Gomaata*, cow slaughter might not occur in your village or town. But the slaughter of the cows of your village occurs in a different city. The slaughterhouse in Mumbai city alone butchers two thousand cows every day and sells that meat. Two and half thousand are slaughtered in Calcutta. In Kanpur, they slit the throats of one thousand and five hundred cows and kill them daily. This daily carnage occurs in several other cities as well. Earlier, during the British period, some Hindu kings had prohibited cow slaughter in their domains. But now, after Independence, even that law at the level of the Provinces has weakened.'

Venkataramana's mind recalled the cow slaughter at Kalinga's farm four days ago. When he first came to know of the matter in Kalenahalli, he had thought of filing a police complaint against Kalinga. But he was unaware of this portion of the law. *The government is favourable towards Kalinga. What kind of government is this? What sort of law is this?* Venkataramana's mind was boiling now.

The speaker was saying: 'And to stop this business which is completely opposed to dharma, we have started a massive organization called the All India Cow Protection Committee. We plan to collect signatures from the people of the entire country—that is, from a minimum of twenty crore people—to "prohibit cow slaughter". And then on the next Gokulashtami Day—the birthday of Lord Krishna—we will take out a procession in Delhi and submit these signatures to the president. If the government doesn't prohibit cow slaughter even after this, we'll launch a severe agitation. Our volunteers will come to your homes very soon. And apart from signing your name and the names of your family members in the book they'll bring with them, I pray to all of you to also get the signatures of all the adults on your street, village, and neighbouring villages. We request that those who wish to assist us may please provide their name and address to any volunteer present in this assembly. Jai Bharata Mata—Jai Jai *Gomaata!*'

The assembly sat there calmly even after his speech was finished. Venkataramana carefully scanned the assembly. A few Rashtriya Swayamsevaks were seated in an orderly manner amidst the people gathered there. Wearing khaki knickers, white shirt and a black topi on the head, they comprised both boys and young men. Venkataramana had no acquaintance with the Rashtriya Swayamsevak Sangh. But when he was in Mysore, he had seen them doing the drill and singing patriotic songs during evenings in a few public grounds. He had greatly appreciated the manner in which they recited Sanskrit *slokas* flawlessly as a group. From the English newspaper that he read, he had learnt the names of the founders of that Sangh as also the names of its prominent people whenever they appeared in the news and other writing.

He turned around. Even in the outer perimeter of the assembly, some Swayamsevaks were standing in a disciplined manner. It was getting late for the cart. He crouched and walked noiselessly, exited the gathering and wrote his name and address in the book that a Swayamsevak was carrying with him. Then he said, 'When you visit our village for collecting the signatures, please come to our home,' and then headed for the marketplace.

2

On the very second day after this, two people visited his house. Apparently, they were both still high school students. Attired in khaki knickers, white shirt and a belt around the waist, they had come here from the Taluk on foot. When Venkataramana asked, 'But there's a motor?' they said, 'Our Cow Protection Committee has no money sir. The committee gives these books for free. The Swayamsevaks need to bear the cost of travel on their own.'

'Are you poor students?'

'We aren't poor at all sir. Our father has a farm, wetlands and a house. But our committee people have told us that this sort of work has to be done as much as possible with physical strain.'

Venkataramana felt happy listening to this. His mother served meals to the boys. His mind desired that the first signature for the book must begin with Kalenahalli, and the very first signature must be that of Tayavva. He went to Kalenahalli along with the boys.

Tayavva was at home. When they went in, she was sitting under the roof of the front portion of the house and polishing a large pot to a fine shine. It appeared as if she was stricken with some severe ailment. When he had seen her six days earlier during the episode of the cow slaughter in Kalinga's house, she had appeared just fine. *Why had she become like this now?*

'Why mother, are you unwell?'

She called them in and placed a wooden plank each for the three. She went inside, heated milk, added ghee and jaggery and placed a tall tumbler in front of each and stood there.

'Why're you like this?' Venkataramana asked again. She shook her hands as if it was nothing.

'What shouldn't have happened in this house has happened. Still, you must console yourself. This won't occur again. These boys have brought this book which will help the government make a law that prohibits cow slaughter. Press the thumb of your left hand on it.'

Venkataramana smeared her left thumb with ink and got her to press it in the book. He wrote, 'This is the left-hand thumb impression of Tayavva, the daughter-in-law of the Elder Kalinga Gowda, the owner of the cowshed at Kalenhalli, attested by School Master Venkataramana Shastri.' From there he visited all the houses in the village together with the boys. To them, he explained the speech that he had heard at the Taluk. The village folk were now in an euphoria of victory. Apparently, they themselves had meant to send for Venkataramana. The fine of a thousand rupees that they'd collected from Kalinga was with Yangata Gowda. What had to be done with it was a matter to be decided in the presence of the entire village. It was discussed that apart from the cattle fair that had been organized once the temple was built, none had taken place so far. The *kalyani* was anyway free now. A cattle fair should be organized during the next Sankranti in the empty space by the slope next to the fence of Kalinga's farm. So, it was decided to raise more money in addition to the thousand collected from Kalinga. By then, every single adult—male and female—had either put their thumb impression or made a signature in the book.

Venkataramana lodged the two boys in his home for eight days. He applied for leave from the school. He had a bicycle anyway. He borrowed another one from one of the teachers so the boys could use it. Both of them went around 'double riding' on it. Each morning after finishing puja, they would go on a visit to the villages. Together, they covered sixty villages in eight days and collected a total of 23,500 signatures. All these were villages for which he was the *purohit*. He had not visited them regularly since the last five years. Yet, he was known to all of them. Some would immediately sign the moment he asked them to. Others were scared of the word signature. To them, he would explain the purpose behind these signatures, 'See, you don't need to be afraid. All of these guys have signed.' But some villagers who were under the influence of the Congress party refused to sign. 'Did Nehru ask you to get this signed?' they would ask.

'Had Nehru himself had the conviction to prohibit cow slaughter, he could've made a law to this effect. Because he still hasn't done it, we're collecting these signatures,' the boys would reply.

'That means you're working against Nehru's government.'

'How does it mean we're working against the government when we're merely asking to stop cow slaughter? This is what the majority wishes, so please do accordingly—we're doing this to just show the government what the people wish. This is not against anybody,' Venkataramana would say. Some would agree to this and sign. Others would utter humiliating words to their faces and send them away.

But overall, their sojourn of eight days wasn't fruitless. The notebooks were filled with signatures. When Venkataramana offered to pay them the motor fare, the boys refused and went to the Taluk on foot.

3

On the fourth day after the boys had departed, Venkataramana received a notice from the inspector's office: 'It has come to our notice that you have participated in an activity involving political parties by applying for leave under the pretext of personal work. As a government employee, you have participated in this activity which is against the law. You are to show cause in writing as to why appropriate punishment must not be given to you as soon as this notice reaches you.'

The notice had come via the headmaster. But the headmaster hadn't done any mischief in this matter. As a Sanaatani Hindu, he had expressed appreciation for Venkataramana's work. Now, he said: 'Helping in the effort to collect signatures is a normal thing, which anybody does. This hasn't happened due to this. Somebody has wantonly instigated this mischief.'

'What reply should I give the inspector?'

'Write: I haven't committed any mistake. If this has occurred unintentionally, please forgive me.'

Venkataramana thought that was the right thing to say and sat down to write. But the pen swayed him in another direction without his knowledge. 'It is true that I took leave for my personal work. I helped in the effort of collecting signatures supporting the prohibition of cow slaughter. But that's not the work of any political party. It is the duty of every son of this sacred land. I have committed no mistake. Therefore, the question of awarding me punishment doesn't arise at all.' When the headmaster saw what he had written, he said, 'This tenor is not proper. Write saying that you've done nothing at all; that you had some death rites or some other ceremony at home, and that's why you applied for leave. If you so wish, I'll be a witness.'

Venkataramana thought for half an hour. The work that he had done roaming across the villages over eight days had given him moral contentment. His conscience was opposed to the act of slithering away from admitting this to claim that he had never done it. 'No sir, I'll retain what I've written,' he told the headmaster and sent it to the higher-ups through the headmaster.

On the sixth day, he received an order. The higher officials had given him a severe warning for participating in such political activities. This warning was entered in his Service Register. In addition, they had transferred him to a school in a district that was one hundred miles away, for committing this mistake. Not only this: the moment this order reached him, he had to hand over charge, get relieved and join the new school immediately. The headmaster was also instructed in writing, to relieve him immediately.

Because he didn't get a bus immediately, Venkataramana cycled all the way to the Taluk. The moment the inspector saw him, he exploded in fury, yelling: 'Just because I retained your posting in your own village because you're a local, you went ahead and involved yourself in politics? Couldn't you mind your own business like the poor man that you are?'

Venkataramana patiently explained the whole thing to him. He quoted numerous mantras narrating the sanctity of the cow, and argued that he had indulged in no political activity. When he got a taste of Venkataramana's deep knowledge of Sanskrit, the inspector was not only surprised but developed respect for him. He said with compassion: 'Look, this order hasn't originated merely at the district level. It's come down from far higher levels. No matter what we do, the transfer won't be revoked. You go to the new place and stay there for a couple of years. By then all this would've become stale. After that, you can get yourself re-transferred here.'

He said this much and went home. Venkataramana climbed on his cycle and pedalled in the direction of his village. *Who could've been behind this? Kalinga?* His mind was filled with suspicion. But his inner self didn't believe it for some reason. It could also be the work of the Congressmen who had argued with him during his tour of the villages. But he had no proof to say that it was definitely their handiwork. His mind now turned towards the task of resolving this problem rather than speculating who had instigated this. What would be the fate of the temple puja if he went away for two years? The Elder Gowda had placed his entire trust in him and had given him the responsibility to perform the puja. Not only that, before he departed, he had even given him a land grant and cows so that his livelihood wouldn't suffer and that he could fill his stomach. Now, the puja itself was in peril!

Suddenly, a decision flashed to his mind: *It was a mistake to join this job in the first place. There's no limit to human greed. It doesn't matter from how many directions money flows in, we still feel we want more. My job is to perform the puja. The responsibility for maintaining my family has already been discharged by that same noble soul who built the temple. From now on, I'll perform the puja elaborately, chanting the Sahasranama—the thousand names of the deity—instead of being in hurry to get to school. I'll resign from this wretched job.*

This decision solidified. When he came home and informed his family, his mother said it was the right thing to do. But his wife Meenakshi came forward to utter words of wisdom: 'Won't it help to appoint someone to perform the puja for the next two years?'

But he didn't pay heed to her practical wisdom. He awoke the next morning and wrote his resignation letter. He once again justified the work he had done in the same letter. He chided the government which obstructed such sacred work and informed it to accept his resignation and affixed his signature. When he went for the puja that day, he placed the letter near the deity's feet and later, handed it to the headmaster. He didn't take it back despite numerous appeals to reconsider.

4

The next day onwards, when Venkataramana went to the temple to perform the puja, he began to spend over two hours there. Some days, he would take up some Upanishad or a Vedic *Sukta*—hymn—and chant it loudly after finishing the puja. Now there was no longer the sound of the pump near the *kalyani*. Neither was there any noise from the tractor in the farm below. Sparrows, pigeons and parrots were cavorting and talking with one another on the trees. If he was tempted to study for a longer time in this atmosphere, he would loudly chant the same mantras again and again. After he had joined the school, he hadn't experienced the joy of self-study of memorizing mantras by chanting them aloud. Now he found a new sense of soul-contentment within himself.

If he was bored at home in the afternoon, he took out the cows towards the wetland by himself. He hammered a peg on the ridge, tethered them to it with a long rope and allowed them to graze. Then when he began to chant the *slokas* melodiously, even the cows listened with attention. Other farmers too who were working on the soil lent an ear to it from afar. Now Kalinga, his farm, and even Kalenhalli itself wouldn't feature in his memories.

But late one afternoon when he was sitting on the ridge of the wetland grazing the cows, Yangata Gowda and three other prominent village folk came searching for him. Their faces were all glum. After they sat placing their head cloth on the ground, Yangata Gowda started the conversation. 'Did you hear about last night's news?'

'What?'

'Police had come to our village.'

'Why?'

'I'll tell you why later. In all, they took away four thousand rupees.'

Venkataramana was astonished. Although he didn't know any details of the issue, its backdrop flashed to his subconscious immediately. Yangata Gowda now described it. Last night, the motor of the police had itself arrived. Apart from the inspector, ten gun-bearing constables had come along. They called for the names of the prominent folks in the village, apprehended them together and asked, 'All the village folk have ganged up, raided Kalinga Gowda's farm and ruined his tobacco crop. They pay a special tax for the tobacco crop. The revenue that the government would get this year is lost. An inquiry has come against you from the top. Will you return the government's money or will you indulge in hooliganism?'

'Did that Kalinga make a complaint?' they asked.

'He told us nothing. But it's the government's responsibility to safeguard his mortgaged property. He does business with the government's department. Don't think that's some sort of a game.' They pulled out the handcuffs and threatened to send us to jail. The village folk had no other option. They pleaded that they could only give two thousand and begged for forgiveness. The police didn't relent. Finally, they negotiated hard and the final amount stood at four thousand. There was that thousand that they had taken as a fine from Kalinga. For the remaining three, they collected donations right there, submitted it to them and escaped.

'If you wag your tail again, we'll skin you alive. Careful,' the police warned and departed that very night in their motor.

'Kalinga's work,' Venkataramana said.

'Do we need to even say it explicitly? It seems he went to the Taluk in the motor this morning. His barn servant Putta said so,' Yangata Gowda replied.

'Do one thing. I'll come along. Today evening or tomorrow morning we'll all go and question him about this matter.'

'No. Let's not even go anywhere near that thieving son of a whore,' four of them said, shaking their hands. The fear that Kalinga inspired had now taken deep root in them. No matter how hard he tried to convince them to dispel their fear, it was futile. 'May his home collapse. May his lineage perish. Let that whoreson do whatever he wants. We don't need any sort of relation with him from now on. Neither will we talk to him. Let him eat own his sins and decay,' their conversation ended with these cuss words.

As they began to leave, Venkataramana asked: 'How's Tayavva?'

'O, that old woman will die.'

'Why? What happened?'

'What else should happen? Don't you know why her mother-in-law died, why the Elder Gowda died? She'll also die the same way.'

'She was bleached white like she had some disease when I visited her fifteen days ago. I haven't been there of late.'

'Now she looks more like she's dying. You come, see for yourself.'

I need to go to Kalenahalli tomorrow afternoon and see Tayavva. I'll also take mother along, Venkataramana decided.

5

When he went to the temple the next day, Venkataramana looked in the direction of Kalinga's farm. Till then he hadn't even properly cast a glance that way. He had been thinking last night of meeting Kalinga and speaking to him. Six or seven *bhaktas* had arrived. He gave the *tirtha* and *prasada* to all of them, then offered the coconuts, bananas, and rice to the deity, and leaving the remainder of the *prasada* behind in the temple, he locked the door and descended from the flank of the *kalyani*. It appeared to him that they were digging a new well to the right of the farmhouse. In the entire farm, apart from some stray ones sticking out randomly, the tender tobacco plants that had been plucked out had now become desiccated.

When he stood at the door, Hilda was seated on the sofa inside. But she didn't talk to him. When he himself asked, 'Isn't Kalinga home?', she said, 'Why did you come to this house again? Don't you have any shame?' Venkataramana stiffened for a minute at these words. Then he turned to leave. Meanwhile, Kalinga who emerged from the inner room, called out, 'Come in. Sit down.'

'It's ok,' said Venkataramana, standing there.

'No, it's fine, come. She's just speaking out of anger,' said Kalinga.

Venkataramana stepped inside. Hilda got up, went to the inner room and shut the door. Kalinga leaned against the sofa. Venkataramana sat on the wooden chair. They sat there for five minutes, both not knowing what to say. Finally, Kalinga asked: 'What's the matter?'

'Look, I came here to speak to you about something. I'll say it as your well-wisher. You must speak to me without concealing anything.'

'Tell me.'

'Apparently, a police inspector and ten constables had come at night to the village the day before. It seems they threatened them all and took away four thousand rupees. What's all this?'

'Why? What's the matter? I never knew this!'

'Don't lie. I'm telling this for your own good. Tell me the truth. It's impossible for them to show up like that without your instigation.'

For a minute, it appeared that Kalinga was preparing the answer within himself. Then he said: 'Look, you don't know business matters. You won't learn business merely because you're learned in the Shastras. The government levies a special tax on tobacco. When I planted tobacco, it was already entered in the government records. Now my entire crop is ruined. I informed the government that I an unable to pay the tax. Then the obvious question arises as to why the crop was ruined. Then we were forced to tell them the truth.'

'Couldn't you tell them a different reason, couldn't you save the folks of your own village?'

'Couldn't I save my own folks?' Kalinga repeated his question, stressing upon it sarcastically and said: 'I need to save them because they've saved me, right? For wiping out fifty thousand in just one night, and to top it, for humiliating me to this appalling level... for all this, I needed to lie to the government and save them, right?'

'It was mob insanity that was responsible for destroying your crop. All the elders do agree that it was an unfair thing to do. But who humiliated you? The Dharmashastras say that there is atonement for one who has committed a mistake. Accordingly, they took thousand rupees from you, going by your status. Even that money hasn't been used for anybody's personal purposes. They were about to use it for the temple's work.'

'Venkataramana, you're merely a drab, barren Shastri. You've no notion of self-esteem or respect. You shamelessly do anything, tolerate anything, spouting the excuse of Dharmashastras. But I have esteem, respect... everything.'

'You're using this language to my face... in this tone. I'm not a slave of your house. The food I eat is not the *bhiksha*, alms, that you give me. I've always been doing good to you because you're the Elder Kalinga Gowda's grandson, and because you're my friend. I'm telling you even now. Listen to me. The fury of the village folk subsided that very night. You should've let it go at that. Now that the police had come, the unrest that the village had towards you has resurfaced. I came here to advise you for your own good.'

'Just shut up. Don't drop your grand utterances on me,' Kalinga spoke, now sitting taut on the sofa: 'Don't puff up your chest and tell me that you're not eating alms off my hand. Whose lands are those which give food to your home? Weren't they given as alms to you by my grandfather?'

'That's not alms. It's an endowment left behind for performing the deity's puja.'

'Right! My grandfather endowed you with that grant because you perform spectacularly productive work. You're set for life, aren't you? Given this, given that you eat the food of my house, why did you take sides with the village folk that night? You should've stood by me and reprimanded and sent them away.'

'When the mistake is yours how can I stand by you? You utilized the deity's *kalyani* for your personal benefit. I cried out to you a thousand times not to do that. Husband and wife, both of you dipped your bodies there and frolicked in its water. She could've had her period or whatever other thing. Your wife swam in the *kalyani*. I was constantly getting all the news. Finally, she slaughtered the cow. Am I performing the puja in the Punyakoti temple to conceal all this? Am I performing it to stand by you and justify everything you both do? Instead of questioning me, talk some sense into your wife. Learn how to make your wife behave properly. Be a man for the wife at home first!'

When he spoke the last lines, Venkataramana's voice had reached a crescendo. The swollen veins of his neck were visible. His pitch had reached a peak that threatened to blow the ceiling away. Kalinga went completely still now. For about ten minutes, neither spoke. Kalinga was thinking. 'I'll leave,' Venkataramana said and got up. But Kalinga said, 'Just a minute. Sit down.'

But he still didn't speak for the next five minutes. When Venkataramana himself asked, 'Tell me, what is it?' he said slowly:

'Look, it's not my intention to harm you. But understand something clearly. I know all the paperwork and other correspondence that my grandfather had done. I was twenty-six years old when my grandfather wrote the land endowment for the temple's puja. He didn't ask my consent for it. Neither is my signature present on the endowment deed. The land made out in your name is ancestral property. My grandfather didn't earn even a single acre of land that can be called his own. If I file a case even today stating that you hoodwinked my grandfather and got the land written in your name without my knowledge when I was abroad, I'll win it. You don't have enough respectability to either speak contemptuously to my face or to scold or advise my wife. Get that.'

Venkataramana was feeling progressively dizzy even as he listened to these words as they were being uttered. By the time Kalinga finished his final sentence, he leaned his head on the backrest of the chair he was sitting on and went inert for a full minute. Kalinga didn't notice any of this. After two or three minutes, Venkataramana recovered, sat upright and said in a trembling voice: 'Were you born, O Virtuous Grandson, to pilfer the works of dharma that your grandfather carried out? *Oye*, you uttered all those words, right? Know this much: your own life is your witness. You *will* be ruined. Your lineage *will* be annihilated. This isn't merely my curse alone, it's the curse of your grandfather. It's the curse of your great grandfather and his great grandfather. You'll go to the court? Even I'll see what you can deprive me of in the court. Go! Go away, you undeserving whoreson!'

Saying this much, he got up and came outside without waiting for another word. From there he directly went to the temple, took the vessel of the *prasada* from inside, locked the door, rang the bell in the compound, descended the hill and went straight to Kalenahalli.

When he reached Yangata Gowda's house, his son Maata said: 'Father's gone to Tayavva's house.' Venkataramana too went to Tayavva's house. She was lying on a straw mat. A wooden plank supported her head. Apart from Yangata Gowda, two or three other village folk were seated there leaning against the wall and talking to one another. When Tayavva saw Venkataramana, she tried to get up and sit but she couldn't without support. All of them understood by looking at his attire that he had come here directly from the temple. 'Wash your hands. I'll give you *prasada*,' he said. All three got up and washed their hands. Venkataramana gave a lump of jaggery to each. 'Tayavva, open your mouth. I'll give the deity's *prasada*,' he said. When she opened her mouth, Venkataramana dropped in three small morsels of the *prasada*.

After he was seated on a wooden plank, Yangata Gowda asked: 'You came like this directly from the temple? What, had you been there?'

'Hmm. Yes. He spoke very shrewdly. He even warned me. Seems when his grandfather wrote the land grant deed for the deity's puja, he hadn't taken Kalinga's signature. And now if I don't listen to him and do as he says and support him even if he kills a cow every day, it seems he'll slap a case against me in the court and deprive me of my land.'

'May the home of the woman who gave birth to that whoreson be ruined! The pious lady, his mother, she's still alive. We can take her along and give her statement as a witness. We'll see how he'll take your land away,' all three said in unison. They also assured him that if required all the village folk would come as witnesses.

Venkataramana felt a little comforted. He enquired about Tayavva's health.

When he asked what exactly was her illness, Yangata Gowda said,

'What else? Giving birth to that son is itself a disease in her belly. She won't survive anyway. Remember what happened to the Elder Gowda and his wife? It's the same for her.'

Tayavva's face was bleached dry. She was gazing in a nondescript direction with a bizarre look like she was possessed by a ghost or demon. Her limbs resembled a thin reed. Under the blanket made of sheep wool, her body appeared like a wisp of cloth. Yangata Gowda said: 'The Elder Gowda and his wife died after the motor road was built on top of the graves of the Punyakoti cow and Krishna who'd both died at the hands of the hyena. Although the road was built on the graves, Tayavva visited the spot on the new moon day of the dark fortnight month and offered them milk and ghee.'

When Kalinga had sold the aged cattle to the butcher, she had borne the pain in her stomach. After the cattle at home had been carted off to the new barn, she was anxious every moment regarding the safety of their lives. When the servants described how milk was sucked to the last drop using the machines, depriving the calves of their mother's milk, tears would flow from her eyes. But, she was helpless. What right did she have to either stop her son or speak some sense to her daughter-in-law? But she had somehow borne all that patiently. She lived on thinking within the confines of her mute mind, as to why this wretched life wouldn't end; that she simply couldn't bear to watch all this. But then, cow slaughter occurred at the hands of her own son and daughter-in-law. She went mad when she heard that the cow of the Punyakoti stock—which was the very foundation of their lineage's well-being—had been slaughtered. She went with all the village folk, imposed the fine on the person who had committed this transgression and returned home. Others in the village could forget this episode. But how could Tayavva? Besides, she also learnt of the news that the police had come here and extorted four thousand rupees from the village folk.

Yangata Gowda said: 'She no longer has the will to live, my man. All that now remains is carrying the bundle called the human body. She's anticipating her journey.'

Then Tayavva gestured with her hands. Because she had no strength in her shoulders, her hand movements were unsteady. Even the expression on her face didn't quite match the meaning that her hands conveyed. But Yangata Gowda somehow understood her message and asked, 'Let's see how he takes away the land. Let's go to the court. Right, mother?' She nodded her head conveying a 'yes'.

'Tayavva, don't forsake your life for this. We must stay alive and face everything. If you feel sad to stay here, come to my village. Or come to the temple every day, sweep and clean up the place and serve the deity' Venkataramana uttered these words of solace and left for his village.

By the time he reached home, it was already one in the afternoon. His mother still hadn't eaten anything. He handed her the *prasada* vessel in which a handful was still remaining, and without bothering to sit for lunch, he directly went to the *Shanubhoga's* house. He was aware of all that had transpired so far. When Venkataramana narrated the day's incident, he said: 'It's true that his sign was required. Yet, what the Elder Gowda did was a work of charity. He hasn't lost any property by way of misuse. If he goes to court, I'll also give my statement as a witness. I've made the deed and I've written the B Column in there. He needs to go to the court first. Until he goes, there's nothing we can do. You don't do anything till then.'

6

Venkataramana checked his correspondence tray for ten or twelve days in case a notice arrived from the court. Nothing came. He also constantly enquired whether Kalinga left the village by motor and if so, in which direction. He learnt that he had indeed gone twice to the Taluk by motor. But there was no evidence to show that he had gone to the court to file a case against the land grant.

Venkataramana's mental composure had been disturbed since the day Kalinga had uttered those words. So far, he had bonded himself with love and devotion towards the temple puja. No matter how busy he was with work, he hadn't touched a single drop of water to his lips even one day without performing the puja. Once when he was down with fever, his mother had gone to the temple and had performed the puja with only flowers and fruits minus mantras and ritual procedures. He had consumed medicine only after taking a fully blossomed flower that she offered him. But now, the axe had fallen right at the root of his puja.

At times, his mind speculated whether Kalinga would really file a case in the court. He recalled the exact words of Kalinga: 'Look, it's not my intention to actually file a case. Because you're eating the food of my house, you must stand by me in times of difficulty. You don't have enough respectability to either speak contemptuously to my face or to scold or advise my wife.'

I hadn't gone there to advise him. It was my duty to tell him a few good words out of a feeling of affection because he's the Elder Gowda's grandson. What does it mean... 'stand by me in times of difficulty because you're eating the food of my house?' What's the difficulty that'll befall him? When he sells the aged cattle to the butcher, when he and his wife kill a cow only to satisfy the craving of their tongue, should I justify his act declaring that it's correct? Is it only when I justify his act that the temple's puja will remain with me? Which also means that then he'll no longer touch the land given to me as a grant. And so I'll need to perform puja to that stone idol in the temple, and I'll need to assist in the slaughter of the real, living Gomaata. Which is nobler? There's no loss if the puja of a stone deity halts. But if the real, living Gomaata is slaughtered again, a greater ruckus than last time must be raised. His house itself must be burnt down. These people won't see sense without a healthy dose of fear and pain.

However, his mind could not agree to forego the puja of the stone deity. It was impossible for his mind to accept that the *murti* inside the temple was mere stone. When the Elder Gowda was getting the temple built, even Venkataramana had taken a part in the process of its construction. He used to visit the site regularly and assist in various tasks such as calculating and fixing the dimensions of the temple and the *kalyani* up until its construction was completed. He used to narrate various stories from the Puranas extolling the glory of the cow. From the Shastras, he used to quote verses about the importance of performing puja to the cow to the men and women volunteers, the stoneworkers, the artisan Shivalingachari and the Elder Gowda, and thereby drew out their bhakti and zeal. When the *murti* was consecrated, he had meticulously participated in all the rituals involving mantra and tantra.

From then, up until now, he had performed the *Nyasa* rite of anointing the Punyakoti *murti* as the Divine Cow and the three other *murtis* respectively as Brahma, Vishnu and Shiva. Indeed, the *Nyasa* didn't need to be performed afresh now. Venkataramana had conducted the puja ever since, in the spirit of this devotion. And now, how could they remain as mere stone idols? It was true that the cow slaughtered in Kalinga's farm and the ones which might be slaughtered in future were all living deities, but the one inside the temple was a symbol of these forms of the same deity. So how could one regard that symbol as a mere stone?

An inextricable bond had grown between Venkataramana and the temple. It was impossible for him to let go of it. Kalinga had threatened to snatch away the grant made for performing the puja and not the actual puja itself. And so, even if the grant went away, the puja would still remain with him. Yes! The moment this revelation dawned upon him, his mind rejoiced like it had found light amid darkness. *Let him take his land if he wants to. I'll perform my puja at any rate.* He made the decision.

But, what about food? Mother, me, my wife, my two kids... how can I manage my family? I made a mistake. Should I plead with the government to please accept my apologies and revoke the resignation I have given? But the next instant he reasoned, *they transferred me only because I participated in the movement to prohibit cow slaughter. Which means if I plead with them to revoke my resignation, I need to admit that I made a mistake. Kalinga too, is asking the same kind of admission of guilt in order for me to enjoy the land grant. Both the government and Kalinga are demanding the same sort of obedience. And in a haste to free myself from Kalinga's clutches, I shall fall in the whirlpool of the government. If I need to really free myself, I need to free myself from both.* He was now resolute.

Both his mother and wife were aware of the turmoil he was going through. When he asked what needed to be done now, his wife said: 'You can still approach someone at the top and tender an apology. You'll retain a comfortable salaried job. You'll also get pension in old age. Why do you need all this trouble?'

But his mother said: 'Child, we don't need to vacate the house that's come down to us from ancestors and go elsewhere. I've served food to Kalinga for four years. Let's see if he listens to my counsel. Don't go to court. I'll tell him to not snatch away the dharma that Elders have done. You don't oppose him from now on. Be tactful.'

'Mother, why should I oppose him needlessly? Should I stay quiet even if he slaughters the cow?'

His mother couldn't think of a reply. 'Bad times have descended upon the world,' she said and left it at that.

One morning after finishing the puja, Venkataramana was sitting on the temple veranda and loudly chanting the Kathopanishad to his heart's content.

Peetodakaa jagdhatrunaa dugdhadohaa nirindriyaah |
anandaa naamate lokaastaan sa gacchati taa dadat ||

Those who gift such cows which are so weak due to old age,
that they cannot drink water, eat grass or yield milk,
such people will go to the joyless worlds.

The young boy Nachiketa in the Upanishad asked his father who was gifting these cows, *tata kasmai maam daasasyi*—whom will you donate me to? When his father replied angrily, 'To death', the boy obediently journeyed to Yamapuri, the abode of Yama, the Deity of Death. And before setting out on the journey to the home of Yama, he consoled his father saying:

Anupashya yathaa poorve pratipashya tathaapare |
sassyamiva martyah pachyate sassyamivaajaayate punah ||

Look at how men lived in the past and how they live in future,
They rot like vegetation and will be born again like vegetables.

And then he calmly went to the abode of Yama, the Deity of Death.

Aah, the steadfastness of Nachiketa! thought Venkataramana.

Instead of chanting, Venkataramana's mind remained busy in deep contemplation for about a half hour. Then, as if he had arrived at a decision, he stood up, took the *prasada* vessel, locked the door, rang the bell in the compound, came outside, stood on the summit and looked on. The construction work of the well next to Kalinga's house in the centre of the farm was briskly progressing. Twenty or thirty labourers were working with pickaxes and pans. Kalinga was standing on the bank and supervising the work.

Venkataramana went home directly. He gave the *prasada* vessel to his mother who was still wearing her Sanctified Garments, and opened the wooden trunk in the inner room. He extracted a thick envelope from it and came outside holding it in his hand. Then he walked again towards the hill and reached the temple. He placed the envelope on the temple's threshold, perambulated thrice and prostrated at the door. Then he held it in his hand and descending from the direction of the *kalyani*, reached Kalinga's farm. The work on the well was still in progress. Kalinga was still standing there.

When the labourers saw this temple priest who was wearing his sacred puja garments, his hair cascading down after being knotted at the tip and bands of *vibhuti* smeared across his forehead, biceps, chest and shoulders, they simply stood there looking at him. Although Kalinga tried to pretend that he hadn't seen him, he found it impossible to do so and turned in his direction. It was only Hilda standing near the well and overseeing the work who ignored his presence and stood there as if she was peeking into the well. Venkataramana neared Kalinga and handed over the envelope in his hand. Assuming it was some letter, Kalinga accepted it and asked, 'What's this, Venkataramana?'

'It's the land grant deed written by your grandfather for carrying out the puja of the temple. Remember you told me that day that if I didn't obey you, you'd slap a case and take away the land? I won't obey you. I simply won't shut up if you kill cows at your home. You don't need to go to the court and spend money on lawyers. Take these papers. From today, the relationship with that land and me has been severed. I'll inform this to Honna, who's tilling it under a sharecropping arrangement. You may do as you please with it.'

Not only was this act and the words that accompanied it unexpected but they also evoked astonishment in Kalinga. But before he could say something, Venkataramana himself spoke powerfully: 'Look, I know that you've also made out to your name the land on which the temple has been built. Although I've given up this land given to me as a grant, I won't stop conducting the temple puja. So far, I was performing the puja and eating the meal that emanated from it. Today, I've cut off all ties with that profane meal. Now, I'll retain ties with just the puja. You might try to even deprive me of the puja because the temple land is in your name. Or, you might even take control of the entire temple itself. And from now on, if you feel a desire to eat the flesh of a cow, you can slaughter a cow right inside the temple, right before the Punyakoti deity, cook it right there and eat it. After that, both of you husband and wife can frolic in the *kalyani* till such time that all the fat that you've eaten melts away!'

After saying this much, Venkataramana turned. The labourers were standing rock-still, listening to him. Now even Hilda was looking at him with a fixed gaze. Venkataramana, who had walked a few steps, suddenly halted remembering something he had to say. Returning, he thundered, 'Look, the temple and the *kalyani* land might be in your name. It's also true that the Elder Gowda spent money for getting it built. But, just like how the *kalyani* fills up and overflows with water, the women and men of Kalenahalli have shed their sweat and laboured for building both. Now the temple has become a *Punyakshetra,* a Sacred Pilgrimage Spot, in the surrounding hundred miles and devotees are flocking to it. So get this straight: if you try to take over the temple just like how you did with the land grant, your skull won't remain intact. Tomorrow I'll tell the folk at Kalenahalli to erect a strong fence between this side of the hill and your farm and around the temple including the *kalyani.* And if you try to intimidate us by calling the police... by calling anybody, you *will* suffer cane lashings. I'll myself stand in the frontline with a cane. Then we'll learn the true extent of your manhood.' He turned and stormed away. By the time he had taken twenty steps, Kalinga called out from behind, 'Venkataramana, stop for a bit.' But he didn't stop. Without turning back, he yelled, 'If I even look at the face of a scum like you, I'll accumulate a non-existent sin. Stay away.' He doubled the pace of his steps and walked off.

At home, he didn't tell anybody what he did that day. After eating a hearty meal, he fed straw to the cows in his own house, spread a blanket and slept. In the evening, he took a pleasurable walk on the embankment of the lake and returned. That night after everybody had drifted off to sleep, his mind began to ponder: *All these days, I had neglected astrology. Although people's faith in dharma and karma had dwindled, there's an increase everywhere in the number of people getting their horoscopes read and making enquiries about their future. If I study well and write a kundali I'll get ten rupees. If I write a complete future prediction of a horoscope, anybody will pay a hundred rupees. An astrologer must necessarily worship a deity. I don't need any other deity. Each morning, if I get up and perform puja in the Punyakoti temple, that's all it'll take to develop the mental poise to calculate and draw up a kundali. There's always some path to fill the stomach. And now, there's no place where the cows can graze. If I ask Kalenahalli's Yangata Gowda, they can graze in his pasture or on a knoll in the field near our village. During Ugadi, when I narrate the Varshaphala—the prediction of rains and seasons, crop and harvest for the year—I can ask folks to give me extra grain and pulses. Not only will the folks at Kalenahalli agree but even if those in other villages give five kilos per house, it'll be more than sufficient.*

Together with this thought, he calculated what was available in the storage in his house. He had saved two-and-a-half-thousand rupees from the salary he had earned so far. His mother had sold the excess corn that came home from time to time and had passed on her necklace, bangles and other ornaments to her daughter-in-law. This was valued at one thousand rupees. The ragi and rice at home would last for the entire year. What more was needed? Human need is limitless. With this consolation, he tried to prepare his mind for slumber.

But then he recalled the words he had spoken to Kalinga that afternoon. *That's all fine but why did I utter such ferocious words to him? I could've handed over the papers and said whatever I wanted to say patiently, gently.* One strand of thought advised this. But another strand was justifying his anger: *Does that wretch understand gentle language? So what if I displayed anger? What can he snatch from me? Why do I need to fear him? It's natural to feel scared as long as I had the desire for the meal coming from that land. Why should a person who has no desire of any sort feel scared?*

And so, it was a long time after midnight that he finally lapsed into sleep.

7

When Venkataramana awoke late the next day, he hurriedly had bath, took the *prasada* vessel and went to the temple. His mind was calm. He performed the puja chanting mantras loudly and when it was time for the *arati*, he sensed somebody running in from outside. But he completed the *arati* without looking in that direction.

It was Yangata Gowda's son, Maata. Still panting, he said: '*Ayya*, it seems Tayavva will die today. You come.'

'How do you know that she'll die today itself?'

'My father said so. It seems she said she wants to perform a *Godaana* before dying. One of the guys went to your house looking for you. I came here. Come. Let's go.'

Venkataramana took the *tirtha* tumbler along with the *prasada* vessel, locked the temple door, rang the large bell in the compound and left with Maata for Kalenahalli still wearing the Sacred Garments. Tayavva's time was fast closing in. His head filled with worldly worries. Venkataramana hadn't been to Kalenahalli in the last thirteen or fourteen days. It was just yesterday that his mind had found solace. He would've anyway visited the old woman today or tomorrow. *But has her time neared so quickly?* When he reached the spot with these thoughts in his head, about fifty to sixty people had already assembled in front of her house. All of them made way for him the moment he arrived. Inside, the frail body of the old lady was lying on a blanket. Although she didn't have strength enough to move her limbs, her eyes were radiant. She sensed that Venkataramana had arrived. Because she had no strength to sit up, she didn't even try. Four women from the village were sitting near her head. Yangata Gowda was seated leaning against the pillar while six or seven prominent folk from the village had congregated near the wall. A woman placed a wooden plank for Venkataramana.

Yangata Gowda said: 'Swami, why did you do such a thing yesterday?'

'What did I do, my man?'

'The servants who had gone to dig the well told me. Why did you return the land grant papers to him? If he'd gone to court, all of us village folk would've come as witnesses.'

'*Ayya*, instead of all the village folk coming there as witnesses and tiring yourselves out, if each one of you gives this pujari a basketful of ragi, can't I fill my stomach? Have I also abandoned the puja because I gave up that land? See, I'm coming here directly from the temple with the *tirtha* and *prasada*. There'll be no impediment for the puja. You don't worry.'

'I know that. When Tayavva heard this yesterday from the servants, her sorrow began to fester. Last night, she gestured with her hand that she'll die now. I got up in the morning and came here. Then she signalled with her hand that she'll donate all the cows in her home and that I should send for you, *Ayya*.'

Venkataramana thought for a minute and said: 'Look, if someone wants to perform the *Godana*, one mustn't decline it without reason. One must decline it only if the person donating is a miser or isn't giving it away with a pure mind. Tayavva will donate with a pure heart. But the head of the family, you know his mentality. That's why I won't accept this charity.'

The moment she heard these words, tears filled up the eyes housed in a withered Tayavva's body. Everyone near her noticed it. Yangata Gowda said: 'How does he become the head of the family, Learned Sir? Let him have all the property, gold... whatever, and waste away. But the Punyakoti stock? That belongs to the Elder Kalinga's ancestors. If that can't be cared for with devotion by the people in this house, it must be given away in charity. The mistress of the house has that right. You *must* take it.'

Tayavva made an expression on her face indicating that those were her words. Venkataramana said: 'In that case, get me the items for puja. Flowers, sandalwood, milk, ghee in a pot, a titbit of gold, all of these. If Tayavva is unable to have bath, wipe her body with a wet cloth even as she's lying down. Wipe this courtyard and decorate it with *rangoli*. So many folks have already assembled here. We can make some *prasada*.

Grate seven or eight coconuts, add crushed jaggery, and if available, mash some bananas as well.'

The women stood up to prepare Tayavva for her bath. The menfolk stepped outside. Two boys ran to get flowers and leaves. Maata climbed up the attic in his house, extracted eight coconuts and skinned them. While all this was happening, Venkataramana sat on the platform built around the Pipal tree opposite the house.

All the preparations were completed in an hour. Seven Punyakoti cows, two calves, one bull calf that had weaned off milk, six calves that hadn't, and the orphaned calf of the slaughtered cow had all been bathed and the *kumkum* applied on their foreheads. They had been brought to the inner courtyard, now wiped clean and decorated with *rangoli*. The cow and the two calves were tethered. In another portion of the courtyard, a bed was made at some height and gunny bags were folded up into a roll and placed on one side of the head. Tayavva had been bathed and was made to recline on it. Venkataramana came in. Yangata Gowda and other prominent village folk came in and sat wherever space was available. After examining the puja ingredients, Venkataramana began rubbing the sandalwood stump on a tile, to extract its paste. After sucking the teats of their mother once, the calves crept under the stomach of the other cows. After watching them for a minute, Yangata Gowda asked Tayavva: 'That brown calf? Isn't it the one orphaned?'

Tayavva nodded her head saying yes. Then Yangata Gowda said: 'See that? It still doesn't feel that its mother is dead. No matter to which other mother's teat that it latches its mouth, none of them kicks it. It regards it as its own child and licks its body and feeds it milk.'

Still rubbing the sandalwood, Venkataramana said: 'Gowda, isn't that why the cow is known as everyone's Mother? You know it right? Back then, before the Punyakoti cow went to the tiger, it addressed all other cows in the barn: "My mothers, my elder sisters, my siblings, treat this orphan as your own baby." Then all the cows had given their word, "Listen O Mother Punyakoti. Your baby is our baby, why the melancholy in your heart? Stay serene, Mother." Right? Where did this occur? In the barn, in the backyard of this very house. Then Punyakoti went to the tiger to offer herself. When the tiger on the slope of the mountain realized the cow's steadfastness to truth, it cursed the craving of its own wretched stomach and gave up its life. But now, the tigers who have built a house at the foothills of the same mountain have killed a Punyakoti cow of this house and filled their stomachs. But see, the cows preserve the memory of the promise that their ancestors have made. If any calf in their barn is orphaned, they regard it as their own baby. But it's only humans who forget the good deeds their ancestors had performed, the promises they had given, even though they are fully aware of it. Isn't this the only difference between humans and cows?'

Venkataramana had lowered his head, rubbing the sandalwood as he was speaking. Everyone was looking at the orphaned calf as they listened to his words. Yangata Gowda said, 'Sinful bastards, Swami. Vile whoresons!' By then, Venkataramana scooped up the sandalwood paste with his right thumb and naturally turned to his right. He was astonished: Kalinga was standing there, having entered from the backdoor—that is, from the door to the barn. Nobody had noticed him. Now everybody saw him. Venkataramana's speech stopped at that.

When Kalinga heard from the servants that his mother would die today, he couldn't restrain himself. He had anticipated that the menfolk and the womenfolk would have gathered at this house in the village. He felt his face contorting with embarrassment to go there in front of all of them. But then when the mother who had given him birth was giving up her life, he felt that he had to be near her and serve her in some way, or to call the doctor and save her. He had left his farm with this decision. When he had spotted from afar all these people gathered at his house, he thought it was best to enter from the backdoor. He had thought that her life had already ebbed when he saw the throng of people. But when he came in, a different scene was unfolding. All the cows and calves at home were standing on the floor that was wiped clean and decorated with *rangoli*. Venkataramana was getting the puja ingredients ready. Maata was seated near the heap of pulses and grating coconut slices. Kalinga was aware of the custom of performing *Godaana* before one died. But, what was the reason behind his mother giving away all the cows and calves at home in this fashion? But before this question even arose, his mind had already figured out the answer. Although his self-respect told him to just leave the place and return to the farm, he found himself unable to lift his feet. Some unfathomable power bound him with this scene.

'Shall we begin?' asked Venkataramana to which Yangata Gowda said, 'Hmmm, yes.' A woman left and returned with a large lit earthen lamp filled with thick ghee. Maata was still grating the coconuts. After Venkataramana chanted the *Shuklambaradharam Vishnum* mantra uttered in the worship of Lord Ganesha, he announced the *sankalpa*: the solemn vow that he was about to conduct the puja of the cows at that auspicious time and day, in order to obtain religious merit as stated in the Vedas and the Puranas in the manner prescribed by various sacred texts. Then he chanted the mantras of meditation, invocation and installation, procured water for washing the feet, hands and for drinking, and performed the accompanying rites for each of these steps. Then he offered water for the ritual bath and furnished clothes. Then he stood up and applied the sandalwood paste to each cow chanting the appropriate mantra. He turned to Tayavva and said, 'Mother, now I'll chant the *Nyasa* mantra, which means mentally assigning a deity to each part of the cow's body. Listen with devotion. I hereby assign Brahma and Vishnu to the base of the horns, all the sacred rivers to the tip of the horns, Mahadeva or Shiva to the forehead.' He simultaneously explained the meaning of the mantras that he was chanting and described which God or Goddess resided in which organ of the cow. With her eyes wide open, Tayavva was watching each cow as if the deities in its body were visible to her.

And then, after the incense and the lamp was lit, the *naivedya* was offered to the deity, which was followed by perambulation and offering of water, Venkataramana asked, 'The puja for the cow is complete in all respects. Now shall we start the *daana*?'

Tayavva moved her eyes as if to say, 'Please start'. Despite suffering from extreme weakness, she was observing everything with pointed focus, leaning on just one side. The fatigue and pain that was always visible on her face had now stilled. Kalinga was leaning against the wall near the backdoor and watching everything.

Venkataramana chanting the mantra:

Gorme maata vrushabah pitaa ve divam sharma jagati me pratishtaa

The cow is my mother the bull my father, may auspiciousness be established in this world

He then untied a cow along with its calf and positioned it such that its tail was near Tayavva. He sat facing north, filled a vessel with ghee and dropped the gold titbit in it. Then he held the cow's tail together with the vessel and told Tayavva to touch it. The women nearby held her up in a sitting position, lifted her hand and touched it to both the ghee vessel and the cow's tail.

Yagna saadhana bhootaayaa vishwasyaagha pranaashinii | vishwaroopah paroodevah priiyataamanayaa gavaa ||

Chanting this, Venkataramana touched a spoon filled with water to Tayavva's hand and then poured the water onto his palm. Then, he said, 'Look. Now you must think these words in your mind: *Gomaata*, you're my form as well. There's no separation between you and me. Therefore, by giving you away as *daana* today, I have given myself away as *daana*. *Yaavaiyooyam sohamadaiva Bhaavoyushmaandatvaa caahamaatma pradaata.*' He then took the ghee vessel from her hand together with the tail of the cow and holding it in his hand, said to Tayavva, 'I'll tell the cow: you who can assume both gentle and fierce forms, now this donor's mind is no longer set upon you. That means, the sense of attachment is gone. You have now become an object of my affection and attachment. Therefore, please bestow the desired prosperity and be propitious to the donor and me.'

The *Godaana* was now complete. After this, the rest of the cows were brought one after the other. Tayavva's hand would touch their tails following which Venkataramana would hold them in his hand. After he had accepted all the cows, he said, 'Maata Gowda, you take them outside and stand there. I'll give the *tirtha* and *prasada* to everyone.' The cows went outside along with their calves. With his finger, Venkataramana applied a dot of sandalwood paste on Tayavva's forehead and as *prasada,* placed an oleander flower upon her right ear. Then, he dropped a spoonful of *tirtha* in her mouth. He mixed the *prasada* that he had got from the temple with Maata Gowda's coconut and jaggery mixture and fed a pinch of this to Tayavva. After this, all the folk who had assembled there came forward and took the *tirtha* and the sandalwood paste. Venkataramana himself got up and distributed the *prasada* to everyone. He didn't even look at Kalinga who was leaning against the wall, still standing there; nor did he give him the *prasada.* Still unable to walk away, Kalinga remained rooted to the spot.

After everything was finished, Venkataramana said, 'I'll leave now, Mother.' From where she was sleeping, Tayavva indicated with a nod of her head that she wanted to perform *namaskara* to him. He moved forward and stood close to her head. The women around her lifted both her hands and placed them on his two feet. As her shrivelled white hands resembling the skeleton of a thin reed touching his feet, Tayavva closed her eyes. Venkataramana couldn't recollect the appropriate mantras for uttering the *ashirwada,* the benediction upon her. He tried for a minute to recall the mantra but it had eluded his memory. But as if something surged inside him, he suddenly laughed out. His eyes were filled with tears.

'You're like my mother, what *ashirwada* can I give you? You've never committed a single wrong deed in your entire life. You're truly virtuous. Like a cow you don't know how to speak and like a cow, you've lived a sinless life of *punya.* Still, because you've done *namaskara* to me, I must utter some words of benediction. You've decided not to live any more. Pass away as your heart desires. May you attain a quick and tranquil death bereft of any pain. May your soul reach the womb of a cow.'

Having said this much, he bent down, held both her hands and repositioned her on the bed comfortably. Kalinga remained standing where he was. Venkataramana didn't even look in his direction. He took the vessel of the *prasada* and came outside. He combined all the ropes of the cows that Maata Gowda was holding and held them in his hand and chanting the *Gomati* mantra loudly, he left:

Gaavah surabhayo nityam gaavo guggula gandhikaah |
gaavah pratishtaa bhootaanaam gaavah swastyayanam mahat ||
annameva param gaavo devaanaam haviruttamam |
paavanam sarva bhootaanaam rakshanti ca vahanti ca ||

Venkataramana forgot himself as he walked on, chanting the mantra in a high pitch.

The hooves of the cows left a trail of dust in their wake as they followed him. The little calves followed behind, running and suckling their mothers' teats, happy and playful.

VOLUME 16

1

Kalinga remained standing even after Venkataramana left. No one spoke with him. Those who had gathered outside the house ate the *prasada*, washed their hands and went to their respective homes. To the women sitting near Tayavva, Yangta Gowda said, 'You all stay right here. Maybe this evening or tomorrow morning, life will go out of this body. I'll go home for a bit, eat and I'll be back. Make her drink some milk.' Tayavva was drowsy. When they shook her shoulders and asked her, she said she didn't want anything to eat.

Kalinga felt a tug in his heart. He wanted to sit near his mother and talk with her. But if she didn't reply, he would feel insulted. Neither was he prepared to undergo humiliation in the presence of all these women. Nor did they show any sign of getting up and vacating the place. He thought of asking them to leave and telling them that he'd take care of his mother. But if they responded sarcastically, 'It's because you took care of her all these days that your mother has fallen to this state', it'd be a far greater humiliation.

Still rooted to the same spot, he lacked the will power to even turn back and go away. He was unaware of the power that had fettered him like a prisoner to that spot since the last three hours. Finally, he summoned all the strength of his personality and forcibly lifted his feet and walked out of the backdoor. The expansive, ancient barn at the rear of the house, standing since his grandfather's time, didn't have a single cow remaining. The last of the few cows that had remained had been given away as *daana* today. The oxen had gone out to graze. Standing there for a minute, he experienced an intense emotion. But before he could be swept away, he summoned his usual state of mind and brought himself under control. He then wore the shoes he had left outside and exited the village from the rear side. He walked across the stream and reached his new barn. But unwilling to stay there, he walked to his farmhouse.

The work on the well was in progress. The servants were clearing out the water that was welling up and digging still deeper. Nearby was a heap of bricks that had arrived that morning. Kalinga went straight in and lay down on the cot. Hilda came in and asked: 'Dear, you haven't even had lunch. Get up.'

'I don't want food.'

'Why, did you eat something there? How's your mother now?'

'She'll die today or tomorrow.'

'Why should we let her die? Can't we call a doctor? Or can't we call an ambulance and get her admitted to the district hospital?'

'No, no, you won't understand. Now be quiet,' he said indicating that he didn't want to talk.

'Sorry, please calm down,' she said and left the place.

He didn't get up in the evening as well; neither did he eat anything. He was experiencing an overpowering sense of defeat. His willpower had vanished. When Venkataramana was accepting the *daana*, a thought had arisen in his mind: of going ahead and holding the cow's tail thereby becoming a participant in the *daana* ritual. But then, had he done that and Venkataramana had yelled back, 'I will not accept a cow which this wretch has touched,' what would've been his fate? Scared, he had refrained. He had also thought of turning back several times and returning, while the puja was in progress. But he lacked the willpower to do so. Ultimately, he was like an impotent, torpid cripple who was unable to participate in the ritual—to assist or even oppose. He only stood there watching it from a distance and had to struggle to even get away from the place. *Should I go there again?* He thought. That place, that atmosphere, and his mother on her deathbed. He felt a bizarre attraction towards them, but lacked the mental poise to get up and walk towards the village.

He initially said no to dinner. But thinking that Hilda would be upset, he got up and sat at the dining table. When Hilda noticed that he was in no mood to talk, she too lapsed into silence. When Jack attempted to talk to his father, she shushed him.

Kalinga did get sleep at night. But he couldn't figure out whether it was really sleep or an unconscious state. One needs mental composure to sleep peacefully—one's willpower needs to be firm. In his case, both were depleted. Yet, he spent the night without the worries that befall one in their wakeful state.

He got up in the morning, washed his face, drank coffee and went to the barn. He had found another person to do Jamal's work, a Lingayat youth about twenty-five years of age. Malleshi had worked as a cleaner in a Motor Service bus in the Taluk. He had no parents. He had learnt motor driving and knew how to drive the tractor. When Kalinga offered him a monthly salary of seventy-five rupees, free meals, snacks and a place to live, Malleshi came with him. A pure vegetarian, he cooked his own meals. He would sometimes eat in the hotel, but he never even touched the coffee in Kalinga's house.

By the time Kalinga arrived, Malleshi was supervising the milking of the cows using the machine. He stood watching as the servants filled the cans with milk and took it to the road. Malleshi was washing the tubes of the milking machine. At eight, the large bell of the temple on the hill sounded. Halting the work he was doing, Malleshi turned in the direction of the hill, closed his eyes, joined his palms and stood there. He remained standing till the sound became feeble and could no longer be heard. Then he resumed his work. Kalinga became curious about Malleshi. He wore khaki knickers and a half-sleeved check shirt with a belt around his waist. He could drive the motor. Because he had worked in the bus service, he even spoke Urdu. He smoked *bidis*. But Kalinga wasn't aware that he was endowed with such deep religious faith.

Without speaking a word with him, Kalinga went home. The servants were working on the well. Hilda was supervising their work. Feeling piqued to stand there, Kalinga went in and lay down. Loneliness and its consequence, ennui, enveloped him.

By ten in the morning, Hilda came in and said: 'Look, a whole lot of people are going to the temple today. Is there some special puja today? I saw the *pujari* finish his work and return a long time ago.'

Kalinga got up and came outside. More than two hundred people—men, women, old folk, were climbing up the slope of the *kalyani* from the outer path. All of them were from his village. What was special today? He cast his sightline further ahead. Four people were carrying a corpse on a bier. It was clear now. *Mother has died. Perhaps it was her wish to be buried near the temple, not in any of their fields and farms! That's why they're carrying it there. But who'd pour earth in her mouth and close the grave? Couldn't the village folk call him for that rite at least? Aren't they aware that I'm right here? Or should I go there myself?* he thought. But then he recalled yesterday's experience and remained standing where he was.

Meanwhile, about twenty servants working on his well ran past where he was standing and joined the folks carrying the corpse. None of them were from Kalenahalli. They were from other villages in the vicinity. They wouldn't be directly acquainted with Tayavva. But because she was the Elder Gowda's daughter-in-law or because she was a virtuous old woman or the mistress of the house that built that temple, they'll all go on their own accord even if they are uninvited. And as a mark of respect to the corpse, they'll offer it a fistful of earth. By then the group had reached the top. The solitary Malleshi ran from behind and joined the group. It was only twenty days since Malleshi had come here and joined work. He was not connected with Kalenahalli in any way. His *jati* was different, his district different. *Has he gone there to merely witness the burial? Or has he gone there to give some earth, thereby offering his devotion to the corpse?*

Kalinga couldn't stand there. He came home and lay down. Hilda entered and asked: 'The servants told me that your mother died. Is that true?'

'Yes.'

'The village folk were supposed to call you, right?'

He didn't respond to this.

'What right do they have to perform the last rites to the corpse without calling you, my dear? You can take action against them for doing this.'

'Hilda, you won't understand this. Just stay quiet.'

'You only say I don't understand but you won't make me understand. Tell me, what's it?'

'I'm in no mood to talk now. Just stay silent.'

'I am sorry', she said and went to the kitchen with Jack in tow.

At about twelve thirty in the afternoon, Malleshi opened the door of his shed and went inside, perhaps to cook. The tin door would make a loud noise each time it was opened and closed. After first getting it purified with cow dung and urine, Malleshi began to live in this same shed in which Jamal used to live earlier. His menu was not fixed. If it was just curd and rice, so be it. If he was in the mood for it, he would prepare a vegetable broth and eat it with ragi *mudde*. Else, he would prepare *rotis* made with rice flour and eat them with coconut chutney. But no matter how hungry he was, he never ate a single morsel cooked in Kalinga's house.

Kalinga went to his shed and asked: 'Why had you gone there?'

It appeared that Malleshi was frightened by this question. 'It was a mistake, sorry sir', he said.

'I didn't ask you because it's a mistake. Tell me everything they did there.'

Putting down the rice vessel in his hand, he said: 'They didn't do anything sir. They lowered the corpse once in front of the temple. Then the Revered *Pujari* came and opened the door. It looked like he'd already come there earlier and performed the Puja. He poured a spoonful of *tirtha* on the body and placed a flower of *prasada*. Then they all took the corpse and buried it.'

'Where did they bury it exactly?'

'The Tiger Cave behind the temple. They dug out a pit beyond it and buried there. Isn't that the place where the tiger waylaid the cow and said I'll eat you? Isn't it the same place where the cow gave her word that it'll go to the barn, give milk to its baby and return?'

'What did they do after burying the body?"

"The Revered *Pujari* had a bath and then performed an *arati* with ghee wicks. Two strongmen filled two pots each with water from the *kalyani.* Then, after making all the men sit on the bank of the *kalyani,* they poured it on their heads.'

Malleshi's head was wet, too. His khaki knickers and checks shirt had been spread out to dry on the rope in front of the shed. Now he wore a scrap of *dhoti* and a white shirt. Kalinga didn't speak further. He came home. When he turned in the direction of the temple, it appeared that everybody who had come there were gone.

2

On the eleventh day after Tayavva's death, nobody came to work on the well. It wasn't hard for Kalinga to fathom the reason behind it. Nor was it unanticipated. But Kalinga hadn't thought about it one bit. His mother's *shraddha* was scheduled that day. The village folk would perform it themselves by pooling in the money for expenses. Or they would take out the grains and pulses in their homes and use them for the ceremony. But none invited Kalinga. And if he went on his own, nobody would even speak to him.

That morning at about eight, some ten or fifteen bullock carts went towards the hill from Kalenahalli. They were filled with enormous vessels, sacks of groceries and firewood. Kalinga saw them on his way to his new barn. He understood that they would perform the ceremony near the temple. When he saw Malleshi just returning after dispatching the milk cans to the motor, he asked: 'What will happen near the temple today?'

'It seems that from morning onwards, puja will be performed at the temple. In the evening, there is a grand feast for everyone coming from the neighbouring villages. About five or six thousand people from all *jatis* will gather there. They will prepare a separate feast for people from my *jati* as well. I'll go there for my meals.'

Kalinga didn't question him any further. He went home. Hilda was in the kitchen. He told her: 'Come. Let's go to the Taluk or to some other place, stay in the Government Traveller's Bungalow and return tomorrow.'

'What's this, all of a sudden?'

'It seems they'll perform my mother's after-death rituals right here, near the temple. There is a feast in the evening for about six thousand people. Neither will they invite us nor will they mingle if we ourselves go there. For some reason, I don't feel comfortable staying here. It'll be a sort of change for us as well.'

'Why should we be scared and leave the place? Why do we need to be afraid of anyone to stay in our own house?'

'It's not fear. I won't feel at peace if I stay here. Just come.'

Hilda was in her seventh month now. But there was no restriction for travelling by the motor. Jack had turned dull of late. He had no companions after Jamal and his wife had left. The newly arrived Malleshi didn't display affection towards Jack.

There was a motor at ten. After locking the door and informing Malleshi to guard the house with care, they reached the road. Hilda asked: 'I really don't understand the ways of these people. They say there's extreme food scarcity in this country. But the number of mass, public feasts that happen here, happens nowhere else. Four thousand people if there's a marriage. Four thousand if there's a death. Now you say that six thousand people will gather today. Unlike us, there's no need to even arrange for plates, forks and spoons. They serve food on a forest leaf. It's true, it's very easy. But why should one even feed so many people?'

Kalinga was aware of the answer that people would give to this question. But he himself lacked the conviction required to explain it to her. 'Isn't all this a waste?' she asked. To this, he said neither yes nor no. She lapsed into silence, thinking he wasn't in a mood to talk.

Hilda got herself examined by the lady doctor at the Taluk. Now a cinema hall had arrived there. The three of them went there. It was a Kannada film. Even this contained scenes depicting Gods, sages, animals talking, and thousands of people eating together.

After spending that night and the next afternoon at the Traveller's Bungalow, they took the evening motor and returned to their farmhouse. When Malleshi returned to his shed after finishing his evening work, Kalinga asked: 'How did everything go yesterday?'

'Very well. They'd organized a grand festival itself. *Dhotis*, copper pots, plates... all kinds of gifts. Mother had already performed the *Godaana* before dying. The Revered *Pujari* said it wasn't necessary to give any other gift again to enable her to cross the *Vaitarani* river to reach Heaven. They donated an ox to the village.'

'Who gave the bull-calf?'

'Nobody. There was a motherless calf when the Mother donated all the cows.' Suddenly, Malleshi bit his tongue and fell silent. He had known the background from the other servants that this was the calf whose mother had been slaughtered in his master's house. When Kalinga himself prodded, 'That's ok, tell me,' he said: 'They embossed a trident symbol on both its thighs. Then they untied it and set it free. Still, it wandered around suckling the teat of the cow that was with it. "Let it be like this for a year. Then we'll release it on a grazing field," said the Revered *pujari*. Despite this, it seems they won't tie the rope around its neck.'

'What else happened?'

'Nothing else.'

'Was I discussed?'

Malleshi said nothing in response. He remained that way even when Kalinga asked again. 'It's okay, tell me, I won't be displeased with you.' When he insisted the third time, he said: '"What kind of a seed is that guy born to? The grandfather built a temple for the cow. This whoreson slaughters the cow and eats it. The one who died is a virtuous woman. She'll definitely attain Heaven." This scoundrel whoreson and his wife… worms will fall in both their mouths. They said this and other stuff as they were eating.'

'Who?'

'All of them.'

Then Honna arrived there. So far he was tilling the land that was given in grant to Venkataramana on a sharecropping arrangement. Now it appeared that his head had been completely shaven yesterday. He stood at a distance from Kalinga and said: 'There's ragi and beans in the field. We need to scatter seeds in the wetlands by the *Pushya* month, around December. Coconuts have matured in the farm. We need to cut them. Where should I put them?'

'Which wetland, which farm, man?'

'Venkataramana's. The *Jois* told me, "I've returned all these lands to him, from now on, you deal with him in this matter."'

'When did he say this?'

'Twelve days prior to today. Then, after Mother died, I was busy with chopping firewood, arranging for the items and lots of other work. I never went to the fields. When I went to the home of the *Jois* this morning, he said, "Didn't I tell you the other day, man? I've given up those lands. Whatever you need to ask, ask that fellow."'

Kalinga was at a loss on how to respond to Honna. Suddenly, he felt dizzy and realized he'd fall down if he continued to stand there. He quickly walked home and reclined on the sofa. After he recovered, within five minutes Honna stood before him again. 'I'll send for you later. You go now,' said Kalinga and sent him away to the village. After he had gone, Kalinga got up, went to Malleshi's shed and asked: 'Why has this Honna shaved his head?'

'He shaved it yesterday to perform Mother's obsequies. Yangata Gowda asked who was to take the place of the son and perform the ceremony. "My man, the Mother has served me milk and ghee and reared me. I am her son. I'll get my head shaved," he said. The Revered *Jois* assented.'

Kalinga once more felt a deep sense of discomfort in his body. He was scared that he'd feel dizzy again and went back to his house and reclined on the sofa. Jack arrived there and leaned against his thighs. He was unable to understand the grief churning in his father's mind. Having no one to eat and play with, he came close in silence. His father said, 'I'm not feeling well. Go in and stay with your mother.'

Then Yangata Gowda's son Maata came to the outer door and stood before him. He was wearing shorts that covered his knees, a full-sleeved green shirt and thick slippers on his feet. He wore red earrings. A gold bracelet with the thickness of a thumb was shimmering above his right elbow. His plump lips were closed stiffly, and he was holding a long bamboo stave in his hand. It appeared from the manner of his stance that he had come here spoiling for a fight. But he didn't use provocative language. He extracted a large key from the pocket of his shorts, flung it so that it landed in front of Kalinga and said: 'Your house is locked. Go, open the door, and take whatever is there. All these days, the oxen in your house were tethered there. "Tether them in the barn or do whatever you want with them", my father said this to your servants yesterday. If you want, you can slaughter those oxen and eat even them.'

Maata paused for half a minute. Kalinga didn't say anything. Then Maata spoke as if he had recalled something: 'Look, after your mother died, everything in your home is as is... paddy, ragi, beans, chillies, everything. No bastard son of mine has touched it. All the village folk pooled in pulses and groceries for your mother's ceremony. As a mark of his devotion, Honna offered four bags of ragi, two sacks of rice and fifty rupees. Beware of making an allegation against us tomorrow that "the village folk took away the grains and groceries from my house after my mother died." You open the door yourself and check everything. The entire village is a witness to me giving you this key. Yeah!'

Having said this, he turned and left in a spirit of having accomplished his task. Kalinga mulled over the reason he had come with the bamboo stave. *Perhaps he had anticipated that I would pick a fight with him.*

Kalinga spent the entire day lying down, not speaking to anyone. He had a feeling that everybody had abandoned him. Not just Venkataramana and the village folk, but this mountain, the foothills, and even the wafting breeze had pushed him towards loneliness. All of them had gone far, far away from him. No matter who came to see him, it appeared to him that they would all come merely to tell him that they had nothing to do with him anymore.

That evening, two people from the *Kole Basava* troupe arrived at his house. One of them leading a Rama ox and a Sita cow was a young man of 23 or 24. The other was a girl aged 17 or 18 carrying a baby on her waist. Both Hilda and Jack stood watching the curious costume they wore as well as the way the ox and the cow were decked up. 'Is this the home of the Master Kalinga *Golla*?' Kalinga emerged from inside when he heard this question. 'Are you the grandson of the dead old Gowda, Little Gowda?' he asked in the manner of addressing his ox.

'Why?'

'Look, the old Gowda had given a loan of fifty rupees for our wedding. We held the tail of our Mother Sita and gave him our word. Take your money back now,' he said, pulling out a cloth containing a wad of rolled notes from the inner pocket of his striped coat. Then he said: 'When we took the money, we made an oath holding Mother Sita's tail. Now you utter, "I got back the amount" holding her tail.'

Kalinga simply stood, saying nothing. The *Basava* youth held out his hand containing the notes and asked: 'Why, Little Gowda? Don't you want the money?'

'How do I know what my grandfather gave you?'

'Why should we give you the money without any reason? Take it.'

Kalinga stretched his hand forward. 'First, you hold the cow's tail and utter that the money has reached you,' the other man insisted.

'What'll you do if I don't touch the tail and utter those words?'

'I won't give the money. I'll use it to buy a striped sari for my Mother Sita and drape her with it.'

'Who told you I was here?'

'We'd been to your home in the village. The village folk told us.'

'What else did they say?'

'It's none of my business what *else* they said. Take your money.'

Kalinga felt crestfallen. *Even this Kole Basava person knows everything. The village folk have narrated their complaints against me even to this fellow. Now these guys will go around tom-tomming it to the entire country,* he thought. Then Hilda said: 'You came from that direction, right? Where did you come from exactly?'

'We'd been to the temple that your husband's grandfather built. It's the temple of our Mother Sita. We visited it, prostrated before her and came here.'

'Who opened its door now?'

'The Revered *Pujari* is right there. He's sitting in the temple and chanting mantras.'

When he heard this, Kalinga felt crestfallen yet again. He said: 'Look, I don't want this money. Give it to the temple's *pujari*.'

'*Ayya*, the grandfather's loan must be handed over to the grandson. You take it.'

'I'm telling you I don't want it.'

'Even if you say you don't want it, we will not relent. The *pujari* rejected the land grant that your grandfather gave him. Will he ever touch this money?' Even as the *Basava* youth uttered this, his wife said, 'Why are you concerned with all that? Shut up.'

The youth placed the notes in front of Kalinga and said, 'Although you didn't utter that you received the money, I've still given it to you. My Mother Sita is herself the witness.' Then he signalled to the ox, 'Come, let's go Rama,' and walked away. His wife walked behind Mother Sita.

Kalinga stood there as if struck by lightning. *Who gave this Kole Basava fellow the right to speak with such audacity?* Outraged, he felt like slapping him. But by then they were far away. Kalinga walked twenty steps in their direction. Hilda asked, 'Where're you going?' He paused and turned around to answer her. But he was unable to find any response. By then the thought of slapping them had vanished. He silently went inside the house and lay down on the cot.

3

Kalinga felt orphaned after his mother's death. Children become orphans after the mother dies; that is, they have none to look at them with warmth and attachment. He had heard these words since childhood. But now he realized that their meaning went far deeper.

In reality, as long as Tayavva was alive, there was no visible relationship between mother and son. Earlier, he used to think there was nothing he could speak with that mute woman. After being educated, he felt there were absolutely no topics on which he could converse with her. After he returned from America and established a new farm, she took the side of the opposition at every stage of his work. From the time of selling the cattle to the butcher right up to getting the pump removed from the temple's *kalyani*, she stood by the village folk and Venkataramana. Fumes of unexpressed anger had been fanning inside him against her. But then she died and even after her death, the village folk kept him at a distance, performed her obsequies, and announced in the neighbouring villages that he was no longer connected to that family.

Kalinga was burning with humiliation. If it was merely an insult, he could've borne it. But then he had drowned in a feeling that he had no one left to call his own in this land, in these surroundings and indeed, in this country itself. When he was studying in college, he had led an active social life with scores of friends after distinguishing himself as an excellent sportsman. But after returning from America, he suffered from acute loneliness. But as long as his mother was alive, his village, his house, the village folk, all of them lived in his conscious awareness. A couple of times he had thought of not informing the police about the incident of paying the punishment fine for slaughtering the cow. That would've ended the matter and everything would've been fine. But then he had been unable to wipe off the suspicion that had he left it at that, the village folk would summon the guts to engage in similar hooliganism in future. Yet, despite all this, he had a latent self-confidence that he would be able to pacify them. But even that collapsed with his mother's death.

Now he felt completely desolate. The servants worked for him just for the sake of their livelihood. They could never regard him with affection from the perspective of culture and conviction. Then there was Venkataramana. He was one person with whom the relationship could've perhaps been renewed. But even that possibility was unthinkable now. Whenever he thought about the village folk, Kalinga didn't feel even an iota of fear. But with Venkataramana, a sort of unfathomable fear would envelop him. *He quit the school job for the same reason. He's also courageously tossed aside the land grant for this very reason. I didn't ask him to leave it. Because I merely warned him, 'If you take the side of the village folk and try to harm me, you might lose your land,' he took the decision to give up the land on his own. He hasn't abandoned the puja even after the land was gone. He's always been devoted to bhakti, puja, traditions and customs from the very beginning. Although he doesn't have much to eat, he walks one-and-a-half miles each day, comes here, and does the puja. What must his mother and wife think of me!*

One day, Kalinga walked up towards the temple as usual. About forty or fifty servants from Kalenahalli were engaged in some work, hoes and crowbars in hand. Without going close, Kalinga stood observing them from afar. They were erecting a fence of agaves blocking access from the farm to the *kalyani,* the temple, and cordoning off that flank of the hill. Nobody could access the temple from the farm now. After digging trenches, they were planting agave stalks in them. As if that wasn't enough, they had planted acacia reeds between each stalk and were fastening a mesh of bamboo thorns around them. Venkataramana was personally overseeing the task. Several women workers were watering the agave stalks, drawing water from the *kalyani.*

Kalinga understood immediately. He recalled Venkataramana's

S.L. BHYRAPPA

words: *Don't you dare come this side. Beware if you try to usurp the region of the temple and the kalyani. That's why we're erecting this fence.* Unable to stand there any longer, he went home and lay down on the bed. Had he continued to stand there, he would've been spotted either by the village folk or by Venkataramana. But what'd happen if he was spotted? He couldn't get himself to think of this question.

He lay there in that position for over an hour. Then Hilda came inside as though she was looking for him and said: 'You're right here! I searched for you everywhere.'

He continued to lie down, without speaking. She sat close to him leaning against a pillow and said: 'Look, there's only seventeen or eighteen days left for my delivery. During this period, it's your duty to make sure that I get adequate rest and mental peace. You've been doing nothing of late. How can I manage everything on my own?'

He still said nothing. She continued: 'The work on the well is complete. All that remains is the installation of the pump. I can't do that in this condition. Can't you call the cement workers and get it done? After your village folk ruined the tobacco crop, that is, since the last four months, the entire farm has fallen into disuse. The life of anyone who engages in this sort of economic negligence is shameful. If we'd taken out water from the pump and moistened the farmland, Malleshi would've driven the tractor. Have you thought about what we'll grow this time?'

He didn't speak even now. Hilda herself spoke again: 'Well, there's nothing to think. We had filled the farmland with manure last time, but the crop was destroyed when it had grown about a quarter. But the essence of the manure hasn't been lost as the soil has been well-preserved over these four months. Let's plant tobacco this time as well. Bring even better quality seeds. What's the point of my staying here if we don't harvest a profit that'll compensate for last time's loss?'

Kalinga found a new zeal the moment he heard her words. He sat up. But before he could open his mouth to say something, the zeal dissipated and he sat in silence, a dreary expression on his face. Hilda asked, 'Kaling, my dear, what has happened to you, tell me.'

He stayed quiet. She embraced his head and placing it between her breasts, she whispered consoling him: 'You've been like this for so many days. Tell me, tell me baby.'

Grief broke out from within Kalinga at these words. Burying his face in her chest, he said: 'Loneliness. I'm all alone in this whole world, in this entire life. Everyone has rejected me. Who's there to feel happy for anything I've accomplished?'

'Why do you say that? Am I not part of your life?'

'You are. But you can't cure my loneliness.'

Hilda became serious at hearing this. The gloom that had struck Kalinga also struck her now. But without losing her mental composure, she said: 'I understand your feelings. Didn't I tell you earlier? This is just how this country is. Even I'm suffering from loneliness here. Only, I haven't told you. Neither have you attempted to understand it. Let's do as I say.'

'What?'

'Let's sell all this for the best possible money and take it all there. Come. Let's start a new life in America.'

Kalinga looked at her face and smiled at her as if in sarcasm. Seeing this, she asked, 'Why?'

'I've thought about that as well. I'm lonely there too. Because I'm black-skinned, they won't fully admit me in their circle. And it's not just that. Had it been before my mother died, perhaps I would've come there. But now, no matter what I do, it's impossible for me to get out of here. I feel like someone has tied me up.'

Hilda considered his words and thought about them seriously. Tears filled her eyes. She said: 'Kaling, you're simply uttering meaningless words. You say you're lonely. You also say you're bound to this land. You said even I can't cure your loneliness. Neither do you have the memory of the sacrifices I've made for you. I left the land of my birth, all the people I considered mine and I came here. Neither do I have any friends; no companions. No pastime. Nor can I hear my mother tongue. Despite all this, I've remained patient and I'm doing all this work. So, apart from being irresponsible, you're telling me to my face that "even you can't cure my loneliness" and hurting my self-respect.'

Comprehending nothing, Kalinga was watching her face. She said, after thinking something: 'Not here. Come, let's go there, to America. If you're unable to come with me, I'll go alone.'

'What... what're you saying?' Kalinga asked stupefied.

'It's rather simple. I don't utter words after chewing and swallowing them like you do. That temple's *pujari* out there? I speak like him, directly, like breaking a twig into two. I'll take Jack with me and return to my native country. You stay here; find a girl from this country, marry her and be happy. Your loneliness will disappear. Goodbye,' she said, pointing her hand at him like she was issuing a command. Then she went to the other room, shut the door and began to sob. Dumbfounded, Kalinga stood silently outside the door.

Jack who was then playing in the soil near Malleshi's shed, came inside. Despite calling out mummy twice, she didn't respond. Kalinga took him along, washed his hands, legs and face, and seated him before the table and served food. After he was told that his mummy had finished her food, Jack began to eat from his plate.

Hilda didn't emerge even after two hours. Tired of waiting, Kalinga went to the bedroom with Jack in tow and lay down. Jack drifted off to sleep in half an hour. Hunger had joined forces with the shock that had hit Kalinga. He couldn't sleep. Everyone had become an alien to him in his own land. But today, even his wife had uttered words of abandoning him. *If the words 'walking out' are uttered even once, it means the marriage has cracked,* he thought. Hilda might well go away. What would be his fate then? And like she said, he could marry some girl here. Even the very thought of this possibility appeared unbearable to him. He fell in love with Hilda and married her. They had imagined that they would come to this country and together, accomplish all sorts of miracles in farming! Now, she would go away, rejecting him; and he would marry a local girl!

His mind drifted towards Hilda's joys and difficulties. After Jamal left, she was not getting to eat meat regularly. Not a single servant in the house would go to the butcher to bring it. On some occasions when he visited the Taluk, he would get it from there. That was all the meat that she got. Even in that case, when he got it packed and brought it in the motor, if someone detected the odour, they would complain. When

Jamal and his wife were here, they had bred chicken. Almost every day, they got a supply of eggs they required at home. Now, along with all the other work, Hilda found it impossible to take care of the chickens and so their breeding had stopped. No eggs for either breakfast or meals. Without the diet that she was accustomed to since birth, with no kin, and no friends, she too was suffering from loneliness. Indeed, both were lonely. But why was it not possible for both of them to be one another's companions? When this thought arose in his mind, he felt excited, as if he had stumbled upon a new question. But he couldn't find an answer.

4

By evening, he heard noises indicating that Hilda was in pain. When Kalinga went to the door of the room, the bolt was unlatched. Going inside, he asked: 'What happened?'

'Labour pains have begun.'

'You said there were still 17 or 18 days?'

'I did. At times premature delivery might occur due to mental trauma. The kind of shock I experienced today isn't trivial.'

Unable to figure out anything, he quietly went close to her and gently stroking her head, said, 'Get a hold of yourself, darling.'

'If there was at least a van or car in this dense jungle, we could've quickly gone to some hospital. Arrange for a doctor now. Run.'

Kalinga got up and stepped out of the room. Hilda called out to him again and said: 'Look, in this situation, it's the duty of the husband to serve his wife appropriately. It's the duty of love. But the time for you to carry out that sort of duty has long passed. So do it with the feeling a common citizen would have for a helpless woman in distress. I won't ask for your support for much longer.'

Kalinga said nothing. Her face was contorted in pain. He went to Malleshi's shed, climbed on the cycle and reached the road. About one-and-a-half miles down that road was a camp of the Electricity Department. It was possible to talk to the Taluk's Electricity Office from there. He talked to the camp supervisor and then spoke to the Taluk Office: 'Get any vehicle that you can immediately find and bring a doctor and nurse. Labour pains. It's impossible to bring the pregnant woman there. It doesn't matter what the doctor's fee is.'

The Taluk's Electricity Office assured him that they would definitely send a doctor. Kalinga pedalled back home. By the time he returned, Hilda's pain had escalated. Jack was sitting dumbstruck, unable to comprehend anything. Hilda had herself made arrangements for the preliminary items required for delivery. When Kalinga informed her of his phone conversation, she felt relieved for a bit, but the moment she saw his face she became agitated yet again. 'Get out of here. Don't show me your face,' she yelled shrilly. Scared, he stood outside the room. Inside, she was writhing in agony.

In half an hour, she called him in. Her whole body was drenched in sweat. She said: 'Look, you've studied veterinary science. You know how delivery takes place, right? I'll keep giving you instructions, just do accordingly. If I become unconscious by chance, do what you think is appropriate. All the materials are here. Jack might feel scared. Send him to Malleshi's shed.'

Then a worker from the Electricity Department's camp called from outside. When Kalinga stepped out, he said to him: 'The doctor and nurse will come in the car. It seems they've just left.'

Kalinga came back in and conveyed the news to Hilda. But her pains had reached the final stage. Even then, without losing her composure, she described everything that he needed to do in detail. When the time came, she didn't lose consciousness. He carried out everything with deftness. Completely drained, she slept. She didn't have energy even to ask the gender of the baby. Kalinga looked at the baby. A girl. But unlike Jack who was red, her colour was like Kalinga.

The doctor's car arrived by the time Kalinga had boiled water on the electric heater in the kitchen. The nurse took over from there. After examining the new mother's blood pressure and other parameters, the doctor told Kalinga, 'She's hugely agitated. Give her some liquid first. Then you need to give her a sleeping pill.'

Half an hour later, the doctor returned in the same car. The nurse would return in the motor tomorrow morning. She was living with her mother, who had also served and retired from the same profession. The nurse told him that her mother was ready to come and stay here for fifteen days. Apart from paying her four rupees each day, they would also need to pay the return motor fare and give her meals and tiffin. Kalinga agreed. The nurse assured him that she would send her mother in the next motor immediately after returning home the next day.

Perhaps the doctor had prescribed a heavy dosage of the sedative because it was about ten in the morning next day when Hilda awoke. The nurse had left by then. Kalinga himself made bread and coffee for Hilda, who was still feeling drowsy. When she saw the baby again, it didn't feel attractive to her. Like every newly born baby, even this infant was fair and red. But then it was evident that in the future, instead of becoming like the Red People, this baby's colour would be black like the people of Hindustan. But her current state of drowsiness didn't allow her to think further. She loosened her body and closed her eyes.

It was night when she awoke again. Meanwhile, the nurse's mother, the old nurse had arrived. Filled with milk, Hilda's breasts were feeling heavy. But one shouldn't feed the infant the first round of milk. Hilda sucked out the milk from both her breasts using the breast pump that the nurse gave her. When she lay down after eating food, she drifted off to sleep again.

The next day when she woke up in the morning, the baby was wailing in a high pitch. The nurse said: 'You must feed breast milk. You lie on your side.'

Her eyes still sleepy, Hilda turned on her side towards the baby. The baby fixed the nipple between its tender jaw. 'You press it gently,' said the nurse. But that was unnecessary. Milk oozed into the baby's mouth. In five minutes, the baby began to suckle properly. Then, it firmly pushed against the mother's breast with its mouth and tugged. Hilda felt a pleasant pain that made her say *Aah*, as she clasped the baby's head with her left hand.

5

Hilda was aware that labour pains had started because of the mental trauma she had experienced. But then she didn't change the decision she had taken that day. She had firmly made up her mind to leave for her homeland along with Jack a couple of months after the delivery.

She hadn't closely observed the baby immediately after delivery. When she awoke the next morning, she felt a little unenthused when she noticed its colour. This girl child would eventually turn black, she thought. What would she do with it if she took it to her homeland? Amidst her own people, this baby would become a symbol reminding her of her previous life. She felt sleepy even as this thought vaguely arose in her mind. It came to her yet again when she awoke at night and began to pump out milk from her breasts. Another bizarre question came to her mind: *why did this baby take birth from my womb?* It wasn't as if this sort of thought hadn't occurred to her when she married Kalinga—indeed, it was possible that her womb could give birth to such children. But the enthusiasm then was completely different. Back then, the picture of leaving him and returning to her homeland and living separately wasn't present in her imagination. But now, her mind was telling her that somehow there would be no place for this child there. She couldn't muster attachment and love for this baby. She glanced at it once with a sort of negligent abandon and closed her eyes.

But when the baby began suckling her breast the next day, that negligence disappeared. When it punched her breast with its mouth once with enormous strength and tugged, not only did the last wisp of negligence extinguish, but love gushed forth towards the baby along with the milk that flowed from her breast into its mouth. As she held its head in her left hand to prevent it from punching and hurting her again, she also embraced it tenderly.

The nurse stayed there for fifteen days. By then Hilda had begun to perform her routine tasks. The evening that the nurse left, Jack was playing with his little sister standing by her cradle. Kalinga was seated on the sofa outside engrossed in some thought. Since the day Hilda had spoken about leaving him, Kalinga no longer spoke to her looking at her face directly. Fear, disappointment, melancholy, disinterest or whatever—he was constantly torpid, thinking within himself. 'Call papa,' Hilda told Jack. As if duty bound, when Kalinga went inside, she held his shoulders and seated him on her bed and asked: 'How far has the work on the well progressed?'

'It's where it was', he said lowering his head.

After remaining quiet for a minute, Hilda said: 'Why are you neglecting work like this?'

He said nothing. She continued: 'Look, the more you're like this, the worse I feel. Work with the same enthusiasm as before. Be my partner in it. Take my advice. Then even I'll feel like I'm together with you. And you'll feel the same. Our mutual loneliness will go away.'

Kalinga turned his head and looked at her face. She spoke: 'Think about me as well. If you stay dull like this thinking that your loneliness is greater, who'll dispel my loneliness? Start work from tomorrow itself and install the pump for the well. Get the tractor moving quickly. At least its sound will help overcome this silence, this boredom. Else, life gets very tough in this forest.'

Kalinga squeezed her hand tightly. Both remained that way for two minutes. Then the baby began to cry. Seated near the cradle, Kalinga himself lifted it up and laid it down on his lap.

Hilda asked: 'It's already seventeen days. What do we call her?'

'You tell me.'

'Jacqueline? How about Esther? Is there no Padre nearby? If no, we can go to the church in the Taluk after a few days.'

Kalinga shook his head in disagreement at these words. 'Why?' asked Hilda.

'Have you observed the baby closely? Its face, eyes, nose, forehead. Everything is my mother's.'

'Kaling, how's that possible?'

'Why not?' even as Kalinga asked this, Hilda said: 'Yes, my brain isn't functioning properly lately. Not only is it possible, but natural as well.'

Kalinga was gazing at her face. Then he said: 'Let's name her after my mother.'

'What's her name?'

'Tayavva.'

'That means mother, right? How appropriate is it to call a baby—mother?'

'Even I don't know. But when my mother was born, her parents called her Tayavva. I don't know from what sense of propriety they called her that. If we ask folks like Venkataramana, he might explain it in detail.'

S.L. BHYRAPPA

'The possibility of asking him no longer exists, right?'

Kalinga went quiet. The baby wailed again. Sitting up and feeding it milk, Hilda said: 'What do they do here if they want to name a baby?'

'They inform Venkataramana the day and time of birth. He makes calculations accordingly, and if it's the first male child, the name of the grandfather and if it's the first girl child the name of the grandmother is taken into account and then he suggests a suitable name. That name stays.'

'In that case, if we inform someone the date and time, will they suggest a name?'

'Perhaps no', he said, laughing once.

'Why did you laugh?' she asked.

'For the state we're in. Of being unable to decide a name for our own baby. The baby's face resembles its grandmother. Therefore, the name that you suggest won't fit. But neither do we have the freedom to name it directly after its grandmother. The *purohit* who needs to perform the naming ceremony and give the infant a place in social life has become our sworn enemy. What a situation to be in!'

Unable to say anything in response, Hilda stared at him blankly.

6

In fifteen days, they installed the pump and watered the land. Having no tough labour to perform so far, Malleshi now climbed the tractor. Hilda began to walk around outside but felt a little fatigued. 'Our women spend six months in convalescence. What's going to happen if you work like this just after a month?' asked Kalinga.

'I don't need the customs of this place, dear. After Jamal left, there's been no meat regularly. You go to Karim one of these days and inform him. Let him send it here daily through a delivery boy. We'll give the boy some wages every month. How can I work without adequate protein?'

Kalinga complied accordingly. Hilda savoured the new food that she ate daily. Even Kalinga began to feel the earlier enthusiasm returning. He said he would take care of the tobacco saplings and the harvest work this time around. Because it would give her the requisite walking both in the morning and evening, Hilda agreed to oversee the work at the barn. Besides, as Malleshi had now begun doing the tractor work, she remained in the barn supervising the milking machine.

The cowshed was now in complete disarray. After Tayavva died, they had crowded this place with all the oxen that were being tethered earlier. Although some servants were using the oxen for tilling the lands in the village, Kalinga had never supervised their work personally. He was averse to visiting village lands in the presence of the village folk. But now Hilda began to mull over the problem of the cattle that had newly arrived in this cowshed. When she calculated the cost of the amount of grass they fruitlessly ate every day, she felt that it was completely disproportionate to the profits they gave in return. That apart, four cows in their shed had become infertile. Despite having been inseminated three times, they failed to become pregnant. Upon inquiring, the servants informed that they had crossed the age of becoming pregnant again. *So what had to be done with these? Who'd buy them?*

Two more months elapsed. Then Hilda's health failed. Initially when she was feeding the baby, both her breasts experienced extreme pain. Now it felt like something was hardening from within. Thinking that it would get better if she completely stopped feeding the child, she did so. But in exactly one day, the tightness increased from within. The infant too began wailing stubbornly. It wouldn't allow the milk in the bottle to even touch its lips. Hilda breastfed the baby only to reduce the tightness in her breasts. The baby calmed down, and the pain in her breasts reduced slightly as well, but it didn't fully subside. She administered hot water press to herself and felt a little better.

She told Kalinga, who inquired about the pain everyday: 'When Jack was a baby, I never fed him so much milk. He grew up on bottled milk and baby food. This child is totally attached to breast milk.'

'This is a child of Hindustan; it's like the calf of a cow.'

'Don't joke dear. But then I feel what you're saying is true. When it's drinking milk, it punches solidly, it bites, just like a calf does to a cow! It doesn't even touch any other food. Perhaps the mammary nerve endings are exhausted with all this relentless suckling.'

'But the women of this country feed any amount of milk to their babies. Why doesn't this happen to them?'

'I don't know about that. I'm not from this country. All I'm saying is: I need to reduce the milk I'm feeding the baby. Apparently there's not even a surrogate nurse who can feed milk in this wretched country. That's what that nurse told me.'

Kalinga went quiet.

The work of planting tobacco saplings in the farm was now complete. Kalinga's time was occupied by carefully examining and giving water in an optimal quantity to the tender plants among them. The supervision of the cowshed was now completely in Hilda's hands. Apparently, there was some ragi grass in the region behind their house in the village. But because there was no one to supervise it, it was taken away by random people. The grass in their barn which was set up in a scientific manner was not enough to last this year for the cattle inside it, including the new ones. *The time for this season's harvest is also nearing. Next year onwards, the village farmlands need to be tilled with the tractor; else, the fragmented lands have to be sold and a single tract of fresh land spacious enough for the tractor has to be purchased,* thought Hilda. *Now what is the use of this excess cattle?* When she informed that she intended to sell them, the servants themselves fetched buyers. The oxen which still had strength to work were purchased. But there was no buyer who came forward to purchase the twelve old oxen and the four old cows, completely useless for any sort of work.

She told the boy who came home daily to supply meat to tell Karim to see her. Rejecting her offer to buy the twelve aged oxen and the four aged cows, Karim said: 'What do I do after buying them? If the townsfolk learn that they've been slaughtered, they'll burn my house and celebrate the Holi festival. Do this: There's a cattle seller in the Taluk. I'll send him here. Sell them to him.'

'What'll he do?'

'He'll transport them to Mumbai in the train. They'll slaughter them at the abattoir there, pack the meat in boxes and sell it.'

'Send him.'

The cattle seller arrived on the fourth day. Nobody in Kalenahalli knew that he was a butcher. Ten rupees for a cow and fifteen for an ox. He counted out the money and took them away. To the servants he encountered outside the barn, he said: 'I'm taking them to the *Goshaala*. We perform the last rites for the old cows on the banks of the river.'

The servants said nothing.

1

By afternoon that day, Hilda's breasts started to pain again. While inside her right breast it felt like there was a hard lump, yellowish milk began to flow from her left. Unable to bear the pain, she began to writhe uncontrollably. The reason for it was beyond their grasp.

'One way or the other, I think it's good to show it to a doctor,' said Kalinga.

Immediately, both of them reached the road with their children in tow. They sat in the motor, reached the Taluk and went to the government hospital from where the doctor had come for Hilda's delivery. Throughout the journey, Hilda fought back her tears with great difficulty and bore the pain. By then, unable to withstand its hunger, the baby too began to wail.

After examining the patient, the doctor said: 'This might be breast abscess. A lump has formed in the right breast. There seems to be nothing in the left. Can't say anything definitively. I'll give an injection for now. It could be breast cancer. It's advisable to visit a bigger hospital.'

Hilda was aghast. No cancer patient survives. One of her mother's elder sisters had died from it. *Perhaps the same disease has struck me.* Tightly embracing her baby, she let out all the tears that she had bottled up so far. Kalinga too stood there, drained of all strength. The doctor who had given her the injection said: 'I am not an expert in women's ailments. You first go to the district hospital. There's a gynaecologist, a specialist. Take his opinion and then go to some cancer treatment institute.'

Hailing a taxi, Kalinga immediately went to the district hospital with Hilda and the children. They admitted her in the hospital. However, they were informed that the specialist who examined such diseases was on leave and it would be three days before he would return. Kalinga took accommodation in a hotel near the hospital. The baby was hollering in hunger. The lady doctor took the initiative and enquired with a nurse there, who had a six-month-old baby. She agreed to feed milk to this infant. Hilda assured her that she would pay her generously.

Hilda's pain temporarily subsided from the injections they gave her. But, neither she nor Kalinga were free because of anxiety till the specialist examined her. She was convinced that she would definitely die from this ailment. She had studied zoology and veterinary science. Medical science was still unaware of when, to whom and how cancer struck. Doctors who were extraordinary specialists could help postpone the death of cancer patients by a few days or a few months. But, they couldn't save lives. Even if death was postponed, the suffering, the physical and mental agony was hellish. Instead, an early death was welcome. It was simply enough if the specialist told her that she indeed had cancer. *I myself must refuse to take treatment. There's a gun at home. I can bid goodbye to life within a minute.*

With this thought of death, Hilda recollected the memories of her life from the beginning. Her birthplace, her upbringing, education, falling in love with Kalinga, marriage, arriving in this companionless country, the vandalism that the villagers inflicted on their farm, Jack and then the birth of this still-nameless infant—all these thoughts flashed in her mind. *This baby was born without anybody's help, by her own husband who did the work of a nurse. Is this a premonition that it would be orphaned in future? How will it survive after I'm dead? Who will give it breast milk? Who will hold it until it falls asleep? Who can it call it its own?* The whole hospital was quiet in the middle of the night. A bulb was burning dimly in the special ward in which she tried to sleep. The nurse who had agreed to feed milk for a fee had gone home after informing that she'd return early in the morning. Hilda turned once and looked at the infant. Its colour was now turning to that of the Hindustanis. Already three months, its face clearly resembled that of Kalinga's mother. *Why did it take birth in my womb?* The question arose in Hilda's mind.

What will be the fate of this baby? There may be institutions to raise motherless children. But no matter with what pristine care they were raised, they still were orphans. This baby's nature is indeed strange. Since the time of its very birth, it stubbornly insists that it won't touch anything other than breast milk. Where did it get this obstinacy? I could've died without worrying much if it was a baby that drank whatever was given to it. But this baby's nature is making my death that much more agonizing. I mustn't die. No matter what it costs, I must live. I mustn't allow it to become an orphan, she decided. But no matter how much money was spent, no medicine had yet been discovered to ensure that cancer patients definitely survived. When she realized this fact, she began to sob uncontrollably. The baby awoke to the sound of her sobbing. It too began to wail immediately. And now, the only way to console it was to feed it her breast milk. Patients in other wards too, awoke to the sound of the infant's cries. The duty nurse who was leaning and asleep in the easy chair in the corridor outside ran in. She carried it and sprinted to the nurses' quarters in the hall.

By next morning, the pain in her breasts was unbearable. The other doctors didn't know the reason for it. Neither could they figure out anything after taking an X-ray. 'It could well be cancer. But wait till tomorrow evening till the specialist arrives,' they said.

A pale Kalinga was sitting in the ward. Hilda was speaking bizarrely in an effort to forget her suffering. Hugging Jack, she began to cry, 'Baby, my baby, you'll be orphaned. You didn't drink breast milk. Yet, how will you survive? It's certain. I'm going to definitely die.' At this, even Jack began to cry. When Kalinga said, 'Don't talk like that. The boy will needlessly be frightened.'

'Kaling, my dear, I'm speaking the truth. Death is not merely a future possibility. To me, it's the present truth. I'm already dead actually. Tell me definitely. Will you be the mother for this baby? *Can* you be?' she watched his face. Then she said, 'No, no, no father in this world can ever become a mother to children. But a mother can become a father as well.'

Meanwhile, the nurse who was outside came in and said, 'You mustn't create a ruckus by becoming hysterical like this. Please remain quiet.' Still, Hilda didn't stop talking.

By night, her agony had touched impossible heights. The doctor affixed the breast pump and sucked out all the milk from both her breasts, ignoring her pain. Although it felt better for a while, the pain resurfaced. Finding no other way, the doctor gave her sleeping pills and Hilda drifted off to slumber by about eleven in the night.

Till the next evening, she writhed like a dying frog. She spoke of death and suicide scores of times. After the specialist arrived by the evening train, Kalinga immediately escorted him to the hospital. After listening to the disease history and then examining the patient personally, and then sucking the milk out and examining it as well, he said: 'I don't think it's cancer. My diagnosis is different. I'll give the required medication immediately. You should be able to see the results in two days. If not, let's think about what we can do in the future.'

Hilda suffered one more day. Then the pain subsided. The specialist said: 'My diagnosis was accurate indeed. It's not cancer. The patient will need to stay in the hospital till she's fully cured—that is, twenty more days. If you wish, you can go back to your village.'

Kalinga remained there for four more days. After removing the lump through surgery, her pain subsided substantially. The lump in her right breast had grown visibly. There was one growing in her left breast too. The doctor said that it would also be surgically removed. Hilda urged Kalinga to return home. 'The nurse will take care of the child. You go home with Jack. Who knows what's happened to the tobacco? Visit me here once in two or three days with Jack,' she said. Kalinga went home.

2

Kalinga had instructed Malleshi to get food for him and Jack in Hilda's absence. Malleshi systematically prepared rice and vegetable broth and delivered it to both of them in aluminium utensils.

One day when Kalinga and Jack returned home from the district in the evening's motor, someone had left thirteen gunny bags in front of the house. When he went near and examined each, it became clear: one had beans in it, the other had legume, and the rest were filled with ragi. He called out to Malleshi and asked: 'What are all these bags?'

'Honna from the *Agrahara* came with two carts, unloaded them here and went off. Apparently this is half the yield from sharecropping. He asked where the ragi grass should be delivered. I told him I don't know. I told him to ask after the *Saavkar,* the Master, came.'

'Why didn't you tell him not to dump this stuff here without asking the *Saavkar?*'

'I did tell him that. But he said there wasn't place in his house.'

Kalinga closely observed Malleshi's face. *Does he or does he not know the background to this? All the servants know it. This fellow also keeps visiting the temple. Even he knows,* thought Kalinga and said: 'Look, take the cycle and bring Honna with you right now.'

Honna arrived at seven in the night. 'Why did you dump this here?' asked Kalinga. Honna said: 'Where else should I put it, my man?'

'Couldn't you ask the *Jois?*'

'It's been many days already since he even looked in the direction of the land. I did ask him. He said: "Why should I look at that after the debt is torn?" In fact, I myself cut the coconuts in the coconut grove. It's now one and a half thousand.'

Kalinga had indeed anticipated this answer. Yet, he had sent for Honna out of some desire unknown to him. 'I'll get the grass and dump it in your yard,' said Honna and went away.

After eating the food that Malleshi brought at night, Jack and Kalinga slept. Hilda was now recovering. Relieved, he had come home today. But his sleep was ruined by those sacks of provisions that Honna had dumped here. No matter how many times he changed sides, he simply couldn't sleep. He questioned himself whether he had accurately understood Venkataramana's nature. *When he used to teach me lessons in childhood, he had been a gentle boy. When he was studying in Mysore, he used to be immersed in his studies like a dunce and never engaged in any mischief.* On occasions, Kalinga even thought that he didn't have adequate resolve. In the past, Kalinga had even thought that unless one travelled abroad, studied science, a person wouldn't develop resolve. But now he himself didn't have the strength that Venkataramana possessed, thought Kalinga, adding more twigs to the fire of his worry.

It wasn't just Venkataramana. He recalled the memory of his mother as well. Venkataramana has at least studied Sanskrit. He also learnt English. But his mother knew nothing. *She was a mute. But she possessed such extraordinary willpower! How fiercely she'd opposed me towards the end, joining forces with the village folk! On the day she gave away all the cows to Venkataramana as daana, she had ignored me even when she'd seen me. And even after she died, the same disregard towards me has continued. The village folk too have behaved with the same contempt towards me. The agave fence that has been built between my farm and the temple is evidence enough.* Then the thought that came to his mind was that despite so many days after his mother's death, he still hadn't performed her last rites. But it appeared that the village folk had taken a decision to not have it performed by him. And even if he had perchance said he wanted to perform them, none would turn up.

He then launched into a self-introspection as to why he was unable to sleep even after midnight had passed. He could've regulated such worries if Hilda had been here. Her mere presence at home would influence his mental makeup. Now she's not here and perhaps even his willpower wouldn't survive without her! She had decided to forsake him on the very day the baby was born. What would've been his condition had she actually gone away?

He slipped into slumber for a bit by dawn. But he awoke the moment Malleshi switched on the water pump of the well. As there was no tractor work, Malleshi was going to the barn to extract milk from the machine. When Kalinga got up and came outside, the sacks that Honna had dumped were still lying there. The question of what to do with them remained unsolved.

When Malleshi returned at eight-fifteen, Kalinga asked: 'Look, do you still visit that temple?'

'No.'

'Don't lie. I won't object if you visit.'

'I do visit.'

'What does the Revered *Jois* do?'

'Shall I tell the whole truth?'

'Tell.

'After giving up your land, he stays at the temple for longer hours. He sits right there and writes horoscopes and birth charts of various people. Now, lots of folks come there for offering puja and taking sacred vows.'

'Does he still prepare the *prasada* for the deity just like he used to earlier?'

'Hmm. He prepares it every day. When he arrives for the puja, he leads all the cows in his home up here. He grazes them atop the hill, stays till evening and returns. After finishing the puja and after giving *prasada* to the devotees, he eats a bit of the remainder. He saunters behind the cows chanting mantras loudly. Else, he lets the cows loose and sits around writing horoscopes and birth charts.'

'Do you know what he does for his livelihood?'

'It seems he gets money for writing horoscopes. It seems the village folk have decided that from now on they'd give him twelve kilos of pulses from each house for predicting the rain, harvest and health of the people in the ensuing year at the time of the Ugadi festival. It seems folks from the other villages have offered to give as well. This year, folks of Kalenahalli gave two bales of grass each for his cows. The guy who ploughed the field, Honna? He offered twenty-five kilos of ragi, five bales of grass as a mark of his bhakti towards the *Jois*.'

Kalinga was speechless when he heard this. Not knowing what to say further, Malleshi stood there quietly. Kalinga asked: 'Look, all his cows give milk. Do you know what they do with all that milk?'

'Not all cows give milk. They don't milk the cows completely. They milk only that quantity that remains after the calf drinks to its stomach's content. That itself fills a large pot. They bring some of that to the temple for puja. The rest, everyone at home drinks twice a day. If something still remains, they make buttermilk and then extract butter.'

'Don't they sell milk?'

'No. "*Gollas* can sell milk, but I shouldn't," he says. Even if a female calf is born, they don't sell it. Only after the bull calf grows up he gives it away. In the past month, he sold two large bull calves. He got four hundred rupees.'

Kalinga asked nothing further. Because he had to light the stove for cooking, Malleshi went to his shed. But after half an hour, Kalinga himself went to his shed and said: 'Look, you need to do something.'

'What?'

'I'll give you money today. You go on the cycle and buy lots of flowers, fruits, rice, sugar, raisins, almonds, incense sticks, all of this for puja and hand it to the Revered *Jois* at his home. After he performs puja at the temple tomorrow, you bring me the *prasada*.'

Malleshi said nothing at all. 'Why are you silent?' Kalinga asked.

After being suspicious for five minutes, Malleshi asked in a tone of asking forgiveness: 'Sir, would you get angry if I tell you the truth?'

'No, tell me.'

'If I even utter your name, he won't accept those items. Neither will he perform puja in your name nor give *prasada*—I know everything.'

Kalinga felt like he'd just been slapped with these words. But he controlled himself and said: 'I didn't mean it that way. You do it as your own *seva*, offering. Say that you're doing it in the name of your father or your mother. Say that you'll eat some at home and bring the *prasada*.'

Malleshi agreed to this suggestion. But what if some day, the Revered *Jois* learned of what he'd done! If that happened, the *Jois* would never speak to him again. But then he found it difficult to refuse his master's words. *Why's he getting all this done now? Has he made some vow because his wife had taken ill? Or, is it because he hadn't performed his mother's rites that his wife was struck with disease like this? Maybe this was to atone for that.* Malleshi made some guesses of his own. It appeared thrilling to him that he was playing a part in this situation.

When he reached Venkataramana *Jois'* home on the cycle in the evening after buying all the items, he was at home. When the *Jois* asked, 'What's special tomorrow?'

'Nothing. I had a dream to perform puja in my mother's name. Her name is Basamma,' he said.

The next day, Malleshi awoke, had bath and went to the temple. After the puja was finished, the *Jois* tied the *prasada* in areca leaves. The quantity was so large that he didn't need to cook food both in the afternoon and at night. The ten or twelve folks who had come at puja time that day got ample handfuls of the *prasada* from Malleshi's *seva*.

Kalinga too had fasted and taken his bath. When Malleshi came home, he donned the role of a *pujari* and gave him and Jack the *prasada*. *Had Hilda been home now...* this thought came to Kalinga's mind even as he was eating the *prasada*. He also got the suspicion that *had Hilda been here, would I have the puja performed in this manner? Why is it like this?* When this question arose in his mind, he began to seriously ponder over it.

3

Hilda returned home with the baby after staying in the hospital for twenty days. Her ailment had been cured. But in the process of curing it, the doctors had to stop breast milk secretion. It wasn't possible to heal the wound without stopping the milk. 'Perhaps you might face the same situation when milk is produced after your next delivery. We can't say anything now,' they had said.

The baby's problem remained. The nurse who had been feeding it milk couldn't quit her job and come to Hilda's home. Nobody else was willing to feed the milk meant for their own baby to this infant even for a fee. Not just Kalinga, but even the doctors were unable to fathom this baby's temperament. Even if the softest nipple was fixed to the feeding bottle placed in the armpit and an attempt was made to feed, the infant would simply refuse to touch it with its mouth. It needed milk straight from the breast. The nurses had concluded that it would die because of this obstinacy.

By the time they reached home, its clamour had touched indescribable limits. Fruit juice, sugar water... she declined them all. Hilda said: 'Dear, this child is born to harass us. I feel hatred when I see its stubbornness. But when I see the helplessness that it creates through this obstinacy, my hatred melts and turns into pity. That pity generates love.'

'That's correct. The joy of being father and mother is filled with such pain, right?'

Even as they were analysing their experience, the screams of the baby reached a shrill crescendo. It didn't stop for even a moment when Kalinga picked it up and rocked it on his shoulders in a swing-like motion. When Malleshi emerged from his shed and watched this, he said: 'Put its mouth to some cow's teat. It'll suckle it *ploch ploch ploch* and go quiet. I've seen it done like that.'

Kalinga suddenly felt like he had seen new light. He recalled memories of him drinking from the cow's breast when he was a kid. But why had this solution never occurred to him till now? Why had this plan, which had occurred to Malleshi within a fraction, disappeared from his mind? 'That's right!' he said aloud.

But Hilda said: 'Although what you say is correct, that milk isn't good for health. Who knows how many germs are there outside the teat! Who knows what kinds of bacteria are living in the milk itself! The milk must be boiled, cooled, its fat separated, and then it needs to be fed to infants.'

'I had drunk it as is. Nothing happened to me. It's enough if this baby survives', said Kalinga and lifting the baby, walked in the direction of the barn. Hilda instructed Malleshi to watch over Jack and the house and followed her husband.

Both reached the barn. Hilda selected a healthy cow. After thoroughly washing its udder, Hilda herself held the baby's mouth to its teat. Startled, the cow kicked and leapt. Nothing happened to the infant. Hilda, who was squatting beside the animal holding the baby, was hit by the cow's hoof on the knee which swelled up. Kalinga tethered the cow and brought another. They washed its udder as well. But it behaved akin to its predecessor. But because they were cautious this time, nothing happened to the infant and neither did Hilda suffer injury. Despite trying with four other cows, not one permitted feeding the baby. Then, with another cow, they sent its calf to suckle. But the moment the calf punched the teat once, the cow kicked it. Hilda said: 'This baby does exactly like the calf. Like it, even this used to punch my breast painfully and suckle.'

Kalinga, deep in thought, asked: 'Did it merely pain? Didn't you feel happy when it punched like that?'

'Dear, don't ask questions of psychology now. Of course I feels happy. Now, no cow allows itself to be suckled, right? Tell me why? What you said about cows letting human infants suckle them is false.'

'It's not that. These cows are now accustomed to getting milked from that machine's rubber tubes. The cow that has no experience of even suckling its own calf... how will it permit human infants near it?'

'Perhaps that's true as well. What do we do now?'

Kalinga thought for a minute and said: 'There are several cows in the nearby villages who do allow human babies to suckle them. But nobody will give them to us. Another thing: not all cows are that gentle. It has to be a cow of a specific stock. Remember we had a breed called Punyakoti? Doesn't matter which cow from that stock. It allows this kind of suckling.'

'Which is that?'

'The same one which you instructed Jamal to slaughter.' Even while he was uttering these words, Kalinga had no intention of mocking or inflaming her. Yet, Hilda, instantly fierce, said: 'Even *you* found this occasion to denounce me? Didn't you *also* eat its flesh?'

'No, not to denounce you. I merely stated the fact. Didn't my mother take away all the cows of its stock? She donated them all to Venkataramana before she died, right? To my knowledge, there's nobody apart from him who has a cow of that stock.'

Hilda was answerless. The baby was shrieking shrilly. And, because it was screaming continuously, not only were the veins in its neck swollen, both its eyes had distended and turned red. Trying to mollify it, Hilda said: 'In such a time, even Venkataramana might thaw. Go ask him.'

'He won't. Not just that. Hilda, I can't descend to that level and subject myself to experience the worst ever contempt in my entire life. Doesn't matter even if I die.'

Hilda was paralysed for a minute. But by then the baby shrieked once again, its breath catching. She said immediately: 'Dear, this isn't a question of your death; it's the question of this baby's death or survival. If a father regards his self-respect greater than his own baby's life, it amounts to sheer arrogance.'

'In that case, you go yourself.'

'I'll go. But you tell me as such in your own words. Is there no relationship at all between this baby and you? You keep reminding me, telling me that its face resembles your mother's face!'

Kalinga could find no answer. Humiliation, self-contempt and a realization of irony, his mind was now stifled with numerous emotions tinged with dejection. Despite the futility of all her attempts, Hilda continued to attempt to pacify the baby. Standing numbly for five minutes, Kalinga then said: 'It's now three-thirty. Venkataramana will be at the hill together with the cows. You go home with the baby. I'll go to the hill.'

4

Venkataramana was sitting in the grove below the *kalyani* with the cows untethered. He was wearing the Sacred Garments of the kind while performing puja. He had some book in his hand. Kalinga suddenly came from behind and stood before him and said: 'Look, you can tell me anything now. Because of a boil in my wife's chest, there is no more breast milk. The four-month-old infant won't touch anything other than mother's milk. It's almost dying after wailing continuously. Give me just one of your cows. I'll try and get its teat suckled.'

Venkataramana was aware of Kalinga's wife's ailment and the infant's problem. Yet he sat there quietly as if he didn't know anything.

'Now you must save the baby,' Kalinga asked again.

'Why, are there no cows in your shed?'

'There are. But they don't allow the baby's mouth to touch them.'

'Why?'

Kalinga was in a state of heightened anxiety. Standing here after summoning all his strength, he said without thinking: 'Having been accustomed to being milked by the machine, it appears as though they find it bizarre if a baby puts its mouth.'

'In that case, put the machine's pipe in the baby's mouth.'

Realizing the sarcasm in his words now, he said: 'Venkataramana, you can now mock me in any manner you wish. I'm standing here before you as the father of a dying infant. In this situation, if you have even a shred of humanity, you'll simply give me a cow without uttering petty words.'

'Indeed! Humanity, divinity, everything dawns upon parents especially when the baby of their own flesh and blood is about to die. But when their own parents are in distress, no lofty ideal occurs to them. Correct? Kalinga, you're younger to me; you're a boy who grew up learning the alphabet under my tutelage. Don't preach me Dharma. Go, this world will suffer no loss if your baby dies.'

Kalinga had absolutely no answer that he could give Venkataramana. His lips trembling for a minute or two, Kalinga opened his mouth to say something. But Venkataramana said: 'Your progeny, the one born to you, the one that developed in your wife's belly, the more it dies, the better it is for Dharma. Let's say, today I give my cow to save it. In future, your same progeny, the children born to it, its grandchildren, its great-grandchildren will slaughter thousands of cows and eat them. I'm not an idiot yet to be responsible for that sort of cow slaughter even if indirectly. Just go away.'

Kalinga indeed wished to go away from there. But he had no strength to lift his legs and retrace his steps. He remained standing like how he had stood for over three hours, as if he had been imprisoned, absorbed by humiliation on the day his mother died after performing the *Godaana*. Venkataramana spoke again: 'Each day during puja, I used to pray for the continuation and prosperity of the Elder Kalinga's lineage. You know what I pray for now? Let this lineage end. When bad progeny begins to grow in the belly of good people, that lineage mustn't survive. The Elder Gowda, Tayavva, both of them have attained *mukti*, spiritual liberation. And now, merely for the *one* reason that you and your progeny have been born from their blood, there's no necessity for you and your progeny to survive and flourish. God has put you in this situation for good. Go away. You didn't have the fortune to bury your own mother's corpse. Seems that same mother is born as this baby. Seems her face has verily become this baby's face. I've heard everything. The house servants narrate everything. After it dies, bury the baby properly. You'll at least discharge your mother's debt.'

Kalinga hadn't anticipated that Venkataramana could even speak this savagely. With each sentence, he was directly stabbing his innards. Tears filled Kalinga's eyes. He said: 'I'm asking you the last time. Just tell me. Will you or will younot give, just tell me that. Will you behave at the standard of merely taking out your anger at me or will you behave at a higher level? For the last time, just tell me this much.'

Venkataramana felt ashamed at these words. Thinking within himself for two minutes, he said: 'Look, I'll give you one cow. But understand this well: it's mine because it came to me as *daana*. I'll leave it with you for four days only out of compassion for the baby. That's about it. I won't place it under your control by trusting either you or your wife. Your servant Malleshi—get him here. I'll put it under his care. I have faith in him.'

Kalinga went near the *kalyani*. But the agave fence was standing there with its roots deep in the ground, separating this area from his farm. It wasn't an easy task to pluck it out, to make an opening and squeeze through. Besides, would Venkataramana stay quiet if he learnt that an opening was made in the fence explicitly built to isolate his farm from the temple? Kalinga felt scared. He spotted Hilda standing afar, still trying to pacify the baby. He signalled her to come near. Then he shouted out asking her to send Malleshi.

He said to Malleshi who reached there, sprinting from his shed: 'There's no space to creep inside this fence. Come from around it.'

'No sir, there's space here,' said Malleshi, and lifting aside the bamboo thorns placed between two agaves, squeezed through and crossed over.

'Who made this space? How did you know?"

Embarrassed, he said: 'The servants have themselves done it, sir. We squeeze through from here during the puja time and all of us drink *tirtha,* eat the *prasada* and return.'

Venkataramana told Malleshi who was now standing before him: 'Look, go to my house. You see this white cow here, right? It has a young calf. It has a mark of *gopichandana, a* yellow ochre on its forehead. Bring it here. Wait, my folks won't give it if you just ask them. Give this book and this vessel as a mark of identification and tell them I told you.'

Malleshi ran to the *Agrahara.* Not knowing what to do till he returned—although Kalinga thought of going home—he found it impossible to walk away. By then, Venkataramana himself walked behind a cow that had strayed a bit. Venkataramana had tied tiny bells around the necks of all his cows. In the serene atmosphere of the hill, their soft melody filled his mind with an otherworldly feel. To Kalinga, this sight was nothing new. When he was still a young boy, he had seen his grandfather also decking up cows in the same fashion. 'When they come to graze, the sound of puja must emanate from their neck. That's why the bell is tied,' his grandfather used to say. When they returned to the cowshed at night, they removed the bells.

In an hour, Venkataramana's cows had drifted in the direction of the village slowly grazing along. By then, Malleshi reached there, leading the calf. Taking Malleshi along with him to the calf's mother, Venkataramana said: 'Look here, you must make a promise, holding its tail. If they slaughter and eat it, you'll accumulate the most horrible sin and go to hell. Tomorrow by the hour of puja, you must bring both cow and calf here and return them. You must tether them both in your own shed.'

Kalinga arrived by the time Malleshi was uttering the words of his oath, the tail of the cow in his hand. Venkataramana didn't speak to him. He went away, leading the other cows. As the cow that remained behind tugged at the rope in an effort to join her sisters, Malleshi caressed its face, embraced its neck and whispered words of comfort. After this, it walked behind him. Kalinga asked: 'What's this, you're going that way? Can a cow squeeze through that fence?'

'Yes, we can squeeze it in, come sir.'

Malleshi first removed the bamboo thorns and walked ahead. The cow followed right behind. The fence opened up just like that. After Kalinga followed with the calf, Malleshi didn't close the open fence— Hilda was standing close to the fence. Having bawled nonstop and with no energy left now, the baby had gone quiet. Spotting Hilda, the cow trembled a little. Malleshi himself took the infant in his hand. Hilda stood at a distance. Kalinga let the calf go. It bolted and fastened its mouth to the udder on one side. Squatting on the other side, Malleshi put the baby's mouth to a teat. Suspicious, the baby didn't drink. After Malleshi himself squeezed the teat, milk dribbled into its mouth. It seemed that the infant swallowed the milk. Malleshi slowly squeezed the teat again. The infant then began to suckle.

Watching from afar, Hilda was not just surprised, she was also curious. *This baby goes quiet after suckling milk from this beast's teat. Why can't it drink from the nipple of the bottle? What outlandish sort of baby is this?* She questioned herself but found no convincing answer.

5

After drinking milk again at night, the infant slumbered without noise and fuss. But Kalinga couldn't sleep.

He recollected his own childhood experience. He had drunk from the teat of a similar Punyakoti cow—by relationship it could well be the grandmother or great grandmother of the cow whose milk his child had suckled. This childhood memory of drinking from Punyakoti's teat kept coming back to him. With it also came the memory of his mother. He recalled the incident of his grandmother speaking with another woman in his presence. It seems milk had dried up in his mother's breast in just one year after his birth. A mere infant, it seems he stubbornly demanded only breast milk. Having become accustomed to drinking from the cow's teat, he kept drinking from it for countless days from then on. And, with the memory of his childhood days, he also remembered his grandmother and grandfather. The memory of his mother surged. Today, he detected a new meaning in the commonplace fact that he had suckled her breast for a year.

Unable to sleep, he looked at his watch using the torch nearby. It showed two-thirty in the night. From her wriggling, he knew that Hilda too was unable to sleep. He asked: 'You said you sold the old cattle twenty days ago, right? What's that guy's name?'

Recalling, Hilda said: 'It seems he's from the Taluk. Shukoor Saheb is his name apparently. Why?'

'Nothing.'

He felt sleepy by the time it was dawn. When he awoke at seven in the morning, he got up and rinsed his face. By then Malleshi had brought the cow to the front of the house, and was suckling the baby with its milk. Wearing his shirt and slacks, Kalinga filled his pockets with money.

Hilda asked: 'Where're you going suddenly?'

'I need to visit the Taluk,' he said just this much.

Travelling by the morning motor, when he eventually traced Shukoor Saheb and asked him, he said: 'Sir, it's twenty-two days since I bought them. I sold them the same day to the big contractor at the district.'

'In that case, you also come with me. I'll give him any amount he asks. I need all of my cattle.'

'I'll come. But the beasts won't be with him either. As soon as the

S.L. BHYRAPPA

number reaches fifty or hundred, he'll load them directly into the rail wagon and dispatch them to Mumbai.'

'So, these are all slaughtered and sold in Mumbai?'

'They do it elsewhere as well. But, our big contractor dispatches it only to Mumbai. The kind of profit from there, we don't get anywhere else.'

Kalinga climbed into the motor with Shukoor Saheb and reached the district. The contractor said: 'It's already ten days since I dispatched this lot to Mumbai. I can't say whether you'll get them or no.'

'Why?'

'If they've reached Mumbai by now, they'd have already been cut and packed. If a traded beast is kept needlessly even for one extra day, it's a huge loss—all that grass, water and everything.'

'No matter what happens, I'll search. Tell me what I need to do.'

'I'll write a chit. There's a big contractor in Mumbai. All the cattle business from this region is his. His people come here and transport the beasts themselves. Even if you find your beasts, they'll take money from you for transport cost, labour charge, expense on grass and water for all these days, and on top, his cut of profit. You need to pay all these.'

Kalinga hadn't anticipated that he would need to go to Mumbai for this work. He did have money in his pocket, but he had no clothes. Besides, he hadn't informed home. Taking the note from the contractor, he took the motor immediately available and came to the Taluk with Shukoor Saheb. From there, he sat in the motor and went home directly.

It was four in the afternoon. A motor was available at six that would go to the preceding Taluk. He decided to travel in it and then take the train from the Taluk. But, Hilda wasn't there when he came home. Malleshi who arrived there by then told him that she had gone to the cowshed. Kalinga stuffed four pairs of clothing into his small leather suitcase, took more money and got ready. He then went to the kitchen, served himself whatever food was available, ate it and then, taking the briefcase, walked towards the road. By the time he reached the road, he met Hilda on the opposite side. The infant was in her arms. Jack was following her, playing along. 'Dear, where're you headed to? You never tell me anything at all?' He said, walking ahead, 'Come, I'll tell you by the roadside.' And, as she followed behind, he said: 'You had sold those old cattle to the butcher twenty days ago? I'd gone to get them back. It seems he has dispatched them all to Mumbai. Now I'm going to Mumbai to bring them back if they've not yet been slaughtered. *If they're still alive.*'

'What's *happened* to you?' she asked, astonished.

'Hilda, can't you still understand it?'

'You tell me what it is.'

'The mother-cow saved our baby that was on the verge of death, by feeding it from its teat. Shouldn't we care for such mother-cows in their old age just as we care for our own mother? The cows and oxen that you sold are all such mothers and fathers.'

When she heard these words from *his* mouth, Hilda was dumbstruck. After remaining quiet for two minutes, Hilda said, 'You've changed because of that *pujari*, my dear. Your mind is now perhaps in an emotional turmoil. Think a little calmly,' and proceeded to grab the suitcase in his hand.

But clutching it tightly, Kalinga said, 'Actually, I haven't changed because of him. Indeed, there's really nothing to change. This is the conviction that was within me since childhood. Only, I'd forgotten it for a few years in the interim. This baby has reinforced it. That's about it.' He bent and kissed the cheek of the infant in her arms with great emotion.

They had reached the road by then. By the bank of the road, he sat near a banyan sapling that was growing slightly. Hilda who sat nearby said: 'Dear, you're still speaking emotionally. Think about what's going to happen to the economic balance of animal husbandry if you do this. Whatever you're seeing since yesterday is no miracle. An infant insisted on drinking milk only from the breast. And a cow—all cows are typically gentle—remained quiet and didn't kick even when the infant put its mouth to its teat. Several gentle creatures remain quiet just like this. People in hilly forest regions drink goat milk. Infants drink milk by suckling on goat teats. But don't they ever slaughter that goat and eat it? There's no fundamental difference in drawing an animal's milk from its udder into a vessel and drinking it or drinking it directly from the udder. You mustn't get so agitated over this.'

Kalinga sat there silently. Waiting for an answer, Hilda herself said when he didn't speak: 'All the science you learnt, the education you got in America, will you chuck it all into the whirlwind of your emotional frenzy?'

'No, I need all this electricity, this scientific manure—all of this. I also need the medical science that cures animal diseases. But we need to throw to the winds the notion that animals exist solely for human utility.'

Hilda was sitting quietly. After thinking for a minute, Kalinga said: 'When he was alive, my grandfather used to tell me. Venkataramana says the same thing as well. If conviction needs to originate from within, one needs spiritual refinement for that too. It appears I had this refinement from birth. When I was studying in college at Mysore, I once unknowingly ate a meal that had beef in a European principal's house. After I confirmed it, my mind wasn't at rest until I atoned for it by drinking *panchagavya*. But when I went to America, my conviction changed. Now, the earlier conviction has re-established its strength.'

Hilda remained quiet. That she was engrossed in some serious thought was evident on her face. Kalinga said: 'I know your conviction is different. That's why you didn't develop the conviction that I did. Both of us are experiencing the same thing since yesterday. But why're you unable to believe it?'

Tears filled Hilda's eyes. Unable to restrain herself, she shrieked, weeping: 'Merciless, Kaling, you're merciless, you're a butcher. You're killing me.'

'Darling, console yourself.'

'Console myself? What kind of consolation? You brought me here from such a far-off country. You placed me on a proud pedestal saying "you're the director of my intellect". Now you're telling me right to my face that I'm different, my conviction is different from yours? Shouldn't you have some marital commitment?'

'Where did I tell you to go away? Don't you know how much I love you? Darling, please understand what I'm saying.'

'No, no. Your conviction wounds me intellectually. I can't adjust with it and live happily. I myself need to go away from here.'

'I won't let you do that. Besides, what'll you do with this baby?'

Hilda said crying yet again: 'I trusted you and got married. I became your baby's mother as well. You tied me down with numerous bonds. Now you've taken the route of your conviction. And, I can't come to that route on my own. But I must walk on that unknown path, bruising my body, getting yanked by you. Else I need to tear away in the opposite direction and go my separate way. No matter which one I choose, it's painful. It's cruelly painful for me, Kaling. This isn't called loving your wife.'

Then they heard the sound of the bus. Jack who was playing at a distance shouted, 'motor'. Kalinga stood up. Holding his hand, Hilda said: 'You must not go now. If you do want to go, you must convince me and only then leave.'

The bus was stopping close by. 'The old cows won't survive till the time I convince you. Besides, no matter how much I debate, you'll never agree. I'll go by this bus itself,' he said, climbing in. Hilda tightly gripped the suitcase in his hand. Because he didn't want to fight in public, Kalinga left the suitcase in her hand, got in, and shouted, 'Right!' The bus which hadn't completely halted, moved forward. 'Cruel, butcher, oaf!' Hilda yelled once more. Through the glass at the back of the bus, he could see her weeping.

6

Kalinga found a place to sleep in the train which he boarded that night. Although he hadn't had any sleep the previous night, he was still unable to sleep. He felt like a new man. He was now endowed with a sentiment that he belonged to the same strain of conviction as his grandfather, grandmother and mother. But he couldn't fathom the reason behind such fierce opposition to his conviction from Hilda. It didn't matter if she couldn't develop the same conviction that he had developed. *What would she lose if I bring back the old cattle and protect them? Why should her mind be hurt at this?* he thought. *Will Hilda leave me and go away for just this one reason?* His mind was churning with this question. *Should I get down at the next station and return, just to please her?* Although this thought flashed on occasion, he remained lying down unable to get up. He drifted off to sleep a little after midnight.

By the time he awoke the next morning, the train was at a large station. There was a goods train right next to the platform at which his train had halted. Every single wagon was filled with aged cows and aged oxen, tethered inside together. While other passengers alighted to wash their face and have breakfast, Kalinga sprinted to the goods train, climbed in and examined all the wagons. He couldn't spot his cattle. *All these days, maybe they've reached Mumbai*, he thought, then sprinted back and sat down in his train. But as the train moved, he recalled something: he hadn't even properly seen the cattle that Hilda had sold. Even if he examined them now, there was no guarantee that he could identify them accurately. During the time that he was busy in the tobacco plantation work, he had never been to the barn. It was during that time that the servants had brought the oxen home from his village and tethered them. Neither had he properly seen these oxen earlier. He was familiar only with the four old cows in his own barn. Now, he was sitting in the train and looking out the window with a confidence that he could identify his cattle based on the weight of this evidence: his familiarity with the cows and on the district cattle-contractor who had sent the oxen away with these cows.

His train didn't stop at all stations. A cattle goods train was standing at a station that passed in between. Even as the thought arose that perhaps his cattle would be in it, his own train zipped past it with great speed. It didn't halt anywhere for the next forty miles.

Getting down at Pune, he took the train to Mumbai without stopping even to eat. When he reached Mumbai in the evening, he inquired the address on the paper he had with him and set out. By eight in the night, he found the house of the big contractor. Living on the second floor of a large building, the contractor appeared to be enormously wealthy. When Kalinga considered the board outside, the spread of the *diwankhana* inside, the telephone and other items, he calculated that this tycoon must be worth a few crores. Expansive *diwankhana*. Posters of Lakshmi, Saraswati, Badarinath, Kedaranath on the walls. Soft carpet on the floor, sofas. The contractor was home and watched Kalinga with disregard. After two days of train journey, he was unshaven without a change of clothes. After reading the letter that Kalinga gave him, he said: 'We don't know where they are.'

Despite not being invited, Kalinga sat on the sofa and spoke English in an American accent: 'I've come from so far. You must search them wherever they are. The district supply contractor has sent me here reposing faith in you.'

The Seth couldn't understand this English. Still, he said in his Hindustani English: 'Why do you need them?'

'We don't sell cows for slaughter. The servants at home have sold them without our knowledge.'

'Come here tomorrow morning at eight. I'll send a servant. Go with him and search. We don't have any details of which cattle belong to you, or whether they've even arrived or no. Our overseer does all that work. We merely supervise. That's it.'

Kalinga stepped out of the house, lodged himself in a hotel, took a bath had his meal, washed his upper garments himself and slept off. When he woke up in the morning, he wore the clean clothes, had a shave in a barbershop, combed his hair after getting oil applied to it and exited the hotel room. When he arrived at the contractor's house, the tycoon said: 'Go with my servant. We don't keep the cattle separately for many days. There's no stock in the cowshed now. There's some land belonging to us in front of the slaughterhouse. Check the stock there. It's your fortune if you find them there. Else, we know nothing.'

Kalinga went to the slaughterhouse at Bandra with the servant. They had tied thousands of cattle, sheep and goat in the vast field in front of the slaughter platform. There were also enclosures made with bamboo. Leading Kalinga to one enclosure, the servant said, pointing, 'This is ours.' Over three hundred oxen and cows. Kalinga examined every single animal. But he couldn't identify his cattle. There were several cows resembling his own aged ones, but he found it impossible to identify even one among them and declare that it was his. Not a single cow exhaled and licked his body with love when he went near it. *It's all right if I can't identify them; can't they at least identify me?* he thought. But then it flashed to him instantly: not once had he scratched the neck of the cows in his barn, not once had he hugged them, kissed their face

S.L. BHYRAPPA

or put straw in their mouth with his own hands. True, on numerous days, he had himself drawn milk from them using that machine. But was that enough to make the cows remember him and identify him? *My own cows have deteriorated to the extent that they don't even have the ability to recognize me*, he thought.

He recalled suddenly: there's a difference between teats that are milked using a machine and those using hands. *Can I identify them using that yardstick at least?* With this thought, he bent down and examined the teats of all the old cows. Teats milked by hand will sag. Teats milked with a machine will be thin. But because they were stricken with old age, all the teats more or less looked alike.

Even as Kalinga was examining the cows, the servant who had brought him here said: 'It's getting late. Shall I leave?'

'The cattle loaded into the wagon from my district ten days earlier... when will they arrive here?'

'Sethji told me about your matter. We can't say. Sometimes, they arrive in just four days. The moment they arrive, we get a certificate from the veterinary doctor and send them for slaughter immediately. If we keep them for an extra day, the cost increases.'

Kalinga had no more questions left to ask him. He raised his head once and looked. Cattle in groups of fifty or hundred were joining in the field. People were leading the cattle, which filled the three large alleys that opened out to the field. Kalinga asked the servant: 'This number of cattle, how do you get them?'

'What's the use of the oxen that become old after working in the farm? What's the use of the cows which can no longer give milk? Farmers sell them to our agents.'

Kalinga wasn't unaware of the question he asked as well as the answer he received. Still, he couldn't himself understand why he asked it.

The servant went away. Unable to do anything, Kalinga remained standing where he was. The cows that were being brought for slaughter slowly began to fill out around him. He repeatedly bent down and looked at their aged teats. He examined the shoulders of the debilitated oxen. Suddenly he remembered his baby, followed by the memory of his mother. *Mother shouldn't have died,* he thought. Then he said to himself, *it was true what the village folk said. It was I who killed her. Mother's gone. Will Hilda return to her country or will she stay back with me, respecting my conviction? Considering the mode of her thinking, her intellectual deliberations, her cultural background, she'd definitely go. But the baby? It was born out of her own belly. Perhaps she'd stay back just for that reason.* Hope surfaced. But, the strand on which that hope rested had feeble strength.

Even if she said, 'ayyo', in disgust, it didn't matter. Mother should've been alive. Then I could've adjusted according to Hilda's wishes. But she died and won me over. Now on, Hilda must only adjust to me. But how do I get her to adjust to me? With this thought, he raised his head and looked up. Amid this huge mass of cattle, they were leading the ones in front towards the slaughterhouse. Thinking that there would be one that belonged to him, he went close and looked at them. The face of every cow and ox appeared like the ones that belonged to him. Perhaps they had a premonition of their death. They remained stubborn, refusing to go in. Kalinga gazed at the face of one of the cows. In his memory, the expression on its face resembled the expression on his mother's face as she lay on the blanket on the day of her death when she performed the *Godaana*. It was a blind man's vision to separate and distinguish which among these was his. His mind told him that all these thousands of cattle assembled here, fated to enter the slaughterhouse, all belonged to him. His hand slid inside his trouser pocket. Then, realizing that he didn't have the strength or capacity to take care of all of these old cows and oxen, he took out his hand. The impotence that had struck him on the day his mother died now coursed through his hands and legs.

Feeling dizzy, he squatted down for ten minutes. Then, getting up, he walked towards Bandra Railway Station without looking back. Taking a taxi, he reached Dadar Station and awaited the train to Pune. He thought of Hilda. *Will she stay here or go away?* The question reared its head again. For ten minutes, he was caught in an emotional maelstrom. Then the question came to his mind, pushing away his thoughts about Hilda: *I'm ploughing with the tractor. I'm using chemical manure. What's the use of a cow? If I rear it only for milk, what do I do with the bull calves that are born? How long is it feasible for me to needlessly feed it grass, take care of it? Perhaps the problem would be resolved if the science of bovine genetics progressed such that at most only the female stock would be born. The cows that kept giving milk and then grew old could be given grass and water until they died of natural causes. Some such arrangement could be made. If the human being who escaped the dependency on Basava, the ox, for agriculture, gradually abandoned the habit of drinking cow's milk, there would be no problem,* he felt.

What do I do now? Should I sell the tractor and restart the ox and the yoke of my grandfather's era? But he didn't see any meaning in it. This question doesn't even arise with the Americans. They clearly say and believe that other animals exist only for the utility of man. *But we need both the tractor and the Gopuja.* He was reminded of Venkataramana. And felt pity for him. The strength of his *shraddha,* his faith and conviction, was enormous. But he can't answer this very important question. He would simply say 'smash the tractor to pieces. The *Ambaa* sound of the cow, the sound of the Om mantra, the *gana-gana-gana* sound of the bell—spiritual liberation comes from only this.'

Unable to find an answer, Kalinga's brain was now listless. The train arrived after a while. He ran, climbed in, found a place for himself, and sat down. After an hour, the train stopped at Kalyan station. When it resumed, he spotted a mountain to the right. He was reminded of the Arunadri Hill neighbouring his farm. Suddenly, he was reminded of his mother. He felt his mother shouldn't have died. If he had behaved differently with regard to her, she wouldn't have been mentally affected. He thought it was his fault. But soon another question popped up and this one slid away. This wasn't a question of simply pleasing her with his outward behaviour. Even if he had tried, to what extent could he have pleased her? Only those who shared her conviction could have a conversation with her. In worldly matters, she was indeed born dumb. *After I brought the tractor, perhaps a little before that or a little after, it was inevitable that she would die and I'd become an orphan.* In this thought, Kalinga saw a vast spread of a wave of insight. But unable to grasp its full meaning in that immediate moment, he sat there in the same position, his mouth half-open.